BABY LOVE

"Need some help with the baby?" A wry smile turned up the corners of Sylvester's lips.

"Not from you," Colleen said. "You're supposed to be in bed."

"All I could hear was his bawling. I hate to hear children crying when I can do something about it. Give him to me." He reached for the baby.

Colleen looked at Phillip, red-faced from crying, then had no choice but to hand the baby to Sylvester. The hard rigid muscles of his chest brushed against her forearms. The heat of his body burned right through his shirt and the sleeves of her dress. A memory of another time flooded back to her, when he'd held her against his chest. He'd placed tiny kisses down her neck, all the while pushing the shoulders of her gown and petticoat down.

Phillip stopped crying. The silence jarred her back to the present. She stared at Phillip, noticing him now. He looked content, peeking over Sylvester's broad shoulder. Sylvester hadn't stopped staring at her, and he was wearing a look she remembered well. When he had last worn that look, she'd ended up in the garden with him, half naked, kissing him, succumbing to his passion . . .

—from *Fate's Little Miracle* by Constance Hall

BOOK YOUR PLACE ON OUR WEBSITE AND MAKE THE READING CONNECTION!

We've created a customized website just for our very special readers, where you can get the inside scoop on everything that's going on with Zebra, Pinnacle and Kensington books.

When you come online, you'll have the exciting opportunity to:

- View covers of upcoming books
- Read sample chapters
- Learn about our future publishing schedule (listed by publication month *and author*)
- Find out when your favorite authors will be visiting a city near you
- Search for and order backlist books from our online catalog
- Check out author bios and background information
- Send e-mail to your favorite authors
- Meet the Kensington staff online
- Join us in weekly chats with authors, readers and other guests
- Get writing guidelines
- AND MUCH MORE!

**Visit our website at
http://www.zebrabooks.com**

BABY IN A BASKET

Constance Hall
Candace McCarthy
Jean Wilson

Zebra Books
Kensington Publishing Corp.
http://www.zebrabooks.com

ZEBRA BOOKS are published by

Kensington Publishing Corp.
850 Third Avenue
New York, NY 10022

Copyright © 1999 by by Kensington Publishing Corp.

"Fate's Little Miracle" © 1999 by Connie Koslow
"Cradle Song" © 1999 by Candace McCarthy
"Gambler's Full House" © 1999 by Jean Wilson

All rights reserved. No part of this book may be reproduced
in any form or by any means without the prior written consent
of the Publisher, excepting brief quotes used in reviews.

If you purchased this book without a cover you should be aware
that this book is stolen property. It was reported as "unsold
and destroyed" to the Publisher and neither the Author nor the
Publisher has received any payment for this "stripped book."

Zebra and the Z logo Reg. U.S. Pat. & TM Off.

First Printing: April, 1999
10 9 8 7 6 5 4 3 2 1

Printed in the United States of America

CONTENTS

FATE'S LITTLE MIRACLE

CONSTANCE HALL

*To Mom and Pop, for being the kind, loving
people they are.
And to Donner and Essy—they'll always be
remembered.*

CHAPTER 1

Northumberland, England, 1821

Lady Colleen Davenport hopped off a stile and stepped down into the snow. She gasped, feeling the frigid moisture seeping through the worn soles of her boots. Her wet woolen stockings stuck to her feet and legs, and she'd long since lost the feeling in her toes.

Gusts of frigid wind bit at her face, stealing her breath. A thin mist of sleet began pelting her head, then flakes of snow. Unable to believe it was snowing again, she stared ruefully up at the heavy gray clouds. That's all they needed, more snow. It was only four in the afternoon, but the snowstorm was smothering what was left of the daylight. It would be dark by the time she walked the last mile home. She could have walked home from the village by way of the road, but she'd taken a shortcut across Farmer Britter's field, shortening her journey by a mile.

She sighed loudly, her warm breath blowing a white cloud

around her face. Blinking back the ice sticking to her lashes, she threw the sack she was carrying over her shoulder, then pulled her woolen muffler tighter around her neck and chin. Off in the distance, she could see a hint of the cottage, the chimney rising above a stand of oaks, the inviting black smoke spiraling up through the snow. Colleen focused her gaze on the smoke and tried not to think about her freezing toes, or the pain she would feel when her feet finally thawed near the fire.

The sound of a dog barking drew her attention, and she glanced toward a knoll to her left. Farmer Britter's Border collie, Donner, was herding a flock of sheep toward the barn for the night. They leaped down the glen, jumping up out of the snow. Several headed the wrong way, but Donner, ever vigilant, was right there, barking, nipping them on the bottom, turning them back with the herd.

Thick woods surrounded Farmer Britter's field and absorbed the echo of Donner's barking. The collie moved the sheep along the fence that separated the field. Colleen scanned the field for Farmer Britter, but he was nowhere in sight. He often let his trusted pet herd the sheep alone—especially on a miserable evening like this.

Colleen thought she heard the sound of a baby's cry mixing with the dog's barks. Something moved out of the corner of her eye. Turning, she glanced down the length of the field and saw a gentleman glancing furtively, left, right. He hurried along the fence.

She ducked behind a nearby prickly juniper. Without thinking, she pulled down a thick snow-covered branch to peer at the strange gentleman and a blob of snow hit the hem of her dress. She didn't bother knocking it off. The hem of her dress was so sodden now, what did a little more snow matter? Instead, she watched the man. A basket swung like a pendulum near his side.

There was something sinister in his long, even strides that made a shiver go through her. Worse yet, the wide shoulders and stiff posture of the gentleman seemed familiar. She strained to see past the hooded cloak covering the man's head, but she couldn't see his face. As the man came closer, the crying grew louder. It was a desperate cry, as if the infant feared something.

Colleen was sure now there was a baby in the basket. Galvanized into action, she stepped out from behind the tree and strode toward the man.

He didn't seem to notice her as he drew near the fence gate. When he was in the middle of it, he laid the small basket in the snow. He bent his head and stared down at the basket, then he glanced at the approaching sheep. Colleen realized too late what he was planning. Before she could yell at him, he turned and darted back up the knoll, toward the wood.

"Oh, no," Colleen whispered under her breath, watching Donner herding the sheep straight for the baby. She dropped the sack from her shoulder and ran through the snow. Fifty yards separated her from the child.

The sheep were running toward the gate, Donner urging them onward.

She wasn't near enough. Oh God! She wouldn't make it in time. The lead sheep was twenty feet from the gate and closing fast—

"No!" Colleen screamed, her voice echoing through the dell, scaring a flock of rooks from the forest.

Whether Donner responded to Colleen's voice or she sensed the baby's presence, Colleen would never know, but the dog darted to the fore and turned the sheep, inches from the baby. Confused by the abrupt change, the sheep ran along the fence and halfway up the knoll. They finally paused, billowing into a white mass of wool.

Colleen's jaw dropped open. Her heart hammered against her ribs so violently she felt light-headed. She held her chest and all she could do was sigh.

Donner looked at Colleen and barked as if to say, "There now, I've saved the baby." Then she bent and sniffed at the

basket. With her pink tongue hanging out, she stood by the
child, looking from the basket to Colleen, then back again.
She barked impatiently again. The din startled the baby, for
the wailing grew louder, echoing through the field.

"I'm coming," Colleen said. She reached Donner and patted
her head. Loud enough to be heard over the baby's crying,
Colleen said, "Good girl. You're a wonder of a dog. Don't
tell Sharon I said this, but if you have a litter of pups, I wouldn't
mind having one."

Donner licked Colleen's hand, her dark eyes sparkling, stark
against the white fur around her nose and head.

The baby's loud continuous wail made Colleen turn toward
the basket and drop to her knees. She picked up the basket,
hardly feeling it in her numb hands, and set it across her thighs.
A moth-eaten brown blanket covered the child from head to
toe.

The baby's feet kicked wildly and the clumsily-wrapped
blanket fell open. She caught a quick glimpse of male body
parts, then at the tiny trembling arms clutching helplessly
against a naked pink chest. He'd drawn his fingers into tight
fists. His face was red from crying, his puffy eyes nothing more
than tiny slits. With each deep wail, his lower lip quivered. It
was a frightened wail, crying out for comfort and warmth.

"It's all right. We'll get you warm. They didn't even bother
dressing you, did they?" As quickly as she could, she wrapped
the blanket back around him, then stuffed him beneath her
own coat. She cuddled him, feeling how tiny, and how utterly
helpless he felt in her arms. "There now, little one, I'm here
. . . I'm here," she cooed.

At the sound of her voice, the baby's crying lessened, then
finally stopped. She looked down into his eyes. They were
staring up at her with trusting innocence.

"Look at you. How could anyone not want you?" she said,
peering down into the bluest eyes she'd ever seen. A growing
strangled feeling pulled at her throat and she blinked hard.

Fat snowflakes hit the baby's face and it whimpered. The baby opened and closed its lips, then frowned at her.

She smiled and said, "What funny faces? I remember when Sharon used to make those faces at me, but that was a long time ago. Wait until she sees you."

The infant squirmed and whimpered again.

Colleen held the baby tightly to her breast and picked up the basket. Something made her remember the man, and she turned to see if he was anywhere in sight. The only sign of him was the trail of footprints leading to the wood, and they were being covered quickly by the falling snow.

The baby began crying. Colleen bounced him on her shoulder. "There now," she said. "You needn't cry. I shall see that dirty old man hanged at Tyburn, if it is the last thing I do." She pulled the blanket back over the baby's face, then hurried through the falling snow.

Aggie set the paring knife down on the counter, scooped up the turnips she'd chopped, then leaned over and threw them in a pot. She put the lid on, then turned and glanced out the kitchen window at the thick blanket of snow coming down. "It looks like we're in for a big one."

Lady Sharon was sitting at the kitchen table, her head bowed, strands of her thin straight blonde hair falling down near her face. Seeing her, no one would guess she was seven and ten. She looked more like a young child. Sharon raised her head and gazed at Aggie with wide brown ethereal eyes. Every time Aggie looked into those eyes, it was like looking into the eyes of an angel. Oh, yes, her Sharon was special and too sweet to be of this world.

"Did you say it's snowing again?" Sharon said, continuing to pet the baby rabbit in her lap. The wild creature sat there, mesmerized by Sharon's touch.

"Aye, I said it. And I'm worried about your sister. She's twenty minutes late."

Sharon glanced toward the door, alarm furrowing her golden brows. "I hope nothing has happened to her. I didn't want her to go to the village, but she wouldn't listen."

Aggie realized she'd upset Sharon. "Don't you be worrying about your sister, my pet. Anyway, no amount of talking would have made her stay home. You know how determined your sister is." Aggie's gaze strayed to the rabbit. "You ought not let her see you with that creature in the house. You know how she feels about you bringing home your strays."

"I just couldn't leave him out in the snow without a mama."

"Likely, your sister won't care."

"Oh, Aggie, she cares. Don't let her fool you. She wouldn't leave a baby bunny out in the snow to starve, no more than you could."

Aggie made a face. It was likely Colleen had killed the mother for last night's stew, but she didn't voice her suspicions aloud. Instead she said, "Not everyone has a kind heart like you, my pet."

Aggie glanced at the cage in the corner, where a baby squirrel was curled up into a ball, enjoying the heat of the kitchen. He'd been abandoned by its mother, and Sharon, bless her heart, took up where the mother left off. Spitter and Duke, the stray cats Sharon had found, occupied two chairs beneath the table, their bodies curled into furry sleeping circles. Spitter was missing a tail and Duke had only one ear. Now a rabbit was added to the menagerie, and they couldn't hardly afford to feed themselves. Aggie shook her head, then turned back to the hob, picking up a spoon and stirring the soup.

Abruptly the back door opened.

A gust of wind followed Colleen in from outside. Snowflakes swirled around her head like a halo. Aggie grabbed a tea towel before it blew off the counter.

Colleen fell back against the door, slamming it shut, breathing heavy.

"Oooo! It's bitter out there," Aggie said, then picked up the towel and glanced at Colleen.

She was four years older than her younger sister and much taller and sturdier-boned. Her hair was thicker and darker than Sharon's, with streaks of golden brown in it. Where Sharon looked like a meek little angel, Colleen looked built for sin. She matched Sharon in beauty, but was more voluptuous in all the right places. Unlike Sharon's eyes, that were too velvety brown and pure to be of this world, Colleen's green eyes sparkled with fire, deeply rooted in the tenacity of life. Aye, they were different as chalk and cheese.

Aggie heard Colleen's teeth chattering, then noticed how wet Colleen's clothes and boots were. She hurried over to her. "You must be frozen clean through, child. I told you to let Farmer Britter pick up Sharon's medicine at the apothecary."

"If I let Farmer Britter do us a kindness, then he would expect me to give his son another free pianoforte lesson, and we can't afford that—not if we want to pay the butcher. Anyway, I stopped at Mrs. James's. She had another dress for us to sew."

"You're hardheaded as a stump, I tell you. Surprise me if you don't come down with a cold, or something worse. Give me those wet clothes this instant." Aggie noticed the bulge beneath Colleen's coat and asked, "What's that you got there?"

"A baby." Colleen dropped the sack and basket in her hand, then eased the bundle from beneath her coat. She pulled back a corner of an old blanket and said in a whisper, "See? It's a boy."

Aggie's jaw dropped open as she looked down at the sleeping infant. "It don't look a day old. Who would take out a newborn in this kind of weather? Who does it belong to?"

"Us, for the time being."

Sharon placed the bunny on the floor and jumped up from her seat. "A baby! Can we really keep it?"

"Lord be above," Aggie said, shaking her head. "We can't hardly feed ourselves. How can we take care of a baby?"

"We'll just have to find a way," Colleen said.

"We have Midget. Goat's milk is supposed to be good for an infant." Sharon held out her hands. "May I hold him? What shall we call him? He must have a name." She studied his tiny sleeping face. "What about Phillip? What do you think, Colleen? Does he not look like a Phillip?"

"I suppose he does." Colleen gently placed the sleeping infant in Sharon's arms, then pulled the scarf from around her neck and head.

Sharon stared at the baby and said in a tender voice, "Colleen, where did you ever find the little darling?"

"In Farmer Britter's field."

"Oh, no. Someone had just left him there?" Sharon gazed down at the baby, her soft brown eyes full of concern.

"Yes." Colleen shared a glance with Aggie, then pulled off her gloves and old coat.

Aggie tried to hide the frown on her face so Sharon wouldn't see it, and took Colleen's wet coat and gloves. She strode over to the line strung across the far end of the kitchen. Every step sent a shooting pain up her swollen legs. She grimaced as she hung the wet clothes there, then waited while Colleen took off her wet socks.

Colleen handed them to her, then walked over to the hearth and held her red chafed hands near the fire. When her teeth finally stopped chattering, she said, "Sharon, why don't you go to my hope chest and see if you can find some clothes for Phillip? I know there must be something for him in there."

"The poor little thing doesn't even have clothes? How horrible." Sharon glanced at Colleen and Aggie, a serene and unreadable expression on her face, then she strode from the kitchen with the baby in her arms.

The moment Sharon's footsteps died away, Aggie whispered,

"All right, you can tell me what you didn't want to tell your sister. I want the truth, mind." Aggie raised a curious brow.

"I left out the part about the gentleman."

"A gentleman?"

"Yes, he set the baby down at the gate right as Donner was herding the sheep home. If Donner hadn't turned the sheep, the baby would be dead." A painful light shone in Colleen's eyes, at odds with the fighting expression hardening the lines of her red lips.

"Lord above!" Aggie grabbed her heart. " 'Tis a good thing you didn't tell your sister that."

"As soon as this snow stops, I shall go to the magistrate and tell him what happened. And you can believe I'll have a front-row seat at his hanging."

Aggie felt the blood drain from her face. "This just ain't right. There's all kinds of meanness in this world, but this . . . It makes me blood run cold, it does."

"I know. If I'd had a gun I would have shot him."

"Do you know who it was?"

"I didn't see his face, but he was a tall gentleman, and finely dressed." Colleen's expression grew pensive and her brows drew together.

"I know that look. There's something you ain't telling me."

Colleen hesitated a moment, pushed back a lock of golden hair that had fallen loose from the bun at her nape, then said, "I had the strangest feeling I knew him."

"Don't say it. To think there might be a monster loose like that around here!" She shivered and rubbed her arms.

"It makes my blood crawl. I'm going to have to find a way to keep Sharon from going out on her walks." Colleen flexed her fingers, then held out one foot toward the fire.

"You're right. I wouldn't want her running into such a monster."

A silence settled between them.

Aggie walked to the hob and stood next to Colleen. Colleen

was a head taller than she. Her neck bones cracked as she gazed up at Colleen. The worried expression on Colleen's face prompted Aggie to ask, "What is it?"

"I was just wondering if carrying around the baby would be too much for Sharon's heart."

"I wouldn't try to keep her from it. And it would certainly upset her if there was a baby in the house and she couldn't hold it. She'll be all right and I'll help her with it. She'll be good for him, too. You know she has a strange way with living things."

"I know, but what if she becomes attached to him?"

"We'll have to deal with that when the time comes. Surely she knows we'll have to give the wee one up when we find the mother."

"I'm not so sure we will find her. I wonder if she's not dead and the father meant to rid himself of the infant as well." Colleen's disgust for the opposite sex came through in her voice.

"If she ain't dead, then she's probably wishing she were." Aggie shook her head. "She's probably some poor waif who he's taken his pleasure with and wants to be rid of."

"Men! The lot of them are horrible, unfeeling knaves. . . ." Colleen waved her hand angrily through the air, then she sniffed several times and made a face. "Speaking of horrible things—" She turned toward the pot on the hob. "Is it turnip stew again?"

Aggie nodded. "Aye, and that's the last of them."

"Thank goodness." Colleen rolled her eyes, then looked at Aggie. They both smiled at the same time.

Aggie began to stir the stew, but Colleen took the spoon out of her hand. "Go and sit down. You shouldn't be on your feet. Your legs will start swelling again."

"These old legs ain't worn out yet." Aggie snatched the spoon from her. "They might as well take me out and shoot me when I get so feeble I can't take care of my girls. I've took care of you from the moment your mama put you in my arms twenty-two years ago, and I ain't about to stop now.''

Colleen stared at Aggie for a moment, her pretty face growing somber. Then Colleen did something she rarely did, she pecked Aggie on the check. ''I won't let anyone shoot you, Aggie. You know you're more than a servant to us.''

Aggie blinked, her bottom lip trembling as she felt a wash of tears come to her eyes. A lump formed in her throat and she couldn't say anything.

''I guess I'd better go and change my clothes, I'm wet all the way to my petticoat.'' Colleen turned, took one step, then froze as she stared down at the baby rabbit near her feet. She glanced at Aggie over her shoulder for an explanation.

Aggie shrugged. ''She found it outside this morning.''

''Well, rabbits eat very little, and it might keep him out of our garden this spring.'' Colleen grinned, but the tension never left her lips.

Aggie watched Colleen leave the kitchen, her old faded blue gown flapping limply around her long legs. Even in the old dress, she carried herself like a queen, her back straight, her head high, every bit the highborn lady. Her Colleen may be destitute, but it couldn't take the dignity from her. She was a pillar of strength, always had been. Aggie and Sharon had survived off her strength. But pillars only lasted for so long under pressure. One day life would come crashing down on her. One day. More tears came to Aggie's eyes and she sniffed hard, then she smelled the turnip stew. She wrinkled her nose and slapped the lid back on the pot.

The pounding on the door startled Colleen out of a deep sleep. She felt the baby on top of her chest and hoped the abrupt movement hadn't awakened him. Hearing her heartbeat was the only way she could quiet him enough so Sharon could sleep. She glanced over at her sister to see if the din had awakened her. Sharon hadn't moved, still lying on her side, her feet and arms drawn up into a fetal ball, barely taking up her half of the bed. Aggie might have answered the door, but her room was near the kitchen and she snored so loud a cannon blast couldn't awaken her.

Frowning, Colleen gently eased the baby off her chest and laid him down next to Sharon. He didn't awaken and Colleen breathed a sigh of relief.

Bang. Bang. Bang. The knocking grew louder, more insistent.

The fire had long since gone out in the room. Silently cursing the person at the door, she left the warmth of the covers. The frosty air from the floor hit her, seeping up her thin nightgown and sending goose bumps up her legs.

Turning, she laid her pillow next to the baby so he wouldn't roll off the bed, then hurried out of the room, gently closing the door behind her. She groped her way to the front door in the dark. The cold from the floor penetrated the thin socks on her feet. If she didn't know better, she'd swear she was walking barefoot on ice.

The person banged again as she reached the door. She flung it open, ready to give the impatient person on the other side a piece of her mind.

She gasped and stepped back. All she could see was a mountainous figure standing in the darkness, blurred by the thick snow coming down.

''There's been an accident.'' Abruptly, Colleen was shoved aside as a large man stepped through the threshold, dragging a man he was supporting with him.

''See here, sir, you just—''

''Is there a room my cap'n can be usin'?'' the man said in a heavy Scottish brogue. ''He's hurt. I think he's broke some ribs, bumped his head, too. But he's strong, you need not worry about him dyin' on you. I told him we should have held up at an inn, but he wouldn't hear of it. Determined he was to get home in this snowstorm. A lot of good it did him, too.''

After a moment's hesitation, Colleen shivered, then shoved the door closed, waving the snowflakes that had blown through the door out of her face. "Every room is taken. I suppose you can put him on the couch in the parlor." She rubbed her freezing arms.

The Scot acted like he didn't hear her. "We'll be needin' a bit of light in here, lass."

"I'm not your lass, sir, I'm Lady Colleen Davenport to you." She stiffened her back and frowned at the back of the man's head. When he didn't respond, she strode past him to the kitchen and lit the very last inch of a taper.

Snatching up the wooden candlestick, she cupped her hand around the flame and carried the candle back into the hallway. She could see the Scot clearly now. His shoulders were broad as a barn door, buttressed by a barrel chest that protruded from a short sea-green wool coat. His head almost reached the exposed beams in the ceiling. He looked about thirty or so, with bright red curly hair that was sprinkled with snow. Freckles covered his face and dipped below the reddish stubble on his chin. A small gold earring hung from a pierced ear and gleamed in the candlelight. Snow stuck to his bushy eyebrows, making him look almost comical. Since he'd said his captain was hurt, she assumed they were seafaring men.

Her gaze moved to the hurt captain hanging on the Scot's arm. He was not anywhere near the size of the Scot, but he was a large man, his wide shoulders hidden beneath the five capes of his black wool greatcoat. Shaggy raven-black hair hung down to his shoulders. A full thick beard, the same color as his hair, hid the lower half of his face. His head hung down, tilted slightly against one shoulder. His long dark lashes made wide crescents on his cheeks. Tan doeskin breeches were tucked beneath a pair of black mud-covered Hessians.

She felt the Scot's gaze on her and glanced over at him. His gaze flicked down her nightrail then up again. His aqua-colored eyes brightened several shades as they twinkled back at her; then a wide appreciative grin spread across his mouth.

Her cheeks burned as her fingers tightened around the sides of her threadbare nightgown. In her haste to answer the door, she'd forgotten to put on a dressing gown. Now she was standing there exposed, with her hair loose around her waist like any cheap harlot. The blush that had started in her face burned all the way down to her neck now.

"He's gettin' a might heavy, lass." The Scot held one of the captain's arms over his beefy shoulder, while his other arm clamped around the injured man's back and side. He was trying to hold up the dead weight with the side of his hip, but the strain showed on his face.

"I told you, you can put him on the couch."

The Scot stared at her lips intently, then he grunted under his breath and said, "The couch."

"Yes, the couch," Colleen said in her most indignant voice. "It's the only free space we have."

"Point the way, lass." His grin broadened.

"This way, and stop calling me 'lass.' " Colleen shot him the best contemptuous glance she could muster.

He chuckled, a deep rumbling that sounded like muted thunder in his chest.

Her frown deepened as she walked into the parlor and stepped around the Knole-style sofa. It was so old the stuffing on the cushion showed through. The only other furniture in the room was an out-of-tune pianoforte and an ancient oak trunk that they used as a table. She felt the blush on her face deepen at the shabbiness of the room and hoped the stranger wouldn't notice it.

The Scot grunted under the man's weight, but she didn't turn around to help him. If she'd been wearing something more substantial, she might have.

Between deep grunts, he said, "Since I'll be 'ere for a while,

I'd better tell you me name. It's John Robin, but me friends call me Red. I'd like it if you called me that, too."

Colleen didn't bother acknowledging him.

He laid the man on the couch, then his gaze swept the leaking rafters and the buckets sitting on the floor. His face screwed up in a disapproving mask.

"Granted the parlor isn't all that hospitable," Colleen said, growing defensive. "But if you do not like it, you can always take him elsewhere." She grabbed an old moth-eaten blanket from the trunk and wrapped it around her.

He sighed. "He won't be too pleased with this, but then again . . ." He stared at Colleen and that grin was back on his face. "He might like it after all."

"I'll see that he doesn't," Colleen said under her breath.

"I'll have to ride for the doctor." The Scot turned and pulled off his captain's boots and coat. "Is there a doctor to be found in the village?"

"His surgery is the last house on the east end."

"Good, good." He rubbed his beefy hands together, then glanced at the brazier in the corner. "Woo! 'Tis a might cold in here, lass. Do you stay in this room with no heat?" He stared at her lips again.

"One gets used to the cold, sir."

" 'Tis snake blood you'll be havin', then, lass." He chuckled, then rubbed his hands together. "Can we warm it up a bit for the cap'n?"

Colleen's brows drew together, then she said, "I'll see if I can find some coal." She turned to walk back down the steps.

He grabbed her arm. "Nay, I'll be doin' that for you, lass. Just tell me where it is."

"It would take me longer to tell you than to do it myself."

His hand tightened around her arm. "You'll no' be carrying coal, not while I've got me two good arms. Have you no' had a man around to ease the burden for you? Perhaps you're needin' one?'' He grinned again, his eyes twinkling with an impish gleam.

Colleen felt the blood rush to her cheeks. This man was too intuitive by half. Her fingers dug into the blanket around her shoulders as she raised her chin to a haughty angle. ''I certainly do not need a man to 'ease the burden' as you put it. My sister and I survive quite nicely here without a man underfoot.''

He stared at the buckets sitting on the floor. ''I can see that.'' He saw the acerbic expression on her face and his grin widened. ''Now, where is that coal?''

Colleen didn't want to argue with the man any longer. She just wanted the arrogant clod out of her house. Thankful to be rid of him, she said, ''Out back, near the kitchen door. You might have to shovel snow to get at it.''

''That'll be no problem. And while I'm gettin' the coal, perhaps you could be gettin' a blanket to cover the captain.'' He smiled once more, then strode toward the kitchen.

Colleen shook her head, then pulled another blanket out of the trunk and slammed the lid down. She walked over to the sofa and placed it over the captain. His feet hung off the edge of the sofa, and she decided he was taller than she thought. Something about him looked familiar, but she couldn't place his face.

She stared at his brows, black as midnight and flaring above his eyes. His deep-set eyes added a sinister look to his face. His skin was tanned, the color of golden tea. Tiny wrinkles spread out from the corners of his eyes and stopped near his temples. Thick coal-black hair hung down to his shoulders and wisps of it fell along the sides of his lush black beard. A thin gold earring peeked out beneath his left ear. He looked about six and thirty and every bit a pirate rogue just off a ship. Hesitantly she bent over and put her hand on his head to see if he had a fever.

The captain's eyes opened.

Their gazes locked.

Colleen looked into the gray eyes as they narrowed, gleaming at her like icy gray crystals sprayed by searing sunlight. She grabbed her throat, then stumbled back from the bed. Her mouth opened and closed, but no sound would come out.

"What's the matter, Colleen?" he said in a deep drawl. "I've never seen you speechless, but I must admit it's almost as entertaining as when you jilted me."

CHAPTER 2

Sylvester Brock Worthorn Rawlings, the Viscount of Usworth, hoped he was suffering from delusions. But no, he was sure the throbbing pain in his ribs was as real as the witch standing before him.

But what a voluptuous witch she was. The blanket only covered the sides of her shoulders, exposing the prim neckline of her nightrail. He stared at the rise and fall of her heaving bosom, the seductive swell thrusting against the thin lawn. The gown was so threadbare, her dark nipples showed beneath it.

He kept his gaze on the witch's breasts as he said, "Are you going to stand there staring at me, Colleen? I presumed you'd have something to say when we met again. 'Hello' might work."

"I—I . . ." Her words trailed off in a strangled gasp. She clutched her throat as if trying to force out the words.

"Stuttering now," he said, the perverse side of him enjoying every moment of her discomfort.

She stared down at her hands, busily strangling the ends of

the blanket, then glanced up. Candlelight struck her eyes, setting them on fire. Her anger must have taken over, for she found her voice.

"For your information, I can speak, and very distinctly. If I was stuttering, it was because I never expected to see you again."

"Nor I you—especially in bedroom attire. . . ." His gaze flicked over her slowly, making sure she saw him. "You know I used to dream of you like this, though I didn't envision the old blanket. You wouldn't want to remove that for me? Somehow it spoils the moment."

She saw him staring at her and yanked the ends of the blanket together. "How dare you speak to me like that. I won't stand for it!"

"Have you grown prudish?" He raised his brows while his lips twisted down in a sardonic grin. "As I recall, you were anything but modest when we were engaged. Do you remember the way you used to tease me by letting me touch and kiss your breasts? After all these years, I haven't forgotten how they filled my palms. You have a beautiful body, Colleen— and a passionate one, as I recall. I distinctly remember one night in the arbor—"

"Stop it! You're being despicable."

"I suppose I am. I'm not the same man you knew five years ago. I was younger then," he looked pointedly at her, "and a naive fool." He held back the bitterness in his voice as he said, "Now I speak my mind and take what I want—be damned, the consequences."

"I thought you must have a loose screw when I heard you'd bought a ship and were living no better than a pirate. After speaking to you, I'm quite sure you've gone completely mad."

"Been keeping track of me, have you?" One side of his lip twitched in a sneer.

"It didn't matter to me what you were doing, but one hears gossip." She thrust up a haughty jaw. "It is most unfortunate you came home in the middle of a snowstorm. If you had held up at an inn, we would not have had to suffer each other's company.''

"The roads were worse than I'd anticipated," he said, more to himself. "I hoped to get home to my father, but the effort was futile in the snow and sleet."

"Is he ill?" Some of the haughtiness left her voice.

"So I was led to believe in a letter from him."

"I hope you find him in good health. I always liked your father."

"And he, you; though he stopped singing your praises after you left me at the altar."

She stared up at the leaking ceiling, silent, grave, a look of regret on her face.

He stared at her hair, falling down to her waist, the candlelight flickering in the golden highlights, making it look like golden spun silk. Seeing her standing there, barefoot in this freezing hell of a room, wearing a nightgown that should have been used for rags long ago, with a moth-eaten blanket around her, should have given him some sort of satisfaction. But it didn't. He had no idea she'd been reduced to such poverty.

The moment of compassion did nothing to curb the bitterness in his voice as he said, "You never gave me an acceptable explanation of why you cried off. I thought I would have at least received a nasty letter. What made you do it, Colleen?"

"I don't owe you an explanation." Her gaze dropped to him, the haughty mask in place again.

He felt the urge to shake her and probably would have, but for the pain in his ribs and head. "I've gotten over any feelings I may have had for you, so you can tell me the damned truth."

"I don't wish to discuss it with you."

"We'll discuss it, all right. You wouldn't have agreed to marry me if you felt nothing for me, nor would you have responded to my kisses, then suddenly cried off an hour before the wedding. Oh, no, something changed your feelings. I want to know the reason.''

Some of the haughty control slipped, and she blurted, ''You should know.'' She stared at him, indignation burning in the depths of those emerald eyes.

''How should I know? I waited for five damned hours that night for an explanation, but I heard naught from you.''

''No, I was too angry at the time to speak to you. I never wanted to speak to you again. And if your servant—or whatever he is—had not forced his way into this house, I never would have allowed either of you beyond the threshold. Had I one inkling it was you he was bringing in here, I would have told him to take you elsewhere.'' She twisted the ends of the blanket in a white-knuckled grip.

As if summoned by her resentment, Red came in the parlor, carrying four small pieces of coal in a scuttle. He glanced at Colleen, then at Sylvester. He paused for a moment. His brows furrowed, and he looked unsure about speaking. Finally he said, ''Ah, I see you're awake, Cap'n.''

''He's awake, all right. And as soon as the doctor comes, I want him out of my cottage and out of my life.'' Colleen threw the words out like daggers, then she stomped past Red, her hair flying out behind her like a thick gold mantle. She thrust open a door, then slammed it behind her.

Immediately a baby began crying, the high-pitched wail smothered by the closed door.

Sylvester made a face at the door.

''Sounds like there's a wee one in the house,'' Red said, walking over to the hearth, shaking his head. He dumped the few pieces of coal in the grate, then stared at Sylvester.

''I wonder if it is hers?'' Sylvester said, voicing his thoughts out loud.

''Could be why she hates men. One might o' left her flat with a babe. Probably ran her poor man away with her harpin'. And speakin' of her ways, I know she's a bonny thing, Cap'n, but did you have to be gettin' her hair up on her back? There's ten inches of snow, and more fallin'. How will I get you moved?''

Sylvester stared at the door. ''I've no intention of moving. The haughty lady will just have to put up with us for a couple of days.''

''Och! I dinna want to be the one tellin' her.''

''I'll tell her.'' In spite of the pain in his ribs, Sylvester smiled.

''You're smilin' like a cat watchin' a mouse hole. I thought you'd be interested in her. She's a mighty fine-lookin' piece. Got a little too much vinegar in her, though.''

''No one knows that better than I,'' Sylvester said ruefully.

''You've felt her claws, then?''

''You could say that.'' Sylvester's eyes narrowed as he thought of how well he knew her.

''Och! . . . Sounds like she sunk 'em pretty deep.'' Red raised his brows, his eyes gleaming. When Sylvester didn't elaborate on how deep the scars ran, Red turned and lit the coals. His voice grew concerned as he said, ''They didn't have another bit of coal in the bin. I had to scrape bottom to get this. Crofters live better than she does. This is their parlor.''

Sylvester took a good look around the room, now that Colleen wasn't around to distract him. He saw the yellow cracked walls, the bareness, and the buckets on the floor. He glanced up at the roof and watched a drop of water roll along the cracked ceiling and plop into a bucket.

''I've got to go and see to the team and get a doctor in the village,'' Red said, drawing Sylvester's gaze back to him. ''I'll be leavin' you for a time. Try not to get your eyes scratched out 'fore I get back.'' He grinned at Sylvester.

''When you're in the village, hire someone to fix the damned roof, get a load of coal, and make sure the cupboard is stocked. And get a bottle of brandy.'' Sylvester pulled a long strand of golden blonde hair from the quilt and held it between his fingers and he added, ''Better make that a case.''

He watched Red leave, silently cursing that ever-present intuitive smile of his. Red was enjoying this. Not so for Sylvester. Thoughts of seeing her again had plagued him since he hit English soil.

At sea, he'd had a woman in every port to help him forget her. Ravishing women: blondes, brunettes, redheads, raven-haired beauties, hourglass-curved sirens with sweet, giving bodies. They had soothed away the raw memories. But coming face-to-face with The Witch resurrected all the bitter memories. They weren't likely to go away, either. He would never be able to wipe her completely out of his mind until he knew why she had cried off. She owed him that. He was more determined than ever to get it out of her.

Colleen cursed inwardly that she'd slammed the door and awakened the baby. She gently picked him up and bounced him in her arms.

He bawled louder.

Without opening an eye, Sharon turned over and mumbled, ''Feed him.'' She nestled deeper into the covers, then didn't move, looking fast asleep again.

Colleen's brows furrowed at Sharon. All day she had cared for the baby. If she hadn't been exhausted, she would have gotten up with him. Perhaps it was too much exertion for her. On the morrow she would make sure Sharon rested.

She glanced toward the door. A shaft of light flickered beneath it. The only way to the kitchen from her room was through the parlor. She'd rather face a firing squad than Sylvester again. Phillip bawled louder in her arms. Better to face the dragon than keep Sharon awake with a crying baby.

Squaring her shoulders for battle, she strode back out into the parlor, Phillip's distraught screams pounding her ears.

Immediately, Sylvester turned and glanced at her, his eyes like shards of wintry gray ice, his black brows heavy over his eyes. Colleen glanced away and swiftly crossed the room, ignoring his silver-gray eyes boring into her.

"Give me the child," he said in a tone sharp enough to pierce iron.

"No." She paused and tightened her hold on Phillip.

Phillip's screams grew to a fevered pitch now, his face red with anger, his mouth wide, baring his raw gums and pink tongue. She bounced him on her shoulder, but it didn't do a thing to quiet him.

"Either nurse him or give him to me."

Colleen saw Sylvester staring at her breasts and realized, a bit too late, that she was standing before him in her nightgown. Blood rushed to her cheeks as she said, "He's not my baby."

"Then for God's sake, give him to me. I'll hold him while you find something to stick in his mouth."

"But you are hurt."

"I'm not so wounded I can't hold a baby." He swung his booted feet down and sat up, then clutched his ribs, a pained expression on his face. A fine sheen of sweat broke out on his brow.

"That was very stupid of you to get up." Colleen walked toward him, not knowing if he heard her above Phillip's crying, but she hoped he did.

"I'll be fine." He held up his hands and waited for her to give him the baby.

She stared down at his large callused palms and didn't remember them being so wide, or his fingers so long. Those hands had touched places on her body that she didn't care to recall. Her dreams had recalled the memories, though, with vivid, aching intensity, making her wake in cold sweats, panting like a cat on a hot day. A desolate, cold, empty sensation always followed the dreams, an emptiness she feared would one day consume her. Those wicked, sensual hands!

Drawn to them, she found herself placing Phillip in them. The moment Sylvester brought the baby down to his chest, Phillip immediately stopped bawling.

"I don't remember you ever liking children," she said, staring at the baby in disbelief.

"I don't—unless they happen to be mine."

Colleen swallowed hard, while a vision of Sylvester's wife rose up in her mind: a tall beautiful woman with six children tugging on her skirt. Some emotion, which she wouldn't put a name to, swirled in her stomach and made it roil.

"What is the matter? You look as if I've just killed someone in your family." He stared at her intently, his gray eyes shimmering with amusement.

" 'Tis nothing."

Realization dawned on his face, then a ruthless smile made his beard part. "I see, you think I have children—is that it?"

"I would not care if you did."

"What if I told you I had ten of them?"

"I would say I pity your poor wife and the nurse who must care for them."

"Ah, but you still have the tongue of a wasp, my dear." That irritating smile on his face grew wider until his white teeth gleamed at her. "It's such a pleasure to hear it again."

She narrowed her brows at him and bit back a retort. He was baiting her and she wouldn't stoop to his level. "Since Phillip is so happy with you, I'm going to the kitchen to get his milk." She turned abruptly, but his voice stopped her.

"Wait." He glanced down at Phillip with mild interest. "Who does this belong to? Have you started taking in orphans?"

In short, clipped tones, Colleen told him how she'd found the child and added, "And I mean to see the man arrested."

"The scoundrel needs arresting. I shall see the magistrate myself on the matter."

"Thank you, but this is my problem. I shall speak to the magistrate."

"You still have that dignified independent streak." The words were complimentary, but he said them with a tainted edge, hinting it was a flaw in her character. "That hasn't changed, has it? I would have thought your circumstances would have broken you of that iron self-reliance, but you don't need anyone, do you? I see you haven't changed at all."

"Oh, you would have liked that. That's the reason you ordered your solicitor to buy Westmoreland. You wanted to humiliate me because I wouldn't marry you."

"I bought it because it was auctioned off at a cheap price."

"How do you know?—you left England. You told your solicitor to buy it in your stead at any cost. You wanted revenge." Some of the anger left her voice as she said, "What I can't figure out is why you didn't stay to bask in it." She would never tell him that she had swallowed her pride, went to confront him the next day, and found he had left the country.

"Did you expect me to stay here and be mocked and ridiculed by every scandalmonger for miles?"

"No, I wouldn't wish it on anyone." She stared down at her hands. To still her trembling fingers, she balled them into her fists. She said, more to herself, "I wish I could have escaped."

"Was it uncomfortable for you, my dear? I'm so sorry," he said, his voice laced with sarcasm.

She lost her patience. Anger filled her again as she blurted, "You should be happy with your purchase of Westmoreland. It brought barely enough money to pay off all of Father's debts. But I'm sure your solicitor informed you of that. How you must have gloated over it. Well, let me tell you, I'll always hate you for that. Always!" Colleen turned and stormed from the parlor, feeling a choking feeling in her throat.

She wouldn't cry because of him. Never again. Long ago, hours before the wedding, when she had learned something that destroyed all the love she felt for him, she'd cried until she was sick from it. Then and there, she'd vowed to never cry another tear over him—or any man. And she wasn't about to start now, just because he was in her house and goading her. Hopefully he would leave soon, and if he didn't, she would throw him out. She stomped all the way to the kitchen.

The next morning, Colleen stared down into the pot of porridge she was stirring and wondered what was taking the doctor so long to come out of the parlor. She was desperate to know when Sylvester could be moved. Last night, after she'd fed the baby, she'd taken him back to bed. He'd slept peacefully between her and Sharon. But Colleen had lain awake, seething, knowing Sylvester was in the next room.

She glanced out the window. Dark gray clouds harkened the morning, and snow, thick as the threads in an Oriental carpet, hid the sky. The small yard that surrounded the cottage butted against Farmer Britter's field on all four sides. To block the north wind, he had left a small stand of trees standing in the back and on the sides of the cottage. The tall pines and younger oaks bent against the wind and the snow, their trunks hunched, their boughs touching the ground, looking like elderly people frozen in the ground. Slanted drifts almost buried the fence near the base of the trees, only the top rungs peeking through.

They rented the cottage from Farmer Britter, and the only access to the road was by way of a small drive. It circled the cottage and ended near the small barn out back. If she had not known the drive was there, she never would have been able to find it below the snow. She turned and glanced toward the barn. Icicles jutted down from the snow-covered eaves, making a gruesome smile against the fading gray timbers.

The thought of being snowed in with Sylvester made her turn away from the window and frown down at the pot. She heard Sharon cooing to Phillip and glanced toward the kitchen table.

Sharon held the baby in her arms. He looked content to gaze into Sharon's large brown eyes and suck on the bottle Aggie had fashioned out of a hollowed-out cow's horn. A soft piece of leather on the end served as a teat.

"He's adorable, isn't he, Colleen? Just look at his eyes. They're the color of a clear sky, and so alert. He's going to be a very bright boy when he gets bigger. I found that pretty little outfit Mother made for your firstborn. Doesn't he look adorable in it?" Sharon pulled back a pink flannel blanket, showing an embroidered white frock. A cap that matched the frock framed his little cherub face.

Colleen gazed at the tiny mouth moving hungrily over the leather nipple, at the eyes wide with the newness of life, soaking up everything around him. "He is adorable and I feel sorry for the poor little thing," she said, more to herself.

"Colleen."

"Yes?" She glanced at Sharon.

"Yesterday you didn't tell me everything about finding the baby, did you?"

"What makes you say that?" Colleen wanted to glance away, but she looked Sharon straight in the eye.

"It was obvious. You sent me out of the room yesterday so you could tell Aggie what happened." Sharon sounded hurt.

"I didn't."

"You did. You're lying to me again." When Colleen didn't speak right away, Sharon said, "Just because I have a weak heart doesn't mean you have to shelter me from everything. I appreciate your concern, but please, don't treat me like I haven't a brain in my head."

"No, you're too clever by half." Colleen smiled, but Sharon didn't return it.

"I want you to stop treating me like a child. Tell me what happened yesterday," Sharon said, her usually soft voice tight with annoyance.

Colleen crossed her arms over her chest and rubbed her

elbows. Her brows furrowed as she studied Sharon, then she sighed. "I suppose you'll find out anyway, when the gossip gets around the village." Colleen took a deep breath and told Sharon about the man, then she waited for her reaction.

Sharon gulped hard and the blood drained from her cheeks, but she tried gallantly not to show the shock on her face. In a strangled voice, she said, "Is that all?"

"Are you all right?" Colleen strode over to her and touched her shoulder. "Shall I finish feeding the baby?"

"No, no. I'll be fine." Sharon blinked down at the baby. "The poor little thing. Do you think we'll find his mother?"

Colleen didn't want to express her fears that the mother might not be alive, so she said, "The magistrate will find her."

Sharon hugged Phillip closer to her breast. "We can't go to the magistrate. They'll want to take Phillip from us and place him in an orphanage. I could not bear to see him in an orphanage with strangers taking care of him."

"I would hate that as well." Colleen touched the top of the baby's round little head, feeling the soft fine black hair on his head.

"Then we can keep him?" Sharon's eyes lit up.

"I suppose—but just until I can mount my own search for his mother. If I cannot locate her, I shall have to go to the magistrate." She saw the anxious expression on Sharon's face and added, "But we'll keep Phillip until we find a home for him. You have to admit he deserves a home with a mother and father."

"I suppose so."

The dispirited look didn't leave Sharon's face and Colleen said, "You can even interview the prospective couple. And we can go and visit Phillip."

"That would be lovely. Thank you, Colleen, you are too good to me." Sharon smiled up at her, her large brown eyes exuding so much warmth and unselfishness that her pale face glowed with it.

Moments like these, when so much goodness was directed at her, Colleen found herself awed and frightened of losing her sister. Sharon was the only pure and unadulterated thing left in Colleen's life. Having Sharon near always made her aware of the extreme differences between them. When confronted by so much sweetness, Colleen always felt jaded and abundantly aware of the flaws in her own character.

When Sylvester hurt her, and she lost all faith in love and the human race, Sharon had kept Colleen from becoming like their father, cold and callous. He had not always been so. After their mother died giving birth to Sharon, he had turned into a bitter, crazed stranger. Those horrible fears of turning into a heartless shell of a person still haunted Colleen daily. But being near Sharon kept them at bay. She needed Sharon's guiding sweetness, her giving heart. If she ever lost her sister, it would be like losing that one steady pure light which guided her. Hoping some of Sharon's warmth would wear off on her, she bent down and kissed her sister on the brow.

Sharon bestowed a gentle smile on her. "Colleen, may I ask you something else?"

"Of course—but I hope you haven't found another creature to bring in here." Colleen walked back over to the hob, watching the tiny bunny hopping beneath the table.

"Oh, no. I was just wondering if it has upset you overmuch that Lord Usworth is staying with us."

"So you know it's him?" Colleen raised a surprised brow at her.

"He spoke to me this morning." Sharon picked up a handkerchief and wiped a drop of milk dripping down the side of Phillip's chin.

"Oh." Colleen hoped Aggie and Sharon wouldn't know it was Sylvester, but she realized how ridiculous that hope was. She turned back to the hob and stirred the pot of porridge.

"I would not worry about his injury—"

"I'm not worried about him." Colleen saw the crestfallen

look on Sharon's face and realized she'd just snapped at her. She added, "I'm sorry. It's just I don't want you to think I have any feelings for him, because I don't."

Sharon shot her a dubious look. "Well, if you feel that way. But I hear you at night in your sleep calling out his name—"

"I certainly do not."

Sharon touched Phillip's clenched fist and her lips parted in a serene smile. She kept her eyes on the baby while she spoke. "You do, but go ahead and deny it if it makes you feel better."

"Feel better." Colleen bit her lip to keep from snapping at Sharon. She ground the spoon against the bottom of the kettle. The porridge gurgled up at her, and she saw Sylvester's face outlined on the surface, that derisive smile on his lips.

"Have you told him the reason you cried off?"

"No, and I never shall." She shook the spoon in her hand at Sharon. A blob of gruel flew across the kitchen and hit Duke, who was lounging in a stool by the hearth.

He hissed, shot Colleen an indignant look, then jumped down on the floor.

"You should give him a chance to explain," Sharon said, not daunted by the flying gruel.

"I don't owe him anything. Not after the way he ordered his solicitor to purposely humiliate me by buying Westmoreland only two weeks after I cried off. He did it out of pure spite and I loathe him for it. He had no intention of living there, he'd left the country by then. Not only did it drag us through the scandal columns, it also dragged Father through it as well."

"Father had been dead for a week, Colleen, he didn't know anything. Anyway, everyone knew about his gambling debts."

Abruptly the back door opened. Red entered the kitchen, carrying a huge satchel. He knocked the snow off his boots, then plodded across the floor, plunking down his burden on the table.

"What is that?" Colleen asked suspiciously.

Red acted like he didn't hear her. He'd caught sight of Sharon and looked entranced, watching her with the baby in her arms.

Sharon smiled at him, and then as if she were talking to an old friend, she said, "Good morning. The weather is frightful. You shouldn't be out in it."

Red blinked several times and then a reverent expression passed over his face as he said, "Hello, lass."

"Are you deaf? What's in the bag?" Colleen asked again, walking up to Red's broad back.

Sharon looked at Colleen. "Lord Usworth told me he was deaf. He can't hear you."

Colleen raised her brows at this news, then she felt a tug on her conscience for being so abrupt with him.

Red obviously read Sharon's lips, for he turned and saw Colleen standing behind him. "Oh, there you are." He glanced back at Sharon. "And would you mind tellin' me who this pretty little fairy is?"

"That is my sister, Lady Sharon Davenport. Sharon, this is Red."

"Pleased to know you, little one." Red executed a low bow. "Pretty little babe you have there."

"Thank you. He is adorable, isn't he?"

Red cooed at the baby.

Colleen tapped him on the shoulder to get him to look at her. And she raised her voice and spoke slowly as she said, "You mind telling me what is in this satchel?"

"That would be meat, lass. And there's more coming. I ordered a load of coal, too. George White will be here to fix your roof soon as he can get through the snow. I made use of your barn out back to stable the horses. I hope that don't set your hair bristling."

Colleen squared her shoulders. "I didn't order our roof to be fixed."

"No, but the Cap'n did."

Colleen was about to protest Sylvester's high-handed ways,

but Sharon spoke up. "How nice of him to fix our roof." She shot Colleen a pleading glance.

It never failed. When Sharon gave her that sweet, reproachful look of hers, Colleen always felt like the biggest shrew alive. But the feeling was short-lived as she peeked into the sack and saw a huge ham and a side of beef. She dropped the edge of the sack and said, "I suppose his lordship can't eat what we have been eating."

Red stared at the porridge bubbling in the pot. "Don't take this to heart, lass, but that stuff wouldn't keep a baby chick alive."

Colleen was about to open her mouth, but Sharon touched his arm, which brought his gaze around to her. "That is wonderful. Please send Lord Usworth our thanks."

"I'll do that, little one. I'll go tell him now."

"Oh, no." Colleen grabbed his beefy arm. "I'll tell him in person. But first, he'll eat this porridge like the rest of us." Colleen ladled a mountain of the gray mushy stuff into a bowl, then flounced out of the kitchen, leaving Sharon with a disturbed expression on her face, and Red smiling.

She met Aggie in the hall, her bosom heaving. Aggie obviously had run out of her room and her breaths were coming in great gasps. "You shouldn't have let me sleep in this morning."

"I didn't think you were feeling well." Colleen usually started breakfast for Aggie when she knew her legs were bothering her. She'd never complained before now.

"My hearing's well enough. I heard men talking. Who's come?"

"We have visitors. They came in the night. A gentleman was wounded in a carriage accident. Dr. Collins is here."

"Oh, well, menfolks in the house. Won't that be a nice change. You should have got me up," Aggie said, sounding excited, hurrying toward the kitchen, rubbing her hands together like she was about to open a Christmas package.

Colleen met Dr. Collins outside the parlor. He was a tall,

balding man, as thin as a drainpipe. He paused and said, ''He broke a few ribs and has a nasty bruise on his head, but he'll live.''

''He's too spiteful to die.''

Dr. Collins chuckled. ''You may be right there. He spouted some pretty malignant expletives at me when I bandaged his ribs.''

''When can he be gone from here?'' Colleen asked eagerly.

Dr. Collins popped his hat on his head and hefted his black bag in his left hand. ''Not for a week, I'm afraid.''

''A week?'' Colleen realized she'd yelled this when she saw the doctor flinch.

''Now, don't get distraught. You'll have to learn to live with him for a while. He's a rich sea captain, I take it, and you have to look on the bright side. You can charge him an outrageous rent while he's here and have some heat in this house so Lady Sharon doesn't come down with a chill.'' Dr. Collins chucked her under the chin and looked content that he'd settled the matter, then he went on to another.

''Now, he should stay in bed. Here's a bottle of laudanum. Give him a dose every six hours. I'll check back in a day or two.'' He stuffed the bottle in the crux of Colleen's arm, then stared down at the porridge. ''He'll need something that sticks to his ribs, my dear, not the meager fair you live on.'' He saw Colleen's scowl and added, ''No need to see me out.''

Colleen watched him walk to the door and wondered why Sylvester had kept his identity a secret from the doctor. It couldn't have been to spare her from being the brunt of gossip. And there would have been gossip in the village. After the scandal with Sylvester, she had moved to this cottage twenty miles away. But it wasn't far enough. The gossip had followed her and it would start up like a bonfire if word leaked out that Sylvester was staying in her cottage.

She heard a moaning sound intruding into her thoughts. She frowned and walked into the parlor.

Colleen paused when she saw him lying on the couch. The covers were pulled up to his waist, meeting a thick white bandage covering his ribs. Higher still, she saw the dark patch of hair on his muscular chest, and then the thick brawny shoulders that appeared to be wider than the sofa. She gulped and licked her lips. The sight of him, almost naked, sent a strange pain beneath her ribs and she found it hard to breathe.

"Be careful, Colleen, if you look at a man like you want to rake your claws down his back, you may get that chance."

"I—I . . ." She stuttered and forced her gaze to his face.

Veiled now by the pain, his gray eyes didn't have their usual penetrating coldness, but a cynical sneer stretched his lips tight across his face. His forehead glistened with a fine sheen of perspiration, and his damp raven hair fell down beside his beard in wet strands on the pillow.

She had meant to ring a peal over his head for his high-handed ways in ordering repairs to the roof, but after seeing how much pain he was in, her voice came out sounding oddly polite and caring. "Are you hurting? Is there anything I can do for you?"

He raised a dark brow at her and looked surprised that it was she who had spoken. "I can think of a few things that would take my mind off the pain, if you're willing to do them." His gaze roamed slowly over her, devouring every curve in her body, then inched up again, pausing to stare at her breasts.

Colleen was wearing an ancient bishop-blue day dress that she'd had from her come-out days. Thin and faded, it was too small for her now. The worn material stretched across her breasts and left nothing to the imagination. Blushing all the way down to the roots of her hair, she tried to keep from staring at his chest as she said, "Be obnoxious, see if I care."

"I don't see any harm in trying to take my mind off my misery. And it might do you some good. It appears to me you're starved for a man, Colleen. I bet you haven't kissed a man in five years. That can wreak havoc on a woman as passionate as you."

"For your information, I've kissed dozens of men."

"Have you?" He cocked a brow at her, then smiled and dropped his gaze to her breasts again. "And did you tease them the way you did me?"

"You really are insufferable. Your mind stays in the gutter. There is no speaking to you." Colleen squeezed her eyes closed until they hurt, then she plopped the bowl of porridge down on his chest. When she saw him wince, it gave her a moment of pleasure. In the sappiest, sweetest voice she could muster, she said, "Here is your breakfast. I hope you enjoy it."

She turned to leave, but his arm snaked out and grabbed her wrist. "If I have to eat this stuff, the least you could do is feed it to me."

"If you can spout insults at me, you aren't that injured." Colleen couldn't bear to look at his naked chest any longer, or feel those warm hands on her skin. She twisted her wrist out of his grasp. "But if you really need help, I'll send Red to you." She turned around.

"Witch," he said under his breath.

She whipped around, saw the contemptuous smile on his face, and blurted, "Beast!"

"Teasing termagant!"

"Shark with a beard!"

He opened his mouth to call her another name, but she jammed a spoonful of porridge between his teeth, then turned and stomped from the room, leaving him lying there with the spoon sticking out his mouth. He had goaded her again and she'd let him. She was more angry with herself than with him.

That evening, Colleen walked the kitchen floor. Phillip was fussing and she couldn't get him to stop. Everyone else was in the parlor, enjoying the warmth of a fire in the hearth, something they hadn't done in years. They had always gathered in the kitchen after dinner in winter. Coal was too expensive to waste on warming the parlor just for Sylvester, and Colleen told Red that when she had seen him come into the kitchen lugging a pail of coal. But he said, "The coal bin is full now, lass." Then, ignoring her, he built a fire anyway.

Colleen wasn't about to go anywhere near Sylvester. Before she'd go in the parlor, she'd grow old and rot in the kitchen. The door creaked open. Her mind still on Sylvester, she inadvertently glanced up. Every muscle in her body contracted when those gray, torch-lit eyes swept her from crown to toe.

Sylvester stood in the threshold, his tall frame filling it.

CHAPTER 3

Colleen stared at him. His shirttail wasn't tucked in his breeches and it hung down around his hips, giving him a handsome roguish look. The top of his shirt was open, exposing the bandage on his bronzed chest and the thatch of dark hair above it. His gray eyes gleamed like two frost-tipped icicles. He had shaved, exposing a stubborn square jaw and the deep dimple in the middle. Thick black hair hung in loose waves around his shoulders. He looked more handsome than she remembered. Her breath caught at the sight of him.

"Need some help with the baby?" A wry smile turned up the corners of his lips.

"Not from you. You're supposed to be in bed."

"All I could hear was his bawling. I hate to hear children crying when I can do something about it. Give him to me." He reached for the baby.

Colleen saw his face turn white, then he grabbed his ribs. He took a step and stumbled. While clutching the baby with one arm, she grabbed his waist with the other and supported him.

"You really are a stupid man," she said.

"I don't know whether I like that epithet, or 'shark with a beard.' "

"You're both."

"Not quite. I'm beardless now. You can see all my shark teeth." He grinned at her, his lips stretching wide across his face, showing his white, even teeth.

"As long as you don't sink them in my back, it doesn't matter to me if they are exposed or not."

"Better have a care, your sweet words might make me sink my teeth into you, but I can think of better places than your back," he said, all the teasing leaving his voice. The icy contempt faded from his eyes for a moment.

She was only a head shorter than he. His face was inches from her, so close she could feel his hot breath on her cheek and smell the lingering scent of brandy. That familiar quickening she had always felt at his nearness swirled inside her. Her heart pounded sporadically against her ribs.

When they reached the chair, she breathed a sigh of relief and helped him down into it. "Here, sit before you fall down."

He stretched out his long legs without taking his eyes off her. "Now, give him to me," he said, holding out his arms.

She looked at Phillip, red-faced from crying, then had no choice but to hand the baby to him. The hard rigid muscles of his chest brushed against her forearms. The heat of his body burned right through his shirt and the sleeves of her dress. A memory of another time flooded back to her, when he'd held her against his chest and his hand had glided over her collarbone. He'd placed tiny kisses down her neck, all the while pushing the shoulders of her gown and petticoat down. When her breasts were bare, his mouth dipped down to one of her nipples . . .

Phillip stopped crying. The silence jarred her back to the

present. She stared at Phillip noticing him now. He looked content, peeking over Sylvester's broad shoulder at Duke, who was walking along the butcher table, his long orange-ringed tail twitching over his back.

Sylvester hadn't stopped staring at her, and he was wearing a look she remembered well. When he had worn that look in the past, she'd ended up in the garden, half naked, kissing him, succumbing to his passion. She would always regret that weakness. Wiping her sweaty palms down her apron, she turned back to the counter to peel potatoes for supper.

"I detect a tremor in your hands, my love," he said, his voice thick with a satiny deepness.

"You must be seeing things." She tried to control her trembling hands and concentrate on holding the paring knife still.

"I never thought I'd see you cooking—or living like this."

Her humiliation wouldn't let her look at him. She kept her gaze on the thin line of potato skin she'd peeled. "How was I supposed to live? Father left us nothing but debts. And the purchase of Westmoreland brought us no profit." She fired a pointed glance his way.

"Had I known you were so destitute—"

"Surely your solicitor told you."

"He didn't. I received a missive from him, telling me he had purchased it for a fair price."

"It was highway robbery, but that is in the past. I never wanted your charity, nor would I have accepted it."

"Yes, you have your pride," he said, his voice snide. "But did you think about Sharon and her condition? She shouldn't be living in this damned hovel."

"I always think about her." Her tone grew defensive. "And she hasn't had a spell since we've come to live here."

"But she should be somewhere warm and go to the best doctors. If you didn't want to come to me for money, why did you not go to my father? He would have been glad to help you.''

''I couldn't, not after . . .'' She paused, unable to tell him she would rather die than face Lord Usworth, a man whom she had loved as much as her own father. After she had cried off, she couldn't bear to see the disappointment in his face. The day after she cried off, she'd gone to confront Sylvester. The butler had informed her that ''his lordship has left the country,'' in snide, judgmental tones. Then she'd heard Lord Usworth's bellow boom down the stairs, ''Is that Lady Davenport down there?'' She had run down the front steps, leaped back on her mount, then had rode away from the house like the devil was behind her. No, she couldn't bear to face his father.

He broke the silence between them and asked, ''Why did you do it, Colleen? I need to know.''

''Why don't you ask Lady Sefton?'' She shook the paring knife at him, punctuating each word.

His dark brows met over his nose. ''What does she have to do with your crying off?'' He narrowed his eyes at her.

''Why are you pretending to be innocent? Of course you know why.''

''If I did, would I be asking you?''

''All right, I'll tell you.'' She slammed down the paring knife on the counter.

At that moment, the door swung open and Aggie came into the kitchen. When she looked at Colleen, her bottom lip pouted out, a sure sign she was angry about something. ''Mr. Rupert Spears and Mr. Winston Spears just pulled up in a sleigh,'' she said, her voice unusually stiff.

Colleen's frown dissolved as she smiled and wiped her hands down her apron.

''Who are these Spearses?'' Sylvester asked, sounding mildly interested.

''They're the sons of Mrs. Spears, who was a friend of Lady Davenport's 'fore she died. They've been mighty kind to us—

the only ones from the old days who even bothered to call on my girls after the scandal. They're regular callers. I'm hoping that Mr. Rupert will propose to our Colleen." Aggie nodded at Colleen. "I think it will be any day now. Comes here regular as clock strikes—even in a blizzard." Aggie was still pouting, belying the inordinate amount of pleasure beaming in her faded eyes.

Colleen knew what Aggie was doing and grabbed her arm. "Come on, let's let them in, shall we?"

"Your guests can wait." Sylvester's voice was rapier-sharp. "We're not done with our discussion."

"We are now." She cast him a long hard look, then guided Aggie out of the kitchen.

When they were well away from the kitchen, Colleen rounded on Aggie. "I would appreciate you not playing matchmaker." She untied the apron around her waist. "I'm done with Lord Usworth."

Aggie harrumphed under her breath. "You're in no way done with him. If you were, you would have told me who he was. When I saw that handsome mug without the beard, I knew right away who he was."

"I didn't think it mattered."

"Silly me, now, why should it matter that he's staying right here under our roof?" Aggie leveled a look at Colleen and snatched the apron out of her hand.

"Nothing will come of it, and I'll thank you to say no more about it," Colleen said, growing defensive.

"Well, I've just one more thing to say. It's nice to have a man around here." She saw Colleen's sour look and added, "Well, maybe not his lordship exactly, but that Red—now he's a godsend. There's a kind man—kindness itself. I hated to see Lord Usworth send him away to the old earl—but I suppose he needed to know what happened to his son. The house seems empty without Red here. Do you know he cooks? He helped me make scones.''

''Yes, but we haven't tasted them,'' Colleen said. A knock sounded on the door, and she glanced toward it.

''I'll let the misters in.'' Aggie wrapped the apron around her waist. ''You'd better go and wake our Sharon. She's resting on the couch.''

Colleen found Sharon lying on the sofa. Her arms were crossed over her chest and her legs drawn up the way a young child sleeps. Her eyes were closed. Thin blonde hair fell down along her pale face, making her look much younger than her seventeen years. Colleen gazed at Sharon and wondered if having the baby in the house was too much for her.

She gently shook Sharon. ''Wake up, my dear. We have guests.''

Sharon sat up on the couch, rubbing her eyes and looking disoriented. ''I must have dozed off.'' She patted her hair back in the bun at her nape, then straightened her shoulders.

Rupert and his brother Winston strode into the parlor. Rupert stopped and handed Aggie their coats and a basket laden with food and packages. ''Our mother sent this disaster hamper for the ladies. She was positive they would be snowed under and starved to death.''

''Thank you, sir.'' Aggie graced Rupert with one of her gracious smiles, then glanced at Colleen with something close to regret in her eyes before she left the room.

Rupert strode toward Colleen, smiling. He was a tall man, with a high forehead and thinning brown hair, and looked in his late thirties. He had pleasing blue eyes, which added a degree of handsomeness to his countenance.

Winston looked much like his brother, with the same pleasing blue eyes, but he was younger and possessed a full head of wiry hair. The thick walnut-brown locks stuck out over his forehead and over his eyes. Yellow britches covered his legs and the points of his shirt collar were so high and starched he couldn't turn his head, and it made him look stiff-necked. His waistcoat was yellow paisley and over it, a scarlet coat. Colleen thought he looked like a very foppish sheepdog, unlike Rupert who wore tasteful tans and blacks.

"My dear Lady Colleen." Winston bent over Colleen's extended hand and didn't let his lips linger long on her skin. He stood, then stepped to Sharon, kissing her hand as well.

Sharon's face lit up in a smile. "Mr. Spears, it was so nice of your mother to think of us. Please send her our thanks and our regards. How is your dear mama?"

"Well enough," Winston answered for Rupert. "Lady Colleen, you are as lovely as ever." Winston's eyes twinkled as he bent and kissed her hand. He let his lips linger on her skin.

Winston flirted with anything closely resembling a female. Colleen saw him as no more than a bothersome coxcomb, so she tolerated his hot breath on her hand.

Rupert noticed his brother and his blue eyes narrowed slightly. She wasn't sure if Rupert was angry with Winston for playing the coquette, or because he was jealous.

Winston raised his head and looked directly at his brother. It was evident he liked baiting him. He stepped over to Sharon, but only pecked her outstretched hand in a brotherly way, then stood and said, "Ah, Lady Sharon, I hope you are well."

"Yes, very well, thank you." Sharon smiled at him. "Please sit." Sharon motioned to a spot near her on the sofa.

The appalling lack of furniture in the room grew embarrassingly evident whenever Rupert and Winston visited. Colleen knew they would not sit until she did, so she strode over to the stool in front of the pianoforte and plopped down. Finally they sat near Sharon on the sofa.

To cover the awkward silence, Colleen said, "How nice it is to see you, but you should not have risked getting stuck in a ditch just to call on us."

"That is so true," Sharon said, looking worried. "You are out in all this horrid weather. How did you find the roads?"

"Terrible mess," Winston spoke up. "We could hardly get through with the sleigh. But our mother was worried you were stranded out here in this snowstorm. She would have nothing but for us to come out here and see if we could be of service to you."

"How very kind of her," Sharon said. "She is such a kind and caring person. Ever since Father died, she's been so good to us."

"Yes, well, I believe she treasures that friendship with your mother. She speaks of her often. I'm sure she still misses her." Winston smiled warmly at Sharon.

"Yes, I'm sure she does." Sharon stared pensively down at a pillow near her arm. A look of regret washed over her expression as she ran her delicate fingers over the worn braided edge, remaining silent.

"Tell them your news, Brother," Winston said, then looked over at Rupert.

"What news?" Sharon asked eagerly.

"Rupert is engaged." Winston shot his brother a disapproving glance. "He's been keeping it a secret for months now. He just got around to telling Mother."

Colleen kept the surprise from her voice as she said, "Who is the lucky lady?"

"Lady Caroline Robbins."

"Is that the Robbins family who owns the shipping companies all over the world?" Sharon asked, grinning sweetly.

Rupert nodded. "Yes, I believe she's very wealthy."

"She's an income of over a hundred thousand a year," Winston said, with a bragging note in his voice. "Old Rue has done pretty well for himself." He slapped Rupert on the shoulder.

Abruptly Sylvester entered the parlor, cradling Phillip on his shoulder. Phillip's small head rested against the side of Sylvester's arm, his gaze engrossed by everything in the room.

Sylvester's broad shoulders dwarfed the baby and made him look tinier than a little doll.

Rupert and Winston stared at Phillip, then at Sylvester, taking in his shirt, half buttoned and hanging down around his hips. Rupert's gaze flicked over him, then he stood and executed a low bow. "Ah, this must be your guest. I heard in the village a wounded sea captain was staying with you."

Colleen wasn't surprised that the whole village had learned of her houseguest. Gossip there traveled faster than a posting coach. She made introductions, then Winston stared at the baby and said, "Is that your child, Mr. Rawlings?"

"I cannot lay claim to him."

"I daresay he favors you." Rupert casually eyed the baby.

"Does he?" Sylvester gently picked up Phillip and held him out so he could look at him.

"He does have your dark hair." Sharon smiled sweetly when Sylvester leveled his gray eyes on her.

"The child is not his," Colleen said, too forcefully, which earned her a curious glance from Sylvester. She ignored him and told the Spearses how she had found the baby and ended by saying, "I fully intend to see that horrible man is punished. Sharon doesn't want me to go to the magistrate, but I shall go as soon as the snow melts a bit."

"We'd be glad to look into the matter for you," Winston said, eyeing the baby, then Rupert. "Wouldn't we, dear brother?"

"Indeed, it would give me great pleasure to be of service to you, Lady Colleen." Rupert smiled at her.

"You needn't bother. I shall see the magistrate for Lady Colleen." Sylvester glanced at Rupert, then at Winston, his gray eyes so hard and icy that neither Rupert nor Winston said anything for a moment.

"As you wish, sir." Rupert's head bowed, a succinct gesture that made his chin hit the points of his collar, then he turned to Colleen. His eyes gleamed with indignation as he said, "May I have a word *alone* with you, Lady Colleen?"

Colleen stared warily at him. He was about to scold her for housing Sylvester under her roof, she could see it in his expression. It just wasn't done without a chaperone in the house. Colleen had long since done away with proprieties. She had more important things to worry about, like what they would eat for their next meal.

Before she could answer, Sylvester wrinkled his nose, stared at the baby, then said, "I believe Phillip has made a large deposit. You had better change him. I don't mind holding him, but I draw the line at cleaning up messy bottoms." He strode over to Colleen and gently laid Phillip down into her arms, letting his forearm brush against her breast.

Her nipple hardened instantly. She felt hot warmth move up her breasts, setting her chest and neck on fire. Her hands trembled as she took the baby, then when he didn't move his arm, she shoved it away.

He knew what his touch had done to her, and his mouth twisted in a wicked grin. His back was to Rupert and Winston. Colleen was sure they hadn't seen the indecent gesture, but still her face colored up. She wanted very much to slap the grin off Sylvester's face.

"I suppose we should take our leave, then. It looks like Captain Rawlings is taking care of you," Winston said, his voice tight.

"It does appear so." Colleen glared at Sylvester.

That maddening grin of his widened.

"I'll show you out." Sharon stood and slowly walked out of the room.

After a rueful glance in Sylvester's direction, Winston and Rupert followed in Sharon's wake.

When Colleen was sure they were out of hearing distance, she turned on Sylvester and hissed, "How dare you be so rude? You offended them."

"Did I? I'm sure they'll get over it."

"That is beside the point. They have been very kind to

Sharon and me. And they came all this way in the snow. You could have kept a civil tongue in your head."

"I wonder at their motives. Did either of them propose yet?"

"If they should do, you'd be the last person I'd tell."

"Do you fear I'd ridicule them for being two kinds of a fool proposing to a lady who may not even show up for the wedding?"

"It is none of your business, should fifty men propose to me and I choose not to marry them."

"No doubt you'd enjoy it." He raised a satirical brow at her.

"How like you to stand in my own home and ridicule me and my guests!" She stomped her foot at him.

"I wasn't disparaging you, I was merely pointing out the obvious. And as for your guests, it's plain to see they only call on you because you're titled and their mother has a hope you'll marry one of them."

Colleen knew he was right. They had tried to call on her after her mother died, but her father had refused to receive them. It had always infuriated him that her mother was friends with Mrs. Spears. They were of the nouveau riche class, having made their money in shipbuilding. Mrs. Spears had only started to call on her again after her father died. But she'd never tell Sylvester that. Instead she said, "Did it ever occur to you that Rupert and Winston Spears may be attracted to me for other reasons than my title?"

"I'm sure of it." His gaze dropped to her breasts and lingered there as he said, "What man would not be attracted to a siren like you? I know firsthand how beautiful and bewitching you can be, or have you forgotten about our little sessions in the moonlight?"

"You really are despicable."

"Only when I want something, and I always get what I want." He glanced back up at her face. Some of the gray ice left his eyes for a moment and they burned with a strange light.

"I should go and change Phillip." Something in his eyes frightened her. He used to look at her like that when they were engaged. She didn't want to go back there again, or experience those feelings again. Once she had loved him more than a woman should love a man, so deeply she had wanted to die when she found out how wicked he was. Never again would she care that much for a man—especially him. She shifted Phillip to her right shoulder and stood up to leave.

When he saw that she was leaving, he said, "Which of them is your favorite? The older one seemed more your type. You could probably lead him around by the nose very easily. Are those the puppies you have been kissing?" He smiled, the cynical light back in his eyes.

"I hate you!" Colleen stomped her foot at him.

The sudden movement made Phillip's little face scrunch up; then he opened his mouth and screamed.

Sharon appeared, took one look at Phillip, and hurried toward him. "Let me have the little darling, I'll change him." Before Colleen could protest, Sharon snatched him up. She smiled serenely at Sylvester, then at Colleen, and padded out of the room.

"Now see what you've done!" Colleen cried, knowing she had allowed him to goad her again and scare Phillip.

"It is not my fault you cannot control your temper, my love."

Some of the harshness left his expression; then his face turned pale as snow. He grabbed his ribs, flopped down on the couch and stretched out his long legs, crossing his ankles. He rested his head back against the sofa. When he closed his eyes, she really began to worry.

"Are you all right?" Colleen's brows snapped together as she stepped toward him.

"Perfectly."

"You shouldn't be up. Lie down." She reached out and touched his shoulder.

"No, no. I'll be all right. Just let me sit here a moment. It was just a twinge. It'll pass."

Colleen bent over and placed her hand on his forehead. He felt a bit warm, but he wasn't burning up with a fever.

When she went to move her hand, he said, "Your fingers feel good. Would you keep your fingers there? It'll take my mind off the pain."

She should have drawn back, should have stepped away from him and gone out of the room, but she didn't. Just as naturally as if her hand belonged there, her fingers curled around his high brow and she ran her fingers up past the widow's peak on his forehead. She did it again, this time stroking his brow. The satiny softness of his thick wavy black hair tantalized her palm. She curbed an overwhelming desire to run her fingers through his hair. Five years ago he had always kept his hair cropped short. A good thing—if it had been shoulder-length back then, she would have constantly had her hands in his hair.

"Hmmm! That's better," he said, his eyes still closed. "Could you rub my neck?" He bent his head forward.

"Are you sure this is helping?" She glanced skeptically down at him.

"Yes, but it might help more if you massage my neck."

All Colleen wanted to do was get away from him, but she couldn't very well leave him in pain. She stepped around to the back of the sofa, then began rubbing his neck. Her fingers kneaded the dense, tight muscles of his wide shoulders. The hardness of his body penetrated straight through her skin and caused a warmth to shoot up along her arms and pool in her breast.

"That feels wonderful. A little lower."

Her hands moved to his shoulders and along the corded muscles there. Glancing up at the ceiling, she fought the sharp stabs of desire plaguing her. How much longer? Could she stand much more torture? She squeezed her eyes closed, feeling her heart pounding in her chest.

He groaned, a deep impatient sound, then she grew vaguely aware of his hands covering hers. She could feel the roughness of his skin, the strength in his wide palms and long fingers. He laced his fingers between hers and moved them slowly back and forth. The heat of his callused skin moving against the tender flesh inside her fingers made her feel dizzy and so languid that she could dissolve away at any moment.

Before Colleen knew it, her hands were moving over his chest, the rigid muscles rippling beneath her palms. He was pressing her hands tight against his skin. When her fingers moved along his open shirt and came in contact with his naked flesh, he stiffened. His muscles turned into hard steel under her fingertips, and he increased the pressure on the back of her hands, rubbing her palms harder against his bare skin.

She could feel her hand gliding over a thin film of perspiration on his skin. Her fingers moved of their own accord and entwined in the coarse hair on his chest. The only thing encompassing her mind was his body and how it molded to her fingers. It was sweet torture to touch him again, to feel the heat of him melding with her. Her knees grew weak and she had to lean against the back of the sofa.

''Colleen, my sweet . . .'' His words sounded like a tortured plea. He turned and his hands moved up the back of her arms, pushing the sleeves of her dress against her tingling skin. The feel of his hands, the heat of them, shot through her clothes, through her skin and up her arms. The heat pooled in her breasts and made her shudder.

When his hands moved along the sides of her breasts, she sucked in her breath and clenched her eyes tighter together. Then she felt his hands moving around to her back and up her neck.

One hand moved to cup her nape, then he pulled her head down toward him.

CHAPTER 4

The moment their lips touched, she was lost in the feel of him holding her, in the savage, possessive movement of his lips taking her mouth. Her body gave over to him and she wrapped her arms around his neck. His lips moved against hers, pressing with an urgent hardness against her mouth. Then his tongue slipped between her lips, gliding along her teeth, begging to be let in.

She opened for him and his tongue drove into her mouth, plundering the moist depths. Before she knew it, he eased her from around the back of the sofa, then pulled her into his lap. His hands reached up to cradle her head as his kiss deepened and grew fierce.

Years of suppressed passion erupted within her. She wrapped her arms around his neck and grabbed handfuls of his black hair, feeling his urgency and hers driving her. Growing bold, she plunged her tongue in his mouth, tasting his moist heat. This wasn't a dream, this was Sylvester kissing her, caressing her. She gave in to all the fire he caused in her, and arched her back, pressing her body against his hard chest.

His hands covered her breasts; then he rubbed his thumbs over her nipples, all the while flattening and kneading her tingling flesh.

From a long distance away, she heard someone clearing their throat. Her mind was too drugged by passion to even care that they were not alone.

When Sylvester broke the kiss, Colleen's desire-drugged wits returned in a jolting rush. She glanced past Sylvester's shoulder at Aggie.

She was clutching a tea tray, her knuckles white from the pressure. Her jaw hung open and her eyes couldn't get any wider.

Colleen glanced back at Sylvester and saw the devilish smile on his face. Five years of pent-up ire exploded inside her. She drew back and smacked him across the face. The sound hit the silent air like a whip.

She leaped off his lap and cried, "You did that on purpose. You weren't in any pain. You're an insufferable lout!"

He threw back his head and laughed at her.

She raised her hand to smack him again, but he grabbed her wrist. "Once is enough, my sweet."

"Ohhh! I hate you!" She looked at the red imprint of her fingers on his face and felt a moment of gratification. But it was short-lived as she felt her own hand still stinging from the slap. With an angry jerk, she wrenched her arm free of his grasp. "See if I ever touch you again!" She stormed out of the room, leaving Aggie staring open-mouthed at her, and Sylvester smiling derisively.

Sylvester felt the raised whelp on his face and a wry smile stretched across his lips. He might have deserved the slap, but it was unexpected. One minute he felt her trembling in his arms; the next, she lashed out at him. It was obvious he could still arouse the burning passion in her—as she did in him.

"She didn't mean it, me lord." Aggie hurried into the room.

"She meant it." Sylvester stared ruefully at the empty doorway, and inadvertently continued to stroke his face.

"Nay, she didn't. My Colleen ain't violent by nature. You know that. You hurt her, is all—you hurt her bad. She can't forget that." Aggie leveled a reproachful glance at him, then set the tea tray down on top of the pianoforte.

"I did nothing to her." Sylvester's anger came through in his voice. "She's the one who left me at the altar for pure spite. I knew how passionate and independent she could be . . ." Sylvester paused a moment, then said, more to himself, "That's why I fell in love with her, but I never thought she could be so cruel to do what she did to me."

"Nay, you're wrong. There ain't a mean bone in her body. I know, I raised her. She's like me own." Aggie shook her head, shaking loose tendrils of gray hair from the bun at the back of her head.

"I appreciate your loyalty to her, but I know firsthand just how unfeeling she can be. She left me standing at the damn altar for an hour waiting for her. I had to face five hundred guests, then she refused to come and give me an explanation. I waited for six hours before I left the country."

"She was upset." Tears shone in her faded blue eyes. "I remember her crying her eyes out. It hurt me to see her like that. I'd never seen her cry. She was always the strong one of the two. Even when she broke her wrist that time. You must have been at the shooting party. She talked about meeting you and how kind you'd been to her."

Sylvester was silent a moment, then said thoughtfully, "She was riding right in front of me when she took a fence most expert horsemen wouldn't attempt. I saw her go down. For a moment I thought she'd broken her neck." Sylvester leaned his head back on the sofa and stared up at the ceiling. He remembered how matter-of-fact Colleen had said her wrist was broken after he'd helped her up. She tried desperately to hide the pain, but it had blazed in her vivid green eyes. He found out later she had been only twelve at the time. It was then and there he knew she was different from any female he'd ever met. He'd seen grown men cry over less. He couldn't help but admire her courage.

It made him angry how casually Lord Davenport had treated the accident, though. He had never met the gentleman before the hunting party, and couldn't believe how belligerent he was. He had insisted his daughter's wrist was only sprained. Sylvester had argued with him. That was an argument Sylvester enjoyed winning. In the end Lord Davenport agreed to take her to the doctor. Sylvester grinned, remembering how he'd given the belligerent fool a bloody nose.

"It's a wonder she didn't break her neck. When I saw him bringing my Colleen home, covered head to toe in mud and her arm in a sling, I wanted to thrash him, I did. . . . And him acting so proud of her because she hadn't shed a tear." Aggie shook her head and her voice grew pensive. "He always wanted a son and tried to make her into one. She never cried neither, but I cried for her—especially after what he did in the stable." Aggie grew pensively silent.

"What did he do?" Sylvester raised his head and frowned at her.

"It was horrible. The old bugger got it into his head to shoot the horse. My Colleen begged him not to do it, even jumped in front of the gun." Aggie's eye widened at the memory. "I thought she was going to be killed. He shoved her aside and shot the beast, right in front of her eyes. I don't know how she took it, being so little. You see, it was her horse and she pampered that animal like a baby. I'll never forget her reaction as long as I live. She stood there like a scrawny little soldier, staring at him, her eyes big as rocks, then she stomped out of the stable without a word. She never shed a tear." Aggie's eyes glazed over, and she blinked back tears.

"The bloody bastard," he said under his breath. Every muscle in his chest tightened and he felt a sharp pain in his cracked ribs. He rested his head back down on the couch and tried to relax his muscles.

"He had his moments, all right. Colleen has some of that hardness in her like her father—indeed she does." Aggie continued to rattle on. "But she never had a cruel heart like him. She might not have cried at Lord Davenport's funeral, but it wasn't because she don't have a heart.

"It was horrible him dying so unexpected like that, a week after our Colleen cried off. He ranted so much at her for making a fool of him that it did his heart in—least that's what the doctor thought—what I thought, too. I remember the funeral like it was yesterday. She stood there as stiff as a gravestone, while my Sharon blubbered on her shoulder. People thought she didn't love him, but she did, she just has her own way of grieving. When she got home, she locked herself in her room for a week and wouldn't come out or speak to anyone. That's the way she is. She's not one for showing any kind of emotions—'course, she did that terrible day of the wedding. Blubbered like a baby, she did. I knew something was terrible wrong. I ended up crying with her that day, too." A tear slipped down Aggie's round cheek. She pulled out a handkerchief from the pocket of her apron and wiped her face. "Look at me, shedding water like a drainspout. You shouldn't have let me prattle on."

"Of course I should." Sylvester smiled and glanced hopefully at her. "Perhaps you can prattle on and tell me why she was crying?"

"I don't know." Aggie shook her head, then smoothed back the gray hair from her face. "It happened after that Lady Sefton came to see her the day of the wedding. I tried to get her to tell me, but she never told no one but Sharon—and Sharon would never spill the truth to me. I knew better than to ask.

All I know, it must have involved you, because she said she wasn't going to the parish and she wasn't marrying— Now, how did she put it? . . . She called you 'a lascivious coldhearted knave.' '' Aggie saw his expression darken and added, "Begging your pardon, me lord."

Sylvester leaned back against the sofa and stared up at the ceiling. Lady Sefton had been his mistress for three years before Colleen reached womanhood and blossomed into a beauty. The moment he had clapped eyes on her at her come-out ball, and those flashing green eyes and wickedly beautiful face turned his way, he knew he was smitten. He broke it off with Lady Sefton.

She did not take the news of his engagement well, and vowed to destroy their marriage. She did, all right, but what had she said to Colleen? Colleen must be persuaded they were lies. He had to admit, even after she jilted him, he wanted to possess every inch of the indomitable Lady Colleen Davenport. Tasting the wild passion in her lips, feeling her sensual body responding to him, made him keenly aware that he'd never be satisfied with any other woman. She burned inside of him, a flame he'd never be able to extinguish. He'd have her one way or the other.

That night, Sylvester was trying to sleep. But the hard lumpy sofa poking his aching ribs, and Phillip bawling in the next room, made it impossible. He threw back the old quilt and swung his legs down to the floor. A pain throbbed against his ribs. Grimacing, he stood up.

Colleen was loath to come near him. She had avoided him all day. There was no reason why the babe should suffer because of her stubbornness. Surely he could do something to quiet the child.

He didn't bother knocking on her chamber door, but opened it. Sharon was bouncing the baby on the side of the bed, crying.

She looked so young and distraught, with her thin blonde hair streaming down her back, her eyes swollen and red from crying. Long rivulets of tears flowed down her flushed cheeks and had soaked the high neck of her nightgown.

Colleen was pacing, her long golden hair flowing out around her with each impatient step. When she saw him, she paused and her golden brows narrowed at him.

Sharon saw Colleen looking toward the door and followed her gaze. "Oh, Lord Usworth, I don't know what is wrong with him," Sharon said over the wailing, still crying herself. "I wanted to wake you, but Colleen wouldn't hear of it. What shall we do? The poor little dear will not stop crying. I think something is dreadfully wrong with him."

"Here, give him to me." Sylvester scooped the babe up in his arm, but he didn't stop crying. Phillip's arms were tight to his chest and his face was twisted in pain. With calm deliberation, he laid the babe down on the bed, then lifted Phillip's little knees up to his chest. Phillip broke wind, a loud burst like an adult would give off.

After several hiccups, Phillip stopped screaming. Sylvester put his knees up to his chest again and more air was expelled.

"Oh dear, it was gas." Sharon dabbed at the tears streaming down her face with a white linen handkerchief and grinned endearingly at Sylvester.

"Wherever did you learn that trick?" Colleen asked him, with awe in her voice.

"In Bombay. I stayed with a friend of mine who had a whole brood of children. I saw his wife do this to her son. It seemed to work."

"Well, it worked on Phillip." Colleen strode toward the bed, then stood beside him as she stared down at the babe. "We owe you a debt of thanks," she said, smiling at him the way she used to.

The smile warmed him all the way to his loins. Her hair was hanging down to her waist, shimmering like multicolored gold.

She was wearing that thin nightgown. He could see every nuance of her body, the high proud breasts thrusting against the material, the small waist that tapered to flaring hips, the dark golden hair between her thighs. If she only knew how much he wanted to grab her.

"Now that we know what to do, you can go back to bed." Colleen said, scooping Phillip up into her arms.

"Bed? You mean bed of nails, don't you?" He grinned wryly at her. "I'd rather have a cup of tea."

"We are so sorry about the sleeping accommodations," Sharon said, smiling placidly at him.

"I'm sure Lord Usworth doesn't mind the sofa, since he'll only be with us a few more days." Colleen eyed Sharon.

"Well, the least we can do is get Lord Usworth a cup of tea." Sharon smiled at Colleen, then said, "I'll look after Phillip, while you fix the tea." Sharon gently took Phillip out of Colleen's arms.

Colleen opened her mouth to protest, closed it, then frowned at her sister. "Very well, tea it is." She turned, picked up a candle, and strode out of the room.

"You'd better go with her," Sharon said, grinning knowingly at him.

Sylvester returned her smile and winked at her, then followed Colleen. The candle she was holding cast a wide halo of light around her body. He could see through her almost nonexistent nightgown. The ragged material was not fine silk, but it was more sensual than any expensive silk he'd ever seen on a woman. He watched her long sensual legs and the sway of her hips. Her back was as straight as the spine of a book. Wave after wave of golden hair flowed down her back and bumped against the top of her bottom with each long stride. His fingers itched to touch the silken mass. He remembered very well how soft it was to the touch.

"You need not follow me." She didn't turn around when she spoke to him.

"It will be my pleasure to help you." Sylvester eyed her bottom. His gaze moved upward, then he saw the slight tremble in the hand holding the candle. He grinned.

They reached the kitchen. One of the cats, with a stump for a tail, came over to her and howled, rubbing up against her leg. She set the candle on the counter, bent down, then petted the cat. "Are you hungry, Spitter?" She stroked the cat behind the ears.

Sylvester watched her hands moving over the cat's fur and felt a moment of envy. Then his gaze was drawn to her luscious little bottom, displayed so openly as she bent over. He could see right through the flimsy nightrail, her rounded bottom, the long sensual lines of her legs. It was the last coherent thought he had before he stepped toward her.

As his hands were inches from her bottom, she stood and strode across the kitchen, the cat hard on her heels. "Come on, I'll get you a bowl of milk."

Sylvester dropped his hands and groaned inwardly. He leaned against the counter and watched her feed the worrisome feline, his patience growing thin.

"You should not be on your feet," she said, still not looking up at him.

"I do a lot of things I shouldn't do." He stared at her nipples, the hard little nubs poking out beneath the wispy material.

She made a move toward a pan hanging on a rack. He had stood all the torture his eyes could take. In three long strides, he was at her side, pulling her into his arms.

She opened her mouth to protest. Before she could speak, he bent down and kissed her, thrusting his tongue into her mouth. He felt her pounding on his chest, but only for a moment. The fight went out of her, and she relaxed against him. Her lips softened and her arms clasped his neck in a tight grip. Then she was kissing him back, pressing her body next to his.

Sylvester groaned deep in his throat and plundered the sweet depths of her mouth while he ran his hands through her hair, feeling the silken mass between his fingers. He splayed his hands and moved them around her small waist and up to cup her breasts. He teased her nipples between his thumb and forefinger while he caressed her breasts, feeling her filling his palms.

She ran her hands along his neck and over his bare shoulders. The feel of her hands on his bare flesh felt like fire burning him. It was his undoing.

In his haste to have her naked, he yanked at her nightgown. The old sheer muslin ripped down the center.

"My nightgown. It's my only one. . . ." She grabbed her nightgown and tried to pull it back together.

"I'll buy you a roomful. Don't hide from me, Colleen, I want to see you." He kissed her, until he felt her hands drop from the gown and coil around his neck again.

His hands slid beneath the rag, along the alabaster skin of her shoulder. He felt a shiver go through her at his touch. Grinning, he ran his tongue along the side of her neck, then placed tiny kisses on her shoulder, letting his tongue move along her skin. He eased the torn nightgown down over her shoulders and it fell off her arms and landed in a heap around her feet. He lifted his head and drank in the sight of her naked body. Candlelight played along her creamy skin, making it glow with a golden hue. The full mounds of her breasts jutted out from a flat belly; the dusky-peach nipples quivered slightly with her ragged breaths. A wickedly perfect woman's mound, slightly darker than her hair, formed a flawless triangle of thick short curls between her legs. He had dreamed of seeing her totally naked, but he wasn't prepared for the jolt of lust that tore through him.

Hungry for her, he took a dusky peach nipple in his mouth, suckling, nipping the hard nub between his teeth. He ran his tongue over the edge, again and again. She arched her back and whimpered softly, digging her fingers in his hair, pushing his face closer to her breast.

"I want you, Colleen, like I've never wanted anyone. . . ."

He moved his hands along the smooth silken skin of her belly, feeling her muscles tighten and flex. His fingers slid over the fine sheen of perspiration on her skin, then down to the soft thatch of hair between her thighs.

He tangled his fingers in the golden curls. Her thighs tensed and he said, "Open for me, Colleen . . . I want to touch you."

"No, no, I cannot," she gasped.

He felt her trembling now, and he stared down at her long-lashed green eyes, so frightened and full of passion. He brushed the hair back from her face. His touch made a shudder go through her.

He grinned and placed feather-light kisses on both corners of her mouth as he said, "You cannot deny you're mine, Colleen. I'm only claiming what I should have taken long ago." He kissed her again and pulled her close to his hips.

His hands stroked the sensitive skin along her naked spine. The softness of her flesh felt like down against his callused palms, and he wanted to drown in the feel of it. When he reached her bottom, another shudder wracked her. He steadily backed her toward the table, kneading her bottom, and whispering endearments near her ear.

His hand hit the table's edge. He shoved aside a chair, then moved his hips against hers, trapping her bottom against the table. His hard flesh pressed against her soft folds. She moaned and her hips moved against his.

His thigh slid between her legs, then he opened the soft folds and touched her hot moist heat. She cried out his name and clung to him. He stroked her as he lifted her hips and set her on the table. While he stroked her, he moved his finger inside her canal. Her soft flesh closed around him. The hot wet tightness of her made him groan aloud.

"You're ready for me, my love," he whispered in her mouth.

"No . . ." Even as the word left her lips, she was wrapping her long legs around his thighs and digging her nails into the bandage on his back. Her hips writhed beneath him, then she threw back her head and her whole body convulsed. He kissed her wildly as she found her release. Unable to hold back any longer, he pulled at his breeches and freed his hard aching flesh.

He thrust into her, breaking through her maidenhead, lifting her hips off the table. Again . . . and again, he buried his flesh inside her hot heat, basking in the feel of her womb touching him. She was finally his. All his.

His tongue made deep forays into her mouth, matching the thrusts of his hips. She kissed him back, her tongue boldly driving into his mouth.

They came together. She cried out into his mouth. He stiffened and clung to her, still kissing her. The power of their lovemaking made him weak all over. His heart hammered in his chest like it wanted to break free of his ribs. He grew vaguely aware of the pain in his right side. . . .

And Colleen pushing at his chest.

"Get away from me. What have I done?" she cried, staring up at him as if he were a stranger.

"You've made love to me."

"I shouldn't have." She bit on her lower lip and glanced frantically around her, looking ready to scream at any moment.

He grabbed her and hugged her to his chest. "Don't say that, Colleen. You have nothing to regret. I'll do the right thing and marry you."

"We tried that once, remember? I won't have you marrying me out of some misplaced sense of honor. Heaven forbid, spare me that!"

"We shall marry, and this time I'm not leaving you until I drag you to the altar."

"I don't want to marry you. My stars, what have I done? I hate you!" She pushed back from him and buried her face in her hands.

"Look at me." He shoved her hands aside and tilted her chin up, making her look into his eyes. "You don't hate me.

If you do, you've got a damn strange way of showing it." He stared down at her naked breasts, the peach-tipped nipples quivering with each deep breath, at the small waist and flaring hips, at the delicious triangle of golden hair pressed against his own loins, and couldn't help but grin.

"I do, I tell you. You're cruel. What you did to Lady Sefton—" She paused and squeezed her eyes closed.

"Tell me what I was supposed to have done to her." His grin faded.

She opened her eyes, swallowed hard, and stared up at him with enormous green eyes. "She said you were seeing her the whole time we were engaged. She said you got her with child and when she told you that, you wanted her to destroy the child."

"It was a bloody lie. Do you really think I would do something like that?" He gave her shoulders a good hard shake. "Lady Sefton said that to get back at me. I would never do such a thing. I broke it off with her the moment I started courting you."

She remained pensively silent for a moment, worrying her lip, staring at him with distrust in her eyes.

"It's true," he said, his voice tight with indignation. "You've got to believe me."

"She had the child in her carriage and swore it was yours."

"Hell and damnation! You don't think it was mine? It couldn't have been. I hadn't bedded her for a year. I know of three men who shared her bed. It could have been any one of theirs. But I swear, Colleen, the child was not mine."

"She was sleeping with three men all at once?" Colleen's eyes widened, disbelief blazing in the emerald depths.

"What can I say? Lady Sefton likes variety."

Colleen grimaced, looking disgusted. She stared into his eyes, then after a long moment dropped her gaze and stared at his chest as she spoke. "Then she was lying to me?" she asked, her voice still heavy with suspicion.

"Of course she was. What made you believe such a thing?"

"Well, Lady Sefton was very convincing. She brought Lady Breckonridge with her to confirm her story."

He grunted under his breath. "Lady Breckonridge used to be my mistress. She's as vindictive as Lady Sefton."

"She was your mistress too?" Jealousy and astonishment rang in her voice. "How many mistresses have you had?"

"Enough." He grinned at the sudden scowl on her face, and said, "But they mean nothing to me. Now tell me, what else did those two shrews say to you?"

"Lady Sefton said that if I didn't believe Lady Breckonridge, her servants could vouch for your nightly visits—if I wanted to speak to them. And she had other friends who would also confirm her story. Of course, I couldn't have spoken to any of them. It was all so sordid, I just wanted to forget everything. You, her, the baby—"

"She probably threatened to fire her servants if they didn't lie. I'm sorry she came between us and hurt you." He hugged her tightly and placed a kiss on her forehead. When she didn't hug him back, he pulled back to look down at her. "What is it?"

"There was another reason why I believed Lady Sefton." She gulped hard and stared up at him.

"What?"

"Lady Josephine used to tell me stories about your conquests—"

"What did Josephine say?"

"She just told me stories about your reputation with women," she said flatly.

"They were just that. Josephine lives to cause trouble, you should know that. How could you believe her?" Sylvester grunted under his breath. Josephine was his cousin, and his father's ward, and a more brazen and bothersome creature didn't exist. When he saw her again, he might strangle her.

Colleen looked convinced now of his innocence. A terrible

frown marred her beautiful face as she banged her head against his chest and moaned, "Oh, God . . . What did I do? I ruined our lives. It was all my fault."

He captured her face between his hands and stared down at her beautiful face, still flushed from their lovemaking. "If you keep that up, I'll have more broken ribs."

"I can't help it. It was all such a horrible mess. If I'd just come to you sooner—"

"You came to see me?" He searched her eyes for a long moment, the pain and regret glistening in the green depths tearing at his chest.

She nodded, forcing long thick strands of golden hair to fall down from her shoulder and cover one bare breast. Her beautiful face was flawed by the agony in her expression as she said, "I felt like dying that day after Lady Sefton and her friend left. I couldn't bear to confront you until the next day; then you'd left. Can you ever forgive me for not showing up at the church?" She wrapped her arms around his waist and pressed her cheek against his chest.

He tensed, feeling her soft face and silken tresses against his hard muscles. He buried his hands in her hair, rubbing the velvety texture between his fingers, then, in a voice coarse with wanting her, he said, "Perhaps I can forgive you, if you agree to marry me again."

She leaned back and looked up at him, her vivid green eyes frantically searching his face. "Do you mean it?"

"Of course I do. I've never stopped wanting you, Colleen. God help me, I believe you could try and kill me and I'd still want you."

"I'd never try to kill you"—she grinned up at him—"and I will marry you." Her eyes filled with excitement and glistened with tenderness. "I should have trusted in you. I'm so sorry."

"You say you're sorry, but I'd much rather you show me."

She wrapped her arms around his neck and pulled his head down for a kiss. He felt himself growing hard again. They didn't leave the kitchen for a very long time, while she showed him just how sorry she was.

The next morning, Aggie strolled toward the kitchen. Something was definitely amiss. She could hear her Colleen singing in the kitchen, while his lordship was snoring like a worn-out groom in the parlor. The two sounds were at odds with each other, but telling enough. Her Colleen hadn't sung a note in five years. Aggie might not have ever married, but she'd lived sixty years and courted enough men to know what went on between men and women.

She marched into the kitchen and found Sharon and Colleen sitting at the table. Colleen was feeding Phillip and singing an Irish love song.

Colleen glanced up. The radiance on her face made Aggie gasp and take a step back. The proof of what had happened stared her straight in the face. She grabbed her heart and cried, "What have you done, child?"

"Not a thing." Colleen stared down at the kitchen table and her cheeks flushed red.

Aggie scowled at her.

"Don't be angry," Sharon said, petting the bunny in her lap. Her gaze strayed to Colleen and held there for a moment, then a placid grin spread across her lips. "Lord Usworth and Colleen resolved their differences last night. Isn't that marvelous?"

Aggie's brow shot up. "Depends on how you look at it."

"We're getting married," Colleen said, her voice growing touchy. She took the empty makeshift bottle out of Phillip's mouth, then lifted him on her shoulder and patted his back.

As much as Aggie had wanted to see Lord Usworth and her Colleen come together again, she had a nagging feeling that nothing good would come of it now. It was a curse on the couple for sure, if the two came together before the wedding. Everyone knew that.

"Are you not happy for me, Aggie?" Colleen looked at her, a hurt expression on her face.

"Of course I am." Aggie strode over to her, feeling the numbness in her aching legs. She patted Colleen's arm. "You're just like my own. I only want you to be happy."

"I am now." Colleen smiled at her, a dazzling smile, then she brought Aggie's hand up to her cheek.

That feeling came back—stronger than ever, as Aggie stared down at Colleen's golden hair falling down around her shoulders. She felt tears come to her eyes, and blinked them away.

That afternoon, Colleen scooped up a cup of fodder and dumped it into Midget's bowl. Midget, their only goat and Phillip's only source of milk, *baaa*ed her thanks and dipped her head down into the bowl. Colleen gave her a pat, then broke the layer of ice on her water trough.

It had stopped snowing. The sun shined through the cracks beside the barn planking and cut across Midget's sharp back and long neck. Snow melted from the roof and she heard the steady *drip, drip* along the eaves outside. Long tendrils of hair had escaped the bun at her nape, and she pushed them back behind her ear as she stood.

She heard footsteps and saw Sylvester striding into the barn, a devilish twinkle in his gray eyes. With each breath, she watched a cloud of white condensation billow out of his mouth and nose. A white shirt covered his broad chest. The muscles in his powerful legs pumped beneath a pair of tan breeches. Clumps of snow covered his boots, stark against the dark shiny leather. Red must have polished the mud off his boots. His raven-black hair waved down around his shoulders. He looked wickedly handsome.

Grimacing at him, she asked, "What are you doing out of bed?"

"This was the only place I could have five minutes alone with you. Aggie is like a bulldog on your heels. I thought when she found me kissing you, that she'd take a bite out of my leg."

"Oh, you're horrible. She's just protecting my virtue."

"It's a little late for that." His arms went around her and he drew her close.

She gazed up into his misty gray eyes and saw the possessive gleam in them. The heat of it seared her entire body. She was totally his now. Her finger went to the dimple in his chin, and she felt the stubble there as she said, "You didn't wear a coat, you'll catch your death."

"I couldn't find my coat." He stared pointedly at the thick black coat she was wearing. It hung around her ankles and the sleeves fell down past her hands.

"I'm sorry," she said, looking sheepish. "It was warmer than mine."

"No matter, you'll warm me." He drew her close and kissed her.

Colleen felt his hard flesh pressing against her hips, then his hands were on her breasts. The smell of his bay rum aftershave mixed with the clean male scent of him, and filled her senses to overflowing. She lost all perception of time and space. It was only Sylvester's lips against hers, the feel of his large hands caressing her breasts.

Before she knew it, he backed her into the stall next to Midget's. He deepened the kiss until she was falling back over his arm, then he was easing her down on a pile of straw. His weight settled on top of her, while his tongue caressed the dark recesses of her mouth.

She was vaguely aware of the straw poking the back of her head and neck and his hips undulating against her, touching the center of heat burning through her. Then she was kissing him back, thrusting her tongue in his mouth, tearing at his shirt.

Ping. Ping. Ping. The buttons of his shirt hit the side of the stall. She splayed her fingers along his broad chest and tangled them in the coarse black hair there. At her touch, his muscles stiffened into granite, his heart pounded beneath her fingertips.

"You make me mad for you. . . ." He whispered near her lips and worked frantically at the bulky coat. When he'd pulled it off her, he threw it over his shoulder. One of his hands moved to her thigh as he jerked up the hem of her dress and petticoat.

She tore at his breeches and freed his manhood, driven by the need to feel him inside her. When she touched the velvety hardness of him, he tensed and groaned.

"You can't touch me like that, Colleen," he said in a ragged whisper near her ear.

"But I want to feel you."

He lost control then and kissed her, fiercely, thrusting his tongue in her mouth. His hips settled between her, then he drove into her.

She arched her back, grabbing handfuls of his shirt. He pumped faster . . . faster. She felt the heat growing hotter, her body consumed by it. Her hips moved with his, until she exploded inside and cried out his name.

He spilled his seed, then fell down on top of her. After a moment, he kissed her on the lips and said, "You will kill me on our honeymoon. I see it coming."

"I can always marry a younger man." She kissed the dimple in his chin and felt the coarse stubble against her lips.

"Not if you want him to live," he said, his eyes turning into gray shards of ice.

"I was only teasing you." She laughed and kissed him again.

Abruptly, the sound of horses' hooves plodding through snow made them look at each other.

CHAPTER 5

Sylvester rolled off of Colleen. She frantically pulled down the hem of a faded yellow dress, while Sylvester jerked at his breeches.

Red strode into the barn, leading two horses: a big dappled gray, and a solid black stallion with four white socks. He saw them and froze. His gaze flicked between Sylvester, who was still buttoning up his breeches, then to Colleen, who was picking a piece of straw out of her hair.

A slow, knowing grin spread across Red's wide mouth. "I guess I should have been a little slower in my comin'."

"Why are you here?" Sylvester eyed him with impatience as he helped Colleen to stand. "I thought I told you to tell Father I'd be there in a week."

"Aye, Cap'n, that's just what I did. But your da sent me here and said it was urgent you come home. He said he needed you. He mumbled somethin' about it being life and death and shooed me from the room. The quickest way to travel in the snow is on horseback, so I brought Disaster for you."

Sylvester cursed under his breath and his dark brows furrowed. He turned and glanced at Colleen. For a moment he looked torn, then he pulled her into his arms. "I'm going to have to go. You're not to leave this cottage. Do you hear? Not for any reason."

"Why?"

"I mean for you to be here when I come back to take you to the church. As soon as I can procure a special license, we are getting married. I didn't want to let you out of my sight, but I have to go."

"Don't worry," she said, staring up into his long-lashed gray eyes. "I'll be here waiting for you."

"You'd better be." He bent and captured her lips. The kiss was hungry and intensely demanding. When she was breathless from it, he stepped back and grinned down at her. "Try not to talk to any of my old mistresses while I'm gone."

"Should they even knock on my door, I'll shoot them." She smiled; then it faded as she said, "Godspeed, and hurry back."

As she watched him turn, she remembered his coat and grabbed it from a pile of straw. The thick wool felt heavy in her hands. "Here, you'll need this." He opened his mouth to protest, but she threw it over his shoulders. "Give your father my regards."

"I shall." He grinned at her, kissed her briefly on the mouth, then leaped up onto Disaster's back. The big stallion shied back a step. Sylvester pulled back on the reins, then turned the black stallion and disappeared through the barn doors.

"You've made him happy, lass." Red shot her a wide grin as he mounted. "I'm glad you two are finally gettin' around to doing the right thing."

"How did you know we were previously engaged?" Colleen raised her brows at him.

"The old earl told me. Near about swallowed his tongue when I told him where the cap'n was stayin'."

"Oh, dear."

"Don't you be worryin' your pretty head over it, lass. The shock will wear off." He winked, bowed slightly, then followed in Sylvester's wake.

Colleen's brows furrowed as she stared at the empty doorway. Surely Lord Usworth would object to their wedding. He probably still despised her from when she had cried off and made a fool of his son. If only he could forgive her. No one else's blessing mattered to her, but his did. If Sylvester couldn't convince him to come to the wedding, she would be heartbroken. Something pulled at her clothes. She glanced down and saw Midget gnawing on her dress.

"You insatiable creature!" She jerked the dress out of Midget's jaws and noticed the finger-size hole in her dress. "Now I'm down one nightrail and one dress. I'll have to go to the altar in a shift and stays."

Thinking of the wedding made her glance back toward the door, and a frown drew her brows together. A singular feeling that something might happen to postpone their marriage gnawed at her. Then she shook her head and decided it was just second-engagement fidgets.

Two hours later, Sylvester strode down a hall, his booted steps thudding against the red Oriental runner. The distinct odor of aged wood and stone, lemon oil and beeswax, and his father's cigars braided together. It was the familiar odor of Madison Hall. Home. He took a deep breath and rapped on his father's chamber door.

"Come," a deep voice barked.

He opened the door and strode inside. The room still looked the same, with its huge mahogany four-poster bed resting on a dais. As large as the bed was, it looked swallowed by the massive room. An Elizabethan writing desk and tables towered along the walls. Royal blue swathed the room, even the Tibetan carpet.

Bennington Pendleton Rawlings, the Earl of Usworth, was lying in the bed, with his springer spaniel, Essy, beside him. Essy had her head resting on his thigh. His father hadn't bothered lowering the paper he was reading. Essy raised her head and *whoof*ed at him, the sound muted by her soft drooping lips. Her brown eyes followed him for a moment, then she sniffed the air and her stub started to wag. She jumped down off the bed.

"Essy, it's only James." Lord Usworth chided the dog from behind his paper. "What is it now, James?"

"I left your butler belowstairs haranguing a maid." Sylvester bent and petted Essy's black head, feeling her wet-tongued kisses against his skin.

His father dropped the paper. His eyes widened and twinkled at the sight of his only son. He looked older and frailer than Sylvester remembered. His hair and brows had turned dark silver. Worry lines curved around his eyes and mouth. His broad shoulders curved in a slump, not rigidly straight as Sylvester remembered them. His complexion looked sallow, his cheeks gaunt.

"I'm surprised she still knows you. She doesn't greet everyone like that." Lord Usworth watched Essy making a fool of herself over Sylvester, then he held up his hand and said, "Come here and let me look at you."

In four long strides, Sylvester was at the side of the bed. He clasped his father's hand, then they squeezed each other in a bear hug.

" 'Tis nice to see the prodigal son return."

"I'm glad to be back. How is your gout?"

"As you see, the damned stuff keeps me bedridden now," he said ruefully.

Essy jumped back up on the bed, and took her rightful place beside his father. She rested her head back on his thigh, and watched Sylvester.

"I'm sorry to hear it."

"A lot you care"—his father's faded gray eyes shot him a look of reproach—"hying off to God-knows-where. If you ever leave England again for another five years without producing an heir, I'll disown you."

"That won't be happening, Father. Lady Colleen and I are getting married." Sylvester looked askance at his father and waited for his reaction.

He couldn't have been any more surprised than if Sylvester had slapped him. His gray brows met severely over his eyes and he folded his clenched fists over his chest. It took him a moment to find his voice. "I had thought your servant was dicked in the nob. I couldn't believe it when he told me you were staying with the Davenport chit, but damnation, you're marrying her?"

"Yes."

"Are you sure you want to do that again? You're setting yourself up for another heartbreak. I'll be damned if I'll go to another church and be witness to it. I loved that girl like my own daughter and what did she do? She made a fool of both of us." Lord Usworth shook a finger at him.

"It won't be that way this time. It was all Lady Sefton's fault." Sylvester told his father about the whole sordid affair and ended with, "So you see, it wasn't Lady Colleen's fault."

"She should have had more sense than to believe two of your old mistresses," Lord Usworth grunted under his breath.

"Part of it is Josephine's fault. She bragged to Lady Colleen about my reputation with the ladies. By the by, where is the little termagant?"

His father grimaced and regret flashed in his eyes. He clasped his hands over his slight paunch, then stared down at them as he spoke. "She's gone missing now for three months. She all but disappeared. Didn't you get any of my letters?"

"I only got the one telling me your gout was getting worse and you wanted to see me, but I didn't receive that one for four months. I came as soon as I got it."

"If you'd have stayed in one port long enough, you would have gotten my letters." Another look of reproach, then Lord Usworth waved his hand through the air. "No matter, you're here now. And I need you. You see, when Josephine vanished, I hired a runner to find her. Just today, he told me where I could locate her. She's been right beneath my nose all this time."

"Where is she?"

"In South Shields. It appears she's been staying in a house of ill repute there."

"The devil you say." Sylvester clenched his fists at his sides.

"She turned out very wild indeed. I never thought her capable of such a thing." His father shook his head and his deep voice softened with regret. "I know your uncle has turned over in his grave several times. Had I but known she was so incorrigible, I would have locked her in her room until she turned of age."

"She could have been kidnapped." Sylvester thought of all the ports he'd been in where men captured women and forced them into prostitution.

"I never thought of that." Lord Usworth swallowed hard.

"I'm off, then, and I'll bring her back."

"Do, and take care. The runner told me he tried to rescue her, but the house is so heavily guarded he failed in his attempt. Had a bullet hole in his arm to prove it. It's near the quay. A run-down blue monstrosity. He said you could not miss it." His voice held a deep note of despair as he said, "I wish I could go with you."

"I'll get her back." Sylvester bowed, then left Lord Usworth staring after him with a worried expression.

Twenty miles away, Colleen sat in the parlor, with Phillip in her arms, listening to the *clackety-clack* of Aggie's knitting needles. Colleen cooed at Phillip and tapped the side of one pink cheek. He stared up at her, his eyes glued to her face, then slowly a smile pressed across his little rosebud mouth.

"Look, he's grinning at me, and he has a dimple in his chin. I never noticed the dimple before."

Sharon glanced up from a copy of Sir Walter Scott's *Waverly.* "Does he?" She leaned forward and looked past Aggie. "Oh, he does!"

Aggie's fingers continued their hypnotizing rhythm with the knitting needles as she looked at Phillip. "Glory be, but he looks like Lord Usworth when he smiles."

"He does, doesn't he?" Colleen smiled down at him, then put him on her shoulder and cuddled him. His soft lips brushed against her neck, and his warm breaths breezed across her skin. She felt the small body against her breast, the tiny head on her shoulder, and frowned. If she had married Sylvester five years ago, she could very well have a baby of her own on her shoulder.

The sound of sleigh bells brought Colleen's gaze around to the window.

"Who could that be?" Colleen thought Sylvester might be coming for her. She leaped up, her heart pounding, her breathing rapid. She ran to the window and eagerly looked out.

The sun was still up. Billowy white clouds knuckled across a blue sky. Her gaze landed on the sleigh. She saw the tall red hat and the yellow greatcoat. Her expression fell as she stepped back from the window.

"Who is it?" Aggie asked, thrusting aside her knitting and standing.

"It's Winston Spears. I wonder if something is wrong." Colleen felt the nagging feeling that had been with her for hours plaguing her again. Inadvertently she cradled Phillip tighter to her breast.

"I hope 'tis nothing bad." Aggie screwed up her round face in a frown and hurried to open the door.

Colleen heard Winston knocking the snow off his boots, then Aggie's anxious greeting.

After a moment, Winston strode into the parlor. He flashed a smile at Colleen, then Sharon. His smile faded as he said, "Ladies. I beg your pardon for the intrusion, but I had to come right away."

"What is the matter?" Colleen blurted.

"Rue—you know how stubborn he can be—took it upon himself to find the mother of this baby." He nodded toward Phillip in Colleen's arms. "I told him we were interfering, but since Captain Rawlings was injured, my brother thought he'd take care of the matter for you."

"Did you find something?" Colleen asked, her impatience coming through in her voice.

"Indeed we did, Lady Colleen." He glanced toward the doorway, then lowered his voice. "Is Captain Rawlings here?"

"No," Colleen said, looking frantically at him now. "What is it?" She was going to shake him if he didn't tell her.

"This should be said in private." Winston eyed Sharon, then Aggie, who had just walked back inside the parlor.

"What you have to say you can say in front of me," Sharon said, the sweet lilt in her voice barely detectable.

"Yes, do tell us." Colleen took a step toward him.

"Very well." He splayed his legs and rested his fists on his hips. "Rupert found the mother of the child."

"Who is the woman?" Colleen protectively tightened her hold on Phillip.

He paused, took a deep breath, then said, "Her name's Annie Jackson. She escaped from a ship in port, the *Mariner.*" When the name didn't elicit a response from Colleen, he added, "It's Captain Rawlings' ship."

"She was on Sylvester's ship? Was she a passenger?"

"She said she was Captain Rawlings' mistress, and she ran away from him."

"This can't be true!" Colleen cried. "I don't believe you."

"Rupert is with her as we speak. It is the truth."

Colleen felt the blood drain from her face, while a numbness swarmed down her arms and legs. For a moment she experienced something unpleasantly familiar, and felt the same churning in the pit of her stomach that she had felt five years ago. No. She couldn't believe this story. She wouldn't. Not again. She wouldn't make the same mistake twice. But there was a tiny shred of doubt that gnawed at her insides.

"Holy Mother!" Aggie gasped, and raised her hands to her cheeks.

Sharon gazed at Colleen's trembling arms and jumped up. "Here, let me hold the baby for you."

Colleen was vaguely aware of Sharon scooping Phillip into her arms, then Aggie's hand was on her shoulder.

"Sit down, child."

Colleen's limbs had somehow turned to stone. Try as she might, she couldn't move. Aggie shoved hard on her shoulders, and Colleen plopped down on the sofa. She sat there, frozen, willing the doubt to go away and take the ache in her throat with it.

After what seemed like an eternity, the shock had worn off. Colleen spoke past the tightness in her throat. "Did you say she ran away from him?" Her voice was so deadpan it could have come from a grave.

"Yes. He didn't want the child, nor did he want you to know he'd brought his mistress with him. I suppose his plan was to dispose of both of them, but she ran from the ship. He found her, though, holing up at the old Anson farm. She was giving birth. After the child was born, he tried to destroy it. That's when you saved it."

A memory of the man she had seen flashed before her eyes. The cold calculation in his long strides, the wide swaying shoulders beneath his cape. Then she remembered Sylvester saying, "I'm not the man you knew, I take what I want now." Her fingers dug into the sofa cushion. She heard the old material rip, then felt shreds of chintz tight against her fingers. No, it couldn't be Sylvester. He would never do anything like that. Never!

Winston stared at the material hanging from Colleen's hand. "Rupert is with her now. He asked me to tell you this, and said he would bring the girl to you to confirm the story."

"This is not true!" Colleen said, trembling all over. Lady Sefton had thrown almost those exact words at her five years ago. Her outrage came through in her voice. "Tell him I've no wish to see this girl, until after I've spoken with Sylvester."

"But surely you want to see the mother to confirm—"

"I want nothing of the sort. I'm sure the girl is lying. I'll hear what Sylvester has to say." Galvanized into action by the indignation she felt on Sylvester's behalf, she stood and headed for her room. She slammed the door closed, leaving Aggie, Sharon, and Winston staring after her.

"Did you see the poor thing?" Aggie shook her head and stared at Colleen's chamber door. "I ain't never seen her so pale and upset. She's shocked clean to the bone, she is, and trying her best to cover it. Oh, I pray it ain't so." She shivered and rubbed her arms.

With tears in her eyes, Sharon turned to Winston. "You'll have to forgive me, but I'm suddenly not feeling very well." She breezed past Winston with Phillip in her arms, the rustle of her silk skirt following her out the door.

"I knew it. I just knew it. We're in for it now. Our Colleen's heart is broke for sure. Now our Sharon will get ill over it all." Aggie shook her head, then shared a glance with Winston.

An hour later, Colleen sat before the rickety old dressing table she shared with Sharon, methodically combing her hair and staring at her reflection. She wouldn't think about what Winston had said. If she thought about it, the nagging uncertainty would plague her again. If only Sylvester were here and she could feel his strong arms around her, smell the scent of him, feel his lips against hers. She needed his warmth to dispel the cold sliver of doubt that threatened to pierce her.

She laid down the comb, then braided her hair, taking little care with it. With stiff fingers, she wound the long braid into a bun and shoved pin after pin into the heavy mass. Strands that she missed hung down along the sides of her face. She shoved them behind her ear and pulled on a clean, faded black bombazine, her best dress, then threw a cream-colored shawl around her shoulders.

With calm deliberation, she left her room. Her gaze swept the parlor and landed on Aggie. She was sitting on the sofa next to Sharon, rocking nervously back and forth, her knitting needles working furiously.

Sharon saw Colleen first and quickly stood up. "You've come out. Are you terribly upset?" A worried frown marred her brow, her lucent brown eyes wide as they probed Colleen's face.

Aggie's fingers paused over her needles and she fixed Colleen with a troubled look. "I didn't think you'd be out for a week, but I'm glad to see you've come out. Do you want to talk about it?"

"Not really." Colleen glanced past Aggie's faded brown skirt and saw Phillip's basket sitting on the floor. His little body was nestled in the folds of an embroidered blue flannel blanket, which she recognized from her hope chest. His eyes were closed, his tiny jaw moving as he sucked on his fist.

Sharon rushed toward her. "Colleen, surely you have to say something. You must be devastated by this news. I know I would be."

"Why should I? I know Sylvester is innocent of these charges. He'll prove it, too, when I speak to him."

"I don't want to believe it either, but you must have some misgivings. After what happened before . . ." Sharon's voice trailed off as she wrung her hands and stared down at them.

"I know in my heart he's been falsely accused," Colleen

said, adding enough emphasis to the words to make her own ears believe them.

"We just don't want to see you hurt again, child," Aggie said, thrusting aside her knitting and heaving herself up from the sofa. She grimaced as her swollen legs took the brunt of her weight.

"I shan't be. And you shouldn't be up. Go and sit down."

"Oh, no. I can see something brewing in those eyes of yours—and it ain't just hurt. And you've got your good dress on. Where you think you're going?"

"To see Sylvester."

"But you can't. There's a foot of snow out there! You'll freeze," Sharon cried. "Wait for him to come to us."

"I have to see him *now*." Colleen stared pointedly at her. "I'm sure I'll find someone on the road who can take me as far as Westoe."

"But you can't walk in all this snow. It's another two miles to Madison Hall from there. You won't get there for hours and the sun will be setting soon."

"Surely the mail coach is out. I can walk in the ruts."

"I'm not letting you outta this house in all this cold." Aggie moved faster than Colleen thought possible. Her heavy breasts wobbled against her stomach as she hurried over and stood next to Sharon, blocking Colleen's way.

Colleen narrowed her eyes first at Aggie, then at Sharon. "Neither of you understands, do you? I won't let lies come between us again. I have to hear him say it's not true. If I have to crawl on my hands and knees in the snow for fifty miles, I'm going to see him." Colleen shoved past them, their cries to stop ringing in her ears.

Five minutes later, Colleen pulled her scarf tighter around her head and neck, and watched her breath puffing out around her nose and mouth in blowing white streams. She could feel moisture already seeping through the worn soles of her shoes and she hoped to meet with a mail coach, or perhaps a post chaise—should a driver be so bold as to be traveling in such deep snow. Even though she'd worn gloves, her fingers were already starting to feel the cold. She jammed her hands in her pockets and headed down the long drive that would take her to the road.

There was a strange silence in the air, mingling with the sound of her determined bootsteps crunching in the snow. The setting sun splashed brilliant purples, pinks, blues across the sky. Snow layered the cleared rolling fields on either side of the drive with a pristine whiteness, the tranquil frozen beauty unmarred by footprints of any kind. The smooth, slick surface shimmered in the fading sunshine, puffing along the fence rails in deep sparkling mounds. A tiny sparrow landed on a fence post and chirped at her, its feathers fluffed against the cold.

If only she had a morsel of bread to feed the poor frozen creature—but she had nothing in her pockets but her cold hands. The jingling of sleigh bells sent the little bird soaring up into the air. Glancing down the drive, she saw two huge sturdy-boned grays, their hooves grinding up snow as a sleek black sleigh crept up the drive. The driver's face was hidden by the horses. All she could see were wide shoulders stretched beneath a black coat with eight capes, making the shoulders appear wider than they truly were. Her heart lifted. Sylvester had come for her.

She ran toward the sleigh, but froze as she glanced past the horses' heads and saw Rupert handling the reins. She remembered Winston saying that Rupert might bring Phillip's mother to speak to her. A moment of panic gripped her, until she noticed the empty seat beside him. As yet, she couldn't face that false-mouthed young woman.

When Rupert saw her, he waved and called, "Lady Colleen."

With just a halfhearted lift of her wrist, she waved back, then waited for him to pull up alongside her.

"How fortunate I found you," he said, sounding breathless with excitement. He rubbed the sides of his red cheek with a gloved hand, then licked his blue lips.

"Your brother came earlier and said you were bringing Phillip's mother here." Colleen paused, then said, "I hate to be rude, but I don't wish to speak to her."

"This doesn't sound like you. Are you involved with Usworth again?" he asked, sounding dismayed and a little surprised.

"How did you know who he was?" Colleen arched a brow at him.

"I knew the moment I looked at him. He's not been gone from the country so long that I didn't remember what he looked like."

"You were acquainted with him?"

"We attended Oxford together, but of course we ran in different circles." A hint of envy tainted his next words. "I was never acquainted with him."

"Oh." Colleen frowned pensively. She understood Rupert's bitterness. Sylvester probably traveled in the highest circles of society, a place Rupert would have never been welcome.

"I dare say I lived through the deprivation." Rupert smiled derisively, his engaging blue eyes sparkling at her. "You never answered my question. Are you back on with Usworth?"

"Yes."

"Are you sure it's such a wise idea, with this latest scandal? Once news of it gets out; then it will surely be all over the papers."

"Promise me you won't spread a word of it. I know this girl's lying." She had hoped this horrible mishap would not be bantered about, but Rupert and Winston were close with their mother. Once Mrs. Spears got wind of it, it would be all over Christendom. She was kind, but plagued by a wagging tongue.

"If you met Miss Jackson, you'd know she was telling the truth." Rupert's expression hardened. "If she were my sister,

I would call Usworth out for what he's done. She's very ill. I think she's given up the will to live."

"She has?" Colleen said, feeling a stab from her conscience. She hadn't thought that Phillip's mother might be ill. She didn't trust the girl, but she didn't want her to die either. "Will she be all right?"

"I brought the doctor. He said she was too weak to be moved. He fears she's not well from the birth. I left her at the farm. She keeps asking for her baby. Knowing what a generous heart you have, I knew you wouldn't mind taking the child to her." He cut his eyes at her, the critical gleam in them making her shift nervously on her feet. "It might be her dying wish."

After a battle with her conscience and her heart, Colleen said, "Of course I'll take him to her."

"I thought you would." Rupert's lips parted in a genuine smile. "I so disliked sending Winston with the horrible news. I wanted to tell you myself, but I couldn't leave Miss Jackson, not in her state. She keeps mumbling over and over again how cruel Usworth—"

"Please, I will take Phillip to her, but you mustn't speak to me about what happened. I'd rather not talk of it."

His brows met over his nose and he nodded curtly. "As you wish."

"Thank you." Colleen quickly changed the subject. "It was very kind of you to take care of Miss Jackson. Who is with her now?"

"I found a nurse to stay with her."

She saw how red and chafed Rupert's face was from the cold and said, "When we reach the cottage, you can warm yourself by the fire, while I bundle up Phillip."

"That is very kind, but we must hurry. I'd like to get back to her. I fear we might be losing her, and seeing the child was her last wish. Let me help you up." He leaned over and held out his hand.

She stared at it a moment, then let him help her into the

sleigh. An image of Miss Jackson lying on some dirty cot in a room, calling for her baby, rose up in Colleen's mind. No matter how much she disliked the girl, she must take Phillip to her.

An hour later, Sylvester reined in and watched the waves bashing against the quay. White foam stuck to the ice-covered wall like frothy cotton. Ships bobbed along the dock, their masts rocking with the waves. He could see his ship, the *Mariner*. Her long, sleek, hundred-foot body rocked near the edge of a pier. His gaze scanned the row houses hunched back from the pier. Some of the shoddily-built homes were missing shingles, and the roofs smiled like toothless fools at him. In some of the yards, clothes rocked on lines like frozen pieces of meat.

He spotted the ugly three-story blue house on the very end. Snow puddled in the sagging eaves and dotted the roof. The shutters were drawn over the windows and nailed shut. A guard stood on the steps, speaking to two sailors who were just coming out of the house. Sylvester had seen many such houses in a thousand different ports. He never frequented them.

Red reined in near him and spoke for the first time since they'd left Madison Hall. "Do you have a plan, Cap'n?"

"It looks pretty simple, really. You cause a distraction in the front, and I'll swing around to the back." His hand inadvertently checked the knife tucked in his boot, then the pistol sitting in the waistband of his breeches.

"You'll be careful, won't you?" Red eyed him, then pulled out a flask of brandy from his pocket.

"Aren't I always?" Sylvester said, sounding incensed.

"You always were, but you're in love now. Some men get stupid in the head when they get the itch of a woman in them." Red grinned over at Sylvester, then took a long draw from the flask. He brought it down and doused his coat liberally with the brandy.

"I assure you, I have more reason than ever now to be careful." Sylvester thought of Colleen's beautiful, proud face, those shining emerald eyes staring up at him with love and passion as they climaxed together in the barn. Would he ever get enough of her sweet sensual body? He doubted it, but he had a lifetime to try.

"Och! See what I mean. You got that itchy lost look. And I ain't blamin' you. If I had such a lass, I'd be thinkin' about her, too."

Sylvester felt a slight blush creep into his cheeks at having been caught daydreaming. To cover his embarrassment, he shot Red a dark, quelling glance.

"Donna go eatin' me, Cap'n. I was just makin' a point."

"You've made it, now forget it." He eased the pistol out of his breeches and checked it to make sure it was loaded.

Not one for dropping a point so easily, Red said, "Well, then, I'm hopin' you'll try to keep your mind off the lass and on keepin' yourself alive."

"She's forgotten for the moment."

Red shot a dubious look Sylvester's way; then his bushy red brows curled down around his nose as he stuffed the flask back inside his coat pocket. "I'm off, then." He saluted Sylvester, mumbled something under his breath about beautiful lasses, then kicked his horse.

Sylvester waited until he was close to the front door, then headed for the alleyway. As he drew closer to the blue house, he glanced past the high fence enclosing the backyard. The steps had been cleared of snow, exposing the missing bricks on either side. He didn't see anyone guarding the back door, so he dismounted and tied Disaster's reins to the fence post.

Carefully he opened the gate on the fence, then froze as someone thrust the barrel of a gun in his face.

CHAPTER 6

Sylvester looked down the barrel of the gun, then saw the sausage-size fingers holding it. His gaze moved up a coat-covered beefy arm, past shoulders wider than an ox collar, then landed on the man's face. A full brown beard curled down over his cheeks and jaw and touched his chest. Deep-russet beady eyes gleamed at him from beneath the brim of a black cap. The deep frown lines over his brow and around his eyes bespoke that he was well into his forties. By his bronzed leathery skin and the smell of fish emanating from him, Sylvester could tell he'd spent most of his life on board a whaling vessel. This must be his second job.

The russet eyes narrowed on Sylvester's face, then the old tar's gaze roamed down the fine tailoring of his coat. He smiled and a mouthful of rotten teeth cracked open. "Well, glory be, we got us gentlemen sneaking in the back now."

"I thought there were two entrances." Sylvester glanced over his shoulder to see if there was anyone else hiding behind the man.

"I wouldn't swear that on yer mother's grave, sir." The man stressed the word "sir," then his grin broadened. "Just like your type to be trying to get it for free." A big beefy hand sprang toward Sylvester.

He jumped aside, hit the man between the eyes, then knocked the gun out of his hand. The gun sailed through the air and landed in the snow. The man stood there for a moment. Sylvester raised both his fists and waited for the man to try and attack again.

When he didn't move, Sylvester decided to make the second move. He drew back to hit the man. Right before his fist connected, the man's eyes rolled back in his head and he crashed against the fence, then fell facedown in the snow.

Sylvester stepped over him, listening to Red's feigned drunken shouts echoing from the front stoop. He hurried to the back door and slipped inside. The house was dark and dingy and had the feel of a prison cell about it. The boarded-up windows allowed no light to penetrate the confines of the interior. A lone candle burned in a hallway sconce, glazing the cracked and yellowed walls with a halo of dim light. The smell of cheap perfume and body odor assailed his nose as he crept down the hallway.

He hurried past the closed front door as Red argued with a man on the front stoop. A staircase stood off to one side. Taking the stairs two at a time, he reached the second floor.

The hallway was L-shaped. He turned the corner and saw a large woman in a chair, snoring. She was leaning back against a wall, her hands moving up and down over her protruding belly.

Without making a sound, Sylvester eased up to the door beside her and tried the knob. It was locked. He turned to the woman and clamped his hand over her mouth. She snorted, then started awake. When she saw him, her eyes widened and the fear in her eyes was almost a tangible thing.

"Listen carefully. I want you to open this door. And no screaming—my patience is wearing thin."

She nodded.

The moment he drew his hand back, the woman screamed like a banshee and went running down the hall, her arms bent, her hands shaking wildly near her head.

"Damn," he muttered, knowing the damage was done. He let her go, then turned and kicked the door in. The hinges rattled and jerked as it hit the wall.

He saw Josephine, lying curled up on a bed. She was fully clothed. Her long dark hair was braided down her back. An untouched tray of food sat on a table by the bed. When she raised her head and looked at him, he saw how pale she was. Her blue eyes looked enormous against her gaunt cheeks and the dark circles under her eyes. She was only ten and eight, but the girlhood innocence was gone from her face. She looked thirty at the moment.

"Sylvester?" She muttered his name as if she couldn't believe it was him, then a relieved smile weakly raised the corners of her lips.

"We've got to get you out of here." He ran to her and helped her up, feeling her body trembling from weakness as he scooped her up in his arms.

Loud shouts boomed down the hall, and a door slammed; then footsteps came toward the room.

"Oh, no, they're coming!" she cried frantically. "I've got to get out of here. He'll come for me again—I know it!"

Sylvester glanced at the window and saw the bars over it. "Wait right here." He laid her down on the edge of the bed, then reached for the pistol in his breeches.

The footsteps were closer now. . . .

Sylvester raised the pistol.

Red appeared in the doorway, saw Sylvester was about to shoot him, and said, " 'Tis me, Cap'n—you got your mind on the lass again?" At Sylvester's sour look, he grinned and said,

"Sorry it took me so long, but I had a run-in with a screaming crone, then I had to fight my way past a woman with a whip. I locked her in the room with her customer." Red smiled at this, and said, "Did you find the lass?"

"I found her."

"Good. I'll go and see the coast stays clear." After a quick glance in Josephine's direction, he left the doorway.

Sylvester turned back to her, then picked her up. She felt so small and bony in arms, it prompted him to say, "I'm sorry this happened."

"Not as sorry as I," she said, pain and regret coming through in her voice.

"Who held you prisoner here?"

Josephine hesitated a moment, then said, "Mr. Rupert Spears."

Sylvester felt his chest tighten. Up until this moment, he'd forgotten about his broken ribs, but now he was painfully aware of them.

"I hope you kill him." A tear slipped down her cheek. "He pursued me relentlessly. Your father found out and forbade me to see him. You know how perverse I can be."

Sylvester knew, but he didn't answer her.

At his silence, she said, "I was so stupid. I went riding with him unescorted. I ended up pregnant. He agreed right away to marry me. I knew your father wouldn't approve, but I had no choice. I met him one night, and instead of taking me to Gretna Green he brought me to this horrible place. He had no intention of marrying me. He kept me prisoner here, until I had the baby. He said he didn't want to be forced into marrying me. I told him I wouldn't tell who the father was, but he wouldn't listen to me. He . . ." She paused a moment. Her bottom lip trembled and she looked unable to speak. Finally, in a strangled voice, she said, "He killed our son."

Sylvester's mind raced as he thought of Mr. Rupert Spears. The moment he'd looked at the man, he disliked him—and his brother. It wasn't just his jealousy at work either. There was a detectable ruthlessness in Rupert's eyes after Sylvester had told him he would see the magistrate for Colleen, the kind of ruthlessness he'd seen in the eyes of pirates he'd fought. Nothing short of death would stop Spears from destroying Josephine's baby. He had meant to warn Colleen away from him, but he knew she probably wouldn't have listened to him, at the time.

He strode down the back steps and stepped over the man he'd left in the snow. When he reached his horse, he said, "Your son is not dead."

"He's not?" A spark of hope lit up Josephine's face.

"No. He's alive. I can take you to him." Sylvester set her up in the saddle, then mounted behind her. He had to warn Colleen about Spears. He was the man she'd seen in the field trying to kill Phillip. He'd personally see Spears paid for everything he had done.

Twenty minutes later, Sylvester banged on Colleen's door. Aggie answered. Her gaze flicked between him, Josephine, and Red, then landed back on Sylvester. She leveled her eyes at him. "Come in, but you won't find our Colleen to home."

Sylvester let Josephine go before him, while Red followed in their wake. When they were inside the parlor, Aggie turned on Sylvester. "I'm surprised you've got the nerve to show your face here so soon."

"What do you mean by that?" Sylvester drew himself up and stared back at Aggie, in no mood to bandy words with her.

The hardness of his gaze made her take a step back. Then her indignation came back in her expression and she jammed her hands on her hips. "Well, after what you did, I didn't think you'd come back here to torment our Colleen again. And her defending you so. It broke me heart."

A feeling of dread churned in his stomach. He grabbed Aggie by the arms. "Where is Colleen? I want to speak to her."

"She ain't here."

"Where is she?" Sylvester shook her by the arms. When he heard Aggie gasp, he realized what he was doing and dropped his hands.

"She's gone with Mr. Rupert to take the baby to its mother."

"Oh, Lord! He'll kill my baby! I just know it!" Tears glistened in Josephine's eyes and she grabbed the front of Sylvester's coat. "You cannot let him. Say you will not."

Aggie slapped a hand over her heart and appeared unable to catch her breath. After a moment, she cried, "Oh, no! Say it ain't so. He's always been so kind. He ain't the one who tried to kill the little mite, is he? He said you had done it." Aggie glanced over at Sylvester, her expression contrite.

"I'm sure the bastard tried to lay the blame elsewhere." Red finally spoke.

"Then he means to finish what he started."

"I believe that is his intention," Sylvester answered gruffly.

Abruptly Sharon's chamber door closed, and Sharon called, "Aggie, has Colleen come back yet?"

Aggie grabbed her cheeks and called over her shoulder. "No, child." She turned and whispered to Sylvester. "Please, don't worry her with this news. It'll bring on a spell."

Sharon's footsteps padded lightly across the parlor. When she reached the hallway, she paused. Her thin gold hair was pulled back from her heart-shaped face and tied back with a ribbon. A dull gray gown covered her thin, delicate frame, hardly bigger than a child's.

In the heavy silence, she took in all the eyes trained on her, then said, "What is the matter? I know something is wrong, I can see it in your faces. Nothing has happened to Colleen, has it?"

"No, child," Aggie said, patting her arm.

"I don't believe you. I feel your hands shaking, Aggie. Now

tell me what is wrong. You don't have to shelter me; I want to know."

It was Sylvester who blurted, "Mr. Rupert Spears is the father of the baby."

The tiny pink spots on Sharon's cheeks faded away and she turned deathly pale. She chewed on her bottom lip as tears flooded her brown eyes.

Sylvester turned to Aggie now, his heart thumping against his ribs. "Do you know where he's taking her?"

"Mr. Winston Spears said something about the Anson place," Sharon said, blinking away tears. "We can try there first; I'll show you the way. Just let me get my coat." Sharon turned, her golden hair billowing out down her back. She hurried out into the hallway.

"You must stay here. You're weak," Sylvester said, grabbing Josephine's arm and steadying her swaying body.

"No," Josephine said with desperation in her voice. "You have to take me with you. I've got to see my baby."

"We'll be taking you, lass," Red said, then scooped her up in his arms.

A semblance of a smile touched her lips, then she said, "Thank you, sir."

"My pleasure." Red smiled back at her.

Sylvester wasn't smiling. He was thinking about Colleen and the baby, alone with that madman.

The moon hung in the sky, vivid, bright. Moonlight danced across the new fallen snow, looking like a sea of blue sapphires glistening on the surface. Thousands of stars winked at Colleen from above. It was a lovely night in spite of the task that lay before her. As she held Phillip tight against her breast, she couldn't help but feel sorry for him. He might not ever remember the touch of his own mother, or feel her arms about him. There was something special about feeling your own mother's contact. Even though she had decided to keep Phillip and raise him as her own, and she knew he would be loved, there would always be a cord within him that yearned for his real mother. Just as Colleen would always pine for the touch of her own mother. It had been fifteen years since her death, but still she felt the loss.

The sleigh rocked and shook as they turned into the snow-covered dirt road leading to the Anson farm. Phillip had fallen asleep from the sway of the sleigh. His face was covered, his small head tucked between her arm and breast.

She glanced over at Rupert, who kept his gaze straight ahead. "How much farther?"

"Not long now."

A heavy silence grew between them. Colleen's apprehension about meeting Miss Jackson was growing more uncomfortable. She couldn't stand the silence any longer, and tried at small talk. "I never got to congratulate you on your upcoming marriage to Lady Caroline Robbins."

"Thank you. A pity you can't meet her."

"I'm sure I would like her. I met her once when Father took me to London for my come-out ball. As I recall, she was very pretty and had a pleasing disposition."

"Yes, she is all of that. I'm afraid I fell for her right away."

"I'm sure your mother is overjoyed by the match." Colleen didn't give voice to her true thoughts. Mrs. Spears was probably beside herself with happiness now that they would be connected to royalty.

"Yes, Mother was pleased." He glanced over at her now. His face was in shadow, deepening the sockets of his eyes and the hollows of his cheeks. The moon cast an eerie glow in his blue eyes.

Colleen thought it was the moonlight playing tricks, and glanced up ahead. A dark form rose up in the distance. As they drew closer, the shadow-hazed shape turned into a small cottage, no bigger than a shack. Half of the thatch roof bowed

in from the snow and looked ready to collapse at any moment.
The broken shutters along the windows hung at odd angles along
the windows. It was more dilapidated than she remembered. Not
a light shone in the dark panes, nor was there smoke rising
from the chimney.

Colleen glanced over at Rupert. "You did say she is here,
did you not?"

"Yes, that's what I said."

"The place is deserted."

"You'll find it's not."

Something in his voice made the hairs at the back of Colleen's
neck prick. Every instinct in her cried out that something was
wrong. "I think we should go back," she said, eyeing him.

"Not yet, my dear."

"Take me back this instant."

"Be quiet before you wake the baby. You wouldn't want to
do that, now, would you?"

Colleen swallowed hard, then it struck her. Rupert was the
man she'd seen in the field. It had to be him. The spear of
doubt eating away at the back of her mind left her in a rush.
She wanted to cry out her relief, but then she realized the
danger she and Phillip were in.

Before she knew it, they reached the cottage and Rupert's
fingers bit into her arm as he pulled her out of the sleigh.
"Come along, and no hysterics, please. I can't abide hysterics."
When she was down on the ground, he looked at her and said,
"Oh, I forgot—you aren't the type for hysterics, are you?"
He shoved her forward.

"Please don't hurt Phillip. You can hurt me, but don't hurt
him." Colleen tightened her hold on him. He felt so small and
helpless in her arms.

"He is my flesh, you know. I'll do what I want to with the
brat. I can't let him get in the way of my marriage with Lady
Caroline." He paused, then said through gritted teeth, "I
worked hard to win her hand, and I'll not have him and his

slutty mother ruining my chances for this match. If word of this scandal ever got out, it would be the end of my engagement.''

"You don't love her, do you? You're marrying her for her title.''

"That and her wealth.''

"You need money?'' Colleen asked, and raised an incredulous brow as he grabbed her shoulder and shoved her forward.

He sighed, then said, "We're good at putting up a front, but unfortunately we're going broke. Mother spends way too much money on frivolities; then I have my gaming debts. There just isn't enough blunt to go around since Father died and we had to sell the shipping company. And then there were those little care packages Mother sent you.''

"I don't understand why she did that if you couldn't afford it.''

"Though she doesn't speak of it, I believe she had a great respect for your mother, for she was the only lady who would receive her. Lady Davenport did have a kind heart. She was liked by everyone who knew her. It opened up a whole new society for my dear mother. Thanks to Lady Davenport, she was accepted into some of the finest drawing rooms in England. That is how I became acquainted with Lady Caroline.'' He paused; then his expression lightened as he appeared to realize something. In a faraway voice, he said, "I'll always mourn her death . . . and perhaps yours.'' His gaze moved back to her.

Colleen shifted nervously, feeling his crazed blue eyes piercing her back. Hoping to take his mind off her death, she said, "Who is Phillip's mother?''

"Lady Josephine, of course.'' He sounded proud of himself. "She was very willing to see to my needs. I quite enjoyed our little assignations, but then she became pregnant.'' He opened the cottage door and thrust Colleen inside.

It was freezing cold and dank in the little hovel. The smell of dirt and mildew pervaded the air. She heard him strike a match; then an oil lamp flooded the room with light. The cottage was bare save for a straw pallet, covered by a moth-eaten blanket, and a huge pile of wood near the hearth.

Hoping to keep him talking and plan for a way to escape, she said, "So you took it upon yourself to destroy Lady Josephine and the baby so the truth wouldn't get out."

"That's right. But your meddling had to go and spoil all my plans."

"Was Winston in on this, too?"

"No, I'm afraid he's a naive little fool. He believed the story I told him to tell you."

Colleen didn't want to ask her next question, but it had to be asked, "Have you killed Lady Josephine already?"

"Unfortunately, no. I was saving her until last. She was quite a tasty little morsel, and I enjoyed when she fought me." Evil blazed from his eyes as he spoke. "I couldn't have my fun curtailed, so I left her until I finished this little matter." His gaze dropped to Phillip.

Instinctively Colleen turned to the side so he couldn't look at Phillip.

He chuckled, a vicious, deep sound that boomed against the walls of the little cottage. "Please sit," he said, motioning her toward the pallet. "Sorry about the state of this place, but I can make a little fire to warm you." He turned his back and picked up a piece of wood from a stack near the hearth.

Colleen saw her chance. Gripping Phillip tightly in her arms, she darted for the door. As she reached it, she felt a tug on the scarf wrapped around her neck. The wool cut into her throat and jerked her up short.

Phillip woke up at the sudden jolt and whimpered. She held him tightly, her head bent backward at an awkward angle until it felt as if her spine would snap.

He tightened the scarf, then leaned close to her ear. "Where do you think you're going?" His hot breath brushed the side of her ear and made chills lash down her spine.

"You're insane," she said, her voice barely a croak.

"If you try to leave here again, you'll regret it." He dropped the back of her scarf, then shoved her toward the chair. "Now sit."

She stared at the dirty pallet, then sat down on it. "Please, you can kill me, but don't hurt Phillip. He doesn't know anything."

"I can't afford for this to get out. You know how people will talk if I should be accidentally seen with the child. It's better to tie up all the loose ends and be done with it." His blue eyes shifted to the baby.

She saw the cruel light burning in them and clutched Phillip tighter to her breast. "You won't get away with this. They'll know you killed us."

His lips parted in a smile; then he threw another log in the hearth, then another. "I've thought of that possibility. That's why you're not going to die here with the child. It must look like the illustrious Miss Jackson went crazy and killed the child. Of course, you were so distraught from learning of Usworth's deception in all of this, that you ran away; so did Miss Jackson before I could apprehend her. Once I spread the lies Usworth was the father, and that he tried to kill the child so news of his mistress would not get out before he could seduce you into marrying him again, I'm sure his reputation will be in shreds and he'll be tried for attempted murder. I'm sure Lady Sefton will add credence to the gossip mills for me." He smiled, pleased with himself.

"What are you going to do with me?"

"I'll sink your body in the ocean with Josephine's. No one will ever find either of you, and they'll believe you ran away when you learned of Usworth's deception. What a horrible tragedy," he said, with the same brutal smile stretched across his lips.

"You'll never get away with this."

"You won't live to see if I do or not."

Phillip began crying and he turned and glared at him. "Keep him quiet."

She rocked Phillip in her arms and watched Rupert piling on kindling and logs. It flowed out of the hearth and out into the room. She realized what he was about, and glanced at the door again.

As if he had eyes in the back of his head, he said, "Do not think about it again. Put him down and stand up."

"No." She shook her head adamantly.

He turned, his eyes full of rage; then he came toward her and stood glaring down at her. "Put him down, or I'll put him down."

Her heart throbbed against her ribs. She was torn for a moment, then laid Phillip down on the straw pallet. He stopped crying, while his vivid blue eyes, so like his father's, stared helplessly up at her.

Rupert grabbed her arm and yanked her to her feet. "Come on, we're leaving now."

"No! No!" She drew back and swung at him.

Before her fist connected with his face, he ducked and grabbed her arm, wrenching it around behind her back. He grinned at her, enjoying her struggles, then shoved her over to the fireplace. With an angry swipe, he snatched the lamp from the mantel.

She saw he was going to throw it on the mountain of wood, and grabbed it with her free hand. He twisted her arm farther up her back, until she thought it would be wrenched from the socket. But she didn't let go. He growled and yanked it out of her hand.

Before she could grab it again, he slammed the burning lamp against the bricks of the hearth. Flames erupted as glass spewed out into the room. He shoved Colleen toward the door.

"No! No!" she screamed, hearing Phillip's cries twining with her own.

With an angry thrust, he forced her out the cottage door and slammed it shut. Colleen struggled, throwing her weight against him. He forced her arm tighter until her hand was touching her shoulder blade.

She cried out, feeling the pain shooting up her arm and down her shoulder. He shoved her ahead of him. Colleen dug her feet into the snow and glanced back at the cottage. Flames leaped along the windowsill as smoke rolled out above the door. Phillip was still screaming—a terrified cry, the sound stabbing her heart.

"No, we can't leave him in there! Let me get him!" She fought Rupert again.

He drew back and slapped her, then shoved her forward. "Try to calm yourself, or I'll kill you now," he growled near her ear.

Abruptly she heard the thundering of hooves. Glancing down the road, she saw two riders approaching. They were in shadow, but she could see the four white socks on one of the horses, rhythmically flicking in the night. She breathed a sigh of relief at the sight of Disaster. Her relief was short-lived when she glanced over her shoulder and saw the flames shooting up over the top of the cottage now.

Rupert pulled a gun out from beneath his coat and pointed it at the approaching riders, all the while pulling her toward the sleigh.

"The baby's in the cottage!" Colleen screamed at the top of her lungs.

"Shut up!" Rupert hit her across the face again.

Her head jerked to the side and pain shot down her cheek and into her neck. As she turned, she glimpsed Sylvester leaping from his horse and running toward the cottage. When he opened the door, flames jumped out at him. He used his coat to cover his head, then leaped through the doorway.

Rupert had the gun aimed at Sylvester, but now he turned it toward Red, who was running toward them.

Colleen hit Rupert's hand with her shoulder. The gun fired into the air. Colleen was torn away from Rupert by a pair of large beefy hands, and she was slung several yards away. She stumbled three steps, turned, and saw Red pummeling Rupert with his fists. Rupert fell back into the snow and didn't move.

Crack. Crack. Crack.

Turning around, she followed the sound of the splitting beams. Her gaze landed on the roof. She watched as the center support beam fell a foot, another, then it caved in. Sparks billowed into the air and spewed burning cinders up into the air. Flames dived twenty feet into the sky.

A scream froze inside Colleen's throat, then she saw Lady Josephine running toward the cottage, screaming, ''My baby! My baby!''

Red ran to her and grabbed her arms, holding her back. ''You ain't goin' near there, you'll be killed,'' he said, fighting to hold on to her. Josephine was fighting him so much, he wrapped his huge arms around her and lifted her off the ground.

Colleen felt the tightness in her throat growing. It ripped through her insides and opened up the carefully guarded dam she had held back for five years. Tears stung her eyes, then poured down her cheeks. Her body hunched over with sobs, each one like a fist in her belly. Her legs gave way and she fell on her knees into the snow.

He was dead. They would never know any happiness together, all because she had doubted him that first time and cried off. If she cared to admit it, a small shred of uncertainty had plagued her again, too, even though she knew deep down in her heart Sylvester would never do such a thing. Perhaps she was being punished for it. She would never taste his lips again, or feel his powerful arms holding her. And Phillip.

Dear God! She buried her face in her hands, rocking on her knees, sobbing.

She grew vaguely aware of a gentle hand on her shoulder. ''It's all right, Colleen.''

Sharon's voice sounded a long way away, mixing with another sound. . . .

Phillip's cry.

Through a wash of tears, she saw Sylvester's face, emerging out from behind the flames. He strode from around the back of the cottage, his handsome face covered with soot and smoke. He held Phillip in his arms. Phillip's frightened cries echoed above the roar of the fire. At the sight of them, Colleen felt another sob bubbling up from her throat. Her vision blurred as more tears flowed down her cheeks. She wiped the tears out of her eyes with the back of her hand and watched Lady Josephine run to him.

"Come on, let me help you up." Sharon grabbed Colleen's arm and pulled her up.

Hiccuping loudly, Colleen kept her eyes locked on Sylvester as he handed Phillip over to Lady Josephine. Red was beside them, slapping Sylvester on the back. "We thought you were dead there for a minute, Cap'n," Red's voice boomed above the din of the fire.

"I jumped out a window."

"I knew you wouldn't be dyin' on me."

Sylvester glanced over Josephine's head at Colleen. The corners of his silvery, gleaming eyes crinkled in a smile. His grin beamed all the way down to her soul. The sight of him, alive, looking at her with so much tenderness, made her feel as if she would burst inside.

As she took a step to run to him, Sharon cried, "Behind you, Colleen!"

Before Colleen could react, she felt a large arm lock around her neck and her back hit Rupert's chest. A gun wavered in his unsteady hand.

Red stepped toward them.

Rupert's arm locked tighter around Colleen's throat. She gagged and coughed as he said, "Stay back, or I'll break her pretty neck."

Red froze, his expression a mask of indecision and composed fury. In an almost teasing voice, one he might have used on an irate drunk, he said, "Let her go now. You know you'll not be leavin' here with the lass."

"He's right, you know."

Red and Spears turned in unison and gazed at Sylvester.

Sylvester stood there, his legs splayed, his hand out in front of him, looking down the sights of his pistol, aimed at Spear's brow. "If you drop the weapon this moment, I might let you live." His gaze flitted between Spears and Colleen. His face was a mask of cool concentration, his hand deadly still as he held the gun.

"You wouldn't shoot me with your beloved in the way," Spears said, with arrogant bravado in his voice.

"Would I not? Red, tell him how I like to shoot flies off the top of the *Mariner*'s main mast. It was a little pastime of mine."

"He's tellin' the truth of it. Och! I lost a lot of blunt bettin' against him."

"But this little beauty here wasn't in your way." Spears squeezed Colleen's neck tighter.

She grimaced from the pain. One more squeeze and he'd crush her windpipe. Her heart beat a savage tattoo against her chest as she stared at the gun Spears had trained on Sylvester. She wanted to knock the gun out of his hand, but she was afraid Sylvester might get shot in the process.

"I've shot under worse odds. Red can tell you. You remember that time on the Canary Islands when we had that run-in with One-Eye, don't you?" Sylvester shared a quick glance with Red.

Red's face lit up with understanding. "Aye, I remember the bloody pirate well—he had nerve capturin' three of our mates. You left a goodly-size hole in his head, Cap'n—that you did."

"It appears Mr. Spears here would like some of the same." Sylvester narrowed his eyes between the sight.

"Stop it, Rupert." Josephine spoke as she held a crying Phillip in her arms and came to stand near Sylvester. "You can't win. Now leave Lady Colleen alone. Haven't you done enough?"

Spears' gaze locked with Josephine's for a moment. The light from the raging fire flickered across his face and gave it a ghoulish, reddish hue. Then abruptly his expression screwed up into a snarl. He screamed at her. "This is all your fault! I should have killed you first." He pointed the gun at Josephine.

It all happened at once. With bulletlike swiftness, Sylvester thrust Josephine aside. Red dove for Colleen, knocking her to the ground.

Both guns went off at once.

Colleen landed on her side in the snow. Red landed beside her, one of his sinewy arms still over her shoulder. Out of the corner of her eye she saw Spears collapse behind Red. She raised her head and turned to see if Sylvester, Josephine, and Phillip were all right. Sylvester was helping Josephine up out of the snow and berating her for almost getting herself killed.

At the sound of his deep voice booming over the bluster of the fire, Colleen let out the breath she'd been holding and smiled. When she inhaled again, the cold air grated against her aching throat, forcing her to cough violently.

"You all right, lass?" Red asked, his bushy red brows drawn together in worry. He helped her to sit up, all the while brushing snow off of her hair and arms.

"I suppose so," she said, her voice still coarse and quavering. "Why do I have a feeling you and Sylvester have rehearsed that little maneuver before?"

"Quite a few times, when a mate needed rescuing," Red smiled proudly.

Sharon dropped to her knees beside Colleen and threw her arms around her neck. "I was so worried, are you all right?"

"Yes, are you?" Colleen drew back and scanned Sharon's face. Other than her cheeks being a little paler than usual, her sister looked fairly composed and well, though that pleasing guileless look in her eye that Colleen had so treasured, was marred somehow now. Her baby sister had grown up in the past few minutes. Colleen felt a wash of tears flood her eyes.

Sharon appeared to know what Colleen was thinking, for she smiled sweetly, laid a tender hand on Colleen's cheek, then said, "I'm okay, you need not worry."

"I know." Colleen blinked back the tears.

The loud gunshots had frightened Phillip even more, and his crying reached a fevered pitch in spite of Josephine's attempts to calm him. As Colleen turned to look at him, she heard the crunch of snow behind her and felt strong arms lifting her, then she was swept up in Sylvester's arms.

"How are you, my love?" He glanced down at her, his gray eyes sparkling, stark against the black smut on his face.

Colleen wrapped her arms around his neck, smelling the thick odor of smoke at odds with the starched scent of his shirt and his bay rum aftershave. "Fine, now that you are all right. I wanted to die when I'd thought you'd been burned alive. I've never needed anyone like I need you. Don't ever leave me." She hugged his neck tighter and pressed her lips against his cheek, feeling the coarse black stubble rough against her lips.

"Do you think for one minute I'd be cheated out of the wedding you owe me?" He bent and kissed her. The fierceness of his kiss stole through her, warming her whole body. All she could feel was his strong arms holding her, the soft moistness of his lips, and the powerful pounding he caused in her heart.

EPILOGUE

Three months later, every seat in the chapel at Madison Hall was taken. White orchids and pink ribbons overflowed in every empty space. The rector's voice boomed over the heads of everyone:

"Marriage is not to be entered into lightly . . ."

Lord Usworth sat directly in front of the pulpit, listening impatiently, drumming his fingers against his cane. Next to him, Lady Josephine held a squirming Phillip in her arms. Red smiled at Phillip, then shared a glance with Lady Josephine. The smile she bestowed on him made his eyes glow.

Aggie and Sharon occupied the adjacent row. Aggie mopped at tears, while Sharon smiled serenely up at the front of the church.

Sunlight burned through the round stained-glass window over the altar, shooting a beam of rainbow-colored light down on Sylvester and Colleen. The twenty-foot-long train on Colleen's white satin gown flowed down the steps behind her like a silken waterfall, stark against Sylvester's black coat and breeches. They stood hand in hand before the rector, a short man, round as he was tall.

The rector paused in his booming but eloquent discourse, then said, "Is there anyone here who knows why these two should not be joined in marriage?"

Not a noise stirred the chapel, not a cough, not a rustle of someone shifting in their seat, not even a breath could be heard.

Lord Usworth turned in the pew and eyed everyone seated, daring them to utter a sound. At that moment, Phillip glanced over and saw Lord Usworth's severe expression, and burst out crying. His voice resounded through the chapel like the voices of thousands of saints coming on Judgment Day.

Colleen jumped at the sound. She saw Sylvester grinning. Try as she might, she couldn't stop the laugh that burst out of her mouth. Sylvester threw back his head and joined her.

Their laughs were contagious. Lord Usworth's frown gave way to a grin, then he threw back his head and laughed. Wave after wave of laughter joined them.

All except one voice, that of the rector. He cleared his throat and waved his hands. "I say, this is a marriage ceremony." He eyed the guests, then leveled a harsh look at Colleen and Sylvester.

They sobered, and silence once again filled the chapel.

The rector raised his voice over Phillip's crying:

"I pronounce you man and wife . . . finally." He looked glad to be done with them, and said, "You may kiss the bride."

Sylvester drew Colleen into his arms, then crushed her to him. She knew it would add more scandal to the ceremony, but it was five years too late to care. She wrapped her arms around Sylvester's neck and kissed him back, pressing her body provocatively close to his, letting him know how much she loved him and how glad she was to finally be his wife.

I hope you enjoyed reading Sylvester and Colleen's story. Please let me know if you liked it. I would love to hear from you. My address is:

> Constance Hall
> PO Box 25664
> Richmond, Va. 23260-5664
> or E-mail me at koslow@erols.com

If you would like a response, please include a self-addressed stamped envelope. I hope your future has a little miracle in it and overflows with love!

ABOUT THE AUTHOR

Constance Hall lives with her family in Richmond, Virginia, and is the author of two Zebra historical romances, *My Darling Duke* and *My Dashing Earl*. Constance's newest historical romance, *My Rebellious Bride*, will be published in June, 1999. Connie loves hearing from readers and you may write to her c/o Zebra Books. Please include a self-addressed stamped envelope if you wish a reply.

CRADLE SONG

CANDACE McCARTHY

CHAPTER 1

The Pennsylvania Wilderness, 1732

The warmth of the sun caressed her face as Emily Russell plucked a plump ripe berry from its bush and popped it into her mouth. She closed her eyes and sighed with pleasure. The succulent fruit was a gift from heaven. There was a time this past winter when her food supplies and stock of firewood had dwindled so low she'd thought she wouldn't live until spring. But she had survived, and her life had changed for the better. Now she found delight in the simple things around her.

It was a beautiful May morning, and Emily, widowed and pregnant during the harsh cold months, had found the strength to give birth to a healthy son. *I made it,* she thought with real pleasure. *We made it, Christopher.* As she gazed down at her sleeping infant, she experienced an emotion so overwhelming and powerful, that it brought tears to her eyes. How she loved her child!

Baby Christopher slept soundly in his basket beside his mother's feet. Bundled in a blanket made from his late father's shirt, he was healthy and content. No one who laid eyes on him would suspect his mother's struggle during her last months of pregnancy . . . nor the ordeal Emily had endured while birthing her babe alone.

She crouched carefully to caress her son's cheek with her finger. *So soft, so perfect,* she thought. *My little savior. Just like your papa.* For it was the knowledge of the tiny life within her that had given her the determination to live. Grief had ruled her days . . . until she had felt the tiny flutter of life within her womb. Cheered by the baby growing inside her, she'd found new purpose, a new strength.

Emily cupped the crown of her infant son's head, enjoying the soft, baby-fine blond hairs that tickled her palm and fingers. Christopher wriggled his nose and sighed in his sleep, bringing forth his mother's quiet laughter.

Smiling, Emily started to rise, then winced at the pain in her abdomen, and went back to her berry-gathering. Her flesh was tender. Christopher's birth had torn tissue, and four weeks later Emily was still healing. But the young woman was optimistic. She had weathered the stormy winter and had much to be thankful for. She would handle whatever pain, whatever dangers, lay ahead—even the wild savages she feared, and who remained a constant threat to the area. Nothing, she decided, could be as terrible as being cold, hungry, and so alone.

Birdsong trilled down from a treetop overhead. Emily paused to look up and smile as the songster soared up to exchange one perch for another. A flurry of movement in the brush startled Emily. She gasped and spun around, then chuckled with relief at the antics of two gray squirrels, one playing chase with the other. She watched them scoot up the trunk of one tree and trail a limb to scurry across the branch of another. The animals leapt from one tree to the next, cackling in the way that squirrels do, moving farther and farther away until she could no longer see or hear them.

Scolding herself for allowing a pair of squirrels to frighten her, Emily picked enough berries to fill her bowl. Next, she began to gather the herbs and edible roots needed to restock her supply back at the cabin. She hummed softly as she worked. Her baby was never far from her side. Whenever her hunt took her to a different spot, she moved Christopher with her.

As the morning wore on, she felt a tingling in her nipples as her breasts filled with milk. She glanced down, saw that her baby slept on, undisturbed by hunger, and went back to work. Her breasts weren't uncomfortable; Emily decided to wait patiently for Christopher to awaken on his own.

A light breeze stirred the air. The new lush growth on the treetops rustled; Emily found the sound soothing. She spied some growth near the base of a large tree and hunkered down to gather moss.

She felt a sudden prickling at the back of her neck as if someone was watching her. Her heart began to pound. She rose slowly and looked around, but she didn't see anything. Then she detected a flash of color and movement in the distance, through a break in the trees. Emily grabbed her baby and hid behind a thicket. Her heartbeat thundered in her ears as she peered through an opening for a better glimpse.

Emily gasped with horror. *A savage!* There, a hundred yards or more away, was an Indian. Her thoughts raced as she watched the warrior's approach. *Dear God, what am I going to do?* Tears blurred her vision as she looked down at her sleeping infant. *My sweet baby, what shall I do to protect you?*

Her gaze went back to the Indian. She couldn't outrun the brave while carrying Christopher. In her present condition, she wouldn't get very far, and her efforts would only alert the Indian of their presence. There was also the likelihood that if she ran with her baby, she'd fall and crush her tiny son.

Frantic, Emily searched for a hiding place and saw nothing that would accommodate both her and the babe. A small hollow in the thicket was big enough for Christopher's basket. She could hide Christopher there, she thought, then run, making enough noise to keep the savage's attention away from her baby's hiding place.

As she tucked the basket into the hole left by the natural growth of forest shrubs, Emily fought the horrible mental images that came with remembered tales of capture, torture, and death at the hands of Indians. She offered up a silent prayer that Christopher would continue to sleep peacefully, oblivious to the danger. She rose to her feet, caught sight of the brave's position and, after one last final check on her baby, started to run.

Tears blurred the sight of her path as Emily raced through the forest, shoving trees, brush, and other obstacles out of her way. A twig snapped beneath her feet. She tripped on a stone and fell headlong onto a bed of dead leaves. She quickly righted herself and took off again, crashing through the forest.

The sudden sound of movement behind her, alerted her that the plan had worked. Emily didn't glance back, for fear of losing precious escape time. Now that her baby was safe and the savage was after her, she had to think of her own safety.

She picked up her pace, aware as she did so of the cramping pain in her lower abdomen, the sore tenderness of the area between her legs. She felt a dampness between her legs and wondered if she might be bleeding, but she couldn't stop to check. As she ducked below the low limb of a tree, she looked for a place to hide. She couldn't run much longer. The welfare of her child depended on her own well-being. Christopher needed his mother alive and well to care for him.

Emily could no longer hear the Indian behind her, but she was making too much noise herself. He was there; she knew he could not be too far behind her. James had told her that a red man could sneak up silently on his enemy and slit his throat before the man had a clue that the savage was behind him.

The thought made her own throat tighten as she fought the urge to glance back. Fear gave her renewed strength. Emily ran, her gaze scanning ahead for some brush, a cave, anyplace to hide.

She was fast losing physical strength. The pain in her lower body had become unbearable. She no longer needed to look to know that she had injured herself and was bleeding below. Emily slowed, then had to stop. She bent over, gasping for breath, fighting the waves of pain radiating from her abdomen. *I'm not going to die! I'll not let him catch me.*

She blinked back tears as she searched for an escape from danger. Spying a thicket, she raced for cover and threw herself into the middle of a briar patch. She gasped with pain. Her skin tore in several places as she fell through thorn bushes and came to rest in a small clearing beneath spiked branches.

Emily was afraid to move. She felt battered and bruised. Winded, she tried to catch her breath. The hem of her rough homespun gown had caught in the thorns. Fearing the Indian would see it, she jerked it free, ripping fabric and tumbling to lie in a twisted position on her back. Her face and limbs stung and throbbed where the bramble had scratched her. Those injuries didn't concern her. The pain in her lower abdomen and the burning between her legs were greater. She wondered how badly she'd hurt herself, but she didn't dwell on it. She prayed silently that the Indian wouldn't find her. She had no strength left to run.

Her breath tore in and out of her lungs as she lay unmoving, listening for her pursuer. When she didn't hear him, she waited longer. After minutes, she winced with pain as she rose up to look for him. There was no sign of movement. Not even a bird or animal.

The young woman shifted to get a better look. She checked all sides of the briar patch, choking back a gasp as her skin scraped against thorns when she moved.

There was no sign of the brave, but Emily knew better than to leave her hiding place. The Indian could be watching, lying in wait. It would be some time before she could return to

Christopher. The sudden sharp tingling of her nipples reminded
her that it was well past the time for Christopher's meal. Her
breasts swelled, and she could feel dampness as her milk leaked,
wetting her bodice. Fear for her child and a strong urge to hold
her babe safely within her arms made her close her eyes and
pray harder.

*Sleep, son! Whatever you do, don't wake up! Not until I
return for you. If you cry out, you'll alert the Indian.* Emily
shuddered as she imagined her sweet baby trapped within the
savage's arms. She stifled a sob, but her tears ran freely down
her cheeks. *Oh, Lord, I should never have left you alone! Please
be safe, my baby. Sleep quietly until Mama returns for you.*

Emily huddled within her thorny prison, tortured with worry
over her infant son. She gave little thought to her own discomfort or the blood she could feel seeping slowly from between
her legs to stain her undergarment. Her concern was with Christopher, a tiny babe lying alone and defenseless . . . and within
a savage's grasp.

Forest Thunder stood, frowning, his bow and arrow poised in
readiness of the hunt, as he studied his surroundings. Where
was the animal? Only seconds ago, he'd heard it crashing
through the woods. The sound had been some distance away,
but he was quick on his feet. Once he spotted a buck, he could
easily outrun it.

If his thoughts hadn't been elsewhere, he would have already
found his prey. His mind had been back in the Seneca village
he'd left only hours before. He was a messenger for the Onondaga, and he carried the Seneca chief's response to a message
sent by Forest's sachem, Drumming Fox. He had been on his
way home when the noise startled him. The brave was certain
it was a deer, although he hadn't actually caught sight of it.
Forest followed the direction of the sound, but it was as if the

animal had disappeared . . . and just when it had been within reach.

He stood without moving, listening carefully. The wind rustled the treetops. A crackle in the brush behind him made him spin about, ready to let loose an arrow, but it was only a squirrel. He wanted the deer. He lowered his bow and moved on, with silent feet, his gaze alert and his ear cocked for sound.

If the animal didn't show himself soon, Forest thought, he would have to continue on his way without it. He wasn't on a hunt, but he wanted the deer. His people would be happy to have it.

Forest Thunder couldn't afford the time to search for the animal. He had to return to his village. His sachem, Drumming Fox, waited for the Seneca chief Long Chin's reply. There was tension between the two Iroquois tribes that would be eased with the marriage between Long Chin's brother and Fox's daughter, Rippling Stream. Drumming Fox waited to hear if the bride-price was worthy of his daughter.

The Onondaga suspected that his sachem would be pleased with the Seneca's offer, but he wasn't sure about the daughter's wishes. This situation was an unusual one. He didn't think the young bride-to-be had been told or consulted in this matter. Normally an Indian maiden married a man of her own choosing or a man chosen by the village matrons. He feared the woman's reaction at being forced to marry the Seneca warrior.

A tiny cry behind and to his right drew Forest's attention. A wounded animal, he thought. Perhaps not a buck at all. He headed toward the sound, wondering whether or not the animal would be worth taking.

He paused when there was silence, and listened. The sound came again, odd yet so familiar that it gave him goose flesh. The cries came intermittently, a garbled noise that lured him closer toward a clump of bushes.

Putting his bow away, the brave drew a knife from his legging-strap, then cautiously parted the bushes. His gaze wid-

ened, and he put away his weapon. There, lying in a basket,
innocent and vulnerable, lay a tiny white infant. As if sensing
Forest's presence, the child started to cry loudly. Something
kicked within his gut as Forest moved his gaze from the baby's
unhappy face to the tiny fists moving above the blanket.

The brave reached into the hollow and picked up the basket.
Murmuring soothingly, he studied the child as he sat on the
base of a huge fallen tree and wondered where the baby's
parents were. He stroked the baby's smooth cheek to comfort
it, and the infant turned toward his hand in his search for food.

"Poor *Ex aa,* you are hungry. Where is your mother?" Forest
felt a sudden spurt of anger as he glanced up and looked around.
Where was the child's mother? How could she have been so
foolish as to leave an innocent baby to face the dangers of
these woods?

He raised the baby's covering, felt the damp diaper, and on
impulse checked beneath the fabric to find that the infant was
a boy-child. The baby continued to cry and intermittently rooted
for food. Forest smiled when the infant began to suck on his
knuckle, then frowned when the hungry baby released Forest's
finger to cry again.

The Indian lifted the baby from the basket and rose to his
feet, cradling the child protectively against his chest. He gasped
and then chuckled softly when the hungry infant turned toward
his nipple.

"We must find your mama," Forest murmured in English.
"Poor boy, you are hungry and wet. Where is your father? I
will find him for you. But until I do, what am I going to do
with you?" He looked at the small face, the perfect smoothness
of baby-soft skin, the little eyes and nose ... the tiny mouth
making so much noise. His anger toward the child's parents
grew.

Forest felt immediately protective. He would find the baby's
mother and lecture her on her careful disregard for her child's
welfare. Had she not realized the dangers to a child left alone

in the forest? Didn't she know that there were wild animals who would see their next meal in this sweet baby?

He tightened his jaw in anger, but his hold on the child remained gentle as he set the infant back into his basket. The baby continued to cry and root, and Forest felt helpless. He reached into the leather pouch tied to his loincloth and pulled out a piece of dried venison. It wasn't food for an infant, but it was the only thing he had to offer. Teaching its strength, he gave it to the child. Tiny lips latched onto the meat and the baby found temporary comfort in the simple pleasure of sucking.

Forest studied the content baby with conflicting feelings. Then he picked up the child in the basket and began a search for the boy's irresponsible parents.

Emily waited within the bushes for what seemed to her like an eternity. She was worried about her son and anxious to have him safely within her arms again. She didn't know how long she huddled beneath the briars. She was afraid to move, fearing that if she did, she'd cry out whenever the thorns scratched her. She couldn't risk having the savage hearing it and discovering her.

Where was the savage? She hoped he was well on his way, long gone. She couldn't be too careful. She'd wait just a little longer before venturing outside.

It was well past Christopher's feeding time. Her breasts were oozing at the nipples, the milk filling her to the point of pain. She could only hope that if Christopher woke and started to cry there would be no one—neither man nor animal—to hear him. She inched up to check her surroundings one last time.

There had been no sign or sound of movement for quite some time. Emily looked about and knew getting out of her hiding place wasn't going to be easy. Her scratches from her first brush with the thorns stung. How was she going to get out without hurting herself worse?

Emily couldn't stop worrying about her baby. Concern for his well-being made her rise up through the tangle without hesitation. She cried out as thorns became imbedded in her flesh, then again when she pulled away, but she kept moving. Her baby needed her.

Finally Emily was free and heading back toward her tiny son. She had difficulty finding the spot at first. Then she recognized the clearing and went right to the thicket.

"Christopher," she called softly. "Christopher, Mama is here." Her lips curving, Emily pulled back branches.

Her smile froze in place when she saw that the hollow was empty. Her heart started to pump hard as she frantically searched the clearing. "Christopher! *Christopher!* Where are you?"

Had she come to the right place? She assessed her surroundings. Where had she left her berry basket? Her whole body jerked with horror. Dear God, did she leave the basket where the Indian could find it? Had her carelessness given away her son's hiding place?

"Calm down, Emily," she murmured. "Make certain you are in the right place. Maybe the basket is where you left it." Where had she left it? *Near the berry bush.*

She forced herself to think rationally. Where had she been picking berries? Her gaze spanned the area until she spied something familiar. Within minutes, she found the berry bush. Emily breathed a sigh of relief. The basket was where she left it. Her face went pale as she realized that she had been in the right clearing the first time, had checked the right hollow all along. Her baby was missing. She had a flash of mental images of the savage with her child—then of her baby's basket surrounded by wild animals.

A sob of anguish burst from her throat, breaking the stillness of the forest and disturbing wildlife.

"Christopher!" she screamed, falling to her injured knees. "My God, no! Not Christopher, my baby!"

CHAPTER 2

She would get her baby back. Whatever it took, however far she must travel, she would find and rescue her son. Emily tried to control her tears as she stood. Fear clawed at her throat and a small sob escaped her. *Christopher!* She should have never left him.

Her thoughts raced wildly as she headed back to the cabin. She'd need supplies to travel or she'd die during the search, she thought. What chance would her babe have then?

She was vaguely aware of her injuries as she stumbled through the woods on her way home. The pain of losing her child agonized her. A few scratches were nothing.

Emily wasn't fit to travel, but she would find the strength. Tears filled her eyes as she saw the cabin. When she saw Christopher's cradle inside, she choked back a cry of pain. Weeping, she searched frantically for food and supplies that she stuffed into a small satchel. She could use a blanket; it would get cold at night. She would take only what she could fit in her bag.

When the satchel was full, Emily left the cabin. Stepping into the sunshine, she saw the Indian, with her child, in the yard several feet from the house. She gasped, rushed forward to rescue her son, and then collapsed before the brave.

Forest Thunder frowned as he studied the woman at his feet, then turned his attention to the baby. Exhausted from crying earlier, the infant had fallen asleep, but he started to whimper upon hearing his mother's voice. The brave watched as the baby screwed up his face for a good cry. He soothed the child and glanced at his mother. Both mother and child needed attention, but he couldn't tend the woman without settling her babe. Forest stepped around the woman to put the child in the cabin. He saw the cradle. After calming the infant, he gently laid the boy down. Then, he went outside to get the baby's mother.

She didn't stir when Forest picked her up and carried her to the bed inside. She didn't awaken as he bathed the scratches on her face and hands. He saw her torn gown and raised the hem to check her legs. He tended the scrapes on her knees and the cuts on her calves. He cursed in Iroquoian as he hiked her skirt higher and saw the blood on her undergarment.

The woman didn't wake that afternoon or night. Forest Thunder held the crying babe and wondered how anyone could sleep through the sound. He studied the mother while he rocked her child. He had undressed and bathed her. He had cleaned her wounds. He'd done things for her that would horrify her if she'd known. But he couldn't ignore the blood. The brave was satisfied that she wouldn't bleed to death, but her pallor continued to concern him.

The crying baby demanded Forest's attention. The child was hungry. After setting the boy in his cradle, Forest made a fine mush out of water and the smallest bit of ground corn. He dabbed his finger into the thin gruel and offered it to the baby. The infant latched on to his finger and sucked. Smiling, the brave withdrew his finger, and quickly recoated it with the mush while the baby whimpered. The child rejected Forest's second offering and began to cry in earnest.

Forest felt helpless as he looked at the crying infant. He thought of the woman's breasts, full to overflowing with milk. The child's need overcame Forest's discomfort as the brave brought the child to his mother and opened her nightgown. Forest experienced a warm pleasurable sensation as the baby found a nipple and nursed.

The sudden silence was soothing. The only sound was that of the baby happily sucking on his mother's breast. Forest smiled, sharing the child's satisfaction. After a time, he lifted the child, burped him, and shifted both mother and child so that the baby could nurse from the other breast. He had learned enough from the village matrons to know that it was best for both mother and child to feed from both breasts, satisfying the child's hunger while seeing to the woman's physical comfort.

When the baby's hunger was satisfied, Forest returned the child to his cradle and refastened the mother's gown.

He couldn't stay here much longer, but neither could he in all good conscience leave the woman and child alone. While he waited for the woman to awaken, he would set up snares for small game.

The baby was sleeping peacefully. Forest Thunder sat in a chair and studied the child's mother. The woman lay in bed, still unconscious. The brave would have been worried if she hadn't stirred during the night. He hoped that it was a deep sleep, brought on by exhaustion and not any serious hidden injury which had caused her to faint.

Where was the woman's husband? he wondered. There were a few articles of men's clothing. And there was the babe— someone had to be the boy's father.

Where was this woman's protector? Had he gone somewhere

for supplies? Forest Thunder frowned. An earlier search had told him that supplies were needed; there was little food.

He returned his gaze to the woman. Her face was pale. Shadows below her eyes made her look weak and extremely vulnerable. Yet he found her attractive, and he had met and been attracted to many white women during the two years he'd spent in England with his English father.

Her thick dark lashes formed perfect crescents against her skin. He recalled the spark of emotion in her eyes when she'd first seen him. Brown, he thought. Her eyes were the most incredible shade of brown. That he could remember the color, startled him, as their glances had met and held for only a second before—in sheer panic—she'd rushed forward only to slump at his feet.

Her lips were full and only the hint of pink color. Her cheekbones were high, her skin smooth and unmarked. She would have no need of feminine face powder or cosmetics, he thought. She was pleasing to the eye, if too pale at present. He'd never before seen such beautiful, flawless features. She wasn't at all like the women of his village—nor like the English ladies who had flirted with him two years before.

Forest Thunder frowned. The woman was too thin. His stomach warmed. Except her curves, which were full and womanly . . . with dark nipples against white skin.

He hadn't given much thought to her body when he'd undressed her. He'd been too concerned with her well-being. She could have been his grandmother, for all the attention he'd paid. But afterward, as though a memory of a dream, he could recall how she looked from the top of her soft brown hair to the soles of her small feet.

His brow creased as he worried about her injuries. She had stopped bleeding. *Why hasn't she awoken?* Her continued state of unconsciousness remained a constant concern to him.

Where was her husband?

Frustrated at the lack of answers, Forest Thunder rose and

paced the room. He had to return home. There was no telling what would happen to the relationship between the two villages if he didn't return with Long Chin's answer.

He paused by the woman's bed and gazed down at his patient. It had been a full day and still her caretaker hadn't returned. He couldn't leave her and the babe alone to fend for themselves—not even after the woman regained consciousness. He pressed his hand to the woman's forehead. She felt cool to his touch. Satisfied that there was no infection, he left to check on her baby.

To his surprise, he found the infant sucking his thumb. Forest smiled.

Then he left to check his snares.

It was late. The days were chilly, but the nights grew colder still. James had been gone all day hunting, and Emily worried about him. He should have returned hours ago. She expected him to walk through the cabin door any minute. When another hour went by without any sign of him, she became scared.

Where was he?

He'd kissed her that morning before he'd left, flashing her a smile. Her heart tripped at the memory of his boyish grin. He was a wonderful husband. Gone only one full day, and she missed him.

Their cabin in the woods seemed so empty without him. The forest was frightening; she'd never noticed it before. James had always been there to protect her. He had the ability to make the world seem brighter, better . . . safer. He was more than her spouse; he was her friend and savior.

For the hundredth or more time, Emily went to the cabin door and peered outside, hoping for a glimpse of her husband.

But James still hadn't come home to her.

* * *

She knew before she found his body that he was dead. James would never willingly stay away from the woman he loved, and she had been the one blessed with his affection.

She discovered him the next day, about an hour's distance from the house. He lay, broken and bloody, having been attacked and ravaged by a bear. Emily recognized his clothing as she approached him. He was lying on his side. She turned him over, saw his savaged features, and backed away, screaming.

Forest Thunder was outside when he heard the woman's screams. He rushed inside to see her sitting upright. She wore the blank look of terror of one who was trapped in a nightmare, and she slept on. He went to the bed and took her into his arms. Holding her, he stroked her hair and murmured softly to calm her. She didn't awaken as she responded to his voice and touch. When she was quiet, the brave laid her back down and covered her with a quilt.

He stood, watching over her for a long time until he was satisfied that she was resting peacefully again. Then he went to the baby, who had started to cry when his mother screamed. Forest Thunder picked up the child and rocked him. The baby settled down, and the brave placed him back in the cradle. The Indian covered the little boy with his blanket. As he straightened, he heard a shriek, and spun around as the woman attacked him from behind.

CHAPTER 3

Emily woke up disoriented. She sat up, and placed a hand to her head when she felt dizzy. She blinked and looked about, and horror returned, with her memory, when she saw the Indian leaning over her baby's bed.

Christopher! Terror held her in its icy grip. Fear for her child energized her. She sprang from her bed to attack. Emily lunged at the Indian's bare back and jumped up to wrap her legs about his waist. She snaked an arm about his neck and began to pummel the man's head and shoulders with her fists.

With a gnarl of anger, the Indian threw her off him with a force that sent her crashing to the floor. Her head spun as she got up and launched herself at him again, scratching and kicking.

The Indian grunted under her attack, but was ready for her. He grabbed hold of her arms so she couldn't move.

"Let me be, you savage!" she cried. "Leave me and my baby alone." She fought him, bucking and squirming even while her head spun, but her efforts to break free were ineffective.

Without much effort, the brave hefted her struggling form into his arms and carried her to the bed. He tossed her on the feather tick, then sat on the edge of the bed and pinned her down with his body. He leaned over her, low, until they were nearly nose-to-nose. Emily's heart skipped a beat as he wrapped the fingers of one hand loosely about her throat. His other hand kept her arms stretched above her head and immobile. The Indian snarled at her as they locked gazes.

"Haht-deh-gah-yeh'-ee," he growled.

She couldn't move her legs. She couldn't move her head or hands, but she continued to struggle.

His dark eyes glinted with anger. His lips curled back, revealing teeth. Emily stopped struggling, suddenly afraid when the fingers about her throat tightened. She could breathe, but just barely. "Please," she rasped.

The brave stared at her without moving. She couldn't tell what he was thinking . . . if he'd understood. He eased back some of the pressure. She swallowed and gulped in air.

"Please," she whispered. "Please let me go to my baby."

They held gazes; his never wavered. Emily shuddered and closed her eyes briefly. How could she get through to him so he wouldn't hurt her baby or her?

Gathering her courage, she tried to reason with him. "I will not fight you," she enunciated softly. Did he understand English? she wondered. "Please let me go. I promise not to run."

The Indian didn't move. Tension filled the air during the ensuing long moment of silence. There was no clue that he'd understood her. Emily closed her eyes and began to pray. She was terrified. She and her baby were at the mercy of a savage. She felt the sting of tears. She was going to die; her baby was going to die; and it was all her fault.

She tried not to cry. She didn't want the savage to know

that he'd won, that she was admitting defeat. She lay still with her eyes closed. She would not beg.

Christopher whimpered in his bed. Emily wanted desperately to hold him.

The brave took his hand from her throat and shifted so that he was stretched fully along her length with his hands securing her wrists. His body pressed her into the mattress and his gaze seemed to burn a fiery hole through her. Emily turned her head to the side to avoid it and a tear escaped to trail down her cheek as she struggled to see her child.

The weight of the Indian bore her down further. She could feel every inch of his hard, muscled body, and felt threatened by it. She could feel the rasp of his breath against her neck and the scent of him filled her nostrils. It was strange, but not unpleasant. If she survived, she thought, she wouldn't forget it, or the firm grip of his hands.

She felt movement above her head, and Emily gasped in fear of her fate at the Indian's hands. She flinched when he touched her cheek. She was astonished when he tenderly wiped away the dampness of her tears with his finger. His light touch brought her gaze back to his. His expression was unreadable, but the light in his dark eyes seemed less fierce.

He muttered something in his native tongue. Emily couldn't answer; she didn't know what to say. He repeated what he'd said, and she inclined her head, deciding it was best to pretend that she'd understood. She didn't know what else to do. At her nod, he released her hands and rose, unpinning her from the feather tick.

The brave watched her carefully as he stood by the side of the bed. Emily didn't move, not knowing what he expected from her. She decided that she couldn't help her baby or herself if she antagonized the man.

He kept his eyes on her while he moved from the bed and approached the cradle. With a gasp, Emily started to rise, but the Indian's glare had her lying back down. She nearly cried out when the brave reached into the cradle and lifted her baby.

Emily trembled as he turned to face her, Christopher cradled against his muscled chest. The infant didn't make a sound. She wouldn't have been able to keep still if he'd been crying.

Concerned for her son, she tried to reason with the Indian. She rose and held out her arms. "Please, may I have my baby?"

The warrior stared, but didn't move. He smiled and turned his attention to the baby as Christopher's little hand reached up to touch his face. He shifted the child within his arms, holding the baby away from him while supporting his head with his hand.

Emily stifled a gasp, afraid that he would drop her son. The sound she made drew the brave's glance. He focused his narrowed gaze to her face, and the warning look in his eyes frightened her into dropping her arms. She saw the Indian bring the baby to his breast again, and she breathed a sigh of relief again.

"My son," she said. "Can I hold him?" She folded her arms against her breast as if cradling and rocking her baby.

The brave studied her a long moment before he approached and offered her the child. Emily snatched Christopher from the warrior's hands. Eyeing the Indian warily, she sat in a chair and clutched her son protectively to her breast. Tension filled her frame as the savage held her gaze. Sensing his mother's fear, Christopher started to fuss.

With a grunt, the Indian turned away and left the cabin. Emily closed her eyes and shuddered. Then, she turned her attention to soothing her baby. She sat, clutching her baby, stroking her fingers down his soft cheek, and sang him a lullaby.

"Mama's here, Christopher," she whispered when she was done singing. She cast a brief, cautious look toward the door, relaxing when the Indian didn't reappear. "You're safe now."

Emily rose with her baby in her arms and went to the door to see if the brave had left. She shivered and held her son tighter when she saw the man was still in the yard, roasting meat over an open fire.

"My name is Emily. Em-il-lee." The young woman pointed to her chest and then at the Indian. "What—is—your—name? I am Em-il-lee."

The brave stared at her blankly.

"Em-il-lee," Emily enunciated with a hint of frustration. She'd been plagued by the man's presence for the last two days, and he had yet to say a word she understood. His only means of communication thus far had been an occasional grunt and a few words from him in his native tongue.

Why was he here? she wondered. She had to figure out how to communicate with the man; she had to make him understand her.

"Emily," she said. Boldly she reached toward him, careful not to actually touch him. "Who are you?"

The Indian studied her with his gleaming dark eyes, and she had to fight not to look away. There was something disturbing in those obsidian eyes. Her gaze fell to study his mouth—lips that curved with amusement as she watched. She met his gaze, saw what appeared as a look of admiration. Emily blushed then, and looked away.

Putting some distance between them, she turned to face him again and was unable to ignore the impact the full picture of him had on her senses. Her heart tripped and sped up ever so slightly. *Fear,* she thought, taking a step backward.

The Indian's hair was the color of midnight; it fell long and silky past his shoulders to his upper chest. He stood in the firelight within the one-room cabin, his bare, muscled chest gleaming beneath the golden glow. This evening, his only garment was a loincloth which did little to deter Emily's imagination of what lie beneath. The quiet intimacy of the moment was too disturbing for Emily's comfort.

How did one reason with a half-naked savage who didn't speak a word of English?

"First you make friends with him," she muttered. Then, she needed to have a name. It would help matters if she didn't have to think of the man as "that Indian."

She ran her fingers impatiently through her brown hair, before trying once again to make herself understood. "Em-il-lee," she said softly, with patience. She laid a hand against her breast. "Emily—me." She gestured toward him as she again approached him. "And you are . . . ?"

His gaze lit up with understanding. He thumped his chest hard. *"Kuh-ha-go Ka-wun-do-ta-te."*

Emily blinked. "Kunago Kawandote?"

He looked amused. *"Kuh—ha—go Ka—wun—do—ta—te."*

"Kuh-ha-go Ka-wun-do-ta-te," she repeated, enunciating carefully.

The man nodded and grinned. Emily drew a sharp breath as she reeled under the impact of his smile.

"I am Emily, and you are . . ." She hesitated. "Great," she muttered with wry humor. "How am I going to get out that mouthful every time I need to talk with you!"

He had watched her closely as she spoke, and now a small frown settled on his brow. She offered him a tentative smile. "I'll think of something," she said.

"Em-il-lee," he announced, pressing his finger into her chest.

She beamed at him. "Yes, that's right. I'm Emily."

He thumped his chest with his fist, producing a loud sound like thunder. "Kuh-ha-go Ka-wun-do-ta-te," his voice boomed.

Emily couldn't help chuckling. "Yes, I know, but you see, I'll never be able to call you that. By the time I've finished, I'll have forgotten what I wanted to say." She became thoughtful. "Let's see. What can I call you that's simple?"

He hit his chest again and repeated his name in a thundering voice.

"That's it!" she exclaimed. "Thunder! I'll call you Thunder." She held out her hand. "Pleased to meet you, Thunder," she said with a smile.

An odd look flitted across his expression, before his mouth curved upward in response to her own. He grabbed hold of her fingers firmly and shook her hand, the abrupt movement nearly jarring her bones. "Em-il-lee," he said, still pumping her arm vigorously.

"Yes," she laughed, her simple answer vibrating from the motion of his enthusiastic handshake. "It's nice to meet you too, Thunder."

She felt as if her teeth had been dislodged by the time Thunder had released her hand. Emily didn't mind, though, for he was smiling, and she'd finally gotten through to him . . . even if it was just to teach him her name. As she went to Christopher's cradle, she wondered if Thunder would respond to the new English name she'd given him. *Only time will tell,* she thought, as she caressed her son's head. She smiled as she glanced back toward Thunder. Dare she try to teach him another word?

"Christopher," she said, gesturing toward the baby with her other hand.

Thunder came to stand next to Emily and, in a move that started her, grabbed her hand and placed it on his own forehead. *"Chris-to-fer,"* he said, holding her gaze and her palm against his brow.

The heat of his skin warmed the inside of Emily's hand. She knew she should pull away, but she couldn't. She was held captive by his proud expression and the intensity of his eager glistening gaze. *"Chris-to-fer,"* he repeated as he began to move Emily's hand in imitation of her earlier caresses on her baby's head. *"Chris-to-fer,"* he murmured as he closed his eyes.

Emily's breath got lodged in her chest as Thunder continued

to move her fingers across his forehead. *"Chris-to-fer,"* he whispered as if he enjoyed her touch.

He released her hand, but, caught up in the moment, she continued to move her fingers, held by fascination for his expression. She had difficulty breathing. Her heart raced as she stood by her baby's cradle, caressing the head of a savage Indian—only, he didn't seem at all savage to her right now.

Emily gave in to the urge to slide her hand from his forehead to touch his hair. She trailed her fingers down his cheek and then into his hair again, where the soft, silky black strands tickled and caressed her palm.

Thunder didn't utter a word. As she glanced into his face, she saw that his eyes remained closed, and she could view him without his dark, piercing gaze to unnerve her. She found his sculptured features attractive, in a rawboned way. His nose, cheekbones, and chin looked as if they'd been carved from the rich earth. His dark, feathery lashes seemed long for a man, a delightful detail that softened his rugged face and added to his appeal. Touching him made her skin tingle and burn, but she was afraid to withdraw, perhaps because she was enjoying the caress as much as he.

Thunder opened his eyes, and Emily blinked and started to pull away. Immediately the brave caught her hand against him, sliding her palm to his jaw. Holding her hand in place there, he continued to delve into her eyes and soul with his gaze.

"Chris-to-fer," he murmured, while he covered and rubbed her hand with his own.

Emily shook her head. "Touch," she corrected. "I am touching you." With her other unsteady hand, she gestured toward her son. "Christopher." She moved her fingers beneath his. "Touch."

He transferred his gaze from her to her baby and back again. "Touch," he said softly. "Touch, Em-il-lee."

She nodded, unable to contain the sharp little thrill nor the smile that transformed her lips. "That's right. I am touching you, and you are touching me—Emily." She looked at her hand beneath his and felt an odd little jolt in the pit of her belly. "Great," she said, with wry humor, knowing that he wouldn't understand. "We're finally communicating, and so far you've learned my name and that we're touching."

She shivered with sudden pleasure. Saying that last word aloud had tremendous impact on her nervous system. She started to pull away. Staring, Thunder held her hand fast. "Emi-lee, touch Thunder," he said, startling Emily with his sudden understanding.

"Yes," she said in a voice that was unsteady. "Yes, that's right. Emily is touching Thunder."

Christopher began to fuss, in demand of his mother's attention. Emily was relieved when the Indian released her so she could tend to her son. She picked up her child while avoiding the brave's gaze. For a long moment, Emily held her son without moving and was conscious of her baby's whimpers and the Indian's piercing gaze that watched her as he moved back, giving her room. She needed to nurse her baby, but how could she do so with Thunder watching her?

Thunder stared at her and said something in Iroquoian. He approached and Emily clutched her baby tighter, afraid that he'd take Christopher away. The Indian scowled at her. He reached out and touched her breast with his finger, repeating the Indian phrase.

Emily gasped at his touch, but then she realized that Thunder was telling her to feed her baby. She shook her head. Thunder poked her in the chest harder, his tone sharp as he apparently scolded her in his native tongue. His gaze angry, he started to unbutton her gown bodice.

"No!" she cried, brushing aside his hands. "I'll do it." She sighed. He wasn't going to be satisfied until she nursed Christopher. She recalled that this man had already seen what she was trying to hide—when he'd undressed her and put on her sleeping gown.

Emily went to a chair and sat. Avoiding the Indian's gaze, she unbuttoned her gown and fed her baby. She flushed as she felt the burning heat of Thunder's gaze, but when she looked up, he had turned his attention elsewhere. He sat in a chair near the dining table, whittling a new arrow shaft.

Emily swallowed and brought her gaze back to her son . . . but she continued to be disturbed by the man who made his presence felt with his every movement.

Although he tried, he couldn't keep his eyes off the woman. Forest Thunder cast surreptitious glances at Emily as he ran the blade of his knife over the wooden shaft. The brief glimpse of smooth, white feminine flesh as she shifted the baby to her shoulder to pat Christopher on the back, made Forest Thunder's stomach flutter. He rose, and set the piece of wood on the table. He moved to the open cabin door where he stared out into the woods. It wasn't the first time he'd watched her nurse her child; yet the sight made his face warm—an unusual occurrence for a man used to the village matrons who openly breast-fed their children.

Why was it different with this Englishwoman? He recalled the sound of her sweet voice as she sang to her baby. The song had soothed Christopher. Forest Thunder had enjoyed listening; the tune had made him smile.

Emily, he thought. A smile of amusement curved his lips as he recalled her efforts to communicate with him. She would be furious if she knew that he understood English as well as he did Iroquoian. For the present, it suited him for her to think differently. Emily tended to say her thoughts aloud, a fact that was proving both useful and amusing to him as he learned more about her character. It had been three days since she'd awoken, and she appeared to be well on the mend.

Well enough to travel, he thought.

Forest Thunder glanced back to see Emily gently placing

her son in his cradle. He watched as she took a moment to lovingly stroke the baby's head before she straightened to button her gown. He didn't look away as she met his gaze. He heard her soft intake of breath and noted the way her fingers fluttered helplessly over the buttons. He saw the slight gaping of her gown and had a clear mental image of the flesh beneath. Disturbed by his thoughts, Forest Thunder turned his gaze back to the woods.

It was time for him to return to his village, and Emily and Christopher were going with him. Earlier today, while hunting for small game, he'd found a gravesite and had known instinctively that it belonged to Emily's husband. The man wasn't coming back, because he was dead. How long? he wondered. It didn't matter. Emily couldn't be left alone in the wilderness to fend for herself and her baby. He hadn't told her yet, and he expected a fight. She wouldn't want to leave here. Somehow, he must convince her—no easy feat if he was to continue to pretend he couldn't speak English.

He felt his smile as it transformed his expression. Judging from their last exchange, their next conversation should prove interesting, he thought with silent laughter.

The amusement left him as he contemplated what to do with Emily once he'd delivered the sachem's message.

Take her to the nearest English fort. With that decision made, he entered the cabin and shut the door. As his gaze sought out Emily, Forest Thunder wondered how he'd make her go with him to his village if she refused to leave.

CHAPTER 4

The baby. Forest Thunder tried to ignore Emily's horrified expression as he held Christopher in his arms. "Come," he said, using one of the new words the woman had "taught" him. He gestured toward the satchel of supplies on the bed.

"No," she whispered, her brown eyes glistening with fear.

Forest Thunder hardened himself against her expression. Emily had to come with him; it was for her and her child's own good. "Come!" he commanded brusquely, and cursed silently as her eyes filled with tears.

Christopher lay in Forest's arms, oblivious to the tension between his mother and the man who held him. He gurgled with joy and waved his little hands above the blanket.

Forest saw Emily glance at the bow and quiver of arrows at his back before settling her gaze on her infant son.

"Why?" she choked out. "Why are you taking us? Why can't you just leave us alone?"

"Come."

Holding Emily's gaze, Forest extended his arms, holding the

baby aloft so that the woman would think that any sudden wrong move on her part might cause him to drop the child. He heard Emily's sharp intake of breath.

"No, don't!" she cried. "I'll come with you. Only please—*please*—don't hurt my baby!"

Forest Thunder kept his expression angry; he wanted Emily to think he would hurt Christopher before he'd budge on his decision to take her and the babe. He would never hurt the boy, of course, but Emily didn't know that. As much as he hated the advantage, he'd use it to keep her and her child safe.

As Emily scurried for the satchel and a wrap for her shoulders, Forest Thunder wondered if he was right in believing her well enough to travel. It was a day's journey to his Onondaga village if he ran. With Emily and Christopher, the trip would probably take twice as long.

Fortunately, Drumming Fox had expected him to stay awhile in the Seneca camp; otherwise the Onondaga sachem might have sent out a search party to find him. He had considered traveling to his village and then returning for the woman and her child, but he was afraid to leave them . . . afraid of what he'd find when he came back. It was better to keep them with him, he decided. Emily would hate him for this, but he couldn't allow his own feelings to interfere with her protection.

As he recalled the gravesite he'd found the previous morning, he wondered what had killed Emily's husband. How long had Emily been alone? Not long, he thought, although the earth covering the site didn't appear to be freshly turned.

It doesn't matter how long, he decided. The woman and her child were alone and vulnerable, and whether Emily liked it or not, he—Forest Thunder—had appointed himself her protector.

Emily couldn't believe that the Indian was forcing her from her home—or, worse yet, that Thunder would hurt Christopher.

He looked angry and unyielding, and she wasn't about to risk endangering her baby by refusing to obey him.

If only the man could speak English, she thought, studying his back through tears. Then she would give him a piece of her mind!

But then she still could, couldn't she? Perhaps it was better that the man couldn't understand. She wouldn't be endangering her son to say what she thought.

"You have no right to take us," she said, sniffing back tears. "If James were alive, he'd—" She choked back a sob. "He'd protect us. He'd make you leave us alone!"

Her husband James and she had been runaway bondservants, their indentures owned by Richard Malkins—a cruel man whose obsessive interest in Emily had become a real danger to the young woman. Late one evening, when Emily had shown up at the door to his room in the barn, James had taken one look at the bruised and battered young woman and begun to pack supplies for their escape. Emily had trusted him. He had always been respectful and unstintingly kind. He'd made no secret—at least to her—of his love for her. He'd been her friend, her confidant, and now, her savior. They'd headed away from civilization, into an area reported to be inhabited by Indians.

Frightened and cautious, they escaped one danger for another. They ventured into the forests of the Pennsylvania colony, where they traveled night and day until they felt that it was far enough away from Richard Malkins to stop. The small, secluded clearing near a stream had seemed like the perfect place to settle. They lived out in the open for a time, until James announced that he would build them a cabin. It was during the construction that James asked Emily to marry him. Emily agreed, because she was grateful and had no doubts that her friend would be a good husband. If her heart didn't race quite as fast as it did in romantic tales when she looked at James, it didn't matter. James had done all the right things to be a proper hero. It was she who was lacking as a heroine, for James had given her so much, while she had given back so little.

"Do you hear me?" Emily cried.

Thunder glanced back briefly before concentrating on the path ahead.

"James—he was my protector," Emily continued in an emotion-filled voice. "He always seemed to be rescuing me from something. First, that horrible man, Richard Malkins. Malkins was a cruel devil—is it any wonder we escaped and did not fulfill our indentures?" She stumbled on a rock, but quickly righted herself. She wiped the tears from her eyes with the back of her hand. "James took care of me as we escaped. He protected me from wild animals. He was a good man—I loved him. If he were here now, he'd—he'd . . ."

Emily halted. What would James do? She eyed the Indian's muscled back and knew that James hadn't had Thunder's strength. What could James have done, with only crude weapons and no gun? What chance would he have had against Thunder?

The Indian turned and glared at her. She shuddered. None, she thought, as she started to follow again. James would have been powerless against the warrior. He had always been concerned about encountering savages, perhaps because he'd known that they were unmatched in cunning and strength.

How ironic that the Indian had arrived after James's death— and after Emily had managed to survive the winter and childbirth alone. She shivered, recalling the day she'd found James in the woods, dead, mauled by a bear. He'd been missing over a day when she'd finally located him. His broken body was barely recognizable. Emily screamed, knowing it was James even before she found the small silver medal he wore on a ribbon around his neck. She'd wept bitterly, wildly, for the loss of her husband's life.

Just as quickly as the tears had come, Emily had stifled them to see to James's burial. Using a spade fashioned by James's own hands, she had dug him a shallow grave and then covered him, getting sick only when she was done. Emily had gone back to her cabin and sat, staring without seeing, uncaring of her future, for James was gone. She existed, moving from one day to the next in a stupor, feeling numb at times, other moments overcome with sorrow and guilt. In the days that followed, the wind picked up and the air temperature dropped to a dangerous chill. Winter was on its way with a vengeance, and Emily was ill prepared. She ate little, feeling too nauseous and too tired most of the time to do much of anything but move slowly, dispiritedly, throughout each day.

Then the baby moved within her womb. The tiny flutter took Emily completely by surprise, for she'd given little thought to the child. When the child moved again, Emily woke up from her stupor. There was a tiny breath of life inside her—her baby—James's baby, someone who depended on her. If she didn't eat, the baby couldn't eat. Her health directly affected her unborn child. Baby Christopher had become his mother's lifesaver, as Emily found a reason to live. The baby in her womb became the center of her universe. Because of her child, Emily found the strength and the will to survive.

"You may have the upper hand," she sobbed to the Indian's back, "but I'll find a way to escape you." She had survived till now alone; she would get free. She and her baby would survive this new ordeal.

Forest Thunder listened to Emily and was not unmoved by her tears. But he kept silent. He wasn't about to let her go—not when he thought about the consequences of allowing a young woman with a child to fend for herself in the wilderness. Her belief that he was a cruel savage gave him control of the situation. He heard her quiet sobs, but walked on, carrying Emily's child.

They stopped to rest about an hour into the journey. The Indian instructed Emily to sit. She saw no place other than the ground to rest, so she sat on the damp earth with her back against a tree. Christopher had begun to fuss, and Thunder held him a moment, murmuring to the child in his native language. Then the brave handed the hungry child to Emily.

Emily gazed into the man's eyes as she took her baby. He held her captive for a long moment with the look in his dark, enigmatic eyes before he released her gaze. Shaken, she tried to ignore the brave as she tended to her son. She pretended not to notice that he continued to watch her as she nursed her baby.

It was as she was checking Christopher's wetting cloth that Emily decided she would mark the trail. In the event that she managed to escape, she'd need to find her way back to the cabin. It wouldn't be easy; she couldn't be obvious about it or Thunder would realize what she was about. She didn't know how she'd get free, but she'd find a way somehow. She figured she could find her way to the cabin from this spot.

Emily glanced up and saw the direction of the sun and knew by the hour that they'd been traveling northeast since they left. When she found this clearing again, she'd have to travel an hour southwest and she'd be back home. She couldn't believe she hadn't thought of the idea sooner, but fear for her child's safety must have numbed her thoughts. She frowned. How should she mark the trail?

She could snap a branch or two so that the limbs hung broken from the tree. Thunder would get suspicious if she stopped along the way to do that too often. She'd have to devise several methods of marking as they traveled.

The idea gave Emily new hope. She couldn't kill the Indian, but if the occasion presented itself she could render him senseless. She smiled and felt optimistic as Thunder signaled her to rise and resume the journey, for now she had a plan.

Her good spirits dimmed as the brave grabbed Christopher from her arms, and fear for her son became paramount in her thoughts once again.

* * *

After what seemed to Emily like hours, Thunder called for a rest. Emily was glad, as she had to relieve herself. The moment was awkward as she scurried behind some bushes. She hurried as fast as she could, as she was uncomfortable with leaving her son with the Indian. When she returned, she was startled to see Thunder with a smile on his lips and his face bent low as he played with Christopher's tiny hand, pressing it against his cheek. Emily froze and watched him. The man was a strange contradiction—one minute a savage who threatened her and her child; the next, he was cooing to her baby as a father might do with his own infant.

As if sensing her presence, Thunder looked up, and the smile left his expression, stealing the light in his dark eyes. He gestured for her to sit, and Emily sighed wearily as she complied.

How much longer before they stopped for the night? she wondered. The thought both cheered and scared her. Thunder gave her Christopher. She fed and changed him, and made sure that he was warm.

The sun was low in the sky. Within an hour it would be dusk and then dark. While Thunder was busy foraging for food, Emily carefully marked the spot by digging her foot into the soft earth, making a small hole, and filling it with pebbles. As long as there were no torrential rains, the hole should remain to guide her home.

Soon Thunder returned and motioned for Emily to rise. The young woman groaned as she stood, clutching her son. She was tired, achy, and she didn't want to give up her son.

The Indian stared at her for a long, uncomfortable moment. Emily straightened her back and raised her chin, prepared to fight if he tried to take Christopher. Thunder narrowed his gaze as he looked at the child in Emily's arms, before he raised his eyes to scan Emily's face. Without a word, he turned abruptly

and barked out a command in Iroquoian. Satisfied at her small
victory in keeping her baby, Emily followed the Indian from
the clearing back onto the trail. Her joy changed to chagrin a
little while later, as Thunder veered from the well-worn trail
into the dense forest. Clouds had begun to fill the sky. Although
the sun peered through on occasion, the afternoon looked omi-
nous.

Where was he taking them? she wondered. Thoughts of
Indian sacrifice and murder muddled her brain. She tried not
to panic. If he was going to hurt them, he would have done it
long before now, she reasoned. Still, she couldn't forget his
expression when he'd threatened to drop her baby. She couldn't
assume that Indians thought like white men.

It was hard while holding Christopher, but Emily continued
to mark the path. She knew it would be a miracle for her to
find her marks again in this dense lushness, but she had to try.
A few times, she had no choice but to drag her toe through the
leaves beneath her feet. A hardy wind would surely cover her
traces, rendering her marks invisible, but she didn't know what
else to do.

She attempted to grab hold of a pine branch and break the
limb as she passed, but the limb was too pliable. Hearing the
noise, the Indian had turned around to see what Emily was
about. There wasn't enough time or opportunity after that to
mark the trail. Her previous actions had drawn Thunder's attention. She would have to wait awhile before trying again.

Darkness fell like a heavy cloak, and the forest suddenly
seemed sinister as the night filled with the sounds of insects,
animals, and other wildlife. The wind stirred the treetops, making a rustling noise that gave Emily chills. She shivered and
wondered how the Indian could see to continue, when Thunder
stopped and moved aside. Emily sensed a clearing ahead, and
she realized that the man had chosen this spot to spend the
night.

Thunder grabbed Emily's arm and led her to a wooden struc-

ture set back among the trees. Emily's heart thumped hard. It
was a lean-to of sorts, constructed by some previous traveler—
or perhaps by Indians while hunting. She was grateful not to
have to sleep on the cold, damp ground.

"*Sahd-yenh*." The brave instructed her to sit on the platform
of the structure, built about eighteen inches off the ground.

Emily sat in the darkness and heard movement in the clearing,
which suggested that Thunder was gathering firewood.

Christopher started to fuss, and Emily opened her gown to
nurse him. The baby immediately began to suckle. Emily felt
such a warm surge of love for her son, that for a moment she
was able to forget her predicament. Sound from a few yards
away drew her gaze. As she squinted to better see in the darkness, she thought she could see Thunder working to start a fire.
She realized she was right when she saw a spark flare, and
then the silhouette of Thunder adding kindling to a small flame.
Soon the fire was sizable, crackling and popping as it sent tiny
golden sparks into the air.

The light lit up the small clearing and sent a golden glow
into the interior of the lean-to. Emily studied the man who
added more wood to the fire, and then tore her gaze away to
study her home for the night. The structure wasn't large, just
big enough to sleep three adults comfortably. Emily's pulse
started to race as she envisioned Thunder lying beside her,
sharing the night.

He glanced up in her direction just as she turned to study
him. Their eyes locked. His dark eyes glistened in the firelight.
Emily wondered what he was thinking, if he knew just how
much his presence affected her. As his gaze dropped to her
bared breast and Christopher, she flushed, realizing what his
thoughts were. Flustered, she looked away and did her best to
cover herself.

She felt a jolt when she heard him rise. Her whole body
quivered with anticipation and fear. What was the Indian
expecting? What would she do if Thunder touched her? She

swallowed hard as she glanced back. How could she spend the entire night in such close quarters with this brave?

Pretending she wasn't afraid, she looked down at her baby. She heard Thunder's footsteps as he approached, sensed him as he drew closer.

He stood for a long moment, studying her. She could feel his heated gaze, but she refused to look up and acknowledge him. She wouldn't give him any ideas . . . nor the satisfaction of knowing that she was nervous. She was afraid that he would recognize her fascination with him. She didn't understand it herself. One moment she feared for her life; yet, in the next, she found herself drawn to the man. It was her attraction to him that most frightened her.

Emily knew when he moved away. She chanced a look and saw him disappear into the forest, heard noise that suggested he was hacking at some bush or tree. He returned with thick pine boughs. She expected him to place them on the fire and was surprised when he didn't. He returned to the lean-to and began to stack the long boughs, thick with soft needles near the lean-to before disappearing again into the woods.

Thunder came back with some finer branches. He threw them on the pile and gestured for Emily to get up. Emily struggled to move. She gasped when Thunder helped her, lifting her and Christopher easily down from the platform, setting her carefully on the ground.

Her heart raced wildly as he turned away. He then took the finest, softest pine boughs and laid them over their platform as a cushion against the hard wood. When he was done, he scooped Emily and her baby into his arms and set them down on the platform. To her surprise, the softer boughs made a nice, comfortable bed, and the rich scent of pine was pleasant.

"Thank you," she said, pleased.

Thunder stared at her. She smiled. He grinned, a splash of white teeth against his skin. His good humor made her skin tingle and her heart race. He left her then, disappearing into the forest once again. Emily felt lonely and found she was more frightened without the Indian's presence.

He returned with a small animal; Emily didn't look too closely or watch as he skinned and cleaned it, then roasted it over the fire. She didn't want to know what creature he had killed. The smell of meat was tempting. She was hungry and would eat whatever he gave her.

Emily shifted Christopher to her shoulder to burp him and then moved him to her other breast. She had no idea why Christopher ate so often, but she wasn't concerned or upset. She enjoyed the closeness of having her child nurse from her.

She had finished feeding Christopher when Thunder approached with a piece of steaming meat. He had set the meat on a leaf-lined flat rock. Emily accepted his offering. "Thank you," she said softly.

The brave simply nodded as if he'd understood, and went to get his own meal. They ate steaming meat and some wild berries that Thunder had apparently found while she'd been busy with Christopher. The food tasted wonderful, as it had been a long time since she'd eaten. She was thirsty, though, and wondered whether or not there was anything to drink.

Thunder had a small satchel tied to his waist. He opened it and pulled out a cup. Emily's eyes widened as she saw it was made from tin. She could only assume he'd gotten it from some white man. She shuddered, wondering if the man had had to die to give up his cup.

He caught her staring and must have read fear in her expression, as he scowled at her while he set the cup on the ground before him. Emily was glad he kept his distance. Her feelings, her attraction to the man, were just as unsettling as her thoughts. How could she be drawn to a man she thought capable of murdering for a cup?

Her gaze followed him as he pulled a strap from about his neck and shoulder. She saw it was connected to a water-skin as he poured water into the tin cup. He looked up and captured her gaze as he raised the cup slowly to his lips to drink. Emily's mouth was dry, and she was dying to drink, but she wasn't about to do anything to get it.

When he had drunk his fill, Thunder poured out another cupful. He stood and approached Emily, extending the cup to her with both hands when he reached her.

Emily looked at the cup before meeting his gaze. His dark eyes gleamed in the darkness. She reached out for the tin, and he pulled it out of reach, toying with her.

Her anger flared. She set her sleeping baby on the platform beside her, before climbing from the lean-to to confront the Indian. Thunder's eyes seemed to glitter with mischief as he backed away, and she followed.

"Give me the water!" she cried.

He froze, apparently surprised by her harsh tone. He narrowed his gaze, lowered his arm, and then offered her the cup.

With a growl of satisfaction, Emily grabbed the cup, and Thunder released it. Without thought, she drank greedily, noisily. She gave no thought to the fact that he had placed his lips on the cup before her until after she was done.

The water tasted good. With a sigh of delight, she lowered the cup and gave it back to him. He took and refilled the cup, and gave it back.

With a sound of delight, Emily drank again, sipping more slowly this time to enjoy the slide of cool water against the back of throat.

"Thank you." She handed the cup to him and then returned to finish her dinner. She couldn't control a yawn as she checked on Christopher.

Thunder got up from the fire and picked up the remaining pine boughs in the pile. He began to secure the boughs to the top of the lean-to, draping them over the opening to create a door flap of sorts.

Emily shifted places as he worked until she sat in the only opening left by Thunder's handiwork. She lay down beside her son and could hear Thunder moving about outside, putting out the fire. It seemed he was gone for a long time, but perhaps it only felt that way because she was nervous about sleeping with him inside. She began to relax when he didn't return. Perhaps he'd decided to sleep under the stars, to allow her and Christopher to sleep in the lean-to alone.

She must have dozed, because she was jolted awake when the pine-bough door covering moved, and Thunder eased onto the platform beside her. Emily slid closer to Christopher who slept near the back wall. She froze as the Indian shifted to cover the remaining opening with branches of pine. Her heart beat a rapid tattoo as he stretched out beside her. The air seemed to hum with a strange energy.

He whispered something as if he'd realized she was awake. There was nothing threatening in his tone nor did he make a move toward her. She could only assume that he was wishing her a good night.

"Good night, Thunder," she murmured, feeling anything but sleepy.

Thunder lay on his side, facing the doorway. Emily remained tense even after she heard the even sound of the brave's steady breathing after he fell asleep. The heat of his body warmed her. Sometime later the sound of rain outside and on the roof of the lean-to relaxed her, and she was able to put aside her fear. She lay with her back toward Thunder, listening to the rain and the man's and her baby's breathing, and she fell asleep.

She woke once in the night to hear that the gentle rain had become a serious rain shower. Thunder had moved to his back, and she was facing him. Startled, she flipped over onto her other side toward her baby again. She was grateful to have a warm, comfortable, dry place to rest.

He knew the exact moment she turned toward him in her sleep. The heavy rain shower had lowered the air temperature, and she must have been drawn to him for warmth. He tensed, but then she burrowed against him, all soft and feminine, and he placed his arm around her, holding her. Her hair felt silky against his bare chest. Her soft curves pressed into his side, heating his insides.

Forest Thunder knew Emily would be horrified to wake up in his arms, but he didn't move her. He enjoyed the contact too much.

In an effort to control his desire, he concentrated on the sound of the rain and the scent of pine. He tried not to think about the soft inhalations of Emily's breath that caressed his skin or the image of her awake with warm brown eyes full of passion and vulnerability.

She seemed to enjoy her child. Forest Thunder frowned. He didn't understand how she could have abandoned him in the woods. It didn't make sense; she appeared to adore Christopher.

He felt anger as he recalled the moment he'd found the infant, lying in the forest, vulnerable and all alone. Why did Emily leave her baby? She'd been hurt, but that was no reason to abandon her child. Forest Thunder wanted to demand an explanation, but he couldn't ask her. He wasn't ready to let Emily know he could speak English. There was still much he could learn from the woman who spoke her thoughts aloud.

CHAPTER 5

Emily heard the baby crying and woke up to find herself pillowed on a warm, bare masculine chest. She gasped and sat up, shocked that she'd turned to Thunder in the night. A soft breeze filtered into the lean-to. She stared at the man beside her, and her face became warm. Her gaze flashed back and forth from the Indian to Christopher. She picked up her son and held him protectively as she studied the brave in his sleep.

How long had she lain in his arms?

Christopher whimpered, and Emily quickly undid her gown to feed him. Her baby began to nurse, and her nerves began to settle. She was glad that Thunder continued to sleep. How embarrassing it would have been if he had awakened to find her pressed against him, absorbing his warmth!

As Christopher suckled, Emily studied Thunder. He was an attractive man, she thought. His dark hair framed a face that was ruggedly handsome, with high cheekbones, a sensual mouth, and a firm chin. Long lashes crested his eyelids, lengthy, dark lashes that should have belonged to a woman, but in no way made him less of a man. His hair was shiny and silky, and she resisted the urge to touch it.

Her gaze wandered down his broad chest. There was implied strength in the way his body was formed. She lowered her gaze down his flat stomach and lower. She flushed as she speculated on what lay beneath the loincloth. Flustered, she continued her study. His legs were perfectly formed, his thighs and calves muscular. She had felt the strength of his powerful form when he'd held her down that first day in her cabin. She'd been terrified then, only now she was intrigued as well as frightened because of her fascination for, and her attraction to, the Indian.

He sighed softly in his sleep. Her heart pounding, Emily quickly turned onto her side, facing away from him, adjusting Christopher so that he could nurse on her other breast. She became aware of the chilly morning air and the sound of the rain that continued to soak the forest. Christopher fell asleep as he nursed. Emily didn't move him. Tired, she closed her eyes and drifted back to sleep.

When Christopher started to fuss again a while later, Emily felt Thunder stir behind her and reach over her to pick up her son. She wasn't concerned; in fact, she was surprised that she trusted him with her baby. She was so tired. She heard him croon softly to her child in a low, deep voice as he changed the child's wetting cloth.

Emily closed her eyes. Moments later, she felt Thunder reach over to return Christopher to her side, and she slept with the knowledge that her baby was happy and they were safe. Somehow she'd gone from fearing to trusting the Indian.

When she awoke some time later, she was alone. The rain had stopped, and the light filtering into the lean-to was brighter. Warmth penetrated the structure, heating the inside. Emily sat up, ran her fingers through her hair to put it into some semblance of order, and then pushed aside a pine bough. She squinted against the bright sunlight. Once her eyes adjusted, she climbed down from the platform, her gaze searching for Christopher and Thunder.

To her astonishment, she saw that Thunder had washed Christopher's diaper cloths. He'd held Christopher in one arm, and with his free hand, was draping the last of the wet diapers over a rock to dry in the sun. Emily was amazed to see the Indian warrior looking so natural and at ease as he held her son and did the chore.

Was he married with a child? she wondered with a sinking heart. Why did the thought bother her?

Thunder caught sight of her and smiled. The sudden appearance of his grin shook her to the core. She couldn't recall ever seeing such genuine warmth and humor in his expression. She gasped as her heart gave a joyful thump. Pleasure shivered across her skin like a lover's caress. For a long moment, she was aware of a strong physical pull between her and the Indian. The intense attraction frightened her. She could tell by the odd look in his expression that he was feeling something, too.

Christopher started to fuss in Thunder's arms, and Emily, attempting to banish her new awareness, rushed forward to take him, then quickly backed away. The Englishwoman avoided the brave's glance, but she knew—could feel—his continued regard as she returned to the lean-to to breast-feed her son. She climbed inside and repositioned the pine boughs to enclose her and Christopher inside the structure. As she placed her son to her breast, she recalled the heat that seemed to sizzle in the air between her and Thunder. The comforting tug on her nipple by Christopher's mouth made Emily flush hotly as images of her and Thunder—of a sexual nature—filled her mind.

They were on their way again a couple of hours later. With Christopher's clean diapers repacked in the satchel, and the lean-to left as they'd found it, Emily and Thunder were traveling on a cleared path again. When they'd left their campsite, Thunder had made no move to take Christopher from Emily, and she was grateful to hold her baby. Emily realized that their destination must be near for Thunder to leave her child in her care. She shot him a glance. *Or has he begun to trust me?*

The notion of reaching the Indian village made her increasingly nervous. Emily contemplated her surroundings and knew it would be hopeless to attempt an escape. It wasn't the right place or the right time. She couldn't run with Christopher—that fact hadn't changed. If she tried to sneak away, Thunder would be after her in a minute. She'd not get outside a hundred yards before he'd recapture her. Then, after an escape attempt, he would no doubt treat her more like a prisoner. At least now he seemed concerned for her and Christopher's welfare—an aspect of him that she found endearing. It would be wise not to anger him and lose his trust.

Still, an imp inside of her had Emily slowing her steps to see if Thunder would notice. He didn't look back. She halted and waited. He stopped then, and turned. His eyes narrowed. He came back to her and held out his hand.

"Christopher," he said, requesting the baby.

Emily bit her lip. Why did she have to test him? With a cry of protest, she handed him her son.

Thunder shifted the baby to his other arm and stuck out his hand again.

"Emily, touch," he instructed.

Alarmed, Emily tore her gaze from his face to stare at his hand.

"Emily, touch Thunder," he said softly, surprising her by using her English name for him.

Her gaze met his. She was startled to see tenderness in his expression.

"Gah'-jee."

Staring into his eyes, Emily felt her fear leave her. She placed her hand trustingly within his grip and felt his gentle strength. Thunder led her along the path, closer toward their destination—the place Emily assumed was his home.

The scent of wood smoke and roasting meat filled the air as they left the forest and entered a clearing, where the village was surrounded by a tall stockade fence. Thunder released her hand and gave her the baby, before he took her in through a gate.

Emily studied the village scene before her. Large rectangular birch-bark houses had been built to form a semicircle within the fence. There was a clearing in the center that served as the village yard. A building much larger than the rest completed the circle. Emily thought it must be a gathering place for social or religious events for all members of the tribe. Children ran about, playing in the yard, dogs yapping and barking as the animals chased at their heels. A large fire burned in the yard, just off to one side, not far from the gathering house. A bare-breasted Indian woman stirred the contents of the large communal pot that hung over the fire. Her lack of attire made Emily blush. The Englishwoman saw the woman scold a naked child who ran too close to the flame. Sniffing the air appreciatively, Emily decided that the delicious smell was coming from the contents of the pot.

Emily was surprised by how welcoming the village scene appeared. She glanced at Thunder and saw by his expression that he felt so, too. This was his home, and he was glad to be back. He looked at her, and she smiled. "Welcome home, Thunder," she said softly, knowing he couldn't understand.

He grinned.

A cry from one of the villagers drew their attention. Suddenly Thunder and she were surrounded by the Indians—Thunder's family and friends.

Emily was shoved aside as his friends, in their excitement, questioned Thunder about his journey. Emily and her baby were knocked about and brushed up against. Christopher awoke and started to cry, and suddenly Emily was surrounded by curious women who touched her and her child.

The crush of the crowd stole Emily's breath, and she became

frightened for her son's safety. "Thunder!" she cried. "Thunder, help me!" But she feared that he couldn't hear her. She couldn't see past the women around her. The men had probably already taken Thunder away.

One matron tried to grab Christopher from Emily's arms. Emily screamed and began to bat away the woman's hands.

"Thunder! Thunder! No!" she cried. "Don't take my baby!"

Emily sobbed and held her baby tight to her breast. The crowd abruptly parted and Thunder was there, talking to his people. He pulled Emily into his arms. She went willingly to him, relieved to see him. Thunder represented a safe haven. He spoke softly to her in his native tongue as he led her from the crowd and into one of the longhouses. Christopher calmed as Thunder rescued them.

The longhouse had an open corridor that ran down the center of its length. The building had cubicles or living spaces off both sides of the corridor. There was a fire pit before each cubicle. Safe with Thunder, Emily was able to note her surroundings with some degree of interest. The brave brought her to a living cubicle halfway down the corridor. The living space was lined with platforms on three sides, built a foot or more off the dirt floor. He brought her to one of these platforms, which was covered with a fur, and gestured for her to sit down.

Emily sat and looked around. The walls of the cubicle were lined with sweet-scented grass. Thunder placed her satchel with Christopher's wetting cloths and their remaining supplies onto the platform next to her. Then he touched her cheek and said something more to her in Iroquoian. Emily cried out when she saw his intention to leave her.

"No, Thunder, please don't leave us here alone. I'm afraid!" She wished he could understand.

Thunder stopped and returned to her. He repeated what he'd said to her.

"I don't understand you! I wish you could understand me.

I trust you. Please let me come with you. Don't make me stay here alone."

Tears filled her eyes, and she quickly brushed them away. She felt so foolish, but she was in an Iroquois village and she'd nearly been trampled to death.

Forest Thunder studied Emily with mixed feelings. He understood her fear. He'd experienced raw terror when he'd first gone to London to stay with his English father.

"I wish you could understand me," she repeated. "I wish I could understand you!"

He felt a surge of tenderness for Emily. After days in her company, it was hard for him to equate the Emily he'd come to know with the woman who'd left her child in the forest. He made a decision. He reached out and caressed her jaw.

"Emily," he said in flawless, if slightly accented English. "I must speak with my sachem. Then I will return to you. You will be safe here." He dropped his hand, too conscious of her soft skin.

He saw Emily's shock as she digested the fact that he not only understood English, but could speak it fluently.

Her face reddened. Embarrassment had replaced the shock. "You understood every word I've said!"

He inclined his head.

"Why?" she cried angrily. She was hurt that the man she'd trusted had deceived her—hurt and furious.

"It was in the best interest," he said.

"Best interest!" she exclaimed. "Whose? Yours?"

He stared at her, then abruptly nodded.

"I don't understand."

"It is not for you to understand," he said, his own temper starting to heat. His expression had hardened. "I will be back. Stay here and no one will bother you."

He left then, without looking back, not even when Emily called to him.

Alone, Emily hugged her son to her breast as she eyed her

surroundings. Her first inclination was to go after Thunder. She changed her mind when she saw a small gathering of Indian women watching her from a cubicle across the way.

You will be safe here, Thunder had said. So Emily didn't move. She held her baby tighter and murmured to Christopher until he fell asleep.

Thunder could understand English! She felt her face flame as she recalled some of the things she'd said. She gritted her teeth and glared at the women across the way. How dare he deceive her!

A headache started at her nape and worked its way upward, creating terrible pain along her scalp and jaw. "Thunder," she muttered. "What *is* the man's name?"

Not that she really cared, she told herself. How could she trust him again after the way he'd toyed with her?

He is the only person you know, an inner voice taunted her. She had to rely on Thunder. He was the only person she knew in a village of savages.

The cubicle belonged to Thunder's mother, Water Blossom. The Indian woman appeared a short time after the brave left.

"Emily," she greeted.

Emily gasped and spun. She'd been changing Christopher's diaper, her thoughts preoccupied. She wasn't prepared for the woman's appearance.

"I am sorry to frighten you," she said in heavily accented English. "I am Water Blossom. Forest Thunder is my son."

"Forest Thunder?" Emily echoed.

The matron nodded. "The Onondaga warrior who brought you here."

Emily stared at her in shock. His name *was* Thunder! That explained his look of surprise when she'd first given him a name.

"You are well?" Water Blossom asked. She was an attractive

woman with dark hair that was streaked with strands of gray. She, unlike the matron in the yard, was fully clothed. Her deerskin tunic was adorned with beadwork and porcupine quills. There was a gentleness about her dark eyes that immediately put Emily at ease.

"I am angry," Emily admitted, deciding to be honest.

Water Blossom frowned as she continued to study her.

"You speak English," the Englishwoman said.

The matron seemed startled. "My son's father is a *Yen'-gees*— English."

It explained how Thunder knew the language so well.

"Forest Thunder did not tell me he could speak English," Emily complained.

A twinkle lit up the older woman's eyes. "Forest Thunder was always a child of mischief." She smiled. "He has a good heart. He would not hurt anyone but an enemy."

Emily felt a little chill. *Enemy?*

"My son would not harm you or your child," Water Blossom said.

The Englishwoman smiled. Hadn't she come to believe this herself? If only she'd known earlier, she thought, with diminishing anger. She might be angry with Thunder, but she liked his mother.

Water Blossom's gaze went to Christopher within Emily's arms. "Your baby seems happy here."

Emily's attention went to her son. He was content for the moment. It seemed strange that only a short while ago her baby had been crying.

"Your child knows that no one will harm you here."

Emily met the woman's gaze. "Outside, earlier . . ."

The matron waved the incident aside. "Our people were anxious for news from Long Chin, our Seneca brother. There is to be a wedding, and they wish to know if everything is well."

The Englishwoman was intrigued. "A wedding?" She

thought back to her marriage to James. They'd exchanged vows in the forest under the night sky with only the stars and the wildlife as witnesses. She'd gone to a wedding once, as a twelve-year-old child back in England, when her cousin Maude had married John Clayton Fletcher. It had been a magical event, with food and drink, laughter and emotion. Life was simple then. Her family had lived in a small cottage in Kent. It was a modest existence for her parents and their two young girls. Emily and her sister Mary Elizabeth had been close . . . until her father and mother had died, and her sixteen-year-old sister had married and moved away, leaving Emily to fend for herself at fourteen. After a year's struggle to survive on her own, Emily had indentured herself and gone to America with the hope of a better life. Her circumstances had improved materially. She had food to eat and a house to shelter her. But the brutality of her employer soon had the young woman longing to return to her birthplace.

"I love weddings," she told Water Blossom.

The matron smiled. "Rippling Stream is to marry the Seneca, Falling Rain. Falling Rain has agreed to pay the bride-price. The wedding will take place as planned."

"The groom pays the bride's family?"

Water Blossom nodded. "It is not like your English way. Here a brave shows his appreciation of his bride's worth by giving a gift to her family."

Emily found the subject interesting and appealing. "I think I like the ways of your people better."

The matron nodded. She gestured for Emily to sit down. Emily set her sleeping baby on the fur-covered platform along the back wall, and then sat, facing the Indian woman.

"Why has my son brought you here?"

Sighing, Emily raised her hand to her hair. "I have no idea."

"Where is your child's father?"

Emily felt a tug. "He is dead."

"You lived alone?"

"Yes. The winter was hard, but I made it."

Water Blossom sat down next to Emily. "My son would not leave a woman to fend for her child alone."

"But I was doing fine!" Emily exclaimed.

The matron shook her head. "You were alone."

"I can't stay here."

"I do not know my son's plans for you and your baby."

"Son," Emily said. "His name is Christopher."

The woman smiled. "Christopher," she said carefully, slowly. "It is a good name. A strong name." She touched the baby's forehead. "You will stay here—you and your Christopher—and be welcome until we learn my son's plans."

"Thank you." Emily had to clamp down the urge to say it was her life and that Forest Thunder shouldn't have interfered.

Water Blossom stood. "You must be hungry."

Emily nodded.

"Come, and I will show you how the Onondaga prepare a meal." She glanced at Emily with an impish grin. "It will be a meal fit for an English king."

Emily laughed. She listened and watched carefully as Forest Thunder's mother began to teach her how to cook the Onondaga way.

When he returned to his mother's lodge after speaking with the sachem, Forest Thunder found Emily seated before the family fire, learning how to grind corn. His mother stood behind the Englishwoman with Christopher in her arms, chatting with Emily, occasionally stopping the conversation to instruct Emily with some simple chore.

Forest Thunder felt a little twist in his stomach as he studied the domestic scene. Emily looked unafraid. She seemed to be enjoying herself. He found himself watching for her smile and experiencing warmth as it appeared during her chat with his mother.

Emily glanced up as he entered the living space. The smile left her expression as she spotted him. She quickly looked away, and he stepped past her to speak with Water Blossom.

"She has been no trouble?" he asked in Onondaga.

His mother shook her head. "She has been no trouble." She smiled down at the baby in her arms. "The white woman has a fine son." She raised her gaze in time to see Forest Thunder's nod of agreement.

"Why have you brought her to our village?" she asked.

"Her husband is dead. She gave birth to the boy alone."

His mother clicked her tongue. "She does not understand why you took her."

"I did not take her!"

Water Blossom narrowed her gaze. "She did not come of her own free will."

Forest Thunder blushed. "She is alone with no one to care for her and the babe."

"And you would care for her and the child?" his mother asked, sounding surprised.

"I would see that she gets back with her own people," he replied.

"She needs to know your plans for her."

"She is angry because I did not tell her I could speak her language."

"You must speak with her."

He nodded and turned to leave. "I will tell her as soon as I know what my plans are."

CHAPTER 6

Sunlight shimmered off the lake, brightening the ripples on the surface. Emily stopped by the edge of the water to fill a water-skin for Forest Thunder's mother. The day was warm. A soft breeze teased the loose tendrils of her brown hair and she lifted her face to enjoy the caress of the breeze. She'd been in the Indian village for three days. She felt less threatened than she had when she'd first arrived. Water Blossom was a kind woman who treated her fairly and helped her care for Christopher.

Of Forest Thunder, she'd seen little. After delivering her to his mother, he apparently was content to leave her in Water Blossom's care. He came to visit his mother at least once a day, but he never stayed long, nor did he try to speak privately with Emily. The young Englishwoman felt his presence keenly when he was near, but apparently the brave wasn't affected by her at all.

She couldn't stay in the village. She knew the Indian had other plans for her—what plans? she wondered. She had to admit these past days had taught her that there was much the white man didn't know about the Iroquois.

Her anger toward Forest Thunder had cooled. She didn't understand why she found herself missing his company. Emily recalled the kindness he'd shown her since he'd first stumbled into her life. She could see now that his "savage" behavior had been an act. It wasn't that she didn't believe he was capable of killing if the situation warranted it, but she no longer believed he would have hurt her or her son.

Hadn't he cared for her when she was ill?

Emily rose to her feet with the full water-skin. She stood a moment, gazing out over the lake.

Forest Thunder has an English father, she thought. The knowledge made him more of mystery to her. Who was this man who had chosen life as an Indian over life as an English son?

He'd been to England. Emily had learned this fact from his mother, but Forest Thunder—known as David Forrest to his father's people—had never felt comfortable there. After two years in London, he'd decided to return to the village and the Indian family he'd left behind. His father, John Forrest, had understood and sent him home.

Who was Forest Thunder and why couldn't she put him from her mind? She must be crazy to care for him. They were worlds apart, yet she couldn't abandon the feeling.

The sound of a footfall from behind made Emily spin to see who it was. Big Hair, one of the Onondaga braves, stood a few feet away, his ebony eyes watching her.

Emily's breath slammed in her throat. She didn't like the way he looked at her. Alarm caused tiny pinpricks of fear along her nape, arms, and legs. *Where is Forest Thunder?* It was strange how she wished he were beside her. Despite her anger over his deception, she would seek his protection still.

She gauged the distance to the trail, wondered if the brave would allow her to pass by him.

Why had she lingered at the lake? If she hadn't, she'd be safe in Water Blossom's lodge, tending to Christopher or helping the Indian matron with chores.

Emily felt half naked wearing the doeskin tunic, Water Blossom had given her to wear. Her homespun gown needed to be washed and repaired. Although the Onondaga garment adequately covered her from neck to above the knee, she wasn't accustomed to exposing most of her legs.

With her fingers gripping the top of the water-skin tightly, Emily inched toward the trail and the Indian village. Surely the brave wouldn't touch her?

Her position within the village was an unusual one for a white woman. She was not treated as a slave, and she had sensed some puzzlement at this among the women who bathed each morning in the lake.

She shifted to get past the Indian. When Big Hair stepped to block her, she tensed and debated whether or not she should run.

"Water Blossom needs this," she said with the hope that he'd understand.

Big Hair blinked but didn't move out of the way. Emily felt threatened by him. In a sudden burst of movement, she started to flee. The warrior grabbed her and pulled her back to fit firmly against him.

"No!" she cried. "Let me go." She could feel the panic that was slowly giving way to hysteria as she struggled to break away. She needed to get to the village. There was no one to help her escape the Indian. Big Hair's interest in her made her physically ill.

The brave's eyes gleamed as she fought to free herself. Emily heard herself sobbing and crying for help. *Forest Thunder, where are you when I need you?*

The Indian released her, but stayed near. She knew that Big Hair didn't understand English, so she tried communicating with him using hand gestures. "Water Blossom needs this water-skin," she said. She held up the water sack.

Big Hair grabbed her again, and Emily struggled. With a gleam in his eyes, he stroked his hand down Emily's throat, across her shoulder, and along her bare arm.

She closed her eyes. *Where are you, Forest Thunder?*

She didn't realize that she'd been calling for Forest Thunder out loud until suddenly she was free, and he was there, talking furiously with the other brave. The discussion in Onondaga sounded heated. Big Hair turned suddenly and stalked off, leaving Forest Thunder and Emily alone by the lake.

Emily felt raw. Her altercation with Big Hair had terrified her, but it was the sight of Forest Thunder, watching her closely, that made her feel like weeping.

He looked good—too good, she thought. He was gazing at her, not with anger, but with concern. Emily couldn't help herself; she rushed to hug him. He didn't hesitate; he opened his arms and embraced her. Emily wept freely and held on for dear life.

Forest Thunder held on to the woman in his arms as she cried. He stroked her hair and murmured softly to comfort her. When he'd first heard her cry out his name, he'd felt his insides freeze. He'd hurried to the clearing and became furious to see a frightened Emily imprisoned within Big Hair's arms.

Emily was his responsibility. She was in his care. The pleasure he felt holding her frightened him as much as it excited him.

Her sobs had quieted, but she didn't pull away. He felt her shudder and burrow further against him. He dipped his head, enjoying the brush of her soft, silky brown hair against his chin. He wanted to go on holding her forever, but he couldn't. It wasn't even right that he held her now.

She stirred after a time and pulled away. Forest Thunder was sorry when she stepped back. He longed to hold her again.

"Are you all right?" he asked.

She nodded.

"He will not bother you again."

"How can you be certain?"

His expression hardened. "I have spoken to Big Hair. He will not bother you again, or he will answer to me."

Emily shuddered with the memory of Big Hair's attention. The anger underlying his tone was not directed at her; yet it told her that Forest Thunder would do something terrible to Big Hair if the Indian ever dared touch her again. "Thank you," she murmured.

Forest Thunder lifted her chin to study her. "You look tired," he said with concern.

She tried to push away. She was tired because she hadn't been sleeping well lately—and Forest Thunder was the cause.

Until marriage, sons usually resided in the longhouse of their mother's clan. Forest Thunder had slept elsewhere since her arrival. Where? Emily wondered.

"I'm all right," she told him.

"And Christopher?" he asked.

How easily he'd said her baby's name. It brought home the fact that he'd deceived her. His English was perfect. She recalled his earlier pronunciation of "Chris-to-pher," and started to fume again.

"Why did you pretend you couldn't understand English?" she demanded angrily. She became more furious as she remembered the things she'd said to him since they'd met.

Forest Thunder sighed as he continued to study her. "I didn't know if you would be difficult. If you'd known I could speak English as fluently as Onondaga, would you have spoken your thoughts aloud?"

"No!"

"Exactly," he said, with a hint of smugness.

"Why did you bring me here? Why did you take me away from my home?"

He cradled her face with his hands. "You were alone," he said gently. "I could not leave you."

Again she attempted to pull away. "I could have managed. I survived the winter." She paused. "I gave birth to my son."

"You were alone all that time?" Horror made his stomach churn.

She nodded, and he felt her shiver.

"You were alone all winter."

She didn't resist him when he pulled her into his arms.

"It was a terrible winter. How did you survive?"

She shuddered and pressed herself closer. "I almost didn't." She slipped her arms around his waist. He didn't think she was aware of what she doing.

He set her back to look at her. He saw the memory of the horror and the fear in her brown eyes.

His gaze dropped to her mouth. Her lips looked soft and moist . . . and tempting. "Emily," he whispered, and dipped his head to kiss her.

Emily wasn't afraid as she saw his intent. She felt her body strain to meet him. As his mouth tentatively touched hers, she realized what it was that had been keeping her up nights. It was the image of Forest Thunder kissing her—her longing to be kissed. She had missed being close to him.

When Forest Thunder raised his head, the loss of contact left her feeling dissatisfied. She heard the whimper that came from her own throat as he pulled away. She heard him groan as he came back to kiss her a second time. This time he captured her mouth in a kiss that made her tingle from head to toe. His kiss was gentle, but she could feel the controlled passion, the underlying tenderness. He teased the corner of her mouth and brushed his lips across her cheek. She sighed with pleasure as he trailed soft kisses over every inch of her face . . . across her forehead, her eyelids. He rained gentle kisses along her nose, over her lips to her chin.

She wanted more from him. She wanted those lips, those

wonderful lips, pressed firmly against her mouth. She'd never wanted a kiss this much.

He pulled back as if to release her. She opened her eyes and was shocked, yet delighted, to see the longing in his gaze, the passion in his expression. She found herself reaching to bring his head down, his mouth back to hers. When he groaned deeply, she felt a shaft of pleasurable heat. When his mouth captured her in a kiss meant to possess her, she moaned low in her throat and allowed herself to respond with every fiber of her being. She tunneled her fingers into the silky dark hair at his nape, and leaned into the kiss.

Forest Thunder tasted the soft, quivering sweetness beneath his mouth and experienced a fiery warmth that threatened to consume him. Desire tightened his loins and made him strengthen his hold on her. But it wasn't fear that caused her gasping when he lifted his head. He saw the longing in her expression and the passion glistening in her beautiful brown eyes. The sight stunned him. He dipped his head and felt himself soar as he kissed her.

Nothing, no one—not even her affection for James, her husband—had prepared Emily for her body's reaction to Forest Thunder. She could barely think, could barely breathe, but her body felt alive. Her heart went wild and pumped rapidly; her blood warmed until she felt every nerve ending tingle and sing.

Forest Thunder pulled back his head. Emily leaned into him as she silently begged him to continue holding her, touching her. He set her back and held her shoulders. She heard the way his breath labored from his throat and felt her own desire shoot a notch upward.

"Come," he said, holding her captive with his gaze. "It is time to go back. Your son will need you."

Emily could only nod. Her lips hummed with the imprint of his kiss. Her body burned wherever his hard form had pressed against her. He turned and started toward the path back to the village, and Emily followed closely behind him. Despite her feelings for Forest Thunder, she couldn't forget Big Hair and the danger in his interest in her.

"What are you going to do with me?"

Forest Thunder froze, then faced her. His hot gaze seared her face as he studied her. "You were alone."

"I was fine."

He raised an eyebrow. "Were you?"

She blushed. So she had passed out after seeing him with Christopher. Any white woman would have been upset to see an Indian holding her child. "Yes, I was managing!"

"It is too dangerous in the forest for a woman and child alone."

"I wasn't alone. My husband—"

"Is dead," he finished.

She blanched and opened her mouth to argue. . . . Then she remembered that she'd given away the truth when she'd thought he didn't understand English. "That's not fair!" Anger for his deception reared up inside her again.

Forest Thunder grabbed her shoulders and kissed her. It was hard for her to stay mad at him in the face of their desire.

He broke away. "Do not tell me about what is fair, Emily." His tone was dark, husky. "Some things in this life are too overwhelming to be fair."

She eyed him with growing horror. Why did he have such an affect on her? It gave her satisfaction to see that he was shaken by the attraction between them as much as she was.

"I want to go back."

"No."

"You can't keep me a prisoner."

His ebony eyes flashed fire. "If you were a slave, you would not be living so comfortably in the house of my mother."

Emily felt ashamed for her outburst, but wouldn't admit it.

"You will be free to be with your people when time permits me to take you." He spun and walked away.

My people? she thought. Emily chased after him, her heart

jumping at the sight of his golden back. "Forest Thunder! What people? What did you mean by that?" She was a fugitive bondservant. She couldn't go back. As punishment, she'd have to live with the cruelties of Richard Malkins. Christopher, her precious baby, would be forced into bond service until the age of twenty-one.

Forest Thunder had picked up his pace. Emily hurried after him. "Forest Thunder," she cried. "What people? Where are you going to take me?" He couldn't make her go back. She'd give her own life to protect her child.

The brave acted as if he couldn't hear her. When they'd reached the village, Forest Thunder had disappeared behind a longhouse. She ran to catch up with him, but he was nowhere to be found.

Emily became aware that she was being watched. Several villagers stood a short distance away; among them was Big Hair. She shivered as she saw the brave. She spun and hurried toward the longhouse of the Deer.

Thoughts of Big Hair were put aside as she wondered, worried, about what the future held for her and her baby.

Time passed and Emily became adjusted to life within the Onondaga village. She felt comfortable there. The villagers no longer looked at her differently. She was treated as one of their own and was permitted the same freedom. To make carrying Christopher easier for Emily while doing her chores, Water Blossom had constructed a cradleboard, so Emily could carry Christopher on her back. Emily was able to move about doing her chores with her baby safe, secure, and bundled within his cradleboard. Sometimes she hung the board from a large tree branch and Christopher seemed content to swing gently from the limb while Emily worked nearby.

Of Forest Thunder, she saw little. He spent most of his time with the sachem of the village, Drumming Fox. Water Blossom told her that the brave was somehow involved with his leader's plans for Rippling Stream's upcoming wedding. The memory of Forest Thunder's kiss haunted Emily. She lay awake nights thinking of him, longing for him, wondering if he could ever come to care for her. She could feel the imprint of his hands on her face and body. It felt so real; it seemed as if it was happening. But it wasn't. Since that day by the lake, she'd not been alone with him. *I'm glad,* she told herself. She didn't need her attraction to Forest Thunder to complicate her future.

Future? she thought. She still didn't know what the brave planned to do with her. He'd told her he would take her to her people. What people? She had no people. Because of her past, she wouldn't be safe at an English settlement.

She had to know Forest Thunder's plans. She was losing too much sleep from worrying. Would the brave be honest with her?

Emily felt a tightening in her chest. Or would Forest Thunder try to deceive her as he'd done along the trail?

She'd find a way to talk with him. Perhaps if she asked for Water Blossom's help.

The idea cheered her as she took her turn working Water Blossom's vegetable field. She was stronger physically with each new day. She had already learned she could survive rough living conditions. If she ended up back at the cabin alone, she'd be fine—so would Christopher. She tried not to think of her son facing a winter like the last one. She focused her thoughts on the Onondagas and the kind of life they had in their peaceful village.

As she entered the stockade, she saw the happy children, the contentment of the village elders as they moved about their daily lives . . . and she wished she could stay in the village forever.

* * *

He watched Emily from a distance. The memory of their kiss haunted him, arousing more than his desire. What was it about her that made him want to touch her, hold her, possess her? His fascination with her disturbed him greatly. He'd tried to avoid her these last few days, but he couldn't stay away. He shouldn't become involved with her. She would go back to the English, and he'd never see her again.

She was beautiful. Her soft, silky brown hair fell unbound past her shoulders. She had eyes like the coat of the fox, brown with a hint of red. When she looked at him, he felt warm all over. He was amazed by how well she'd adjusted to village life. He'd seen her working in his mother's field. He'd watched as she left the village for the lake each morning with the Onondaga women.

Water Blossom said that Emily was learning to make moccasins. The white woman had been horrified to work with the skins at first, but she did the tanning without a care now. She understood the value of furs for warmth and clothing; his mother had taught her well.

It was dangerous for him to think that Emily could be happy in his village, he thought—happy with him.

She did feel something for him. He could see desire in her eyes when they happened to glance his way. He had tasted it in her kiss and heard it when she moaned his name as he held and caressed her.

For the baby's sake as well as Emily's, he must take them to the English fort.

Emily turned then, and spied him by the door flap to the sachem's hut. He'd been spending a lot of time with the sachem, preparing for the arrival of their Seneca guests. Since he'd brought Emily to the village, he no longer stayed in the longhouse of the clan of the Deer, the lodge of his mother. If Water Blossom wondered why he'd left, she hadn't mentioned it to him. Forest Thunder suspected that his mother had guessed his feelings for Emily and allowed him his privacy. She had loved an Englishman, Forest Thunder's father, John Forrest. They had been happy for a time, but in the end John couldn't adapt to the Onondaga way of life. He had gone back to his mother's country, leaving Water Blossom to raise their young son.

Forest had seen the sadness in his mother's eyes after his father left. Years later, John Forrest had sent for his only son. With Water Blossom's encouragement, Forest Thunder had reluctantly gone to England. The young man had stayed with his father for two years. He had tried to live like an Englishman, but he'd been raised an Indian. After two years in London, Forest Thunder had wanted to return to his village and the mother he'd left behind.

Only after his return did he realize that his mother had made a sacrifice in urging him to go. When he'd left, she'd felt that she'd lost not one, but two men she loved. The joy in his mother's gaze when he'd come home had told him more than any words could, how much his mother had missed him.

Forest Thunder belonged here among the Onondaga. Emily belonged with the English.

His heart raced when Emily looked his way and approached him. The sun glistened off her brown hair. Her skin looked soft and smooth, and he longed to touch it.

"Forest Thunder."

"Emily," he murmured. "You are looking well. My mother has been good to you?"

Her expression softened at the mention of his mother. "She is a warm and generous woman. She has made me feel welcome."

He nodded. "Good, that is how it should be."

A frown settled across her brow. "You've been avoiding me."

He blinked, because it was true. "I have been busy. There is much to prepare for the marriage of Rippling Stream and the Seneca."

"I need to speak with you."

"Then speak."

"Why am I here? What are your plans for me?"

He looked away. "We have talked about this already."

"You said you would take me to my people. What people? What did you mean?"

"There is an English fort two days' journey from here. I will take you there, where you will be safe."

"And if I want to return to my cabin?"

Forest Thunder frowned. "Your cabin is not safe for you and Christopher."

"We were managing fine!"

He held her gaze steadily. "You left your son alone beneath some trees."

"Because of you!" she cried. "I knew I couldn't run carrying Christopher, so I hid him. Then I ran so you would follow me and leave my baby alone." Her eyes filled with tears at the memory. "But it didn't work like I planned. You didn't come after me. You found Christopher. When I went back for him, he was gone. Gone!" she sobbed. "And you'd taken him."

Something kicked within his gut as he listened to her explanation. *She had done her best to protect her babe. She hadn't abandoned him in the forest.*

Emily's pain transmitted itself to Forest Thunder, hurting him as it hurt her. He took her arm and led her into the shadow between two longhouses. There, he pulled her into his arms.

She fit within his embrace as if she'd been made especially for him. He could feel every inch of her softness pressed against his hard length. His blood warmed as he held her.

"It is all right. Do not cry. Christopher is safe now."

As he held her tightly, Forest Thunder realized that their time together was drawing to an end. He would take her away from here soon . . . before he changed his mind and tried to keep her here forever.

CHAPTER 7

Forest Thunder's arms felt good around her. It had been so long since she'd been held or allowed a man to comfort her. But there was more to Forest Thunder's touch. She experienced a tingle wherever their bodies had contact. Emily loved the clean, male scent of him, the warmth and strength of his hard, masculine body. She felt safe within his embrace. He was indirectly the cause of her worries, yet she was comforted by him.

I love him. The thought popped into her mind, startling her. Did he care for her—just a little?

Why had he kissed her? Was it just desire? She recalled the urgency in his caress. She wasn't so foolish to confuse love with desire, although she knew that each could be wrapped up with the other.

She was afraid to move. She didn't want to break the contact. She wanted him to kiss her into a state of mindless passion. She wanted him to tell her it was all right, that he would keep her here, care for her. She would never have to worry about Richard Malkins or her own safety again.

He shifted to set her away from him, and she was horrified to hear herself groan with protest. She kept her eyes closed, for she was afraid to read his expression, afraid of seeing his amusement. She opened her eyes when he gently caressed her cheek. Emily's breath became lodged in her throat. She saw no humor in his face. His dark eyes glistened with emotion and a desire that appeared to match the heat flowing through her own body. His face—his wonderfully handsome, rough-hewn features—was taut with passion. He cupped her head with both hands while his gaze caressed her face, gleaming as it fell on her lips, darkening when he raised it to look into her eyes.

Emily's heart began to beat faster. Her stomach warmed, and she felt tiny frissons of pleasure along her skin. She wanted him to kiss her. She wanted him to touch and hold her . . . and more. "Forest Thunder—"

His kiss cut off her flow of words. His mouth was hot, searing, yet incredibly gentle, with a hint of the effort it was taking him to control his desire.

Emily whimpered and leaned into the kiss. Her head spun with the hot, clawing pleasure of his mouth against her own. She clutched him tightly, rejoicing in the feel of him against her, his desire for her.

She cried out when he lifted his head.

"Emily," he gasped, before he took her mouth once again. His kiss was more urgent and filled with need. Emily was dizzy with sensation. She could barely breathe, but gloried in the wonder of it.

A sound behind them drew them apart. They turned just as two of the village matrons came around the side of one long-house. Emily stepped back to put distance between her and the brave.

Her gaze met Forest Thunder's.

"Meet me here tonight," he said, "after the sun sets and the people are sleeping."

Her heart leapt with joy as she nodded. She'd find a way to do as he'd asked. The matrons glanced their way, but didn't look twice at seeing them together. Emily decided that everyone knew of her presence and Forest Thunder's role in bringing her there.

The night seemed a long time away. Emily's thoughts churned with joy and fear . . . with anticipation and concern.

As the hour grew late, and everyone within the village but the guards settled down for the night, Emily no longer worried about the consequences of the meeting. She wanted to be with Forest Thunder. Tomorrow she might have to leave, but tonight, at least, she would enjoy being in his arms. She would store up memories for the long, lonely months ahead. And she wouldn't feel a moment's regret.

He waited silently between the longhouses for her arrival. Would she come? She had responded to his kisses, but perhaps she'd just been caught up in the moment. She must miss her husband terribly. Did she have regrets after their kiss?

Emily waited until everyone was asleep before she got up from her bed. She rolled up the fur covering and placed it beside Christopher so that he wouldn't fall off the platform. Then, with a silent prayer that her son wouldn't awaken during her absence, she left the cubicle and headed down the long corridor toward the door. Softly glowing embers from family cook-fires gave her just enough light to see. Careful not to step in any fire-pits, she hurried toward the door opening with the hope that no one would see her and question her.

Outside, there was a slight nip in the air, but it felt wonderful to Emily. She looked up at the night sky, saw the stars twinkling against the black backdrop, and knew that whatever fate might bring to her in the future, this evening would be special.

She didn't realize how afraid she'd been that Forest Thunder wouldn't come, until she saw the outline of him in the dark distance. As if sensing her presence, he turned and opened his arms. Emily rushed into his embrace, moaning softly when he held her tightly and stroked her hair. Tears came to her eyes as he set her back and lifted her chin with his finger.

"What is this?" he asked huskily, dipping his finger to wipe away a teardrop.

Emily shook her head. How could she explain that being with him alone again overwhelmed her with happiness?

He frowned. "You did not want to come?"

"No!" she gasped. "I wanted to come." When she saw that he wasn't going to let up until he had an explanation, she said, "I'm just happy to see you."

His brow cleared. He looked surprised, but pleased.

"Then you are no longer angry that I deceived you about the English?"

She shook her head.

"Come," he said, grabbing her hand. "Let's go from here, where no one will hear us."

She was disappointed that he didn't proclaim his own pleasure in being with her, but she kept silent and followed his lead. She had a moment's doubt about being out of range of hearing Christopher, but she dismissed it. Her son would not be harmed should he awaken and cry out. He was in the good hands of Forest Thunder's mother.

Forest Thunder led her past several longhouses and across the village center to the stockade gate. Emily felt her face warm as they passed through the gate and Forest Thunder said something to the guards. She wondered what the Indians thought, then realized that she didn't really care. They weren't Englishmen, who would judge and condemn her for being alone with a man. They were the Iroquois, who had a different view of the world around them. She loved Forest Thunder; she wanted to be with him. His people would not care if he chose to spend time with the Englishwoman late at night. If they did care, it wouldn't have made a difference in her decision to come.

Her eyes had become fully adjusted to the darkness as they left the compound and headed into the woods. Emily felt the warmth of Forest Thunder's grip and her body tingled with anticipation. She didn't know exactly what he had in mind, but she hoped he wanted to do more than just talk.

Wanton she might be, but she wanted to feel his touch. Just the thought of what he might do made her breath quicken and her heart race. Suddenly Forest Thunder halted. "Are you all right?" he asked.

She nodded.

Forest Thunder eyed the woman before him and wondered if she was well enough to be out late at night. It hadn't occurred to him that she might still not be feeling up to standard until he heard her breathing. He frowned as he continued to study her. "Emily?" he said, his accent thick in his concern for her.

"I'm all right," she said breathlessly.

And then he saw what he'd missed before—the hungry look in her eyes that mirrored his own desire. He felt the heat in his loins, a tightening in his chest. In a bid for control, he squeezed her hand and continued through the forest. He took her to a spot near the lake, a secluded area where he went whenever he wanted to be alone. He'd had a lot to think about in years past—the knowledge of an English father, his decision to go to England, his feelings when he'd come home.

It was a beautiful night. The lake glistened with moonlight. The air was scented with forest vegetation and the clean smells of late spring. He heard Emily's sharp little intake of breath as he led her into the clearing. The view of the lake was breathtaking. He turned to her.

"It's so beautiful here," she whispered, sounding awed.

He smiled. "You are beautiful, Emily." He enjoyed looking

at her. He was surprised by how much pleasure he felt when he was with her.

"Come," he said. "Let us sit."

The grass was matted as if Forest Thunder came here often to sit and reflect. Emily sat down on the grass and waited while Forest Thunder got comfortable beside her.

They looked out over the lake for a time, neither one speaking. Emily was conscious of Forest Thunder's slightest movements. After a time, she sensed his regard, and turned to meet his gaze.

His dark eyes seemed to glow in the darkness. There was no smile in his expression, but there was a tenderness that nearly unraveled her. He reached out and drew her head slowly, gently toward him. Then he kissed her, a sweet kiss full of gentleness and promise. Emily closed her eyes and allowed his lips to wreak havoc on her senses. He kissed her mouth, her cheeks, her chin, and her eyelids. Then, when she was moaning softly and gasping, he recaptured her lips.

The sweetness turned to passion. Forest Thunder's mouth became more demanding, and Emily was only too happy to give. He pulled her onto his lap and nuzzled a fiery path down her neck. She slipped her arms around him, enjoying the sensation of her palm against bare skin, the heat of his back warming her.

He wasn't rough. His passion was restrained, but the knowledge of it simmering beneath the surface fueled Emily's desire.

They were both breathing heavily when Forest Thunder eased her off his lap in an obvious effort to gain control. His breath was harsh as he focused his gaze on the lake.

"I am sorry," he said. "I should not have done that."

Emily felt a painful pang. "I'm not," she admitted softly.

His gaze shifted to her face. "You are not well yet."

She shook her head, her heart brightening with the hope that he had set her away only because he felt it was too soon to be with a man. "I am fine. There is nothing I can't do if I wanted to."

He stared at her a long moment, as if trying to gauge the truth for himself. "You were hurt; I cared for you."

"I am better. There is nothing wrong with me." She felt as well as saw the shudder that went through him. The knowledge of how he'd cared for her no longer embarrassed her; she was grateful and amazed by how kind he'd been.

"Thunder," she whispered with longing. She boldly touched him, trailing her fingers down his jaw, her gaze following the path her hand took as she continued her caress down his throat and onto his bare chest. "Thunder," she repeated, "don't be afraid."

His muscles contracted wherever she stroked him. She heard the increased, labored sound of his breathing and experienced an odd little thrill.

"Emily," he murmured. "We should go back."

"No." She continued to touch him—his belly, which constricted under her fingertips, back up to his chest and his nipples, which hardened as she stroked them. He closed his eyes and groaned, clearly enjoying what she was doing to him. It gave her a heady sense of power; she'd never taken such pleasure in touching a man. What was it about Forest Thunder that churned up everything inside her and flushed her with pleasure?

Love, she realized. She loved him, passionately, deeply, a grown woman wanting, needing a man.

When she sought to touch him more intimately, Forest Thunder grabbed and stilled her hands. As they stared at one another, Emily could see the war raging inside him. His fingers were warm rings about her wrists, firm but not hurting. She saw the changing expressions on his face. She hoped, prayed, that she'd see the one she wanted, the one that said he'd given in.

She cried out with joy when he gave a tug and tumbled her against him. His groan of desire was loud in the silence of the night before he caught her in a fiery kiss that seared and branded her.

"Yes," she murmured when he released her mouth to kiss her neck. "Oh, yes, Thunder, touch me."

She wore a doeskin tunic that she'd slipped on before going to bed. Forest Thunder's hand found her bare leg below the hem, and Emily nearly shot up off his lap as his fingers created a wild tingling of pleasure from her calf, traveling upward to her thigh. As his hand settled on her upper leg, Emily held her breath in anticipation. He shifted his hand downward and, disappointed, she caught his hand and brought it back to her thigh. She kept her hand covering his and began to move his fingers upward, raising the hem of the tunic. She wore nothing beneath the garment. As the doeskin shifted upward, her bare flesh was revealed. Forest Thunder made a sound that was half moan, half gasp, as he saw and felt what only seconds before the tunic had concealed.

Emily shivered as she released his hand, which continued on its own. His fingers brought her every nerve-ending to life, making her blood heat up and her whole body come alive.

Forest Thunder grabbed the bottom edge of her tunic and raised it from her body. Spreading it on the grass, he reached for Emily and lifted her onto the garment. Then, he stretched out beside her and kissed her. When he was done with her mouth, he began a slow downward journey of lips, tongue, and fingertips on her quivering flesh that had Emily arching off the tunic, gasping, and crying out his name.

He didn't think Emily was ready to join with a man. Forest Thunder found such pleasure in touching her that he allowed himself the fantasy. He would not find release this night. He could not take her without guilt. Soon she would be leaving, and there would be no child to complicate their parting.

Her response to his lovemaking overwhelmed him. If he didn't know she'd had a son, he would have thought that she was experiencing passion for the first time.

He couldn't stop touching her. His hands were drawn to her again and again. His mouth enjoyed the taste of her lips, her flesh.

"Thunder," she gasped. "Please!"

He was rock-hard and swollen, but he wouldn't take her. Battling down his own desire, he sought to give her release. He kissed, caressed, and stroked her until she was crying out his name to the night.

She'd never been loved that way before. Emily lay within Forest Thunder's arms, her body still pulsing in the aftermath of ecstasy. He had brought her pleasure with selfless disregard for his own. As he stroked her hair, she became aware of the tension within him. She pulled away to sit up and study him.

"Thunder," she murmured softly. Her hand reached out to touch the bulge in his loincloth. "Let me touch you. Pleasure you."

He shook his head.

"Please," she pleaded. She cupped him, stroked. When he groaned, clearly enjoying her touch, she untied the strings of the breechcloth, freeing him.

"No, Emily," he gasped, but he didn't try to stop her. Emily was awed by his response to her caresses. She bent her head to kiss him and began a journey of discovery of Forest Thunder's body. Her love for him swelled as she brought him satisfaction and he convulsed and cried out her name.

"You did not have to do that," he said huskily as they lay within each other's arms a short while later.

"I wanted to give you pleasure." She could sense his smile.

"You gave me pleasure," he admitted.

She couldn't control her own smile. "Good." She was warmed by the thought of their time together. They had each sought to give to the other. They hadn't joined as man and wife, but they had experienced the intimacy, the pleasure, of each other's touch.

"You did not want to join with me," she said, shifting away and onto her back. "Why?"

Forest Thunder rolled onto his side, propping his head up with his arm. "You think that I did not want to be inside you?"

She looked away, feeling suddenly shy. He turned her to face him with a touch on her chin.

"It wasn't long ago that you had a child," he said softly.

"I am fine."

He shook his head. "You are still tender. I did not want to hurt you."

She stared at him and recognized his sincerity. "Maybe I wanted to be hurt," she whispered, with all the longing for him in her voice.

His dark gaze glowed with desire. "You could have had a child."

He didn't want their child? Pain lanced through her as she averted her gaze. She fought for control before she glanced back at him. "You are right," she said carefully. She sat up. "It is late. I must get back to check on Christopher."

He rose to his feet and extended his hand to help her up. Emily took his hand and steeled herself against responding to his warmth, his kindness . . . his nakedness. She stood and then bent down for her tunic. She tried to pretend he wasn't watching her as they dressed.

They returned to the village in silence. As they neared the longhouse of the Bear, Forest Thunder halted and took Emily by the shoulders. "You are angry with me."

Tears glistened in her eyes as she shook her head. She wasn't angry; she was hurt that he didn't share her feelings. She had Christopher; she loved her son. She enjoyed being a mother. The thought of having a child by Forest Thunder could only add to the joy.

"Do not cry, Emily," he said huskily. "There are things you do not understand. Tomorrow I will try to explain them to you." He cupped her jaw and lowered his head to kiss her

tenderly. He straightened and smiled at her. "You rest well.
We will talk in the morning."

Emily nodded, warmed by his words and comforted by his
expression. They continued to the longhouse, but were brought
up short when they saw Water Blossom at the door. The matron
held Emily's baby, who slept in her arms.

She looked from Emily to her son. Her face held no expression as she handed Emily the baby. "The boy was wet. He
cried but his mother was not here to comfort him."

Emily felt her face get hot. "I'm sorry." Feeling properly
chastised, she clutched Christopher to her breast. When her son
whimpered, she eased up her grip. Her gaze went to Forest
Thunder, then his mother. "My baby is hungry," she murmured, feeling like a scolded child. "I will feed him." She
turned to enter the longhouse—and was hurt and disappointed
that Forest Thunder had no other words for her.

"What are you doing, my son?" Water Blossom asked with
concern. "You know the Englishwoman must return to her
people."

Forest Thunder sighed. "I know this."

"You care for her."

He nodded.

"Then it is time to take her away from here. She belongs
with her people."

Everything within Forest Thunder protested. "It is too soon.
She is not well. . . ."

Water Blossom's gaze seared her son's face. "The white
woman is well. She will not suffer from the journey to her
people." Her expression softened as she touched his shoulder.
"You will both hurt if you do not take her soon."

He nodded. "I will take her tomorrow," he said.

"Have Big Hair take her," his mother suggested.

"No!" he said, recalling the brave's interest in Emily when they were down by the lake.

"He will not harm her."

Forest Thunder shook his head. "I will take her. I brought her here; I will take her away."

"It will be hard for you."

"Yes."

"I seek only to spare you pain," his mother said in a voice filled with sadness.

He looked at her more closely, seeing his mother's pain in the memory of her love for his father. "I know," he said softly. He touched her cheek to comfort.

Water Blossom nodded, but her gaze mirrored her concern as she watched her son return to her sister's longhouse where he'd slept since bringing the Englishwoman to their village.

CHAPTER 8

"What's wrong?" Emily asked. "What did you say to him?"

Water Blossom stared at her a long moment before replying. "I reminded him that you are white, and he is Onondaga. He agreed that it was time you rejoined your people. You will leave for the fort in two days when the sun has risen high in the sky."

"You want me to go?" Emily felt a sharp tug on her heart-strings. "You don't think I'm good enough for him, do you?"

The Indian woman looked sad. "It is not your worth or that of my son's that concerns me. You are *Yen'gees*. You and your son belong with your people. Our life here is different. I do not want to see you or Forest Thunder hurt."

The Englishwoman turned to hide her sudden tears. "I thought you liked me." She didn't turn when Water Blossom put a hand on her shoulder.

"You have been welcome in my lodge. You are a good matron who is good to her son. This woman cares for you."

It was Water Blossom's sincerity that made Emily glance back at her. "I wouldn't hurt him," Emily whispered.

"Sometimes caring is not enough. Two people can believe that love is strong to keep them happy, but in the end they learn that this is not so."

Studying the woman, Emily realized that Water Blossom was speaking from experience. She had loved a *Yen'gees* and had a child by the man—Forest Thunder's father. Had they come to realize that neither could be happy living in a culture that was not their own?

But it was different for her and Forest Thunder, Emily thought. She felt comfortable among the Indians. She could easily live the rest of her life in the Onondaga village. Danger awaited her and her child if she was taken to the English fort. Perhaps they'd let her stay if she explained. "Water Blossom—"

"It is late," the woman said, apparently saddened by her thoughts. "Sleep. The journey to the *Yen'gees* fort is a long one."

But I don't want to go! Emily knew then that it was no use explaining anything to Water Blossom. Because of her own lost love, the matron couldn't foresee happiness for her son with an Englishwoman.

There were other English among the Indians, she thought, as she headed toward Water Blossom's cubicle—a young woman called Sun Bird, her blonde hair instantly setting her apart from the other maidens within the village. Was it because she'd been captured when she was young?

Would she—Emily Russell—have been happier if Forest Thunder had taken her prisoner? As she lay Christopher on the sleeping platform and stretched out beside her son, she recalled how she'd once thought she was a captive of an Indian. It wasn't until she'd reached the village and been treated kindly that she'd realized that Forest Thunder had only been concerned for her welfare.

He doesn't realize that taking me to the fort is more danger-

ous to me and Christopher than leaving us to fend for ourselves in the woods.

Would he believe her if she told him? Staring up at the rafters of the longhouse, she frowned. She didn't think he would believe her. He would probably remind her of her husband's death, pointing out the fact James had been an armed man who had fallen victim to the wilderness. How could she expect her and her baby to survive?

They'd managed fine until Forest Thunder had come, she thought. She'd rather take her chances in the forest than risk being sent back to Richard Malkins and his cruelties. Would she have the strength to endure the trip? Would she find the trail marks she'd left behind, or become lost in the forest, a place more deadly in the dark of night? How could she bear leaving Forest Thunder after realizing just how much he meant to her?

Emily realized that she had only one choice now—and that was to take Christopher back to her cabin in the woods. Somehow she'd find a way to get there safely.

As she lay in the quiet darkness, she began to make plans to leave.

The thought of leaving the village made Emily's chest tighten. She had never foreseen that she'd feel comfortable among the Indians, but Water Blossom had been good to her . . . and Forest Thunder . . . He made her feel things she'd never felt before—feelings she'd never experienced with James. She couldn't deny that she'd miss the brave. Would he think of her? When he realized she was gone, would he come after her?

She felt wonderful physically, better than she'd felt in a long while. Christopher seemed to be growing daily. She enjoyed the wonder of his smile and his increasing awareness of the world around him. He was a happy baby; and the Onondaga embraced him as one of their own.

Emily tried not to think how it would be if she were allowed to stay. She concentrated on making plans to leave. She decided to go on long walks to build up her strength. Would Forest Thunder notice her short absences each day?

The first opportunity to go into the forest came one morning after she'd filled the water-skins for Water Blossom. As she'd come to expect, there was a lot of activity by the lake. Early each day the women gathered there to wash and to chatter and laugh. At first shy, Emily had come to appreciate that time of day as much, she suspected, as the village women did. She and Water Blossom had joined the others that morning, and when they were done with the daily ritual, Emily had filled the skins and followed Water Blossom back to the longhouse. Expecting to be given a list of chores to help with, Emily was surprised when Forest Thunder's mother had told her to take the day to rest and enjoy herself. Water Blossom, it seemed, had to attend to some tribal business. Emily suspected it had something to do with the upcoming wedding uniting the Onondaga sachem's daughter with a Seneca son.

With a whole free day before her, Emily decided to take Christopher for a walk in the woods. It was a bright, sunny day. The air temperature was warm. Wildflowers bloomed everywhere beneath the treetop canopy. Insects buzzed, and songbirds trilled their tunes from the branches up above.

Emily loved the woods, but she wasn't fooled by its present friendly appearance. There were wild animals who could kill and maim. The night air's temperature could drop drastically, chilling one to the bone. She carried Christopher in the cradleboard strapped to her back. He felt light and seemed perfectly content to take the ride. She knew that caring for Christopher during the journey wouldn't be easy. She would have to stop and tend to him whenever he became hungry or cried. As their journey lengthened, Emily would feel the weight of the cradleboard more as she tired and her shoulders become sore.

She walked for only a half hour before she decided to go

back. She didn't want to venture too far, lest she draw attention with her absence. As she changed directions and headed back to the encampment, she wondered where Forest Thunder was and what he was doing. He'd said nothing more about taking her to the English fort, but she wasn't foolish enough to believe that he'd abandoned the idea. How much time did she have to prepare to leave?

With each passing day, the marks she'd made would fade— or disappear. The rain during their journey to the village already would have washed out some of her trail markers. She could only hope and pray that she'd somehow find the others and make it safely home.

Was the cabin how she'd left it? Had someone broken into it while she was away? She shuddered and hugged herself with her arms. She didn't want to go back. She was afraid. She'd stay as long as she could, leave as soon as she was ready.

"Emily."

Emily gasped, startled by the sudden appearance of Forest Thunder. She had found a spot to sit near the lake; baby Christopher lay on a grass mat beside her. She had come to be alone and was surprised that he had found her. "Forest Thunder! I thought you went hunting."

She had not spoken with him in two days ... since the intimate time they'd spent together in the night. She had watched him hungrily from afar. He hadn't tried to approach her with plans for their departure or to tell her how he felt about the night's intimacy between them.

He shook his head. "We have all the meat we need for Rippling Stream's wedding feast."

She felt hurt that he was going to send her away. Was that why he wanted to talk with her?

He frowned as he reached out to trace the shadows beneath her eyes. "What is this? Are you ill?"

Her chest tightened as she averted her gaze. "I am fine."

He grabbed her chin and turned her face upward for his

inspection. "Has Christopher been keeping you up at night?" His caress seared her.

"Yes," she said quickly, hoping he wouldn't guess that he was the reason she couldn't sleep. That it was him and his decision to take her to the English.

"You should rest this afternoon," he suggested gently. His finger stroked her cheek, making Emily's skin tingle.

She nodded. She gazed at him while mentally preparing to hear what he had to say. But he didn't say a thing. Her heart gave a little leap as he sat down beside her on the grass. She studied him as he stared out over the lake, waiting for him to speak.

He turned his attention to Christopher, smiling as he took the baby's hand and studied the boy's tiny fingers. "He is growing quickly," he said, meeting her gaze.

She nodded and was unable to control a smile. "He is more aware of the things around him. See how he grins?"

The two exchanged looks that might have been shared by doting parents.

Encouraged by the moment, Emily reached out to touch Forest Thunder's hand where it now rested on the mat beside the baby's head. "Did you want to talk with me about something?" she asked.

His dark eyes glowed intently. She felt her body sway slightly in his direction. She heard his soft moan and saw him lean toward her. "Forest Thunder," she whispered with longing.

He caught her face, tipped it upward, and looked as if he were going to kiss her. But then he was muttering something in Onondaga and pulling away. He rose to his feet without looking at her.

"Thunder?"

Her hurt tone drew his gaze to her face. Forest Thunder saw the pain and confusion in her soft brown eyes and cursed silently. "I am glad to see that you are well. In three days Rippling Stream will wed the Seneca. After the wedding feast,

I will take you to an English fort where you and Christopher will be able to join your own people."

"And if I don't want to go?" she challenged.

"It is for the best," he said, wondering why she played with his emotions. "You will be happy there." He wanted her to stay, wanted it too much to believe that she would be content to live here in the village with him. Still he looked for some sign that she truly, sincerely, wanted to remain.

"I was happy in my cabin," she said, sounding as if she was still upset that he'd taken her away.

"The forest is too dangerous for a woman and a child alone."

She didn't say a thing as she turned to gaze out over the calm waters of the lake.

"Emily?"

The way he said her name made her pulse skitter before it thumped steadily again. She looked at him then with dull eyes. "I will be ready to leave in four days," she told him.

He would have liked to believe that she was upset about leaving the village—upset about leaving him. He knew he'd been foolish for hoping that she wouldn't become angry at the reminder that he'd taken her away from her home.

They stared at one another for what seemed to Forest Thunder like an eternity, as he looked for some sign that she could be happy staying here with him. He didn't speak about that night. If it had meant more to her than a pleasurable experience of shared desire, she would say something about it, anything.

He started to open his mouth to bring up the subject, but quickly closed it. She'd been a married woman. Physical satisfaction was nothing new to her. If her time with him had meaning, she would have mentioned it.

A rumbling in the distance drew his attention to the sky, which suddenly looked dark across the lake. The impending thunderstorm seemed to mirror the emotional storm brewing inside him.

"A storm comes. Do not stay here too long. My mother will be worried."

A hurt look entered Emily's expression. "Tell your mother I will return to the longhouse shortly."

He was frustrated when she averted her gaze and refused to look his way again. "Emily."

She didn't turn. "I am coming, Forest Thunder. I know I must shelter my baby from a rainstorm." Christopher whimpered then started to fuss.

Any reply he might have made was lost to deaf ears, as Emily dismissed his presence to tend to her son.

She couldn't wait any longer. The wedding feast was the next day, and she needed to leave that night. There would be too much activity for anyone to notice her absence. Tonight was the perfect time to leave.

For the last two days she'd been secreting supplies and hiding them in the woods. She had stored enough dried venison, corn cakes, and beans to see her through the journey home. In the same forest clearing, she'd hid Christopher's cradleboard. This afternoon, while Water Blossom was occupied elsewhere, she had packed a satchel with supplies for Christopher. She had even tucked in a small fur to keep her baby warm at night.

Emily shivered as she contemplated the dangers of the journey. But what else could she do but go? She would not be taken to the English settlement and risk having her son sold into bondage. And what of their safety? Richard Malkins was an evil man, who would abuse not only her, but her child.

Perhaps I can convince Forest Thunder to let me stay, she thought. She shook her head. It had become apparent early on that Forest Thunder had made up his mind that the best place for her was the English fort. He hadn't asked her to stay after that wonderful night spent in each other arms. What made her think that he'd allow her to stay because she'd asked him?

He said he is concerned for my welfare. No, she couldn't risk it. If he knew the truth and insisted that she had nothing to fear at the English fort, then she would have lost her last chance of returning to the cabin. No doubt he'd keep a closer watch on her, because of her reluctance to go.

When the villagers had settled down for the night, Emily rose from the sleeping platform, slipped the strap of her satchel over her arm, and carefully lifted Christopher. She prayed her baby would continue to sleep peacefully until they were safely away from the Onondaga village. She still had to get past the Iroquois guards. They might not stop her if they saw her, but she didn't want to be seen.

She hurried out of the longhouse and into the night air. Emily paused a moment to look up at the sky. It was a clear night with no threat of rain. She breathed a sigh of relief and headed toward the stockade gate, her gaze alert for signs of movement.

Guests from the Seneca village had been arriving daily. Would the guards be less vigil, perhaps preoccupied because of the impending wedding? Emily hoped so.

She was relieved to find that God and luck was with her. There was no sign of the Onondaga guards. Emily headed quickly toward her stashed supplies. She wanted to get them and be gone before her absence was noted. What would Water Blossom do when she found her gone? Would she tell Forest Thunder, or believe Emily's departure was for the best and allow her the time to get away?

She found the supplies and tucked what food items she could in the satchel, after having made room by removing the fur for Christopher. It was a beautiful night. The moon was bright enough to light up the trail. Emily wrapped Christopher in the fur and then strapped him into the cradleboard. After lifting her baby to her back, Emily picked up the satchel and left the Onondaga village in the direction she thought was the way home.

The trail was surprisingly easy to follow. On the way there, they'd followed a well-worn path for a large part of the journey. She found the path easily enough.

It was the detour into the woods later that concerned Emily. Trying not jump at every little sound, Emily headed home to the cabin she'd shared with James Russell. The image in her mind wasn't that of her late husband James, but of the man she'd left behind in the Onondaga village.

The village was a hive of activity as the Onondagas began their day along with their Seneca brothers. The two Indian tribes would be united by the marriage of a daughter and a son. Everyone was involved in the final preparations for the ceremony and the feast that would follow. Water Blossom rose from her bed to join the other women down at the lake. This morning the village matrons and maidens would take part in the bathing ceremony of the bride. Water Blossom saw that Emily and Christopher were gone from their bed. With the belief that Emily had awoken earlier and was already down by the water, the matron gathered the clothing she would wear that day and headed to the lake.

She didn't see Emily at the lake, but she wasn't concerned, as the water was crowded with women from both the Onondaga and Seneca villages. She laughed and chatted with the rest and helped prepare the bride for her wedding. It wasn't until much later that afternoon, after the ceremony, that Water Blossom gave thought to Emily and her son. She went looking for her to see if the Englishwoman had enjoyed the wedding ceremony. She asked others if they'd seen Emily, and started to worry when no one confessed to having seen the white woman that day. She hurried toward her cubicle and found the baby's cradleboard missing. She wouldn't have been alarmed, except she knew that Emily had been unhappy lately. . . . Since the night the Englishwoman had been with her son.

Water Blossom went back to the gathering to continue her

search for Emily. She spoke with several matrons, who hadn't seen the white woman or her baby. She began to fear that Emily had left the compound to find the fort on her own.

"*Uk-no-hah.*" My mother.

Water Blossom spun to face her son. "Forest Thunder! I'm glad you're here!"

Forest Thunder frowned. "What's wrong? What is it?"

"The white woman—Emily. I think she has left our village. She wasn't in her bed this morning and no one has seen her all day."

"Gone?" he said.

She nodded. "No one has seen her. The cradleboard is gone." She closed her eyes briefly. "A water-skin is missing."

"Have you checked by the lake?"

"Yes. She did not come to bathe today. I did not see this at first, for the matrons were busy. But I have asked many, and no one has seen Emily or her child since before last night."

Water Blossom saw the emotion that transformed her son's face. *He loves her,* she thought. She recognized the agony, the knowledge of love lost.

"I will find her," he vowed.

"You will go to the English fort?" she said with concern.

Forest Thunder shook his head, suddenly recalling Emily's reluctance to go there. "She is heading home," he said. "She did not want to leave her cabin." He saw his mother's surprise. "I made her go."

"You cared for her even then?" she asked.

He felt the jolt in his insides, as he realized it was true. From the first, even though he thought Emily capable of abandoning her child, something about her had drawn his fascination and desire. As he'd learned more about the woman, the desire became a longing so intense it nearly consumed him. With his fascination had come respect and admiration for her. Soon he recognized his feelings as love. He couldn't forget their night, when she'd given of herself so sweetly ... and concerned herself with his pleasure and satisfaction. Still, he had wanted to deny his feelings to protect himself. He had seen how his mother had suffered from love. He had wanted to shield not only his own heart but Emily's. But it was too late, he realized. The thought of her gone was unbearable to him. He would find her and bring her back . . . and convince her that she would be happy staying with him—forever.

"I care for her," he admitted. "I love her and want to take her to wife. I love the boy."

Water Blossom's eyes filled with tears. "Forest Thunder—"

"Do not worry, Mother. I am willing to risk my heart if it means having some time with her."

"No," she said. "You don't understand. It is my fault that she wanted to leave. She loves you. I saw this and became afraid. I told her you would be taking her away from here."

"As I agreed I should," he said. "The fault is not yours. I could have told her of my love, but I chose instead to protect my heart." He smiled as he touched his mother's cheek. "My heart is in her hands. I cannot take it back."

Water Blossom managed to smile through her tears. "Then you had best find her and bring her home again." Her smile faded. "Hurry before something happens to her. There are dangers to Emily and the baby in these woods."

Forest Thunder's expression was sober as he nodded and lowered his hand. "I will find her."

"Take others with you," his mother suggested. "Big Hair. Soaring Bird."

He inclined his head, before he turned away.

"Forest Thunder!" Her voice had drawn his gaze again. "Emily and her son are good people. May the spirits guide you and bring all of you back safely."

For the first time, Forest Thunder grinned. "When this wedding feast is over, you must prepare for another. I will find Emily and Christopher and bring them back to start a new life."

* * *

Clutching her son tightly, Emily shook like a leaf in a thunderstorm. She and her baby were up in a tree. Pacing on the ground below her was a black bear, a big hungry, angry bear. The same kind of animal that had killed her husband James. Fortunately she'd heard and seen the animal before it heard and saw her. She had managed to climb the tree to relative safety before it caught a whiff of her scent. Injured, the animal was crazed with pain and bloodlust. But as the bear began to paw the tree trunk, Emily began to wonder whether or not they were high enough to be safe. *Bears can climb trees,* she thought. *Not this one—he's hurt.*

The animal growled with a trumpeting roar and stretched his long legs as if to climb the tree. Emily shrieked and tried to climb higher, but the branches up above were thinner, less sturdy. Fear of breaking branches under their shared weight kept her from climbing too high. She imagined falling to the ground with her baby, their broken bodies easy prey for the hungry bear's large jaws. She shuddered as she recalled James's mauled body. She wouldn't allow that to happen to her baby. She would sit up in the tree all day and night if she had to. Eventually the injured bear would tire and move on—she hoped and prayed for it.

Christopher was fussing, had been for a long time now. Her baby was cradled between the tree and her body. Fortunately, earlier she had stopped to rest and had taken him out of his cradleboard. When the bear had appeared, she'd sought safety by scrambling with her baby up the tree.

Emily had no idea how long she'd been up on the tree branch. She was aware that her limbs felt numb, and she'd spent what seemed like an eternity trying to calm her crying baby.

Fear and frustration made Emily cry.

"It's all right, baby," she sobbed. "Mama's here. I've got you."

She had a cramp in the arm that held her son, but she didn't dare try to shift him. She wouldn't move until she'd reached the point when the arm might give out.

Christopher was hungry. No doubt he had soaked his wetting-cloth, but he would have to endure it a little while longer. The bear gouging the bark at the base of the tree made it impossible to consider making Christopher more comfortable. So she had to endure the fear and the noise until someone came to help, or the bear left.

She felt dizzy and closed her eyes. She had been up in the tree for hours. She could still hear the bear below. Every muscle in her body ached. Christopher had fallen asleep after crying himself to exhaustion. His discomfort and tears had made Emily weep openly.

How much longer could she hold on? She was afraid that her strength was drying up and soon she and her sweet baby would be at the mercy of the hurt bear.

She'd done nothing but reflect on her life since she'd been in that tree. She suffered regrets . . . for not being able to love James the way a wife should . . . for not staying and acting on her love for Forest Thunder. She had never told him how she felt. It might have made a difference. He might have felt the same way, and asked her to stay.

She would never have an opportunity to tell Forest Thunder of her love, never see her baby grow up to become a man, to find his own love and have children.

Emily realized that she was in serious danger of giving up. She took her last bit of energy to pray silently. It was her only hope—the miracle that would save her and Christopher from the bear. She had been foolish to head back to the cabin on her own. She should have told Forest Thunder about her indenture to Richard Malkins. Why hadn't she? Because she was ashamed. It had been humiliating enough giving an account of Malkins's attack to her friend James. Telling the story to Forest

Thunder, the man she loved, would have been impossible, for she'd feared how he would view her after learning of the attack.

"Emily!"

She thought she was dreaming Forest Thunder's voice, her longing for him making her hallucinate.

"Em-i-lee!" he called up to her. "Don't move."

The sudden roar of the bear had Emily opening her eyes to gaze blearily down at the ground. She blinked. Was that Forest Thunder and two other braves facing the animal?

Emily stared, but could barely see. It looked like Forest Thunder and two of his friends, but were they real? Or was she delirious and seeing things?

She decided it could be real.

"No!" she cried. "Stay back. He'll kill you!" Hallucination or not, she had to warn him.

One of the Indians drew his bow. He shot an arrow, which struck the bear in the neck. The animal bellowed loudly and faced its attacker up on its hind legs. Another brave let loose an arrow, which pierced the bear's flesh close near the first one.

Blood gushed from both wounds. The animal, weakened by his previous injury, lost strength. Staggering, it dropped to the ground with a thud. After several seconds, Forest Thunder rushed forward with a knife to make the sure that the animal was dead. Emily couldn't look, wasn't sure what was real or just wishful thinking.

She clung to the tree as if frozen, with her eyes shut, and her baby now awake again and crying within her arms. She felt the branch beneath her bend. She cried out and was immediately encircled by a strong arm. She turned her head.

"Forest Thunder!" Tears of love and joy welled up in her eyes, blinding her to his expression. "Are you real?" she gasped. "Or am I dreaming you?"

His laughter was too close, too heartfelt to be anything but real. "I'm here, my love, and I've come to take you home."

"To the cabin?"

"To the village, where you belong." He had lifted himself up on the branch below hers. He bent and kissed her lips. . . . and then her tear-wet eyelids. He lifted his head. "I love you."

"You do?" She was stunned. It must be a dream. Surely something this wonderful couldn't be happening to her. She blinked to better see him. She prayed that it wasn't a dream.

Forest Thunder nodded. He couldn't smile. He was still reeling with fear from when he'd first spied her up in the tree with the bear below. It hadn't taken them long to find her. He, Big Hair, and Soaring Bird could travel like the wind; they were known and respected for their running ability within the village. He thought of what could have happened if another hour had gone by before he'd learned of Emily's absence. He experienced a gut-wrenching fear so great that it gave him pain.

He banished his fears to tend to Emily. She was trembling. He could see her weakness, feel her pain. He must take special care with her. He needed to get her down from the tree.

He called on Big Hair for help, because of the brave's strength. The tree swayed as the brave climbed up the other side. Emily gasped when she saw the Indian, probably remembering their encounter by the lake. Big Hair knew better now. If he hadn't known it before the search for Emily, he knew now that the woman belonged to Forest Thunder.

She refused to move at first. Forest Thunder encouraged her to release her baby into Big Hair's care. She finally relented, and handing Christopher into the brave's arms told them all how much she trusted Forest Thunder.

When Forest Thunder saw that his friend had brought the baby safely to the ground, he turned to the woman he loved.

"Come, love, it's your turn," he said gently. "Put your arms about my neck, and I'll carry you down the tree."

"I can climb down," she insisted.

"Then we'll climb down together," he said, "but please put your arms around me and hold tight."

He moved back to gaze into her face and was astonished and delighted by her sudden mischievous smile. "I like holding you tight," she admitted softly.

Heat warmed his insides—heat and a tenderness for the woman in his arms. "Then I'll never let go of you," he said.

"You promise?"

"Before your God and the Great Spirit," he vowed, with a sudden intensity that stole Emily's breath.

"I thought you'd never come," she said.

"You couldn't have stopped me from following."

"Because you love me?"

His eyes glowed. "Because I love you."

"It's a miracle," she whispered, "because I love you, too. I thought you wanted me to go."

"Never," he said, as he began to guide her down the tree. "Never even for a minute did I want to send you away from me."

They turned to each other when they were safely on the ground. "Marry me?" Forest Thunder asked.

Christopher was crying. Emily looked at her son, and knew that he could wait just a second longer. She needed to answer Forest Thunder; she'd been given the gift of his love. She wanted to return it.

"I'll marry you," she said, leaning forward to kiss him.

What started as a gentle kiss became a fiery exchange, fueled by their love for each other and their last moments of fear.

Emily broke away, gasping. "I must see to our son," she said without thinking.

Forest Thunder's sharp intake of breath had her facing him with Christopher in her arms after she'd taken the child from Big Hair. She saw his expression and smiled.

"James was a good man, but he isn't alive to be Christopher's father. You don't mind if I think of you as my baby's father, do you?"

Big Hair and Soaring Bird had moved away to give the

couple privacy, perhaps sensing that they needed to be alone after their ordeal. Emily opened her gown to allow Christopher to nurse.

Forest Thunder shook his head. "I am honored to be his father, just as I will be honored to be your husband."

Emily smiled as she felt an overwhelming joy. "Just as I will be honored to be the Onondaga wife of Forest Thunder."

ABOUT THE AUTHOR

Candace McCarthy lives with her family in Dover, Delaware. She is the author of many Zebra historical romances, including *White Bears's Woman* and *Irish Linen*. Her newest historical romance, *Sweet Possession*, is now on sale at bookstores everywhere. Candy loves to hear from her readers and you may write to her c/o Zebra Books. Please include a self-addressed stamped envelope if you wish a response.

GAMBLER'S FULL HOUSE

JEAN WILSON

CHAPTER 1

Deidre Parfait paused in the schoolhouse doorway to catch her breath. Although the school board frowned on her practice of giving the children an afternoon recess, she needed the fifteen minutes' reprieve to muster the strength to finish the day.

With shouts of laughter, the youngsters scurried to their seats. One boy tossed a pine cone which landed at Deidre's feet. A hush fell over the room. She resisted the temptation to fling it right back at the mischiefmaker. Instead, she tucked it in her pocket and counted heads.

A quick glance told her that two black-haired hellions were missing—Peter and Paul Christopher, misnamed brats she referred to as Lucifer I and Lucifer II. If there was trouble in the class, the pair were usually the instigators. What else would one expect from six-year-old identical twins being reared by Mr. Radcliff Christopher? Their uncle's reputation as a womanizer, gambler, and rogue was legendary.

Before she framed the question as to their whereabouts, Sally Jane Hansen stood and announced to the class, ''Peter and Paul are down by the woodshed.'' The eight-year-old tilted her nose and planted her hands on her pudgy hips. ''My ma says they need to go behind the woodshed for a good licking.''

''That's quite enough, Sally Jane,'' Deidre said, not willing to voice an agreement. In the two months since Deidre had been forced to take the position as teacher in the small mining town of Blissful, Colorado—a town that so far hadn't begun to live up to its name—Sally had tattled on every child in the eight grades. Of course, she also reported the teacher's every word and action to her mother. Mrs. Hansen served as head of the school board, as well as being Deidre's landlady at the boardinghouse.

As she reached for the bell to summon the boys, twin cyclones barreled past her, nearly tumbling her from her feet. Peter and Paul dashed to their seats and shoved a wicker basket under their chairs. Paul whispered to his brother, and Peter elbowed him in the ribs.

Deidre didn't dare question them on the basket's contents. Nearly every day the pair brought one surprise or another to class. In the past weeks, they had been graced with snakes, insects, a kitten, a raccoon, and even a nest of tiny birds. With only an hour until dismissal, she chose to ignore their latest discovery.

''Please take out your slates for our spelling lesson,'' she instructed, with the schoolteacher tone she'd developed over the past weeks. As many times a day as she raised her voice to get the children's attention, it was a wonder she had any vocal cords left. Ruining her voice would spell disaster to a dream already in shambles. ''Who studied the list of words I gave you yesterday?''

As expected, Sally Jane was first to stick up her hand. Most of the girls followed suit, and a few of the boys. ''Peter and Paul never study. That's why they're so dumb,'' the girl announced. ''Their housekeeper quit and their uncle stays in the saloon all night.''

Peter stuck out his tongue at the girl. "We do so study. We can say the ABC's all the way to *m*, we can count to a hundred."

Not to be outdone, his brother Paul added, "We know a bunch of ways to add to twenty-one, and that a full house beats two pairs."

"Yeah, and you never draw to an inside straight."

Deidre groaned. Their education left a lot to be desired, as did their home life. "That's enough," she said. "All of you, sit down." At times she felt sorry for the orphaned boys. It wasn't their fault their parents had died and left them with an irresponsible uncle as their guardian.

After the children spelled half of their assigned words, a whimper came from the side of the room. Deidre ignored the sound, certain it came from the basket under Peter's chair. As the lesson continued, the sound grew louder, and became more insistent, until the "critter" let out a loud squeal.

She jumped. Peter reached down and jiggled the basket. "Shhh," he whispered.

Every child in the room stared at the twins. The girls giggled and the boys snickered. The noise grew louder and more insistent. Deidre didn't like critters, and she was certain she wasn't going to like the creature that screeched like a dying wildcat.

Paul leaped to his feet and snatched up the basket. "Miss Teacher, we gots to go."

She caught the boy by his nape and hauled him back to his seat. "What's in the basket?" The noise sounded like a baby's cries. Almost afraid to look, she lifted the corner of the pink blanket and dropped it like a hot potato. Her eyes must be deceiving her, she thought. Lifting the blanket higher, her heart stopped beating. Small arms flailed the air, and tiny legs fought to be freed from a long white gown. The little round face crowned with a head of dark fuzz was twisted in anger and damp with tears.

The twin's critter was a tiny infant—a human baby badly

in need of attention. It was either hungry, dirty, wet, or all three.

Over the baby's screams, she questioned the pair. "Where did this come from? What are you doing with a baby? Did you steal it?"

"No, ma'am," Peter said. "We ain't never stole nothing."

Paul added, "A lady gave it to us."

By then every youngster in the class had gathered into a heap, each straining for a look at the baby. The girls murmured how cute the infant was, and asked to hold it. Deidre ignored them.

"What lady?" she asked.

"We ain't never seen her before." It was Paul who answered—or was it Peter? She was getting as confused as the situation.

"Where is she?"

"She left. Said we was to take the baby to our uncle."

Deidre picked up the child and the crying stopped. Tucked in the corner of the basket were a half dozen or so squares of cloth. Quickly she changed the diaper and returned the baby girl to the basket, all the while wondering what kind of woman would give her child to two little boys.

Clean and dry, the baby waved her arms and made funny noises. Not sure how to handle the situation, she wrote a note, demanding Mr. Christopher's immediate attendance. The twins and their find were his responsibility. Let him handle this problem. She had more trouble of her own than she could manage.

Handing the note to Peter, she ordered him to find his uncle and return immediately to class.

After the disruption, Deidre knew it was useless to try to teach. She dismissed the class early and settled at her desk to await Mr. Christopher's arrival.

* * *

Rad Christopher sipped the liquid in his glass and tapped his hole card. His eyes burned from the smoke and stale air. Only his girls knew he never drank alcohol, and that he sipped tea all night long to stay awake and alert. Nor did he frequent their rooms. When he felt the need for female companionship, he visited an old friend in Denver.

The card game had begun after midnight, and continued into daylight. He hadn't made it home this morning, so he'd sent Della, the woman who supervised "the girls," to his house to see that the boys were fed and properly attired for school. At last check it was three o'clock in the afternoon. This hand should wipe out his single remaining opponent—a man too stubborn to quit when he was ahead, and now stood to lose a bundle. The pot hinged on the turn of one card.

"Psst, Miss Della," a young voice broke his concentration. "I needs to give this note to Uncle Rad."

Ignoring his nephew, Rad waited for the card that would either win or lose the game. Nearly every day the pesky new teacher sent a note accusing the twins of one offense or another. Didn't the woman understand that boys would be boys? They were no worse than he and Walt had been as youngsters.

"Tell the teacher I'm busy. She can do whatever she thinks is best," he threw over his shoulder. Rad hadn't slept in over twenty-four hours, and he was in no mood to bother with the woman. Let her earn her keep. After all, he personally paid half her salary, just to keep a teacher in Blissful.

He studied the pile of chips in the middle of the table. Overnight, half a dozen cowboys had lost their month's pay and a prospector had lost the gold it had taken him months to mine. Only he and Henry Abrams were left in the game. The rancher was too shrewd to bet more than he could afford to lose, and played conservatively and close to his vest.

Rad dealt the last card. Unless Henry had an ace-in-a-hole card, Rad's three kings beat Henry's pair of aces. With a disgusted grunt, the other man tuned over a deuce.

"Looks like you got me, Rad. I'm busted."

Chewing on the unlit cigar, Rad stuck out his hand to a formidable opponent. "Tell you what, Henry. Let's play one more hand."

"No, thanks, Rad. I've got nothing left. I'm not like that other bunch, and gamble away everything I've worked thirty years to get. Why, the missus would have my head on a silver platter."

"I'll bet the entire pot against the thoroughbred you brought from Texas."

The rancher narrowed his eyes suspiciously. "Black Star? He's only worth half this much."

"Then sell him to me."

"Now, Rad, what do you want with a racehorse? You never ride, and he's too temperamental to hitch to that fancy buggy of yours." Henry took Rad's offered cigar and shoved it into his shirt pocket.

Rad rubbed a hand along his thigh. After being up for so many hours, it ached like a rotten tooth. Since he'd been thrown from the horse ten years before, the bone had never healed properly and he was forced to walk with the aid of a cane.

"Call me sentimental. I was brought up on a Kentucky horse farm. Black Star is a reminder of home."

The thoroughbred stallion was a dead ringer for the one that had nearly ruined Rad. He'd lost the race and, in the bargain, any chance of salvaging his family's farm. Maybe he was a glutton for punishment in wanting the horse, or maybe he wanted to prove something to himself. He was too tired to understand which.

While Henry studied on the proposition, Rad wondered what rule the twins had broken this time. In the six months since their parents had died, he'd done his darnedest to care for the boys. After all they'd suffered in losing their parents and being shipped halfway across the country to an uncle they didn't know, he didn't have the heart to discipline them as he should.

As their only living relative, it was either Rad or an orphanage. There was no choice at all.

He'd built a house on the land he owned outside of town and hired a housekeeper. Unfortunately, the women he hired, widows all, ended up marrying newly wealthy gold miners, and left him high and dry. The latest had left three days ago.

Henry finished his drink and slapped his hand on the table. "Rad, you have a deal. Seven-card stud—nothing wild."

Deidre let out a sigh of relief when Peter raced into the classroom. By then the baby was stirring and sucking her fists. She would soon have to be fed.

"Uncle Rad said he was busy and that you was to do what you please."

Now, why did she expect Rad Christopher to show up and act responsible when so far he'd shown total disregard for her notes and instructions? This time he wasn't going to ignore her.

The boy looked from the baby to Deidre. The youngsters had the darkest eyes and hair—the exact color as their uncle's. That was no surprise since their father and Rad were twins. "Are you gonna whup us?"

"No." However, she was tempted to whup their irresponsible uncle. "We're going to find your uncle and let him decide what to do."

The basket on her arm, she closed the schoolhouse door and started down the path toward their home. "He ain't at home, Miss Teacher," Peter informed her. "He's at the Silver Spur."

She slowed her steps. At the saloon, in the middle of the afternoon? Everybody knew the action didn't start until after dark. Did the nefarious activities now extend into the daylight hours? Changing directions, she headed straight down Washington Avenue, Blissful's main street, and approached the saloon.

After the early dismissal, she was certain that word of the

twins and the baby had spread like the plague among the gossips. She ignored the curious glances and marched right up to the open doorway of the saloon. She was acutely aware that decent women did not frequent such establishments. As the schoolteacher, however temporary, she had to maintain a spotless reputation.

Standing on the boardwalk, she called out, "Mr. Christopher, are you in there?"

The baby started to squirm and any second would demand a feeding. From working in her father's Fort Smith general store, she knew all about nursing bottles and canned milk. At least Rad would have a way to feed the baby when he accepted responsibility. His many lady friends could offer advice and assistance. As for Deidre, she couldn't wait to rid herself of the burden.

"I'm busy. Go away," a deep male voice shouted from somewhere in the dim interior.

"I must see you. Now."

No answer. The man clearly intended to ignore her. A woman clad in a green satin gown with an immodest amount of bosom showing, appeared at the door. "Rad said—"

"I don't give a fig about what Rad said," Deidre cut her off. "I'm going to see him, now."

"You can't."

"Want to bet? That's what he does here, isn't it?" Shoving past the overly made-up redhead, she stalked straight through, into the devil's very own lair.

The large room was virtually empty. Chairs were piled atop tables, and the floor was freshly swept. In a corner two men sat at a round table, red, blue, and white chips piled in the middle between them. Both looked up at her approach. Although she'd only come face-to-face with Rad Christopher a couple of times, she was always struck by his dark, dangerous good looks. She'd been duly warned to stay away from the notorious man. Not that she needed a warning. She'd been taken in by good looks once, and she'd learned a cold, hard lesson. The good women of Blissful had nothing to worry about.

The other man, Henry Abrams, leapt to his feet. His eyes bugged out like a toad's. "Miss Parfait, what are you doing here?" Henry's daughter Henrietta and two sons were in the class, and he was a member of the school board. So much for her reputation.

Rad rose more slowly, and leaned heavily on the edge of the table. "Get out of here, woman," he said, in a voice soft and decidedly dangerous. As always he was dressed entirely in black and white. His suit fit to perfection, but today was wrinkled, and his waistcoat was open over his white shirt. A silk necktie hung loose to his wide chest.

"I'll not have you continue to disregard my notes, Mr. Christopher. This time it's too important."

Ignoring her, he returned his gaze to Henry. "Deal that last card. My concentration is shot." He settled back in his chair and tossed back the contents of a glass. "Then I'll take care of you," he shot at Deidre.

She refused to be intimidated by a man who drank in the middle of the afternoon, gambled away a fortune, and who knew what he did with the women who worked the upstairs rooms.

As Henry flipped a card from the deck, she set the basket on the table. The baby let out a lusty howl that would surely raise the dead. "Now are you ready to listen?" she asked, her temper on its last notch.

"Looks like you won yourself a racehorse, Rad," Henry said on the turn of a card. His gaze shifted to the baby. She'd thrown off her blanket and was waving arms and legs in protest. "And a lot of trouble, to boot."

Rad bit back a string of curses. "Are you touched in the head, woman, bringing a baby in here?" Ignoring the stack of chips that totaled nearly a thousand dollars, he glared at the schoolteacher. In a plain brown dress and her hair tucked under a bonnet, she resembled every spinster he'd ever encountered. It must be some kind of uniform, or rule that a teacher should be plain as white bread.

"Don't yell at me, Mr. Christopher. Talk to these two. They brought this into my class." She glared at him, her blue eyes flashing fire. Most decent women wouldn't bid him the time of day, much less barge into the saloon and face him toe-to-toe. The woman had grit, that was sure.

The twins darted behind the teacher's skirts for protection. He'd never taken a hand to either boy, but there was a first time for everything. They often brought home strays, but never before a baby.

"Where did you get this?" he asked. The baby was crying, tears streaming down her cheeks. "Do something, will you, woman?"

"I do have a name." She picked up the baby and it began rooting at her bosom.

He ignored the sarcasm. "Well?"

Paul spoke up first. "A lady gave it to us. We didn't know it was a girl."

As if being a girl or boy made any difference. "What lady?"

"We don't know. She called us behind the woodshed and gave it to us."

As the baby howled, the teacher stared at him as if he'd grown horns. Rad suddenly developed a splitting headache. "Exactly what did she tell you?"

"That we should bring the baby to you," said Peter.

Paul continued. "She said for you to take care of it. That you're the papa."

CHAPTER 2

She should have known. The notorious lothario had gotten caught in his own trap. For a second she felt sorry for the man. Under a day's growth of whiskers, his bronzed face paled. Rad stumbled back and dropped into his chair. She knew about his bad leg, that he limped and walked with a gold-handled cane. Although she had no idea how he'd come about the injury, she wouldn't doubt the cause was a woman. He'd probably gotten shot in the leg by an irate husband.

Henry gasped, and the red-haired woman shot the gambler an angry glance. The baby continued to cry, her howls growing more and more lusty. Deidre had to do something. It seemed that the other so-called adults in the room had become paralyzed.

"Peter and Paul," she instructed in her schoolteacher voice. "Go to the mercantile and tell Mr. Hansen to give you a can of milk and a nursing bottle. Have him charge it to your uncle's account, and bring it to me immediately." She jiggled the infant, hoping to quell the angry cries. "Do not dillydally. Your little cousin is starved."

Rad regained his composure. "Cousin? Now listen here, woman, I'm not that child's father. And you don't give orders around here."

Ignoring the man's angry retort, she gestured to the twins. "Go."

They glanced at their uncle's furious face, and darted out the bat-wing doors. As if the baby's cries were a signal of some kind, men began to trickle into the saloon, while women craned their necks like ostriches above the doors. She glanced at the gathering spectators.

"Is there anyplace we can go for a bit of privacy? We'll also need a stove to heat the milk."

"No," Rad replied, his voice hard and cold. "Get out of here, and take that kid with you."

She cooed to the baby. "It's all right, sweetheart, the big man won't hurt you." Then she lifted her equally angry gaze to the coldhearted gambler who would throw out his own child to the wolves. "Mr. Christopher, this is your child. I'll go, but the baby stays."

Henry Abrams backed away from the commotion. "Rad, you'd better do as the teacher suggests. You're attracting a crowd. I'll bring Black Star out to your place in the morning."

"That is not my child. I don't know what kind of scheme you're pulling, woman—"

"My name is Miss Parfait, and I had nothing to do with this latest mischief your nephews have concocted."

"Miss Parfait," he ground out from between even white teeth, "I repeat, that is not my child."

"How can you be so sure? The boys said the woman told them it was yours." She stopped short of accusing him of having so many affairs that he couldn't keep up if he tried.

"Who was the woman?" he demanded.

She set the baby at her shoulder and swayed as if dancing. The cries stilled momentarily. "I have no idea. Not only did

I not see her, I do not know all the women that you've— I believe that you understand.''

"I understand that I'm being accused of fathering a child by an unknown woman. And you're charging its food to me."

"Would you rather an innocent infant starve to death? Or die of exposure and neglect?"

His lips thinned to a slash across his handsome face. "Of course not. I'll pay for the milk, then we'll find the sheriff and let him handle the situation."

The color drained from her face. "We will not turn this child over to an old man like Sheriff Lindsay. He's a bachelor, and besides, he's off working his claim."

"Well, I don't want it," Rad declared.

Deidre's gaze shifted from the totally selfish man to the face of the hungry little girl. "Until we find the mother, and get to the bottom of this, you're stuck with her."

As if she knew they were discussing her, the baby resumed her howls. Deidre resisted the urge to shove the child into Rad's arms. But she wouldn't wish that man on a dog, much less an infant. At that moment, the boys darted around the milling crowd and skidded to a stop in front of their uncle.

"We gots the milk," said Peter.

Paul shoved a glass bottle toward Deidre. "And a funny-looking bottle with this thing." He held up a rubber nipple.

The red-haired woman touched Deidre's arm. "Come with me, honey. I've got a small kitchen upstairs. We can heat the milk, and get you out of the limelight."

A relieved sigh escaped from Deidre's lips. She'd fully expected Rad Christopher to toss her and the baby out into the dusty street. At least his woman had a bit of civility. "Thank you," she said.

Before she'd taken three steps, an angry female voice came from the doors. "Miss Parfait, you aren't going up there, are you?"

She stopped, and turned around. Mrs. Hansen stood outside

the dreaded establishment, several other women at her side. "Unless you want to take this baby home, and feed her, I suppose I have no other choice. I don't know when she was last fed, and it's clear she's starved."

"But you don't know what goes on up there." The woman shot an accusing stare at the only person who'd offered even a bit of assistance.

"I have a pretty good idea. But the baby won't notice." She turned back to the redhead. "Please lead the way, Miss . . ."

"Just Della, honey." The woman sidestepped Rad and, lifting her skirts to show an immodest amount of leg, she led the way up the stairway. "Boys, bring that milk and bottle," she called over her shoulder. "And Rad, you can carry the basket."

The murmur of male voices and female gasps followed them up the stairs. The tap of his cane and the uneven gait told her that Rad trailed behind them.

How had he gotten into this mess? Rad wondered, as he snatched the basket and obeyed the woman's orders. There was no way the baby could be his. Over the years, he'd been more than careful in his liaisons. Not only did he not sleep with his "girls," he also never had anything to do with the women of the town. Yet, since his nephews had found the baby, and the mother blamed him, he was obligated to at least try to get to the bottom of the situation.

When he reached the small kitchen where the girls prepared their meals, Della and the teacher had already begun to heat the milk and sterilize the nipple and bottle. The baby was rooting at the teacher's bosom, and crying because there was nothing there.

His gaze followed the baby's mouth nuzzling at the woman's bosom—a very nice bosom under the dampness spread by the baby's rooting mouth and cries. He turned his gaze away, appalled at the direction of his thoughts. Rad was in a mess, and he had no business thinking of the schoolteacher in such a manner. Looked like he needed another trip to Denver. But not until he got this mess straightened out.

He'd known that Della was a pretty good cook, but he hadn't expected her to know anything about babies. As the teacher filled the bottle with milk, Della offered instructions on how much water to add, and opened a jar of honey. "Babies like a little sweetness. Makes it digest better, too."

Miss Parfait smiled her thanks. It was the first time he'd seen the woman do anything but frown or fuss at the boys. Her face transformed into that of a woman much younger than he'd supposed. And pretty, too. She'd removed her ugly bonnet, and stray wisps of wheat-colored hair had escaped the tight bun at her nape.

"Here we go, sweetheart," she crooned. The baby's mouth grabbed at the nipple and she sucked noisily. Peter and Paul knelt on chairs to watch the baby. Their eyes were wide with interest.

"How come it can't eat with a spoon like the rest of us?" Peter asked.

" 'Cause it's a baby, you dope," his twin announced. "Babies have to drink milk, and their hands are too little to hold a glass."

"Boys," Rad admonished, knowing that a confrontation was about to erupt.

Della laughed. "Looks like you've got a full house, Rad. Or at least two pairs."

"Don't get smart with me, woman. How do you know so much about babies?"

"I didn't always do this for a living, you know," she said, a note of sadness in her voice. "I had brothers and sisters, once upon a time."

He filled a cup from the coffeepot on the stove. Della had been with him since he'd won the Silver Spur a couple of years ago. When he'd first hired her, she had assumed they would be lovers, but he soon made it clear that their relationship was strictly business. It never was his style to mix business with pleasure. That was a sure way to lose an able employee and get into trouble. Della was good with the other girls, and kept them in line. She seldom took customers, preferring to supervise and run the saloon. The woman had a good head for business, and Rad didn't want to ruin a perfectly good friendship. He couldn't have managed the Silver Spur and the twins without her help.

Now it looked as if added responsibility had been heaped onto his already full platter.

While the baby drained the bottle, Della sidled up to him. "Rad, we'll be opening soon, and things could get worse. When the girls get wind of the baby, they'll be in here adding to the confusion. And that Mrs. Hansen didn't look any too pleased."

"Exactly where am I supposed to take the baby?" He watched the baby in the teacher's arms. Her hands were soft and sure as she patted the infant's back and made it burp.

Both boys laughed aloud. Then each did his own version of a loud belch. Rad shot them a quelling glance.

"Your house. Where else?"

"My house? No indeed. I don't even have a housekeeper."

The teacher changed the infant's diaper and wrapped her in the pink blanket. Unexpectedly, she shoved the child into Rad's arms. "That's your problem, Mr. Christopher. I'm going back to the boardinghouse."

He shoved the squirming bundle toward her. "Take her with you."

"I can't. Mrs. Hansen owns the boardinghouse, and I'm certain she won't allow me to board an infant."

As she turned to leave, he caught her arm with his free hand. "Oh, no you don't, lady—I mean, Miss Parfait. You brought this mess on me, and I expect you to help fix it. You're going home with me."

Her blue eyes grew as wide as saucers. It was the first time he'd seen her lose control. "I can't go home with you." She gestured to Della. "Take her with you."

"I have a business to run, honey. Besides, I think you're better qualified to care for a baby." Della backed away and exited through the doorway.

"Pete, run down to the livery and have Smitty hitch up my buggy and bring it around back." He tugged the teacher to the table and shoved her down into a chair. "You can fill in until I get a housekeeper, or until the runaway mother returns."

She shook off his arm, and tilted her nose into the air. "I'm not a housekeeper. I have a class to teach. What will the school board say?"

"You'll soon learn that I don't give a d—fig for what those old biddies say. I'm paying half your salary, so they won't very well go against me." The baby in his arm weighed so little, he hardly noticed he was still holding her until she started to make cooing sounds and blow bubbles. She wasn't bad looking, with brown eyes, and a brushing of dark hair. Her skin was milky, and when she opened her mouth, her toothless grin was kind of funny.

"Can we keep her, Uncle Rad?" Paul asked. The baby grabbed his finger and tried to pull it into her mouth.

"No. As soon as the lady comes back, she'll have to take her baby to her own home."

"What if she doesn't have a home?" Miss Parfait asked. "What if she was so desperate and afraid, she gave the baby to a father who didn't want her or his child?"

Before his bad leg gave way, he sank into a chair and set the baby back in her basket. "I repeat. I am not the father. But if you want me to look after it, you'll have to come home with me and lend a hand. Surely you wouldn't want to turn an innocent child over to a lecher like me, or two demons like the boys, now, would you, Miss Parfait?"

She bit her lip as if considering the problem. "Until you

find a housekeeper or some woman willing to look after the child, I suppose I can lend a hand.''

''Mighty generous.''

He finished his coffee, and waited in silence. Paul spoke softly to the baby, and she answered him back. The teacher sat ramrod-straight, her mouth pulled into a frown.

After what seemed an eternity, Peter raced back into the room. ''Smitty'll be here in a minute,'' the boy said, out of breath. ''Can I play with it when we get home?''

The teacher stood and picked up the basket. ''You'll have to be very gentle with her, or you could hurt her.''

''We ain't never hurt a puppy or a kitten. Or even the little birds in the nest.''

''This isn't a puppy or kitten. She's a sweet little girl.''

Tired of all the sugar-coating, Rad stood and herded the boys to the door. ''We'll go down the back stairs and wait for Smitty.'' He picked up the basket. ''You might as well carry the diapers and milk, Miss Parfait.''

Deidre didn't know how she'd gotten involved with Rad Christopher's problems, but there she was, smack in the middle. She preceded him down the stairs, and waited in the alley for him to catch up. The twins raced ahead, shoving and pulling on one another. ''Boys,'' she called. ''Behave.''

They looked her, then at their uncle. He gave them a hard look, and immediately they quieted. In a jingle of harnesses and horses' clops, Rad's fancy buggy appeared. She'd seen it any number of times. It was solid black, with brass trim. Matching black horses were hitched to the lines. The livery owner leaped down, and Rad gestured her up. She climbed easily on the low step fitted for easy access. He handed her the basket, and climbed up beside her. The twins piled in on the other side, shoving her indecently close to Rad's large and surprisingly muscular frame. She'd thought a saloon owner and gambler would be soft, fleshy. However, this man was well built, and the arm pressed against hers was as sturdy as a tree trunk. She tried to shift away from him to give him more room, but that only caused his arm to brush against her breasts. The twins shoved back, and pushed her even closer to the man.

Thankfully he followed the rear alley rather than subject her to the curious stares of the town. Deidre knew she'd already caused a sensation by entering the saloon, but going to the man's home was sure to bring the wrath of the entire school board down with a vengeance.

Her gaze dropped to the innocent child, now sound asleep. She couldn't deny a child in need. That would be wrong. Why, her poor mother would turn over in her grave if she'd known her beloved Deidre had even entertained such a thought! However, since Papa had died, she'd done other things that would appall the saintly woman. Selling the store and running off with Anthony was the least of her sins.

Unaware that she was frowning, she looked up to find Rad staring at her. "We really aren't that bad, Miss Parfait. You look as if you're headed for the gallows."

She let out a sigh. Being alone in a house with two hellions and a handsome rogue could seal the fate of her teaching career. Not that she wanted to be a teacher. It was pure fate that she'd landed the job when she'd been dumped in Blissful without funds or a job. She'd faked her qualifications, forged references, and just plain lied about her ability. She'd done it all to earn enough money to make it to San Francisco, and fulfill her lifelong dream. Deidre had thought herself through with keeping house, cleaning, and cooking when her father had died. "I am not a housekeeper," she stated in no uncertain terms.

"All you need do is look after the boys and that baby until I can work something out."

"Do you know how to cook good stuff, Miss Teacher?" Peter asked.

"Yes," she replied.

"Can you bake cakes and cookies? Our other housekeeper wouldn't fix us nothing but oatmeal," Paul continued.

"Boys, quit bothering your teacher." Rad clicked the reins, brushing his arm against her breasts. His leg pressed against her in a far-too-familiar manner. Tingles raced over her. Next time they rode in the buggy, the twins would sit in the middle. Deidre would take her chances with falling out rather than endure the torture of Rad's casual touch.

Since she would be stuck at the gambler's home, she might as well try to make the best out of the situation. Gaining the youngsters' trust and assistance would go a long way in making the predicament easier. "What kind do you like?"

"Chocolate cake—"

"And any kind of cookies."

"I'll see what I can do. Although I won't be long at your home. The lady might be waiting at your house right now to take back her baby." She hoped and prayed so. Her reputation would be mud if she had to spend the night under the same roof with the infamous Rad Christopher.

CHAPTER 3

About a mile out of town, Rad turned the buggy down a narrow lane that ran through a stand of tall pines. She'd never seen his home, and was mildly surprised at the neat white house with the wide porch across the front. Everything about the place looked new—the freshly painted house, the large barn, and even the fence posts that stood in a straight line.

Sadly missing, though, was any hint of a woman's touch. Not one flower grew in the grassy beds, nor did a single swing or rocker grace the porch. Set apart from the house were a barn and corral, plus the usual woodshed and cellar house.

Rad pulled to a stop, and leaped down, landing on his good leg. Reaching up, he took the basket from her and offered a hand. His touch was firm and mannerly—as if assisting his elderly grandmother. He released her immediately. At least the man had a modicum of courtesy.

A twin jumped from each side, Peter nearly knocking Deidre off her feet. She staggered, landing flush against Rad's wide chest. Her fingers clutched his black coat for balance. He braced his legs and stood as solid as a tree. His free arm circled her waist. Her eyes were level with the most intriguing patch of black curls that peeked from the open neck of his shirt. Abruptly he steadied her on her feet.

"Pete," he called. "Careful. You almost knocked both of us to the ground."

"Sorry," the boy yelled on his way around the house. His brother followed, hot on his heels.

Rad picked up his cane and gestured toward the porch steps. She hesitated at the door. He reached around her and shoved the door open. One step across the threshold, she stopped, afraid to proceed.

"Go on in," Rad ordered from behind her.

"Did a tornado go through here?" she asked. Clothes, toys, books, and other things she would rather not identify were strewn on the floor, the davenport, the chairs, and the tables.

"Yes, named Peter and Paul." He tossed a pair of trousers off the davenport and set the basket down. "Peter, Paul," he called. "Get in here and clean up this mess."

"Has your housekeeper only been gone three days? I would have thought it took a month to make this mess." She backed toward the door, needing to escape before she got lost in the mess.

"Where are you going?" He shot her an angry glance.

"Out of here. I agreed to help out, but I'm not a miracle worker."

"Lady, you aren't going anywhere." He threw his cane across the doorway, effectively blocking her path. "The boys and I will help clean up this mess. The Chinese laundry picks up once a week. All you'll have to do is keep an eye on the twins and that baby, and cook for them."

"That's all? In addition to teaching school."

"I'll pay a salary. Name your price."

A salary. She hadn't considered that he would pay her. From the first she'd been told that Rad Christopher paid half her teaching salary to keep a teacher for his nephews. With the extra money, if only for a short time, she would have enough to pay her way to San Francisco and survive until she was able to pursue her dream.

She decided to test his mettle. Just how serious was the man? "I'll take twice what you paid your last housekeeper." That should stop him in his tracks.

The man didn't blink an eye. He lowered his cane. "You've got it."

"Another thing." She folded her arms across her chest. "I want a free hand with the boys."

He tilted a dark eyebrow and nodded his assent. "Anything else?"

After a moment's consideration, she continued. "They should attend church."

"It's a deal. You can start cooking their supper while we get started on this mess."

Everything was happening so suddenly, her head was spinning. "Just one minute, Mr. Christopher. I need to get my things from the boardinghouse. Where am I to . . . Oh my." She hadn't considered the sleeping arrangements.

"You needn't worry. We have a private room for the housekeeper. You'll stay there." He led the way down a narrow hallway and opened the door at the end.

On the way, she glanced into the other rooms. A large bedroom, neatly furnished and spotlessly clean, must be his own room. The other door opened to a room in total disarray. Clearly, this room belonged to the boys.

"Hope it suits you." He turned on his heel and headed back to the parlor.

In truth, it was much larger and nicer furnished than her room at the boardinghouse. Covered with a colorful quilt, a comfortable-looking iron bed dominated the room. A walnut bureau and matching mirror was against the wall, and the commode held a fine white bowl and pitcher. Plain calico curtains draped the windows, and a rag rug sat beside the bed.

"By the way, Miss Parfait, we also have an indoor bathing room with running water," he called back over his shoulder.

If the lovely room didn't entice her, having a bath close at hand would do it. She removed her bonnet and gloves and smiled into the mirror. Maybe things could work out, after all.

She returned to the parlor to find the boys busy picking up their discarded belongings. They grumbled and complained, but their uncle kept them busy. "After you finish, you can help me brush down the horses."

"Can we ride?" One of the youngsters looked up from the floor, his eyes pleading his case.

Rad's mouth pulled into a thin line. "No. You're too young."

Paul set his fists on his narrow hips. "Our pa was teaching us. We ain't too little."

A play of emotions swept across his uncle's face. "I'm in charge now, and I'll let you know when you're ready." He stalked toward the door. "Come to the barn when you're finished in here."

What a strange reaction, she thought. Boys and girls younger than the twins often rode to school. With all his money, one would suppose each boy would have his own horse.

"Just because Uncle Rad is scared of horses, ain't no reason we shouldn't ride."

The words stopped her in her tracks. Rad Christopher didn't strike her as a man afraid of anything.

"Yeah. He thinks we're babies."

At the mention of babies, Deidre remembered the infant she was supposed to tend. Thankfully, the child was still asleep. She picked up the basket and carried it with her into the kitchen. At least the kitchen was a little neater than the other rooms. Since losing the housekeeper, they must have taken their meals at Patsy's Cafe in town or with the women at the saloon.

She picked up the few cups and dishes from the table and

set them in a dishpan. The modern cast-iron stove was much nicer than the one she'd had at home in Fort Smith, or the one Mrs. Hansen had at the boardinghouse. She built up a wood fire and made a pot of fresh coffee. Searching the pantry, she found a small assortment of canned goods, flour, potatoes, eggs, and bacon. With the limited larder, she set about to fixing supper.

A half hour later, Deidre wiped the perspiration from her forehead with a scrap of cloth. Without an apron to cover her brown skirt, it was dusted with white flour. Her fine blonde hair had escaped its tight coil, and her face was flushed from the warm oven. At least she'd managed to prepare a decent meal for their supper.

After setting four plates on the kitchen table, she peeked into the parlor. To her surprise, it was reasonably tidy. The boys had finished their chore in record time. She turned toward the window that overlooked the barn. Leaning heavily on his cane, Rad walked slowly toward the house. The twins ran circles around their uncle.

She studied the man who'd run roughshod over her. He'd removed his coat and waistcoat. The sleeves of his once-white shirt were rolled to his elbows, revealing muscular arms. Shiny black hair hung in damp waves in his eyes. With the dark shadow on his cheeks and jaw, he looked every bit as dangerous as she'd been warned he was. Her heart leaped in her chest. As quickly as they came, she tamped down the same kind of flutters that had gotten her in this mess and landed her in Blissful. She'd learned her lesson about handsome men. And from all she'd heard, Rad Christopher was the worst of the lot.

"Supper's ready," she called from the rear porch. Like the front, not a single amenity graced the porch. She supposed they were lucky to have curtains at the windows and quilts on the beds. "Wash up."

"We already did," he said. "I hope you found enough to cook. We're starved."

"It's simple but plentiful. I'll make a list for the general store. We can pick up what we need tomorrow." Since the next day was Saturday, and there was no school, she didn't have to wonder what she would do with the baby. In the next two days, anything was possible.

He nodded.

They'd just settled at the table, when the baby again demanded attention. Deidre jumped up. She'd already heated the milk and filled the bottle. Returning to her chair, she cuddled the baby and fed her.

"Can she have biscuits and gravy?" Paul asked.

"Not yet. She's a mite young."

"How old is she?" Peter stuck his head closer to the infant's.

"Three or four months, I suppose." She looked up at Rad, a question in her gaze. Just who had he been with about a year ago? she wondered. And how could he forget so easily? However, he was a man, and men were different from women. None of them could be trusted any farther than she could throw this house.

He caught her gaze and paused in shoveling the eggs and bacon into his mouth. "It isn't mine."

After feeding the baby and changing her diaper, Deidre served coffee to Rad. His eyes were lined with fatigue.

As she cleared the table, the sound of hoofbeats and the jingle of harnesses came from the long drive. Rad jumped to his feet. It was nearly dark, but neither of them had lit the lamps in the parlor.

Deidre followed and peered around his wide shoulder. A wagon pulled to a stop in front of the porch. Mrs. Hansen perched on the high seat. She frowned when she saw Rad.

"Mr. Christopher, is Miss Parfait here?"

"Yes, ma'am. I'm here," she said. By the look on the woman's face, she hadn't come on a social call.

"Do you intend to live with this man?" she asked, her voice hard and full of condemnation.

"I'll stay until he can get a housekeeper. Somebody has to look after the baby."

"You know this is cause for dismissal from your position. We can't have our teacher living in questionable circumstances."

Rad stepped forward. "Mrs. Hansen, in case you don't remember, you insisted that Miss Parfait sign a six-month contract. You can't fire her unless you're willing to pay her salary for that amount of time. And, of course, leave the children without a teacher."

"Well, I never." The woman ended the sentence with a loud *humph*. "If you insist in staying here, you can just fetch your belongings from the boardinghouse. And when he's finished with you, find another place to stay. I'll rent your room out to a decent woman."

"I am a decent woman," she cried. "You have no right to treat me like this."

The woman narrowed her eyes. "I wouldn't be surprised if that baby isn't yours." She pointed a finger. "And his."

Deidre stuttered, at a loss for words. Rad stepped forward, his face a mask of anger. "Madam, that child isn't Miss Parfait's, nor mine. If you give us some time, we'll get to the bottom of this. Until then, Miss Parfait will act as my housekeeper, and retain her position as teacher. She'll return to fetch her belongings within the hour."

After one hell of a day, Rad finally settled down for the night. From the previous night's card game, he'd won close to a thousand dollars, and a racehorse. As he punched his pillow to gain a bit of comfort, he didn't know what had come over him in wagering for the horse. He hadn't ridden in years, and he had no intention of doing so again.

He rubbed his leg, the pain finally subsiding. Then the teacher had shown up with a baby, accusing him of being the father. To top it off, the woman was asleep in the next room. His usual choice for a housekeeper was a widow old enough to be his mother; a safe, older woman who didn't have to worry about her reputation.

Miss Parfait was exactly the opposite. She was young, and attractive, a nice lady, the kind he'd steered clear of since he'd left Kentucky ten years ago.

Funny, she didn't look or act much like a schoolteacher. When the last teacher had quit, they had telegraphed for a replacement. Up until the day school was scheduled to begin for the season, they hadn't received a single reply. Thinking it might be the low salary, Rad offered to match the town's pittance, so the twins could get a decent education.

Then, out of the blue, Miss Parfait had shown up. She had come on the afternoon train, and the next morning had learned about the opening. Was it a coincidence that she presented letters of recommendation, and qualifications for the job? Since they were desperate for a teacher, she'd been hired on the spot.

The house had quieted, the boys settled in their beds, and Miss Parfait had finally gotten the baby to sleep. After Mrs. Hansen had left, he'd hitched up the farm wagon and returned to town to fetch his new housekeeper's belongings. So much for a long hellish day.

A narrow beam of moonlight slashed across his bed. He rarely got to bed before three or four in the morning. All-nighters in the saloon were common. However, since he'd gotten custody of his brother's sons, he tried to be home to see them off to school in the morning, and greet them after school. Since he was all the family they had, he wanted them to at least know he cared.

Rad had just fallen asleep, when a noise from outside the house woke him. The old dog the boys claimed had followed them home one day started barking. Since he wasn't often home this time of the evening, he wasn't sure if that was normal or not.

He listened to other night sounds. Insects, an owl, a horse's whinny, normal noises. Again he punched the pillow. This time he was certain he heard footsteps outside his window.

He sat up. A shadow fell across the curtain. Quickly, he picked up his cane, and pulled the Derringer from the handle. The scrape of a window being opened came from somewhere in the house.

Moving as fast as he could, he'd reached his door, when a scream came from the next room. Miss Parfait. Wearing nothing but a pair of drawers, he threw open his door, and raced down the hall. Flinging open her door, he aimed the small, but deadly gun at the intruder who had one foot inside and one outside the window.

"Please don't yell," a female voice said. "I ain't gonna hurt nobody."

In the pale moonlight, the schoolteacher was sitting up in the bed, a sheet hugged to her chest.

"Don't move," he ordered. "Who are you? What do you want?"

Deidre reached over and turned up the wick on the lamp. She snatched up the basket that was resting beside her on the bed. "What's happening?"

"That's what I'm trying to find out." Remaining in the shadows, he gestured toward the woman half in and half out of the window. "Are you alone?"

"Yes . . . yes sir. Ain't nobody here but me." She threw her other leg over the sill and cowered against the wall.

He moved past her and looked out the window. Nothing moved in the yard. "Who are you?"

She swallowed; her face turned pale. Long dark braids draped over her shoulders. Her plaid dress was tattered and worn. "It's me, Mr. Rad, Franny Maguire, don't you remember?"

Miss Parfait hugged the covers to her chest. "What are you doing here?"

The girl started crying, covering her face with her hands. "I come to see my baby."

As if things weren't already confused enough, the twins darted around his legs. "That's her!" Peter shouted. "That's the lady what gave us the baby!"

Rad staggered, and caught the window frame for balance. "Are you the mother?"

The girl hiccuped between sobs. "That's my baby. And yours."

CHAPTER 4

Deidre didn't believe the situation could get worse. But it did. The noise and commotion woke the baby and she started crying.

"Let me take her, please, ma'am," Franny said. "I got to feed her."

Taking one tentative step toward the bed, the girl stepped into the dim light. She was very young, too young to have gotten involved with the likes of Rad Christopher. Her hands covered her breasts, swollen with milk. Damp spots darkened the front of her gown. Rad stood in the dim light from the window, and for the first time she noticed that he wore only a pair of summer drawers.

Her mouth gaped. Unclothed, his shoulders were wide and muscular. Her gaze followed that intriguing thatch of black curls across flat male nipples, and down a taut belly into the top of underdrawers that did little to hide the very male part of him. Heat flowed over her. She pulled her gaze back to his face. "Mr. Christopher, get out of my room this minute. You—you're almost naked."

He shifted his attention from the girl and glared at Deidre. "Woman, this is the way I sleep. At least I was trying to sleep until I heard a noise and then you started screaming."

She jiggled the baby's basket, while trying to cover her own state of undress. The nightgown was worn and thin, allowing an immodest amount of her body to show through. "Please, put on some clothing, and meet me in the parlor to straighten out this mess." She turned her angry glance to this Franny—a woman who'd so carelessly given her baby away. "You can stay in here and feed the baby. Then we need to hear your side of the story."

"Her side?" Rad glowered at her. "She's lying, accusing me of something I didn't do."

The twins ran barefoot across the floor and stared up at Franny. "You gave us the baby. You can't take it back. Indian giver."

Rad snatched both boys by the backs of their nightshirts. "Go back to your room. Get to sleep."

"We wants to keep the baby," Peter declared.

"Go!"

Deidre's glance slipped back to Rad's incredible body. Pure masculinity oozed from the man like sap from a tree. Her stomach quivered. As handsome as Anthony had been, he'd never affected her like Rad. She forced away her improper thoughts.

Rad shoved the small gun back into the cane. "I'll meet you in the parlor." He pointed a long finger at the girl. "You'd better be ready to tell the truth."

Franny cowered from him, and shot a pleading glance at Deidre. "Ma'am, I'm telling the truth. He's my girl's daddy."

Deidre felt like judge and jury. She was stuck in the middle of a situation that involved the life of an innocent baby, a vulnerable young woman, and a licentious man. "Please, Mr. Christopher, wait for us in the parlor."

He turned on his heel, but paused at the door. "Don't try to run away. I won't have you spreading rumors about me."

"Afraid it will ruin your good reputation?" Deidre asked, unable to hold her sarcasm.

"No. People might begin to think better of me. I am not a father. I'm a gambler, a saloon owner, and a scoundrel. That's all I'll ever be." Shadowed in the doorway, his gaze shot a warning. "You'd best not forget it."

There wasn't a snowball's chance in Hades that Deidre would forget who and what Rad was. She'd been taken in once by a man with the same moral fiber. That would never happen again. As the door closed softly behind him, she turned her attention to Franny.

Her eyes damp with tears, Franny picked up the baby from the basket. "Mama's here now, sugar." Immediately the infant stopped crying, and began to root at the woman's breast. There was no doubt that they were mother and daughter. Franny opened the buttons of her ragged dress and the baby sucked hungrily.

Deidre turned away and searched for her wrapper. Once she slipped her arms into the sleeves, she tied the belt at her waist. She studied the young woman nursing the infant while seated on the edge of the bed. She spoke softly to the child, touching the cheeks with a gentle finger.

"Franny," she ventured, "what's your baby's name?"

She lifted a shy glance. "I call her Christy."

That stood to reason. The child had been named for her father. Deidre's heart went out to the mother and child. Another woman who'd been used and tossed aside at the whim of a cad. Only, Deidre had been wise enough not to give herself fully to the man who'd promised the moon and delivered green cheese. When she'd refused his advances, Anthony had run off with her money and abandoned her in Blissful.

What kind of man was Rad Christopher to seduce a woman

so young and innocent? Then to abandon her and his child? He was a cad of the worst kind.

"Where do you live, Franny?" she asked.

"In the hills with my pa." The woman's stomach growled.

"Have you had anything to eat today?"

She dropped her gaze. "Just some bread I brought with me."

"As soon as you finish feeding Christy, I'll fix you something."

"You don't have to do that, ma'am."

"I want to." And it was time Rad took responsibility for caring for the girl. "My name is Deidre."

"That's a funny name. Are you a foreigner?" The baby's eyes closed, and she fell asleep. Franny buttoned her frock and held the baby to her shoulder.

Franny would never understand why her mother had given her the French name. She said it would be perfect for a performer to have an unusual name. "No, I'm from Arkansas."

"Where's that?" She tucked the baby into the basket. "Across the mountains?"

"Yes. East of here." She opened the door. "Let's go into the kitchen and get you something to eat."

"Do I have to go out there, Miss Dede? Mr. Rad is awful mad at me."

Deidre draped an arm across the young woman's shoulder. "Don't you be concerned about Mr. Rad. He won't hurt you. I'll make sure he treats you properly. And your baby, too."

Rad paced the parlor and sipped black coffee. The twins had returned to their room, but he suspected they listened at the door. Who could blame them for being curious? There it was, the middle of the night and he was pacing the floor of his house. He couldn't wait to confront this Franny Maguire about the story she'd obviously made up. It had all the marks of blackmail. More than one man had been accused of fathering a child, and spent the rest of his life supporting somebody else's kid.

He already had a pair of jacks; he didn't need three females to make a full house. As if they read his thoughts, two of the three females appeared in the doorway. Miss Parfait's wrapper covered her from neck to toe. A row of lace peeked out from the hem, touching her small pink toes. A blonde braid rested on her shoulder. Something twisted in his gut. He swallowed the coffee to gather his thoughts.

In the lamplight, he thought he recognized the girl. "Franny," he gentled his tone. He would never learn the truth if he frightened her. "When did we meet?"

She studied the toes of her scuffed boots. "Don't you remember, Mr. Rad? It was 'bout a year ago. I went to the Silver Spur looking for my pa. You was real nice to me. You even gave me money to eat at Patsy's Cafe. 'Twas the first time I ever ate at a cafe."

Tension had his leg aching. "Sit down, Franny, Miss Parfait."

The teacher edged toward the kitchen. "Franny is starved. I'm going to fix her something to eat."

He waved her away. This was between the girl and him. If she chose to lie about him, he had to know why. "How else was I nice to you?"

She looked away, a blush on her face. "I can't talk about that."

His temper, as volatile as TNT, was a short fuse from exploding. "I think we need to talk. You say you came looking for your father. Did you find him?"

"Yes, sir. You was playing cards with him, and he lost everything he had. He was real mad at you." So far she'd shifted her gaze everywhere in the room except at him. The woman had yet to meet his eyes.

"Maguire?" The name rang a bell. "Magoo Maguire? He

had a small claim up in the hills. He lost it in a game. Said I cheated.''

"That's my pa. He got real drunk, and didn't come home for a week.''

"I see. Exactly when did we''—he glanced down the hall in time to see the boys' door slip closed—''become intimate?''

She started crying and buried her face in her hands. "Mr. Rad, don't make me talk about it. I'm so ashamed.''

"Mr. Christopher.'' Miss Parfait's voice cut like a saber. "Quit badgering the girl. She's tired and hungry.'' The woman laid a gentle hand on the younger girl's shoulder. "Come into the kitchen. I fried some bacon and eggs. That should hold you until morning.''

"Miss Parfait, I want to get to the bottom of this.'' Rad was sick to death of the interfering woman. This whole mess had started when she'd sent that note then barged into the saloon with that baby in a basket.

"I believe you've sunk as low as you can go.'' She softened her voice. "You seduced an innocent young woman, now you have to face the consequences.''

"I did not.'' He stood and glared at the stubborn woman. Why wouldn't she believe him? He wasn't a seducer of virgins, and this Franny Maguire was definitely not his type. Neither was the headstrong schoolteacher. "Never mind. Sooner or later she'll tell the truth. Take care of the girl. I'm going back to bed. We'll straighten this mess out in the morning.''

"Just one moment, sir.''

"What now? You've taken the woman in, fed her and her kid. What else could you want of me?''

"Where is Franny going to sleep?''

He narrowed his gaze. "In the barn, on the floor, back at her father's. I don't give a good—'' He clamped his teeth until they hurt. "She can bunk in with you.''

"But—''

"Lady, I haven't had one hour's sleep in the last day and a

half. I'm not exactly in the mood to discuss sleeping arrangements. Do whatever you want.''

Arms folded across her chest, Deidre watched him limp to his room. He looked like anything but a cad. His shirt hung out of his trousers, and he was barefoot. Fatigue made him look sad and vulnerable. She let out a less-than-ladylike snort. Nobody would ever describe Rad Christopher as vulnerable. The man was outrageous. He continued to deny paternity even when confronted by the mother of the child.

She shifted her gaze to the woman in the kitchen. Something prickled at the back of her mind. Either Rad had forgotten being with the woman, or one of the two was lying. Franny wasn't at all his type. Rad was sophisticated, well educated, and experienced. All Franny had in her favor was her youth and a pretty face. Deidre sighed. For some men that was more than enough.

She almost hoped—wished—that he was not guilty of the accusations leveled against him. Turning her attention to Franny, she wandered back into the kitchen. ''Franny, if Mr. Christopher is Christy's father, why didn't you just come to him? Why did you give the baby to the boys?''

She swiped a biscuit across her plate. ''I couldn't, Miss Dede. He would of throwed me right out just like my pa did. I didn't have noplace to go, and it gets mighty cold in the hills. Christy needs a nice warm house. So I gave my girl to the boys, hoping Mr. Rad would take her in. Then I missed her so much, I had to see her again. That's when I sneaked into your room.''

''Your father threw you out?'' Men! Not one of them had the sense God gave a jackass.

''Yes'm. He said he didn't want no gambler's bad blood in his house. He's still mad at Mr. Rad for winning his claim in the card game.''

Deidre patted the girl's hand. ''You and Christy are safe here. I'll see that Mr. Rad does right by his child.'' Though

how, she had no idea. As long as he denied the child, there
was little she could do except provide a shelter and food for
the pair. "You look tired. You can have my bed for tonight.
Tomorrow, we'll see what we can do."

"No, ma'am. I ain't never slept on such a fine feather mattress. I'll sleep on the floor."

"You certainly will not. I'll get you a nightdress and you
can stay close to your daughter."

Tears rolled down the girl's dirt-smudged cheeks. "Thank
you, Miss Dede. You're a fine lady. Mr. Rad is lucky to have
you for his woman. I promise I won't do nothing to cause
trouble for you and him."

"I'm not his woman," she said. She wouldn't wish that
position on her worst enemy. "I'm merely acting as his housekeeper until he gets somebody else."

"Then I can help you. I'm real good at scrubbing, and I'm
not afraid of hard work."

"We'll talk about that tomorrow. You take my room. I'll
sleep on the davenport."

Rad awoke earlier than usual the next morning. Sleep was
nearly impossible after the turmoil of the night before. Wearing
faded denims and an equally worn plaid shirt, he passed through
the parlor on his way to the kitchen. He wasn't surprised to
see a quilt folded neatly on the davenport. At least Deidre
hadn't given up her bed for that girl.

He filled a cup from the fresh coffee on the stove and headed
for the barn. Henry had promised to deliver Black Star this
morning, and he wanted to prepare a stall for the thoroughbred.
He still had no idea what he would do with the stallion. At one
time he would have welcomed the animal as stud for his mares.
Not anymore. The Christophers had given up horse-breeding
ten years ago when he'd lost Diamond. That dream had been

destroyed along with the stallion. He picked up an old cane he used around the homestead and strolled toward the corral.

As he neared the barn, a noise stopped him. At first he thought it was a wildcat, or an angry crow. Pausing, he looked around for the source of the noise. Then it changed to a human voice—a female soprano. *"Do, re, mi, fa, so, la, ti, do."* The last note hung in the air for what seemed an eternity.

He followed the sound around the barn. A figure stood in the long morning shadows of the trees. Miss Deidre Parfait the schoolmarm stood among the trees singing.

He slipped along the rear of the barn for a better view. Attired in her wrapper and nightdress, she lifted her arms to the heavens. The belt had loosened, and the front of the robe parted. Her pristine white gown clung to her body, the thin material outlining a form to make any man stand up and take notice. After the scales, she began a series of breathing exercises. Her breasts rose and fell, pressing against the fabric of her gown.

The woman was lovely—a goddess welcoming the morning. Desire shot through him. Sunshine filtered through the trees, casting a golden glow on her long, unbound hair. That hair alone was enough to fuel a man's fantasies. He tightened his grip on the cane, when he wanted to stroke his fingers through the silky tresses.

Mesmerized, Rad stared. Then she let out a screech that would scare a bear out of hibernation. Inside the barn, the horses stomped and whinnied.

When the song ended, at least he thought it was a song, she curtsied as if responding to applause. Whoever had told the woman she could sing must have been tone-deaf.

"What's all this caterwauling? You're scaring my animals half to death." He climbed the low hill toward her.

She jerked around to face him, her face flushed. "Caterwauling? I was rehearsing."

"For what?" He leaned heavily on the cane on the uneven ground. Close up, she looked even better. Her face was flushed, and her hair had come loose, tumbling to her waist in soft golden curls.

"For . . . Oh, never mind. You wouldn't know talent if it slapped you in the face." She brushed a strand of long golden hair from her face. The woman was lovely, far too pretty to be a schoolteacher.

His gaze drifted over her. The breeze whipped the thin wrapper around her legs—long, shapely legs outlined by the near-transparent batiste nightdress. Heat surged through him. He wondered how those legs would feel wrapped around him while . . . Rats, the woman was a schoolteacher, and his housekeeper, for gosh' sake. He had no rights thinking about her the way a man thinks about a woman.

"What are you doing out here? Couldn't sleep?"

Hands gripping the front of her wrapper, she faced him eye-to-eye. "I slept very well on the davenport, thank you. I awoke early to take advantage of the opportunity to be alone and perfect a new number. At the boardinghouse, I didn't have a bit of privacy to rehearse."

"Why do you have to rehearse? That didn't sound like any lessons my nephews brought home from school."

She lifted her chin and glared at him as if he were a student too ignorant to understand. "I might as well tell you. After my contract expires, I'll be on my way to San Francisco. I only took the position to earn enough money to reach the West Coast."

If she'd kicked his cane right from his hand, she couldn't have shocked him more. "Why San Francisco?"

"Because of the fine opera houses and theaters. I'm following in my mother's footsteps. She gave up her career for marriage and a family. I plan to pick up where she left off. Madame Rosellini was my voice and diction teacher. She sang at LaScala. She said I'll be the next Jenny Lind."

Rad bit the inside of his cheeks to keep from laughing. "Where are you from, Miss Parfait?"

"Fort Smith, Arkansas."

"And you were on the stage in Fort Smith?"

"There is no theater in Fort Smith. That's why I'm going to San Francisco." She breathed deeply, unaware of the intriguing way her breasts thrust against her thin gown and wrapper. He wondered how he would manage living under the same roof with such an appealing woman.

"How did you end up in Blissful? There's no entertainment here. Unless you want to entertain cowboys and miners at the Silver Spur. They wouldn't know a sonata from an aria."

"Do you, Mr. Christopher? Have you been to an opera?"

He smiled, remembering the diva he'd romanced in New Orleans. "Once or twice. Denver has a fine opera house. Why not audition there?"

Her pretty mouth pulled into a frown. "I did. That manager didn't know a thing about music. He said there were no openings, even in the chorus."

"So what are you doing in Blissful?"

"That's a long story. I think I had best get back to the house. The twins and Franny will be waking soon and looking for breakfast." She tossed her hair and walked away. He fell into step beside her.

"Miss Par-fait." He dragged out the syllables. "Is that your real name?"

She stopped and dug her bare toes in the grass. "Yes and no. My mother was French and she named me Deidre. Parfait was her maiden name, I thought it was more exotic than plain old Parker."

"Deidre. I kind of like that. A pretty name for a pretty lady."

Catching his arm, she pulled him to a stop. "Mr. Christopher, you won't tell anybody, will you? I already have more trouble with the school board than I can handle."

Her warm touch reached past his arm and into his heart. It was the strangest sensation. He hadn't felt that way in years. Since before the accident—since before he'd lost everything.

"Your secret's safe with me, Deidre. And since we're going to be living in the same house, you might as well call me Rad."

She smiled, and his heart tripped. "It's only temporary until you can hire a housekeeper."

"And you can get that audition."

They continued toward the house, rounding the barn. He turned toward the corral, when Deidre gasped and squealed, "Smoke! There's smoke coming from the kitchen."

He stared at the rear of his home. Black smoke poured through the window, thick and ugly. Fear clutched his chest. The children and the girl were probably still asleep. He took off at a run, moving awkwardly over the rocky ground. Deidre picked up her gown and raced past him. Her long legs carried her much faster than his lame ones. He cursed the accident that impeded his progress.

Franny was on the porch, huddling her baby to her breasts. In their nightshirts, the twins were racing toward him. "She started a fire," they said. "We threw water on it, but it just got worse."

Deidre raced into the kitchen. "Stop!" Rad shouted. The woman had no business risking her life.

"Stay here," he ordered, following Deidre into the smoke-filled kitchen.

"It looks like a grease fire," she said, coughing on the heavy smoke.

Water would only spread the flames—what he was afraid had already happened. "Get out of the way." Dropping his cane, he snatched the rag rug from the floor and tossed it on the flames that were shooting about a foot into the air. "The only way to put out a grease fire is to smother it." Within seconds the flames died, and only the thick smoke remained in the kitchen.

Deidre picked up a cloth and fanned the smoke out of the door. Damage seemed limited to the soot-covered walls and a few burned cloths and the rug. He sagged into a chair. "You let that girl stay one night in my house, and she tried to burn it down.'' He shot an angry glance at Deidre. He didn't know which woman was more a menace—the teacher who excited his body, or the girl who claimed he'd fathered her child.

"I'm sure she didn't do it on purpose.''

"Why am I not surprised that you would defend her?''

"There was no real harm done. I'll see that she cleans up the mess, and I'll teach her how to use the stove.'' Picking up the skillet that had caused the fire, she headed to the rear door.

He stood and followed. Franny was sobbing, and the baby was crying. The twins were taking advantage of the day off from school by racing around the yard barefoot and in their nightshirts. "Boys, go get dressed.'' They darted around the house and slammed the front door on their way into the parlor.

"Franny, what happened?'' Deidre asked, gently taking the baby from the girl's arms.

Between sobs, she related that she'd wanted to surprise them by fixing breakfast. But she wasn't used to a modern stove, and the grease popped into the flames. She tried, but couldn't put out the fire. She roused the boys from bed, and hustled them outdoors. At least she had that much good sense.

Deidre patted her back. "It's all right, Franny. We'll clean up the mess, then we'll fix Mr. Rad a fine breakfast.''

"He ain't gonna let me stay, Miss Dede. I just know it.'' Through teary eyes and hiccups, she darted a glance at him.

"Yes, he will.'' Deidre turned her gaze to him. "Won't you, Rad?''

How could he refuse two women and a baby? "You'll stay for now. Just don't burn down my house.'' He picked up his discarded cane and started toward the barn. "Call me when the food is ready.''

CHAPTER 5

"Rad you look like death warmed over." Henry laid his arms across the top rail of the corral fence. "Had a rough night?"

Shaking his head, Rad grunted for an answer. He studied the thoroughbred stallion prancing around the corral, tossing his head to gain the attention of the mares in the meadow.

"Hear tell, the schoolteacher lady is staying on with you. The whole town's in an uproar." The rancher tossed down his cigarette and snuffed it out with his boot heel.

Rad hated everybody knowing his business, but short of moving to a big city, it was inevitable. In the two years he'd been in Blissful, he'd done more than his share to grease the gears of the gossip mills. "They stay that way where I'm concerned."

Henry laughed. "That they do. And all that excitement yesterday about the baby—well, you can't blame them. Did the mother ever show up?"

As much as Rad liked the rancher, one of the few men he could call a friend, he knew that Henry repeated everything to his wife, and who knew where it went from there? "Matter of fact, she did. Magoo Maguire's girl, Franny."

"Franny?" Henry rubbed the stubble at his jaw. "That skinny little kid came around begging for a handout at my place a while back. Said her pa was sick and couldn't work his claim. My boy Hank thought he was sweet on the girl. But I put an end to that. Sent him to stay with my sister in Texas. Just got back this week."

"She isn't skinny, and she isn't a kid. Magoo wasn't sick; he was probably drunk."

"You and her?" Henry's eyes grew wide with disbelief.

"No, I've never touched the girl. And I only met her once."

"Then why is she blaming you?"

Rad threw up his hands, and turned to face the house. At least it was still standing. "God only knows why women do the things they do. I think she wants a handout. I'm letting De—Miss Parfait handle her."

"Now that's another matter, you living out here with a single woman. Can't help her reputation any."

"She's my housekeeper until I can hire a more suitable woman." Suitable for whom, he wondered, the town or him? "Besides, she'll be leaving once her contract expires."

"Didn't know that. We can't keep a teacher and you can't keep a housekeeper." Henry turned his attention back to the corral. "Now that you've won a pureblood, what do you intend to do with Black Star?"

The black stallion tossed his head in their direction as if aware he was the topic of discussion. "Damned if I know," Rad answered. "Could sell him, or put him out to stud."

"Or race him. He's from fine blood, champions all."

The heat drained from Rad's body. "No. I'm not in the racing business."

"Aren't you from Kentucky? I thought everybody there either raised racehorses, or trained them."

Rad turned his back on the beautiful stallion and started for the house. "Not me. I'm a gambler. That's all I want to be."

Henry fell into step beside him. "Rad, now that you've got your brother's sons to raise, don't you think it's time to consider another line of work? You aren't setting a very good example for them."

He gritted his teeth and gripped the cane. "You sound like the preacher or that nosy school board. As long as I have a housekeeper, the boys will be fine."

"I've got boys of my own. They need a strong hand, and a good example."

"Then I'll send them off to military school in another couple of years." Rad had been mulling over the idea ever since he'd gotten custody of the boys. "Probably do them good."

Henry paused at the porch and propped his foot on the top step. "You had a fire or something?" The blackened rug and burnt towels had been tossed into the yard after the fire.

"Franny tried to fix breakfast, and she almost succeeded in burning my house down."

The rancher laughed. "You sure got your hands full."

Rad didn't see any humor in the situation. "You mentioned your boy Hank is back. Think you can spare him until things get under control over here? He can work with Black Star, take care of the animals, and run errands for Miss Parfait. My last hand ran away to look for gold. Seems that gold fever is contagious."

"I'll talk to the boy. I'm sure you'll pay a lot more than I."

"I'm sure I will." Just then, the twin whirlwinds whipped through the kitchen doorway, and barreled into his legs.

"Uncle Rad, guess what?" Peter asked.

"Miss Dede fixed flapjacks," Paul finished the statement.

"And boy, were they good."

"Did you save any for me?" He tousled their hair. His heart tightened. He would miss the boys if he had to send them away to boarding school. Maybe he should consider Henry's advice.

"No. Miss Dede let us eat all of them." Like racehorses at the sound of a gun, the pair took off with a speed that would outrun a rabbit.

"That isn't quite true. I saved enough batter to feed both of you gentlemen." Deidre's voice came from the doorway. "Would you care to join us, Mr. Abrams? I have fresh coffee on the fire."

The rancher flashed a smile that would do a Kentucky colonel proud. He bowed at the waist and doffed his hat. "Why, Miss Parfait, that sounds wonderful. I had my breakfast so long ago, I'm about ready for dinner."

"Then come in, sir. We've gotten most of the soot cleaned up. By this evening, the kitchen will be spotless."

Rad followed at Henry's heels. While he'd been gone, Deidre had dressed in a simple black skirt and blouse. A large white apron covered her clothes, and her hair was neatly pinned at the nape of her neck. For the briefest of instants, he wondered how many men besides himself had seen that glorious mass of golden curls unbound and flowing in the breeze? How many men had buried their faces and hands in the silken tresses and inhaled the sweet fragrance of roses? He tightened his grip on the cane. Whatever she'd done in the past, or planned in the future, was none of his affair. First thing Monday, he would advertise for a housekeeper. A matronly woman as ugly as homemade sin. He didn't need the temptation of a beauty living in his house.

Unable to concentrate on the game, Rad slammed out of the Silver Spur hours earlier than his normal departure. He'd lost more hands than he'd won. His mind simply wasn't on poker. Thoughts of the situation at his home had kept him on edge with everybody in the saloon. He figured it was best to leave before he lost the shirt off his back.

Darkness shrouded the house as he climbed the stairs to the

porch. A dim light came from the housekeeper's room, the one Franny and the baby now occupied. Rad entered the parlor, trying not to wake the woman sleeping on the davenport. Moonlight streaked across the floor, guiding the way to the hallway. Against his better judgment, he glanced at the davenport. Dede—he'd picked up the nickname Franny and the boys used—lay on her back, her golden hair spread on the pillow like a halo. She turned and rolled over, hugging the sheet to her shapely body. The movement sent a well-formed leg protruding from the covers. Unseemly ideas raced through his mind.

He gripped the handle of his cane. It had been a long time since a woman had stirred his blood like this. Not only was she beautiful and desirable, something stronger drew him to her. In the past two days, she'd taken over his household, calmed Franny's demands, and encouraged better behavior in Peter and Paul. She was everything a man would want in a wife—if a man had marriage on his mind. Which Rad definitely did not.

Shaking off his wayward thoughts, he hurried to his room and shut the door. Rad dropped to the edge of his wide bed and tugged off his shoes. Images of the woman a few feet away flashed across his mind. How was he ever going to get any sleep if he kept thinking about the intriguing Miss Parfait? He dropped to the pillows, not at all sleepy. It was hours earlier than his usual bedtime.

Again his thoughts shifted to Deidre—Dede. He liked her name. It suited her a heck of a lot better than Miss Parfait. She couldn't be very comfortable on the horsehair davenport, yet she'd given up her room so Franny and the baby could have comfort and privacy. He let out a sigh. Something had to be done about the situation. He couldn't very well come home night after night and see the woman in her thin nightshift and keep his sanity. Come morning, he would have to see what could be done to remedy the situation. Short of adding on another room, or tossing Franny out, he had only one choice. He would move in with the twins and give Dede his room. On a long groan, he removed his clothes, and tried to enjoy his last night in the comfort of his wide, luxurious bed.

Deidre awoke when she heard Franny stirring in the kitchen. The girl had yet to master the stove, so Deidre hurried from the lumpy davenport before Franny again tried to burn down the house.

Her back was stiff and her legs cramped. Sometime in the early hours she'd heard Rad enter the parlor. The *tap-tap* of his cane on the porch had announced his approach before he opened the door. She heard him pause near the davenport, but she didn't dare let him suspect that she was awake. It was embarrassing enough to think that he'd been watching her while she slept. She wouldn't let him believe that she'd been half awake waiting for his return home. Deidre didn't understand how she was going to manage in the same house with such a devastatingly handsome man. Her only salvation was to remember how another handsome man had swindled her out of her life's savings and left her stranded in Blissful.

Slipping her arms into the sleeves of her wrapper, she entered the kitchen to find Franny struggling to prepare coffee. "Franny, you don't have to do that. I'll fix breakfast in a little while."

Dressed in one of Deidre's nightgowns and robes, the girl stared at her shyly. "I just wanted to help out. If I make myself useful, than maybe Mr. Rad won't run me and Christy off."

Deidre took the coffee grinder from the girl's hands. She was doing it all wrong anyway. "He isn't going to run you off." Not yet, she thought. "I think I hear the baby crying. You go take care of her, and on your way back, wake up the boys. We're all going to church this morning."

Franny backed away a step. "Church? Miss Dede, those

folks ain't gonna want me in their church with them. Besides, I ain't got no good-enough clothes.''

"We don't care what they want. I'll let you wear one of my gowns.''

"Miss Dede, I couldn't.''

Deidre gestured toward the room where the baby was raising a ruckus. "Take care of the baby before she wakes up Mr. Rad. He's liable to toss both of us out on our ears.''

"Yes, ma'am.''

With a few minutes to herself, Deidre took care of her personal needs before starting breakfast. By the time Franny and Christy entered the kitchen, she had hot biscuits, butter, and jelly on the table. The previous day she'd ventured to the general store and stocked up on badly needed supplies.

"Where are Peter and Paul?'' she asked.

Franny shrugged. "They said they ain't goin' to no church. They want to sleep.''

"Sit down and eat. I'll take care of those rascals.''

Tightening the belt of her robe, she headed down the hallway to the boys' room. She knocked lightly, and called in a loud whisper. "Time to get up. We have to get ready for church.''

A muffled voice came from the room. "We're sleepy. We don't want to go to no old church.''

She shoved open the door. Instead of each being in his own narrow bed, the boys were huddled in one with the covers pulled over their heads. Deidre stood at the foot of the bed. "I'll give you until I count ten, then I'm going to drag you out of bed by your ears.''

Identical heads popped out. "Uncle Rad don't have to go to church, and we don't have to, neither.''

It was on the tip of her tongue to ask if they wanted to grow up to be like their uncle. Chances were, they would answer yes. The hellions were well on their way to following in Rad's disreputable footsteps. A small and not-too-clean foot poked out of the blanket. Deidre couldn't resist tickling the arch. Peter squirmed and giggled. He kicked the blanket off, giving Deidre access to Paul's foot. She danced her fingertips along his sole. Both boys broke out in spasms of laughter. "That tickles," they cried.

"Are you ready to give up?" She continued to torture the twins with the tips of her nails.

They wiggled on the bed, and shouted with glee. "Mama used to tickle us like that to wake us up," Paul shouted. He jumped away, and lunged toward Deidre. "Then we would tickle her to make her stop."

Before she could defend herself, they had her on the bed. Each boy grabbed a foot and paid her back double. Between their antics and the sensation on her sensitive skin, she broke out in uncontrollable laughter. "Stop, I'm ticklish!"

"What's going on in here? Can't a man get a decent night's sleep?"

The boys stopped the game and jumped away. Deidre wiped the tears from her eyes. Her gaze lifted to tight denim trousers, then flew to a flat stomach and wide bare chest covered with dark curls. Her stomach lurched and her mouth went dry. She met Rad's stare. Midnight eyes shifted from her disheveled hair to her bosom and down to her legs. Heat shot through her as much from his torrid glance as from the realization that the robe had parted, leaving her bosom nearly exposed. In their playfulness, her nightdress had shifted to reveal the entire length of her legs. She leaped from the bed and struggled to cover her body.

"I . . . I was just trying to wake up the boys."

"And the entire household, not to mention the horses and any stray cows."

In spite of his harsh words, she noted an underlying hint of humor. "I'll try to be quieter next time." She turned to the twins. "Now run along and wash. Franny's waiting for you in the kitchen."

Peter set his hands on his narrow hips. "Uncle Rad, does we got to go to church?"

His gaze dropped to the dark heads of his nephews. "You have to do whatever Miss Dede tells you."

"But you don't go to church," Paul protested.

"I did when I was your age. When you get as old as me, you can make your own decisions. Now get."

They shuffled out of the room, mumbling under their breath.

"By the way, Peter," Deidre called after them, "next time use soap on those feet."

"Now that I'm awake, I might as well stay up," Rad said.

"You're welcome to have breakfast with us."

"Smells good."

She hurried toward the doorway, eager to put a distance between her and the man who had her pulse racing and her heart thumping. "Come to the kitchen when you're ready."

"By the way, Miss Dede." His deep, sultry voice stopped her at the door. "You can wake me like that any morning you please."

CHAPTER 6

Rad tucked his thumbs into the waist of his denims as Deidre drove off in his buggy. He'd allowed her use of the conveyance and warned her about the spirited horses. She'd assured him that she knew how to handle a team, as she'd often delivered supplies for their Fort Smith store when her father was busy.

He didn't envy the boys being forced to go to church, but he agreed they needed the training and moral upbringing. Let her handle it, as long as he didn't have to face the sanctimonious people who looked down on him, but gladly accepted his money for the teacher's salary. Franny had looked scared as a hen with a chickenhawk on her tail. Dressed in one of Deidre's dresses, the girl was rather pretty, in a sweet, youthful way. Cleaned up, and with a decent place to live, Franny might decide to tell the truth and find a man to be a father to her little girl.

Now, Deidre was another thing altogether. In a pretty blue suit, white shirtwaist, and a cameo pinned at her throat, the woman was stunning. She would outshine every woman in town. Rad couldn't deny that watching her had roused the heat in his gut that hadn't quite cooled since he'd seen her in that nightgown. He shrugged off the needs that he had no business entertaining. As soon as things settled down, he would take a quick trip to Denver.

Shoving his battered old hat on his head, he made his way toward the corral. Hank Abrams was supposed to start work that morning as the hired hand. He hoped the boy worked out, as he needed help now that his responsibilities had doubled.

Rad entered the darkened barn and approached Black Star. The stallion was as handsome a piece of horseflesh as he'd ever seen. The years hadn't dulled Rad's ability to identify a quality stud. This one would sire fine stock and build up his herd. If he decided to raise horses again. Which he did not.

As he led the spirited stallion into the corral, a rider skidded his horse to a halt and jumped from the saddle. Hank had grown in the year he'd been away. Now a wide-shouldered young man, he raced toward Rad, his face set in an angry scowl.

"I heard about you and Franny, Mr. Rad. You gonna do right by her? You gonna accept responsibility for your baby?" Hank curled his hands into fists.

Rad knew a confrontation when it stared him in the face. He gripped his cane, ready to defend himself. "Calm down, Hank. I don't know what you've heard, but I'm not the baby's father."

"Franny said you are."

"Franny's lying."

"You're the liar."

He saw the punch coming. Rad ducked and hooked the handle of his cane around the younger man's ankle. With a quick jerk on the cane, he tumbled Hank to the dusty ground. Moving quickly, Rad dropped his knee on the other man's chest, and pressed the cane to his throat. "Hank, I'll forget what you said if you're willing to mind your manners and work for me." Hank glared at him, hands reaching for Rad. "Hold still, or

I'll break your windpipe.'' He locked gazes with the younger man. "I'm not lying.''

Hank dropped his hands to the ground. He nodded. "Sorry,'' he grunted.

Rad stood and leaned heavily on the cane. In spite of his handicap, he'd learned how to defend himself. Reaching out a hand, he helped Hank to his feet. "Do you want to work for me?''

Picking up his hat, Hank slapped it against his leg. "Yes, sir.''

"Then get those horses into the pasture, and we can start training Black Star.''

"You planning to race him?''

"I don't know what I'm going to do.'' He slapped Hank on the back and gestured toward the barn. He didn't understand what had gotten Hank so hot under the collar. Unless what Henry said was true and Hank was sweet on Franny. That would account for his anger. Rad shrugged. He had enough problems of his own to deal with. For a woman a shade under eighteen, Franny had sure upset a lot of lives.

Deidre returned from church with her temper in an uproar. In the short time that she'd been in Blissful, she'd been accepted into the limited society, if a bit reluctantly. Franny and her child were an entirely different matter. The good ladies, led by Mrs. Hansen, had snubbed the girl as if she carried a plague. Their censure extended to Deidre since she was living under the same roof with Franny and Rad.

Rad approached the buggy when she pulled into the yard. "You don't have to check. I didn't damage either your buggy or your fine team,'' she declared as she tugged the horses to a complete halt. The twins jumped to the ground, and tore toward the barn. "Change your clothes,'' Deidre yelled. The pair ignored her as if she hadn't spoken a word.

Rad grabbed the halter. "How was church?" he asked.

"Fine. You should have come. The reverend preached on hellfire and brimstone."

He laughed. "I've been there and back, Miss Dede. I could tell the preacher a thing or two."

"I'm sure you could."

"Are you in a snit because I didn't accompany you?"

Realizing that she'd taken out her irritation on him when she wanted to tell off the snobs in town, she forced a smile. "No. It was the way we were snubbed."

"Get used to it, Miss Dede. I've been snubbed most of my life."

"But you're a gambler."

He lifted a hand to help her down. "You can think of me as a gold miner."

Now on the ground, she gazed into his eyes, humor glittering behind his long lashes. Heat settled in her stomach every time he flashed that crooked, boyish grin. "How do you figure that?"

"Some men mine gold with a pick or pan, I simply mine the gold right out of their pockets."

His analogy brought a smile to her face. "That's one way to think about it."

As she plucked Christy's basket from behind the seat, a brawny young man stepped from the shadows of the barn.

Franny stiffened and gasped. "Hank," she whispered.

Deidre followed the line of her vision. "Franny, what's wrong?"

"Nothing, ma'am. I got to get to the house. Christy is hungry and I got to feed her." Without waiting for help, the girl leaped to the ground, her baby tucked close to her chest.

What was that all about? Deidre wondered. The young man's gaze followed the girl until she disappeared into the kitchen. He walked slowly, with the long easy stride of a man born to the saddle. How different from Rad's awkward gait.

"Miss Deidre Parfait," Rad said, "this is Hank Abrams, Henry's son. He'll be working for us."

Us? It sounded so . . . together, so domestic. So permanent. "I'm pleased to meet you, Hank."

The young man flashed a charming smile. "You're the new schoolmarm? If my teachers were as pretty as you, I might never have left school." He doffed his hat and bowed at the waist. Brown hair tumbled into his eyes.

Rad growled. "Unhitch the team, and we'll see if we can get something to eat."

"I put a roast in the oven this morning. I'll have a meal on the table in about a half hour. I'll call you when it's ready."

"We'll be waiting," Rad said, gripping the side of the buggy. "Let's go, Hank, you've got work to do."

Exactly thirty minutes later, Rad, Hank, and the twins showed up at the back door. The boys had tugged their shirts from their trousers, and the new britches were mud-stained. Mr. Lee, the laundry man, would have a time getting these things clean again. She had set the table, and added the potatoes and vegetables, along with fresh biscuits. As they settled for their meal, she sent Peter to call Franny. Since she'd entered the house, the girl hadn't shown her face. Peter came back with a message that Franny wasn't hungry, and she had to take care of the baby.

When Deidre stood to retrieve the girl, Rad placed a hand on her arm. His touch was gentle, but his words stern. "Leave her be; she'll eat when she's hungry."

Young Hank held Deidre's chair. "Smells mighty good, ma'am." He nudged Peter away and took the seat beside hers.

She returned his smile. "Thank you, Hank. I hope you enjoy it."

The twins pushed and shoved and grabbed biscuits from the bowl. "Boys," she admonished. "We'll pray first."

Rad stopped right in the middle of reaching for the platter

of meat. He glared at Deidre as if she'd told him to throw the food to the dogs. "You pray."

After a short prayer, she nodded and passed the platters around the table. Hank was a polite and attentive young man. From time to time he glanced toward the rear of the house where Franny had retreated on the pretext of tending the baby. Rad spoke little, his gaze studying Deidre across the table.

After the boys and men devoured two apple pies, Hank shoved back his chair and smiled at Deidre. "That was a fine meal, ma'am. Too bad Franny had to miss dinner."

"I saved her a plate," Deidre offered, returning his smile.

Rad folded his arms across his chest and grunted. He'd always liked the young man, who reminded Rad of himself before the accident. Hank was brash and cocky, and a bit of a charmer, witnessed by the way Deidre smiled at him and offered him the last piece of pie. For some odd reason, Rad didn't like that one bit. "Heard that you and Franny used to be close," he said, his gaze locked on the younger man.

A flush crept up Hank's neck. "That was a long time ago, Mr. Rad. Reckon she forgot all about me after I left for Texas. Looks like she's been grazing in greener pastures. Found somebody else and got herself a baby."

With an effort, Rad resisted the urge to repeat his declaration that he was not the child's father. This time, he let it pass.

"She really is a sweet girl," Deidre put in. "It's a shame the way some men take advantage of innocent girls." For a change, she didn't direct her accusation at Rad. Instead, she studied Hank like a bug under a magnifying glass.

"Yes, ma'am," he said. "It surely is a shame."

Having taken all he could stand of the implied charge, Rad shoved back his chair. "Let's get back to work. I want to see if I got my money's worth with that horse."

"Yes, sir. But shouldn't we help Miss Dede clean up?"

"That won't be necessary," Deidre said. "Franny will help out."

He shot a glance toward the hallway where Franny hovered in the shadows. The girl cringed at his glance and backed away. Something was going on between her and Hank. He wondered what had happened a year ago before the young man left for Texas. Rad shrugged. He didn't have the time or energy to speculate about the couple. He had enough problems of his own.

Deidre awoke earlier than usual the next morning. She'd had more than a little trouble falling asleep in Rad's wide bed. He'd insisted on moving into the twin's room, and giving up his chamber for her use. Although she'd protested that it wasn't fair, he'd reasoned that since she was helping him out of a bind, it was only right to give her a decent place to sleep. From the moment she'd closed the door behind him, she'd realized her mistake.

Everything about the room spoke of his bold masculinity. The dark colors, the heavy furniture, the thick drapes to block out the daylight, contained his mark as surely as if he'd signed his name across the room. Most of his clothes remained in the wardrobe as well as in the bureau. A faint hint of tobacco hung in the air. Even the pillows carried the scent of his cologne. She hoped he found a housekeeper soon.

Hard as she tried to deny the attraction between them, the man was the most fascinating male she'd ever encountered. He was a gambler and a rogue—a heartbreaker who had probably left a string of lovesick women from Kentucky to California. Deidre had no intention of joining their ranks. Anthony had left her broke, but her heart remained intact.

Not wanting Rad to catch her in her nightclothes as he had done a few days earlier, she hurriedly dressed in a simple calico gown and covered her shoulders with a shawl. She stoked the stove and put on a pot of coffee before she sneaked out of the back door. This time, she climbed higher on the hill, farther away from the barn and the house. At this hour of the morning only the roosters were stirring.

Secure in being alone, she began her breathing exercises as Madame Rosellini had taught her. The sun had barely crept up the horizon when she practiced the scales. A pale glow of daylight cast long shadows under the trees where she stood. Her voice rose and fell, inviting the day. A blue jay squawked and scurried away in search of food. Her thoughts strayed from her music, to the situation in which she'd been thrust. As her mind searched for a song, she wondered about Rad. She would bet her life that he wasn't the baby's father. Yet he'd taken the girl in, and was providing a proper place for the mother and child.

Too confused to delve into a difficult aria, she chose a popular Stephen Foster number. As she opened her mouth to sing, a movement in the bushes startled her. She backed behind a tall pine. Her heart thudded. Had she disturbed a wildcat or a bear? Her skin grew cold.

"Don't stop on my account." Rad stepped into the dapple of sunlight, leaning heavily on his cane. "That wasn't nearly as bad as the other day."

Fury threatened to choke Deidre. "You scared me out of my wits, Mr. Christopher. Are you following me?"

A wide grin spread across his mouth. The man was a handsome devil with the mesmerizing charm of a rattlesnake. "Actually, I am. We haven't had much time to talk, and I wanted to learn more about you."

She shivered under his gaze. In spite of his smile, his eyes were hard, determined. "What do you want to know?" Her skin heated under his scrutiny.

"Let's head back to the house. I don't want Franny to try to burn it down again." He gestured to the path and fell in step beside her. "How did you wind up in Blissful?"

Deidre swallowed her humiliation. The only thing she'd done wrong was trusting a faithless man. "After my parents died, I decided that I wanted to pursue my career on the stage. My fiancé convinced me to sell my father's store and take the money and go to San Francisco."

"Fiancé?" His voice grew cold.

A chill reached clear to her toes. "A rotten scoundrel who ran off with my money and left me stranded in Blissful."

He stopped and stared down at her. "He stole your money?"

"Yes. He said it would be safer with him. After we left Denver, we came here. You probably met him. I'm certain he gambled away a good part of my money." She planted her hands on her hips and met his intense stare.

"Why did he leave you behind?"

This part was embarrassing. "That's none of your business."

He gripped her arms and pulled her to his chest. "You're staying at my house, so I believe it is my business."

Furious at his boorish behavior, she shook out of his grip. "I wouldn't sleep with that no-account Anthony Winslow without the benefit of matrimony."

"Oh?" He stepped back as if he'd been slapped. "So he abandoned you."

She hugged her arms to ward off a chill. "Left me like a ship on a sandbar. Took my money and left me waiting at the train station. Of course, he'd taken off the night before when I locked my hotel door against him."

"And that day the school board was desperately trying to find a schoolteacher."

"I needed a job, and it just fell into my lap." She smiled at the memory of how the message had flown out of the window and into her hands. "If you must know, I sort of fudged my credentials." Squaring her shoulders, she glared up at him. "If you're worried about your nephews' education, I'm well qualified to teach eight grades of school."

"I don't doubt you are, Miss Dede." He quirked a thick black eyebrow. "So you wouldn't sleep with him."

She poked her finger into his wide chest. "That's right. And don't you get any ideas, either."

Grabbing her hand, he tugged her hard and circled her waist with his free arm. "Lady, you aren't my type."

Her heart raced and her stomach trembled. She was treading on dangerous ground. "What is your type?"

Their gazes locked. Emotion like she'd never seen before, glittered behind his long black eyelashes. "Pretty, blonde, blue eyes . . ." He lowered his head, his mouth inches from hers.

Her breath caught in her throat. She waited, certain he was going to kiss her. In that instant, she debated whether to allow the liberty. Before her mind fully considered the possibility, he stopped abruptly.

"And quiet." He set her away from him. "If you keep up that squealing, the cows will stop giving milk, and the chickens will stop laying."

Embarrassed that she'd actually wanted his kiss, she set her mouth in an angry line. "You don't have a milk cow or chickens, so I don't think there's any danger to the animals from my singing."

"I might get some."

"I'll be gone by then." She lifted her skirts and stalked to the house. The man was a rogue she wouldn't trust beyond the end of her nose.

Rad shook his head. Deidre didn't know that he was in part responsible for Winslow deserting her. Rad remembered the name. He'd caught the man cheating in a card game and promptly escorted him to the depot and deposited him on the midnight train headed east. He hadn't known about Deidre or that he was forcing the man to abandon her without a cent.

What would his housekeeper do if she knew his part in her losing her dream, her money, and her fiancé? Did she love the man? From the way she spoke, she'd clearly gotten over him. He shrugged. Sooner or later Winslow would have left her for the very reason she believed he had. At least she'd gotten a job, and was doing something worthwhile in teaching the children—not to mention helping out in his strange dilemma.

He followed at a slower pace. The woman was quite a looker. And her voice wasn't all that bad. He'd heard worse singers in the various music halls and saloons. In her own way she was an innocent, and she didn't belong in that kind of life. She should have stayed in Fort Smith, married a neighbor, and mothered a passel of kids.

The knot around his heart tightened. He'd almost lost control when he'd gazed into those deep blue eyes. Rad couldn't deny that he'd wanted to kiss her—or more. Good thing he'd come to his senses in time. It wouldn't do to get familiar with the woman who lived in his home as his housekeeper. *Temporary* housekeeper, he reminded himself. As soon as she fulfilled her contract she would be on her way to accomplish her dream.

Rad shifted his gaze to the corral and Black Star. His own dreams had died ten years ago. It was too late for him, but he sincerely wished Miss Deidre Parfait good luck with hers.

CHAPTER 7

That night Rad threw down his cards in disgust. "I'm out, boys." He signaled for Della. "A round of drinks for the table."

Della selected a bottle of his best whiskey, and filled the empty glasses. "Looks like Lady Luck deserted you again tonight."

He grunted. "If you only knew."

She followed him toward the office under the stairs. "How are things going out at your place?"

"Hank Abrams came to work for me." He dropped into the chair behind his desk. "Like everybody else, he thinks I'm a corrupter of young women."

"I always knew you were," Della remarked, her voice ringing with humor. "Except I don't believe you would seduce a woman as young as Franny." She filled two cups with tea. "Now, the schoolteacher, that's another matter."

"I hired her as a housekeeper until I can find a widow willing to put up with the hooligans."

"Two women and a baby." She laughed, a deep throaty sound. "You've got a full house."

He shot her an angry glance. "Tomorrow I expect you to post an advertisement for a housekeeper."

"You could consider marriage."

"Never! I'm a gambler and a drifter. I'll send the boys to military school and sell the homestead first."

"What about Franny and the baby? What's her name—Christy?"

"I'm not responsible for what that girl did. Sooner or later she'll tell the truth. Until then, I'll let her stay at the house." Rad stood. "Take care of things here. I'm going home."

She stared at him. "You never leave this early."

"There's a first time for everything."

As he reached for the door, he heard Della's soft snicker. "For everything."

Rad stopped on the porch and listened to the sounds from inside the house. The lamps were trimmed in the twins' room—where Rad would be spending the night until one of the women left his home. In the darkness, both Peter and Paul were whispering so loud, he heard them from the open windows.

"Lullaby, and good night . . ." Deidre's soft voice whispered in the quiet parlor. It was quite a contrast from the way she'd screeched and bellowed that morning in the woods. He liked this sound.

Through the lace curtain at the window, he spied the woman in the rocker near the fireplace, a pink bundle cradled in her arms.

"Christy likes your singing, Miss Dede," Franny said. "I reckon she's already sound asleep."

"She's such a sweet thing. I love rocking her."

"You'll make a good mama."

Gentle laughter drifted through the window. Rad felt like a

Peeping Tom, but he couldn't help himself. He'd lived alone for so long, his heart warmed at the sound of soft, feminine voices in his house.

Deidre's voice softened to a whisper. "I don't intend to marry for quite a long time. I have plans, goals. What about you, Franny? Don't you believe Christy needs her father?"

Rad pressed his ear closer to the door waiting for Franny to finally tell the truth.

"Yes, ma'am, she does. But he'll never marry me. I ain't good enough for him." The girl's voice tapered off as if she'd left the room.

Footsteps sounded on the wooden floor. The door scraped and was flung open. "You can come in, Rad. No use lurking in the shadows." Deidre glared at him, her hands propped on her hips.

"I just got home. How did you know I was out here?"

"I heard your team a while ago, and saw the lamp in the barn. Aren't you home awfully early? I didn't expect you until near dawn."

"Don't tell me you were planning on waiting up for me?"

"Never." She stepped back and gestured him into the parlor. "Come in, I'm heading to bed."

"How do you like my room?"

With a smile tossed over her shoulder, she paused. "Very comfortable. Hope you like sleeping with the boys."

He started to tell her he'd rather sleep with her. Shocked at the trend of his thoughts, he headed to the kitchen, hoping that there was hot coffee on the stove. Sleeping with two six-year-olds held little appeal, but he would make do for the time being.

By the end of her first full week as Rad Christopher's house-keeper, Deidre was more than a little confused by the man. Every evening he ate supper with them before heading to the saloon. And most nights he returned home while she was rocking Christy to sleep. Franny was still frightened by the man who seldom raised his voice, and she steadfastly avoided Hank. The twins' behavior had improved, as had their grades. Yet they still collected an assortment of critters and often frightened the girls with their finds. The day before, Deidre had ignored the dead snake in her desk.

From Hank she learned Rad was training his new horse for an upcoming race, and teaching the young man how to be a jockey. Every morning as she rehearsed in the woods, she looked for Rad, but since the day she'd told him about her fiancé, she hadn't seen him spying on her. Perhaps he'd lost what little interest he'd had in her.

On Friday, she'd just put their supper on the table when the rear door slammed open against the wall. She jumped back, startled. A slender man badly in need of a bath and shave glared at her with narrowed bloodshot eyes. A shotgun rested on his arm. Franny grabbed the baby and cowered against the wall.

"Pa, what are you doing here?" she said in a shaky voice.

"Come to fetch you home, girl. Ain't got nobody to cook or wash since you upped and run away." He advanced a step toward the young woman.

"I ain't going home, I'm staying right here."

The man reached out a dirty hand. "You're my daughter, and I said you're comin' home."

Showing more bravado than she felt, Deidre stepped between the pair. "Leave her alone. Franny can do as she pleases."

"Stay out of my way, lady," he growled, waving the gun at her. "I don't need a gambler's whore telling me what to do."

Deidre jerked back, repulsed both by the odor the man emitted, and by his angry words. Before she opened her mouth to argue, a soft, deep, and decidedly dangerous voice came from the doorway that led from the parlor.

"What do you want, Magoo?" In his black suit, with his

gold-handled cane in his fist, Rad looked like both savior and menace.

Magoo Maguire stopped cold and turned the weapon on Rad. "I come for my girl."

Rad glanced from Franny to her father. "You want to go with him, Franny?"

Still cowering behind Deidre, the younger woman shook her head. "No . . . no, sir. My pa done threw us out. Can I please stay here with Miss Dede?"

In spite of Rad's calm demeanor, a muscle twitched in his jaw. Deidre guessed he was struggling to remain calm. "It's all right by me." He advanced a step. "Magoo, put that gun down. Somebody might get hurt."

Fear glittered in the miner's eyes. "You done ruined my girl and stole my claim. Reckon you owe me."

Rad eased his body in front of Deidre's. She glanced around for a weapon to use against the man. A pot of water was boiling on the stove. As if he read her thoughts, Rad shook his head in warning for her not to even think about it.

"Magoo, your claim was played out a long time ago, and I didn't ruin your daughter. Get out of my house and off my property."

Magoo waved the shotgun around the room. At that moment, the twins barreled into the kitchen. Careless as ever, they ran headlong into Magoo. Already unsteady on his feet, the man tottered and swayed sideways. Rad grabbed the gun and tossed it to Deidre. Years before, her father had taught her how to handle a weapon. She brandished it in front of the staggering man.

In one quick movement, Rad grabbed the front of Magoo's shirt and hauled him up. "Magoo, listen, and listen good. I don't owe you anything. If I ever catch you bothering either Franny or Miss Parfait, I'll personally string you up by your scrawny neck and let the buzzards finish you off."

Without so much as raising his voice, Rad had everybody's

attention. Even the twins stilled and watched wide-eyed as their uncle tossed the man out of the door. Magoo landed on the seat of his pants in the yard.

The man struggled to his feet, and glared up at Rad's imposing figure. "I'll go, gambler, but you won't get away with this. I'll get the sheriff, and tell him that you're keeping my girl against her will."

"Go away, Pa." Franny jiggled the crying baby, frightened by the excitement around her. "I ain't going home."

Rad brushed his hands together as if to wipe off the dirt. "Go back to the hills, Magoo. Sober up. Franny can stay as long as she wants."

Deidre's heart swelled. Rad was willing to take responsibility for a homeless young woman and a child that was not his. Buried beneath that hard, roguish exterior, beat a lonely heart badly in need of healing. Not many men would try to make a home for their orphaned nephews, provide for their education, and give up his bed for strangers. The Rad Christopher the world knew was a far cry from the man Deidre was coming to know—and love.

The thought of love shook her. She dropped the shotgun to the table as if it were a hot poker. Only a fool would fall in love with a man like the gambler. Look what had happened the last time she'd imagined herself in love. Anthony had left her high and dry without a penny of her own money. Only, she could now admit that he'd left her heart intact. She suspected she wouldn't be so lucky with Rad.

She stared at his back, as straight and stalwart as a tree. In spite of his lame leg, the man was a powerful and imposing figure. He stepped onto the porch and waited until the miner climbed aboard his old mule and plodded from the yard.

"Hank," he yelled. The young man appeared from the barn at a run. "Follow Magoo and make sure he heads for the hills. Then come back for supper."

"Yes, sir," the younger man called back. On a run Hank leaped on his horse and trailed the angry miner.

Rad glanced over his shoulder at the women huddled in the doorway. His heart finally settled to a normal beat. When he'd entered the kitchen and seen the drunken miner with a shotgun leveled at Deidre, fear had gripped his belly. With just the slightest provocation, Magoo could have killed the innocent woman, his own daughter, and a harmless baby. They were all lucky that when the twins rammed into the man he was able to snatch the weapon from Magoo's shaky fingers. He didn't know whether to wallop or kiss the boys.

Leaning heavily on the cane, he climbed the steps. For the first time he noticed that something was different. Pots of red flowers lined the porch, and a couple of old chairs sat against the wall. His breath caught. His mother always kept flowers, a swing, and chairs on the long verandah of their Kentucky home. It was touches like these that made a house a home. Warmth settled in a heart that had been frozen for too long. He liked what Deidre had done to his house, and at the same time he hated it. Rad had no intention of settling down to domesticity. He was a gambler and a wanderer. His stay in Blissful had been his longest in one place since he'd lost the Kentucky homestead ten years before.

"What are you gaping at? Put supper on the table. I've got to get into town."

Franny scurried away when he approached. Deidre stood her ground. "Do you think he'll be back?"

He studied her eyes, wide and blue as the sky, but without a hint of fear. The woman was truly amazing. "No. Magoo is a coward. But just to be safe, I'll ask Hank to move into the barn so he'll be here when I'm away."

"That's a good idea. With a baby in the house, we can't be too careful." She stepped aside. "I'll put the food on the table."

Rad chuckled under his breath. "Magoo is a fool. If he'd

have shown any kind of manners, we'd have invited him to share our meal. Instead, he'll wallow in self-pity and alcohol.''

"I ought to leave," Franny whispered, tears damping her cheeks. "My pa could cause trouble for Miss Dede and the twins.''

Deidre draped an arm over the girl's shoulder. "You'll do no such thing. Mr. Rad said you can stay. And Christy needs a home." She looked to Rad for agreement.

What kind of a mess had he gotten himself into now? Two boys, two women, and a baby, all depending on him. Responsibilities he didn't want were piling on him like snow on a mountain. In another year his hair would be just as white. Already, at thirty-four, he was showing signs of silver at his temples. He shrugged. "Let's eat.''

He settled at the table and the boys jostled for their seats. Franny set the baby into her basket, and turned to help Deidre. At the lack of attention, Christy started to cry. Peter reached for the infant. "I'll hold her," he said. "She likes me.''

Paul shoved him aside. "She likes me better.''

Rad reached past both his nephews. "I'll hold her while her mama is busy. You boys settle down and wait for Miss Dede to fill your plates.''

He lifted the tiny girl into his big hands. The whimpers stopped as abruptly as they'd started. She weighed next to nothing, and he wondered if this was normal. Christy waved her arms and began to blow bubbles from her bow-shaped mouth. Unable to control himself, he bounced her, and she made a noise that sounded like laughter.

"Look at Uncle Rad," Peter declared. "I bet Christy likes him best.''

Paul pressed his face to the infant's. "She ought to. He's her pa.''

Both women stopped and spun to face him. He glared at his nephew. Franny snatched the baby from his hands. "Mr. Rad ain't her pa," she sobbed. Hugging the baby to her chest, Franny fled the room as if the beasts of Hades were hot on her tail.

Rad shoved back his chair. Now that the girl had finally admitted the truth, would she tell them the rest? Exactly who was the baby's father? Deidre stopped him with a hand to his arm. "Leave her alone, Rad. I'll talk to her when she calms down."

"Find out why she lied."

Deidre glanced toward the parlor where Franny had disappeared. "I think she was frightened of her father. And since you'd once befriended her, she chose you as her protector." She slid her fingers to the back of his hand. Her touch both comforted and disturbed him. "You won't throw her out, will you?"

"What kind of ogre do you think I am? Only minutes ago I said she could stay. I may be a scoundrel, but I keep my word." Things were getting too complicated for him. Rad shook off her hand and snatched his hat from a peg near the door. "I'll eat in town. It's a heck of a lot more peaceful."

On his way through the doorway, he brushed past Hank. "Magoo's gone, Mr. Rad. Don't reckon he'll be back." He stopped and looked up at Rad. "What's going on? Did I miss supper?"

Rad growled deep in his throat. "No. I'm going to town. I want you to move into the barn and keep a watch while I'm not here."

Peter and Paul tugged on his coattail. "We don't need nobody to watch us. We's big enough to take care of Miss Dede and Franny," Peter stated in his most grown-up voice.

"And Christy, too. Even if Uncle Rad ain't her pa, we still like her," his brother added.

Hank stared at them. "Franny said that?"

"Yes, she finally told the truth."

The stunned young man looked as if a baby could knock him over with a feather. "Then who is Christy's pa?"

"She won't say. Keep an eye out. I'll be home early."

"Yes, sir. I'll take care of everything."

CHAPTER 8

Franny kept to her room for most of the next week when the others were at home. She refused to give any information about Christy's father except to say that he didn't love her and that he would never marry her. At least Rad was off the hook. To be honest with herself, Deidre was eternally grateful that he hadn't seduced the young woman.

She could never love a man capable of such lascivious behavior. Rad may be guilty of many things, but he hadn't taken advantage of a vulnerable young woman, then rejected her.

After the confrontation on Friday evening, Rad had returned early every night. Although Deidre felt relatively safe with Hank on the property, having Rad handy gave a greater degree of security. Since he'd changed his schedule, she had to admit that she enjoyed having him around. Her heart swelled every time she sat across from him at the table, or listened to him read to the boys while she sang to Christy.

As a child, her own mother had sung lullabies and her papa had read stories. Mother had dreams of being a great singer until she'd married her father and settled in Fort Smith. Deidre couldn't deny that Mama had been happy, but she'd instilled in her only daughter the desire to do more with her life and inherited talent. Getting too deeply involved with the Christophers could stymie all her hard-laid plans.

Word had spread like wildfire that Rad had not fathered Franny's child. Yet there remained speculation as to which of the males in town had taken advantage of the young woman.

On Friday, Mrs. Hansen appeared at the school with a basket of freshly baked cookies. As head of the school board, the woman often showed up unannounced to check up on Deidre and the progress of the children. Deidre suspected that Mrs. Hansen had other reasons for this impromptu visit.

Deidre dismissed the youngsters into the yard to eat their lunches and share the cookies. Sally Jane dutifully distributed the cookies, giving two to the children she liked, and only one to the others. When Peter and Paul started to pout because they felt cheated, Deidre whispered a promise that she would make a batch when they got home that evening.

Mrs. Hansen settled on the steps beside Deidre while she ate her own lunch. It took only a few minutes before her former landlady got to the point of her call.

"I hear that Franny admitted that Mr. Christopher isn't her baby's father after all." Mrs. Hansen tilted her nose and snorted. "In spite of what the others said, I didn't believe that he would do such a thing. Franny is much too young for a man of his sophisticated tastes."

Deidre almost choked on her chuck of bread and cheese. The woman was the biggest gossip in town and had been responsible for spreading the tales about Rad and Franny. "Yes, she is," Deidre agreed.

"Has she identified who is the father of that precious little girl?" The woman feigned sympathy when all she wanted was more fuel for the gossip engine.

"No, and I don't believe she will. Franny has been alone

for much of her life. Her mother died when she was young and her father was often off prospecting. She made the mistake of falling in love with somebody who didn't love her.''

''She hasn't given even a hint?''

''Not a hint,'' Deidre said, struggling to control her temper. Even if she knew, Deidre wouldn't reveal a confidence to the hypocritical woman who didn't care a fig for Franny or Christy. Left to her, both would be out in the street with no place to go. ''If you'll excuse me, ma'am, I'd like to look over my lessons before the children return from their recess.''

The woman stood when Deidre leaped to her feet. ''Miss Parfait, may I give you a word of advice?''

Like it or not, it was coming. Deidre met her gaze without flinching.

''Franny may not suit a man like Rad Christopher, but you're an entirely different story. You're older, a worldly woman, and fair game for a man of his, shall we say, degenerate taste. We can't have the woman who's in charge of our precious children becoming involved with a gambler.''

Deidre shook the crumbs from her skirt and struggled with her temper. ''Mrs. Hansen, just what do you know of Mr. Christopher's taste in women? I'll have you know he has been a perfect gentleman where Franny and I are concerned. And, as far as I know, with the other women in town.''

Mrs. Hansen pointed a finger at Deidre's chest. ''We expect our schoolmarm to be decent and aboveboard.''

''And pure as the new-driven snow.''

''Don't be smart with me, young woman. You'd best watch your step if you wish to remain in Blissful.''

Deidre ignored the threat. ''Have you forgotten that I have a contract? If you break it, you'll have to pay me my full six months' salary.'' Climbing the steps, she glared down at the woman, at a loss for words for a change. ''Thank you for the cookies. The children appreciate your kindness and generosity.''

Trying not to choke on her own anger, Deidre stalked into the classroom. She ignored the muddy footprints that led from the side door to her desk. When she picked up the primer, she simply tossed the pile of feathers that were supposed to represent a dead bird into the trash. These mischievous youngsters didn't bother her a bit. That nosy old biddy had her in an uproar. The idea of using concern for the children to learn gossip about Franny and Rad.

Deidre had her own theory about Christy's father. She often wondered why Hank was so interested in Franny and the baby. Then she'd heard that they'd been friendly before the young man was shipped off to Texas a year ago. The timing was right. And she was certain that Henry Abrams didn't have much use for a poor girl like Franny. Could it be that after Hank had gone away she'd learn that she was having his baby? And with a father like Magoo, she had nobody to help her or come to her aid. Deidre's heart went out to the girl who'd been forced to lie about the paternity of her child to keep the baby safe and warm.

Deidre was still in a snit when she returned home that evening. Not wanting to admit how Mrs. Hansen had upset her, she pasted on a smile, and went about her usual routine. The twins were delighted to have their own batch of sugar cookies, much better than Mrs. Hansen's, if she had to say so herself. Rad had warned them that he might be later than usual that night. Since it was the end of the month, and the cowboys got paid, Rad felt he needed to stay in the saloon and supervise the card games.

As much as she hated to admit it, she missed his presence that evening. After Franny and the boys had gone to bed, and Hank had settled in the barn, Deidre paced the floor in Rad's bedroom. Everywhere she looked were reminders of him. Her gowns hung in the armoire beside his suits and her unmentionables shared the bureau with his.

At about midnight, she threw open the window and breathed

the fresh air. Wrapping a shawl over her nightdress, she leaned against the window facing and stared into the night sky. Stars twinkled and winked on a velvet field. The moon cast its pale glow over the yard. She wondered if the sky in San Francisco was as lovely. Would she like living near the Pacific after her twenty-five years without ever seeing the ocean? Would she miss Blissful?

On a long sigh, she turned her gaze to the dark trees that guarded the homestead. In spite of their continual mischief, she would miss Peter and Paul, and she held Franny and Christy dear. Brash, cocky Hank had become a friend.

Then there was Rad.

Every time she said his name or thought about him, her heart fluttered and her pulse raced. Against her better judgment, she'd fallen in love with the least suitable man in the world.

Surrounded by the quiet room, her thoughts drifted to the past few nights. She and Rad had developed a camaraderie of sorts. He'd quit making disparaging remarks about her singing, and she'd quit ridiculing his lifestyle. She rather enjoyed sparring with him. Rad proved to be well educated and knowledgeable on a number of subjects. Too bad nothing could ever come of their relationship—not that he cared a hoot for her. Deidre had her goals, and come hell or high water she intended to go to San Francisco and make her dream come true.

"Waiting up for me?" Rad's soft voice came from the shadows of the hallway.

Deidre jumped. An unbidden smile curved her lips. "Of course not. There's no telling when you're going to get back. How was the card game?"

He moved into the room. "I won more than I lost."

"I suppose that's good. I feel sorry for your opponents."

"Don't. They're grown men. A man shouldn't gamble more than he can afford to lose." Rad tugged loose his narrow tie, and closed the space between them.

"Do you ever lose?" Her breath caught when his shoulder brushed hers.

"Seldom. I know enough to get out while I'm ahead. And when I'm losing, I know when to cut my losses and quit."

Deidre took a deep breath. That's just what she should do. If Deidre had a lick of sense, she would cut her losses and get away before it was too late. She should go before she fell so deeply in love with Rad that she couldn't leave. But when did a women in love ever do what made sense?

Although his clothes usually smelled of tobacco smoke, his breath never reeked of alcohol. He'd never appeared drunk, or even slightly inebriated. Her stomach trembled. The man was too close for her comfort. Too close to control the needs that bubbled up inside of her. Silence hovered like a warm blanket between them.

"Have you been in Blissful very long?" she asked to break the thick silence.

"A couple of years."

Not wanting him to think she was interrogating him, she turned and glanced at the door. "It isn't proper for you to be in my room."

"I'm not known as a man who stands on propriety." He dropped a hand to her shoulder.

She struggled to not let him see her nervousness. Decency said she should demand that he leave. And she would, after a minute or two. "It's lovely in this valley. You should be proud of your homestead."

"It's a place to live, and a place for the boys. I grew up on a horse farm in Kentucky. This place is second place, at best." His fingers tangled in the strands of hair that had escaped her braid.

"Why did you leave Kentucky?" A tinge of pain glittered in his eyes that even the darkness couldn't hide.

He tapped his bad leg with the cane. "I was thrown from a horse during a race. Broke my leg, and I was laid up for quite a while. I not only lost the race, but we lost the farm as well. While I was convalescing I started to work with cards. Found out I was good, and I suppose I was a natural-born gambler. I always liked the challenge of a bet. Instead of horses, I bet on cards. When I was able, I took off. I've played the riverboats and saloons up and down the Mississippi. I won the Silver Spur in a game. Thought I would sell it, but then my brother and sister-in-law died in an accident, and I inherited Peter and Paul.'' His voice gentled when he mentioned the youngsters who'd obviously changed his entire life.

''So you've made a home for them.''

He chuckled softly, his warm breath tickled her cheek. Tingles skidded down her spine. ''For them, Franny, Christy, Hank, and you, Miss Parfait. Or should I call you Miss Dede.''

''Whatever,'' she whispered. Deidre didn't know whether to move away or closer. He confused her, he annoyed her, but with him so close she felt more alive than ever in her life.

''I sort of like that. Suits you.''

''We should get to bed.''

''Is this an invitation?''

''Certainly not.'' To her own ears the refusal sounded less than convincing.

''I'm not looking forward to that narrow bed and two boys.''

''I understand.''

His hand stroked gently, and moved to the tender flesh at her throat. ''Do you, Miss Dede?''

Her mind went numb. She wanted to tell him to let her go, that she didn't want to enjoy the warmth of his wide chest pressed to her soft breasts. That she didn't want him to kiss her. What she wanted to say didn't make it past the lump in her heart. Of its own accord, her head tilted, and she swiped her tongue across her dry lips.

Rad's dark eyes flashed as his face lowered to hers. His mouth met hers in a kiss that was a mere brush of his breath, as gentle as the whisper of a butterfly's wings. Deidre closed her eyes and shifted closer. Desire whipped through her like the wind before a thunderstorm. Anthony's most ardent advances hadn't affected her nearly as much as Rad's slightest touch. In the back of her mind she realized that love made the difference. And how she loved him. At that moment, she would give up everything if he only loved her back.

He slid his tongue over her mouth, like a hummingbird testing the nectar of a flower. Fire sizzled through her. She gripped the front of his coat to steady her weak knees. His cane clattered to the floor and his arm slid around her waist. With an easy tug, he crushed her against his muscular chest. Her nightgown and his starched shirt only enhanced the delicious sensations that sent tremors to the center of her femininity.

The kiss deepened, and Deidre gave in to the glory of his touch. Heaven couldn't be any better than being in his arms. Expertly he slipped his tongue past her teeth and met her tongue in a slow sensuous dance. Her fingers slid up his chest and looped around his neck. The hair at his nape was soft and curled over his collar. She shifted in his arms, wanting to lose herself in the wonder of his kiss.

Rad ended the kiss, but continued his sensuous assault. His lips nuzzled her cheek, and continued to her ear. His breath sent hot sensations through her entire body. Her shawl slipped from her shoulders, unneeded in the heat that sizzled from Rad's hard masculine body.

He shifted to brace his shoulder against the bedpost. "You taste like sweet strawberries and warm bread," he whispered. His hands stroked her sides, easing up to the sides of her breasts. His teeth nibbled at her neck.

Her breath caught in her throat. His touch did erotic things to her body. She wanted him as she'd never wanted a man— as she'd never thought she could desire a man. The words "I love you," hovered at the tip of her tongue. She wanted to share herself with Rad—to lose herself in his love.

His lips moved lower to the valley between her breasts. The

sensation was so wonderful, she shifted to give him easier access to her body. She wanted this man, and nothing on this earth had ever felt better. Her breathing grew heavy as if her lungs couldn't get enough air.

He lifted his heated gaze. "I want you, Deidre, I need you." His words sounded as desperate as a man asking for water to quench a deadly thirst. And she didn't have the willpower to deny him, or herself, that life-giving substance. It would be easier to live without water than to live without love.

"Yes, Rad." She tugged the tie from his neck, and dropped it to the floor. It was all the invitation he needed.

Rad captured her face in his hands. "Are you sure, Deidre? Do you want to make love with me?"

"Close the door, Rad, and I'll show you."

In a few long strides, he shoved the door closed and set the lock. She watched him move, and knew that she would never love a man the way she did him. Her heart was fluttering when he returned to her, but there was no fear. Her love had chased that away along with her modesty and propriety.

He hesitated at the foot of the bed, as if giving her a chance to change her mind or rebuke him. She read the question in his gaze. Opening her arms, she welcomed the man she loved into her heart, and into her soul. She freely offered her body.

It took only minutes for Rad to shed his clothes. Deidre couldn't stop herself from touching him, stroking the warm, hard flesh that made her feel soft and feminine. She gave of her love, touching him with the same urgency that he touched her. Her kisses were as ardent as his. And when he possessed her body, she thought her heart would burst with sheer joy of being loved by Rad.

Exhausted from lovemaking, they fell asleep, only to wake and make love again. It was nearly dawn when Deidre finally fell into a deep, contented sleep. Held in Rad's strong arms, she felt a contentment that reached clear to her toes. She snuggled closer, and wished the night would never end.

* * *

The next day, Deidre took the farm wagon into town for supplies. Rad had given her use of a wagon and team to drive
back and forth to school and on her errands.

He'd left her room sometime before the others had awakened.
She supposed she should be glad he'd respected her enough to
protect her reputation, but she found it hard to understand how
he could have left without speaking. Yet it was probably for
the best that she didn't have to face him. Her emotions were
all confused, and she didn't know what to expect of him. She
needed time before she faced him again.

Thankfully she managed to avoid Rad. He and Hank had
taken the horses out into the pasture, and she'd left breakfast
on the table for them. She and Franny wanted to get an early
start on their chores. Deidre took her time, checking out the
new merchandise at Mr. Hansen's mercantile, visiting with the
other women who were doing their weekly shopping, and having lunch at the cafe. A meal at the cafe was a rare treat for
the young woman who'd led a very sheltered and underprivi-
leged life.

Rad usually went to the saloon early in the afternoon on
Saturday. When she spotted his fancy buggy passing down
Main Street, she decided to return to his homestead. Of course,
she couldn't hide from him forever, but until she was able to
control her emotions, she would avoid being alone with Rad.

Her purchases in the wagon, she and Franny drove the mile
back to the homestead. As she drove up to the rear of the house,
she noticed that Hank hadn't come out to greet them as he
usually did. The shouts and laughter of the twins came from
the woods. She assumed that Hank was busy in the barn.

As she leaped down from the wagon, a figure appeared from
inside the kitchen doorway. She gasped at the sight of the
bearded and dirty man who approached with a shotgun in his
hand. "Mr. Maguire," she exclaimed.

"Pa." Franny jumped down and hugged the baby to her chest. "What are you doing here?"

Magoo waved the gun in their direction. "Don't get in my way, girl. You, lady, take the baby and get back in that wagon."

"No," Franny slid behind Deidre's back. "This is my baby."

He shoved the gun into Deidre's gut. "Take the baby."

Fear tightened like a rope around her chest. The man was drunk, and anything could happen. "Franny, let me have Christy. I'll take care of her."

Sobbing, the young woman handed over the basket with the infant. Thankfully, the baby was sleeping. "Where's Hank?"

"That young fella is tied up in the barn." He gestured to the wagon. "Lady, you get up there."

Afraid to get him excited, Deidre climbed onto the high wagon seat. "What do you want?"

He heaved himself up beside her and waved the gun toward Franny. "You tell that gambler if he wants to see his woman and his brat again, he'd better bring a thousand dollars in gold out to the old White Rock mine. If anybody else comes, I'll kill them both."

Franny clutched at his arm, her sobs coming in loud gasps. "No, Pa. You can't."

He picked up the reins and the horses took off at a gallop. Deidre clutched the basket and prayed. The man was crazy. There was no telling what he would do to an innocent baby. And there was no telling what Rad would do when he found out that Magoo had kidnapped her and Christy.

"De—" Danny jumped aside once he gave the baby to his sister. "What are you doing here?"

Marco waved the gun in their direction. "Now isn't any way ... well. You know he's the baby and he can kiss my woman."

"No, Danny, don't do that," Doug shouted. "That's my baby."

He shoved the gun into Doug's gut. "Grab the baby."

"Just relax. I like it just around her chest. The trigger was down, and somehow could happen." Danny let her have Chavez. "I'll take care of her."

Soothing the infant, whom she holded over the cradle with the other hand, Harry gave the apartment. "Where are we going?"

"That house has a bedroom in the back." He pointed to the wagon. "... do you see the door."

Marco came to where Denise climbed into the front seat there. "Get in the van with us."

He heaved himself up inside her and stared the engine forward. "Harry." "You will not come in the room to see the women and the baby ..." but before Harry could raise dollars in cold ... Even the old "Why don't you know." It won't go like sometimes, "I'll kill them both ..."

Harry glanced at the uninhabited house sitting in the shade. "Now is your hand."

He stacked up the rig, and the boxes had out of a ... gallon. Unlike Clement the bedroll, and pepper. The road was clear. There was no telling where he would go to with the sick baby. And there was something that Harry would be when he arrived on that Marco had kidnapped her and Chavez.

CHAPTER 9

Rad's luck had changed. He raked in the pile of chips and grinned to himself. Outwardly he wore the same stoic expression that had taken years to perfect. Could having made love with Deidre made the difference? His mouth still tingled from the touch of her lips and his body grew warm every time he thought about her.

He still couldn't believe that he'd taken her into his bed and spent the night with her in his arms. Never had a woman excited him the way she had. Yet the entire situation confused him. Where would they go from here? They couldn't very well continue to share a bed without consequences. Yet he knew he couldn't live under the same roof with her and leave her alone. He couldn't offer marriage. It wouldn't be fair to her. She had dreams, a goal. And he wasn't fool enough to try to stand in her way.

Picking up the deck, he shuffled the cards without thinking about his actions. He'd come to the saloon early, and found several would-be gamblers waiting to challenge him to a game.

In an hour, he'd cleaned out two cocky cowboys, and was working on relieving the foreman of this month's wages.

After dealing the down card, a sound from behind him broke his concentration. "Psst, Uncle Rad," the young voice called in a loud whisper.

He swung his gaze toward his office door. Peter and Paul poked their heads through the opening. On a hard glance, he signaled them to silence. It was Saturday; Deidre couldn't be sending him another note on their behavior. Their deportment had greatly improved, and they knew better than to disturb him at the saloon. He ignored them as usual.

"Uncle Rad!" The voice grew louder, more insistent.

"Della, see what they want," he ordered, flipping the first up card on the table.

Seconds later Della returned. "They said it's important. They have to tell you something."

He slammed the deck of cards to the table. "Sit in for me."

With a nod, Della took his chair. Over his shoulder, he heard the men greet the woman. Della never gambled, but she was no novice. His hand was safe with her. He couldn't say the same for the twins if they'd taken him from his game for some foolishness or mischief.

Once inside his office, he shut the door behind him. "What's so urgent that you disturbed me? What did you do now?"

Each boy grabbed a hand. Both were covered with perspiration, their shirts were pulled from their britches, and they were breathing heavily.

"We didn't do nothing," Peter said, holding his side.

"Franny said we was to fetch you and get right back home."

"Franny? Where's Miss Dede?"

Paul tugged at his hand. "We don't know. Franny was bawling and crying. Hank was bleeding, and moaning. We run as fast as we could."

His blood ran cold. Franny crying and Hank injured. What could have happened in the few hours since he'd left the house?

As he'd entered town, he'd seen Deidre loading her purchases into the wagon. Instincts told him not to waste time in returning home.

"If you can still run, go over to the livery and I'll meet you there in a minute."

Without a moment's hesitation, they were gone. He hurried into the saloon and whispered to Della to cash him out. He had to get back to the homestead. He would try to come back later.

The team was hitched to the buggy when he reached the livery. Both boys waited in the seat. He climbed up, and snapped the reins. Urgency to learn what had happened made him drive as fast as he dared. He followed the rear alley, and passed the slower-moving wagons on the road. His gut feeling was that something was wrong with Deidre, that she needed him. His stomach clenched at the thought.

As Rad tugged the team to a stop, he spotted Hank lying on the front porch with Franny leaning over him. The young woman was sobbing while pressing a cloth to the young man's head. She looked up when he climbed down from the buggy.

Something was definitely wrong. "Where's Miss Dede?"

Franny's wails increased, and she hiccuped. "Gone. Her and Christy."

"Gone? With the baby?" A rope tightened around his chest. Had Deidre taken the baby and run away? That didn't make sense at all. "What happened to Hank?"

Hank shook his head. "He kidnapped her and Christy. Said he would kill them unless you bring a thousand dollars to the old White Rock mine."

"Who?" Fury gripped Rad. If anything happened to Deidre, he would commit murder with his bare hands.

"My pa," Franny moaned. "He knocked Hank out, then he took Miss Dede and Christy."

A string of curses erupted from under his breath. He should have known Magoo was capable of something like this. The man was crazy when he was drunk. Rad hurried into the house. "Hank, saddle Black Star."

The young man staggered to his feet. "I'll go after them, Mr. Rad. That horse is still half wild. You might get hurt."

His own safety was the last thing on his mind. A woman and child were in danger and he held himself responsible. Magoo still blamed him for losing his mine, and there was no telling where he would express his anger.

"You're injured. If somebody else shows up, Magoo might go crazy and hurt them."

"Please, Mr. Rad. Find my baby. Miss Dede was good to me. I promise I'll never lie again."

He ignored the girl's pleas. He had his own guilt to bear. Once inside the house, Rad pulled a hidden stash of gold from a secret compartment in his bureau. Deidre's subtle perfume hung in the air, and her clothes were neatly folded on the wide bed. His stomach dropped to his feet. He pulled out a Colt revolver, and shoved it into his belt. He'd gladly give every cent he had to keep the woman he loved safe.

Rad stopped in midstride. He loved Deidre. As hard as he'd tried to deny his feelings, love had crept up on him and tripped his heart. He loved her and he needed her.

Leaning heavily on his cane, he raced out the rear door to the barn. As he'd done for ten years, he cursed the accident that had hindered his mobility. And the fear that gripped him every time he thought of mounting a horse.

Holding a cloth to his bleeding head, Hank led the frisky stallion from the barn. "Mr. Rad, let me go. I'll ride and take care of Magoo. I'll get Miss Dede and Franny's baby back."

"Hank," Franny said, her voice breaking. "Christy is your baby, too."

"Do you mean I'm her papa?"

"Yes. I didn't want anybody to know."

The young man grabbed the stallion's reins. "I have to go take care of my baby."

Rad shoved Hank aside. "You're hurt. Besides, Magoo might get desperate if I don't show up with the money. Never know what that crazy man will do. You stay here with Franny and the boys."

Rad swallowed the boulder-sized lump in his throat. He grabbed the reins and brushed his hand along the horse's neck. "Easy, boy." His hands trembled and his knees grew weak. Mustering all his strength and courage, he set his foot into the stirrup and swung into the saddle. The stallion danced and sidestepped. Rad tugged on the reins to steady the animal. Fear had no place in his life.

For the first time in ten years, he'd mounted a horse. Sweat broke out on his forehead. He ignored the hammering in his chest and thought about Deidre and the baby. She must be frightened. They needed him. He'd let his family down when he'd fallen from the horse and as a result had lost the farm. Rad wasn't going to let anything happen to the pair.

He dug his heels into the stallion's flanks. The spirited horse took off at a run. For the first time since Rad had got the animal, he let the animal have his head. Rad gripped the reins and held on. As he headed down the narrow road that led into the hills where the abandoned mine was located, he kept his thoughts on his mission. The wind whistled in his hair, and he realized he'd left his hat at home. His coattail waved behind him like a flag in the breeze. Excitement surged through him. As he leaned over the horse's head, his own fear disappeared. His petty anxiety was unimportant in the face of danger to those he loved.

By the time he reached the clearing in front of the mine, Rad realized his fears had flown away in the breeze. He felt more alive than he had in years. His entire being was centered on rescuing the woman and the tiny girl, both of whom had stolen his heart.

Rad reined in the horse in a grove of trees where his wagon and team were tied. Feeling the urgency to catch Magoo by surprise, he slid from the horse and tied the reins to a tree branch. Careful to remain hidden by the bushes and tree trunks, he made his way to the boarded-up mine entrance. His progress was slowed since he'd left his cane behind. The boards were partially torn off the opening. Rad slid along the rock face of the cliff. He stopped and listened. Moans and grunts came from beyond the entry. Rage gushed through him like a crack in a dam. If Magoo so much as hurt one hair on Deidre's head, the man would rue the day he'd tangled with Rad Christopher.

Gun in hand, he slid through the opening and stopped cold. Magoo sat on the ground, his head buried in his hands. He was groaning like a sick bear. Rad shoved his gun in the man's back.

"Where's the woman and baby?" Christy's basket lay turned upside down on the rocky ground.

Blood seeping through his fingers, Magoo lifted his gaze. His face blanched. Rad could smell the man's fear. "She . . . she . . ." He moaned louder.

Rad grabbed the front of his shirt and glared into his bloodshot eyes. "I said, where are they?"

Magoo pointed a finger toward the interior of the mine. Cobwebs hung from the ceiling like a curtain. "She hit me and ran away."

"Magoo, if anything happens to her or that baby, I swear you won't walk out of here alive." He dropped the man to the ground like so much garbage.

"Rad, I swear I didn't do nothing. I just wanted some money. I wouldn't hurt that baby. She's my flesh and blood."

Ignoring the moans and pleas, Rad hobbled into the mine. Broken timbers blocked the path and he stumbled over large fallen boulders. His pulse pounded in his ears. How could Deidre manage over this debris, carrying an infant? "Deidre," he called. Nothing but the echo of his voice came back at him.

The cave was too dark to search properly. He stopped and lit a match to a dry torch left from before the mine was aban-

doned. His hands shook so badly, it took three matches before
he was able to light the torch.

Once he had a bit of light, he proceeded deeper into the
mine. So far there was only one shaft. He called again, and
again. He listened for a sound, her voice. Rad prayed like a
man on the way to the gallows. Only he wasn't praying for
himself, but for the life of the woman he loved and the innocent
child who'd become dear to him.

He took another step and heard it. A soft whimper at first,
then the weak cries of a baby. Relief flooded him. They had
to be nearby, and if the baby was alive, so was Deidre. Holding
the light in front of him, he followed the sound. A hole opened
in front of him. He knelt to the ground and gazed into the pit.
About eight feet below lay a dark figure crumpled among the
debris. And a crying baby. He'd found them. But had Deidre
been killed in the fall? And how was he going to get her out?
The sides were too steep for him to climb down. He needed
help, but he didn't want to leave them alone.

"Deidre, sweetheart, if you can hear me, don't be afraid.
I'm going to look for a rope and get you out of there. Don't
try to move, I'll be right back."

Rad hated to leave, but he had no choice. Somewhere in the
abandoned mine there had to be a rope. Limping badly on his
lame leg, he hobbled to the entrance. He wasn't surprised that
Magoo was gone, that he'd absconded the second Rad had
turned his back. Thankfully, he hadn't taken the wagon and
team. Wrapped packages and baskets of supplies remained
untouched in the wagon bed. He shoved aside her purchases
and located a length of rope. His leg ached and he was heaving
like a stallion run too hard.

Looping the rope over his shoulder, he returned to the mine.
Ignoring the fallen timbers, he again lit the torch and made his
way back to the pit where he'd left Deidre and the baby. Christy
was whimpering softly, probably exhausted from crying.

"Deidre," he called over the edge. "I'm coming down."

He searched for a sturdy timber on which to tie the end of the rope. The roofing was unsteady at best. He was afraid of pulling the entire mine down on their heads. As he tied the rope to a timber, he heard voices.

"Mr. Rad? You in here?"

Hank, followed by Franny appeared in the darkness. "I'm over here." He lifted the torch to guide their way.

"Have you found them?" Skidding to a stop, Hank hugged Franny to his chest.

Thankful for the help, Rad nodded. "The baby seems fine, but I'm not so sure of Deidre." His stomach lurched at the idea she could be hurt—or worse. "I'm going down to get them up."

The younger man grabbed the end of the rope. "Let me."

"No. I'll need your strength and Franny's to pull them back up. I'm not sure that timber will hold our weight. Franny, you hold the light. Hank, handle the rope."

"We'll hold you."

Rad tested the rope. It held. He gripped the rough rope. Hand over hand, his feet against the side of the pit, he worked his way down to her side. Fear unlike anything he'd ever experienced churned in his gut. On the hard, damp bottom, he knelt beside Deidre. The baby was wrapped securely in her arms. He picked up Christy, and she let out a lusty scream. From what he could tell, the baby was fine, if a bit dirty, wet, and probably hungry. Deidre had protected the infant with her own body.

He reached to the woman's throat. Her pulse was strong, and her breathing ragged. At least she was alive, although he had no idea as to the extent of her injuries. Quickly he slipped out of his jacket.

"I'm going to make a sling out of my coat for the baby," he called to the parents waiting for word of their child. "Pull her up slowly." At his full height, he was able to hold the child near the rim of the pit. Franny squealed with joy when her daughter was once again safely in her arms.

Hank untied the bundle and tossed the rope back to Rad. He knelt beside the woman and slid his arm under her shoulders. "Deidre, honey, can you hear me?"

She moaned softly. "Rad? Am I dreaming?"

"No, sweetheart, I'm here." Dirt smudged her cheeks, she was bruised, her clothes torn, but she was the most beautiful woman he'd ever seen.

"Where's Christy? Is she all right?"

"Hush. The baby is fine. Are you hurt?" He quickly ran his hands over her arms and legs, checking for breaks. So far, she seemed in one piece.

"My head hurts."

"And you're probably full of bruises. Don't try to stand. I'm going to loop this rope under your arms. Hank and Franny are going to pull you up."

Carefully he tied the rope around her and helped her to her feet. Unable to help himself, he planted a quick kiss on her mouth. "We'll have you out of here in a minute," he reassured her.

She clung to his shirt. "I'm going to strangle that miserable Magoo Maguire when I see him."

"You already gave him a concussion. He won't bother us again."

"He'd better not."

He lifted her by the waist and balanced her weight while Hank tugged her up. When she was safely on the ground above his head, he gripped the rope and worked his way to the surface.

A timber creaked, and dust flew from the ceiling. "Let's get out of here before we pull the roof down."

Rad picked up a long pole to use as a walking stick. His leg throbbed, but he ignored the pain. Most important was getting out of the unstable mine before something happened. He and Hank half carried and half dragged Deidre while Franny led the way with the torch and the baby. As soon as they left the entrance of the mine, Rad sank to the grass, winded. Wrapping both his arms around Deidre, he hugged her close to his chest and kissed the top of her disheveled hair. He was as dirty and mussed as she, but he didn't care.

Franny and Hank dropped beside them. The baby had stopped crying, and Hank was looking into the tiny face with a lovesick expression on his face.

Deidre buried her face in Rad's chest and wept softly. "I was so scared, Rad. Not for myself, but for the baby. I didn't want that man to hurt her."

"I wouldn't let him hurt either of you."

"But . . . he wanted you to give him money."

Digging into his pocket, he pulled out a hefty bag of gold. "I was prepared to give it to him."

"You were?"

"We'll talk when we get home. I want the doctor to look you and Christy over."

"Mr. Rad," said Franny, "where's my pa?"

"He was there when I went in. I suppose he's running like a scared rabbit. He'd better not stop until he reaches the next county."

Standing, he signaled for Hank. "Let's get them home."

The younger man slanted a glance at Franny. "We've got a lot to talk about. I intend to be a good father to my little girl."

"What's going on?" Deidre asked, as she struggled to her feet. She stumbled and would have fallen if Rad hadn't caught her.

Franny began to cry. "Hank is Christy's papa."

"I said we'll talk later," Rad said. "Hank, help me get this stubborn woman into the wagon. Then tie your horses to the back, and take Black Star into town for the doctor."

"Yes, sir."

As they approached the wagon, a loud rumble came from the abandoned mine. The ground shook, timbers creaked and crashed. Dust flew from the entrance. The noise roared as loud as thunder.

"Cave-in." Rad's voice trembled. If he'd gotten there only minutes later, the woman he loved would have been lost to him forever. And an innocent child would have died before she had a chance to live.

"Come on," Hank shouted.

Within minutes they'd placed Deidre in the bed of the wagon with Franny and the baby beside her. Rad climbed to the high seat, and took off for home. The word had never sounded so good.

CHAPTER 10

Deidre woke the next morning stiff and hardly able to move. The doctor had examined her the past evening, and pronounced her in good shape for having fallen into a pit. Then he'd given her a potion, and she'd fallen asleep almost immediately. She tried to roll over and discovered a large object blocking her movement.

Her eyes slid open, bringing her face level with a wide, male chest—a bare masculine chest covered with a smattering of black hair.

"Rad," she breathed his name.

"How do you feel?" His breath whispered against her cheek.

Shocked. Scared. Sore. And wonderful. He'd risked his life to rescue her. He must love her just a little. Rad brushed the tangled hair from her forehead. His gentle touch warmed her all over. "Better," she managed to say.

"Those bruises and scrapes will heal up in a few days. You'll be good as new."

"Thank you." Deidre lifted her gaze to his face. A night's

growth of whiskers darkened his jaw, and his eyes sparkled with mischief. Exactly like Peter and Paul seconds before they shoved a dead snake into her desk.

She suddenly realized that her hand rested on his waist and her breasts were pressed to his side. She snuggled closer. Only then did she notice that she was under the covers, while Rad lay on top.

"What are you doing in my bed?"

"Dear Miss Dede, I was the soul of propriety. I didn't want to leave you alone after what you'd gone through. The doctor said somebody should watch you in case you had a concussion or other injuries he didn't spot." Heat from his body seeped through the clothes and linens separating them.

"I'm fine, thank you."

His gaze lowered to her lips. "I believe you are." He swung his feet to the floor. "I'll fetch something to eat. Franny and the boys will want to know you're all right."

As Rad moved away from her, Deidre felt strangely adrift without his nearness. He'd rescued her and remained at her side. For a man who claimed to be a rogue, he had a soft side that few outside his family ever saw.

He moved slowly across the room, leaning heavily on the furniture as he retrieved a clean shirt from the bureau. She watched the play of the muscles in his back as he lifted his arms and slid the shirt over his head. He'd slept in a pair of faded denims slung low on his waist. He slanted a glance over his shoulder and caught her staring at him. A crooked, devilish grin played at the corners of his mouth.

"Do you want me to help you up?" he asked.

Deidre swallowed the nervousness in her throat. What she wanted was for him to return to the bed and join her under the covers. Heat surfaced to her face. "I think I can manage."

He sat on the edge of the bed, and studied her for a moment. "What you did yesterday was the bravest and the stupidest thing I've ever seen."

Indignation overrode propriety. She sat up higher against the pillows to face him squarely. "What do you mean, stupid? I was kidnapped by a madman, held against my will, and he threatened an innocent baby. What was I supposed to do? Wait for him to shoot me?"

"No. You should have waited for me to show up." His gaze dropped to the open buttons of her nightdress. Only then did she realize the buttons were loosened to the tops of her breasts. She tugged the sheet to her neck.

"And how did I know you would come? Or that you would find me? I remember how often you ignored my notes when I wanted to discuss the boys with you. What if you were too busy with your card games, drinking, and women?" Jealousy overrode common sense.

He leaned closer, meeting her eye-to-eye. "I *was* busy with a card game. As for the drinking, I don't drink anything but weak tea made to look like liquor. And as for the women . . . you wouldn't understand."

"Yes, I would. Everybody knows you and Della are lovers." Pain clutched her chest. How many other women had shared his bed beside her?

"Lovers?" He leaped to his feet and staggered against the bedpost. Clutching the headboard of the bed, he leaned closer. "Della and I are friends. That's all. She runs my business and she earns a hefty salary for doing so. I don't believe in mixing business with pleasure."

Feeling properly chastised for misunderstanding him, she struggled to regain the upper hand. "I still didn't know if you would be able to find me."

"So you clobbered Magoo and ran into a dark mine. If I hadn't dropped everything and come looking for you, you and Christy might have died in that hole. Or you could have broken your neck when you fell."

"I only meant to hide until help came. I figured sooner or later Hank or Franny would show up. I didn't see the hole."

"You didn't trust me to come?"

She bit her lip to hold back her sobs. She'd prayed and wished he would rescue them, but she'd been afraid he wouldn't care enough for either her or Christy. "I didn't know."

"Know this, lady, as long as you're living in my house I'll take care of you. That goes for Franny and the baby, too."

Tears burned at the backs of her eyes. She didn't mean any more to him than the others he'd taken into his home. How could she love a man who had room in his bed, but not in his heart for her? "Thank you. I'll remember to notify you next time I'm kidnapped."

"Oh, damn." A knock on the door interrupted whatever he'd planned to say. "Come in," he shouted.

The door crept open and Franny stuck her head around the facing. "Can me and Hank come in?"

"Why not?" Rad gestured them in.

The young couple hesitated before stepping across the threshold. Franny glanced back at Hank before approaching the bed. "We want to talk to you all."

Rad sank to the chair beside the bed, and Deidre hugged the sheet to her chest. "How's the baby?"

"She's sleeping," Hank said. "I can't hardly believe she's mine."

Franny's face turned crimson. "Me and Hank stayed up all night talking." She caught his hand in both of hers. She was obviously deeply in love with the young man. Deidre didn't know how she hadn't seen it before. "He wants to marry me and make a home for our little girl."

Deidre let her tears flow. So much had happened in the past day. Who'd have thought that Magoo's mischief would turn out for the best for his daughter? "That's wonderful. But, Franny, why did you say that Mr. Rad was the father instead of Hank?"

"Oh, Miss Dede, you just wouldn't understand. I didn't find

out about the baby until after Hank left. I didn't know where he was, and I didn't want to ask his ma and pa.''

Hank draped his arm over the girl's shoulder. "If I'd known, I'd have come right back. I love Franny. I never stopped loving her. And I was so jealous when I thought that her and Mr. Rad had . . . well, you know.''

"Franny, why did you tell everybody that I was the father?" Rad asked, his arms folded across his chest.

The young woman ducked her head. "I had to tell my pa something. If he knew about Hank and me, he would have caused trouble for Mr. Abrams. But he was kind of scared of Mr. Rad, so I thought he wouldn't do anything.''

"I suppose all of us underestimated Magoo." Rad stood and moved toward the door.

Deidre shivered. It was time Franny had a bit of happiness after the life she'd had with her father. "When are you going to get married?''

"Right away," Hank said. "As soon as we tell my folks and get the preacher. We'd like Miss Dede and Mr. Rad to stand up for us, if you will?''

"We would be honored." She glanced at Rad who looked as solemn as a cigar-store Indian. "Won't we, Rad?''

"I suppose so. I'm going out to check on Black Star.''

Deidre sat up straighter. "I'll get your breakfast as soon as everybody leaves the room and I can get dressed.''

Rad shook his head. "The doctor said you should stay in bed for at least a day. We'll manage without you.''

Her heart tightened. Was this his way of telling her he didn't need her? "I have to get up.''

"Okay, but don't try to work." Rad moved across the room, his gait slower and his limp more pronounced than usual. He'd clearly hurt himself in rescuing her.

"I can get breakfast," Franny said. "You just take it easy, Miss Dede. I owe you a lot for taking care of my baby.''

"I love that little girl. I'd do anything for her.''

"She loves to hear you sing. I couldn't hardly get her to sleep last night."

Remembering the things he'd said about her singing, she wrinkled her nose at Rad. He merely grunted and left the room. Hank followed at his tail.

With Franny's help, Deidre managed to dress and move to the kitchen. She hadn't realized how sore and bruised her ordeal had left her. She supervised Franny as she prepared breakfast. The girl was getting proficient at cooking and keeping house. It wouldn't be long before she could take over as Rad's house-keeper, if he agreed.

In spite of her desire to continue her career, Deidre knew she would miss living on the homestead. While Franny cooked the eggs and bacon, Deidre took her coffee to the rear porch. Rad and Hank were in the corral with the horses. As she watched, Rad mounted the big black stallion. From the twins, she'd learned that Rad had ridden the horse to rescue her at the mine—that it had been the first time he'd ridden since his accident ten years earlier. He'd conquered his fear.

Man and horse made an imposing picture. Rad always cut a fine figure of a man, but on the stallion, he was stunning—like a knight of old on his sturdy charger. Her emotions all in a flutter, Deidre settled on one of the chairs she'd dragged to the porch. The morning sky was a deep blue, and a breeze whispered through the trees. It was a magnificent day. For several minutes, Rad pranced the horse around the corral like a showman in a ring.

Suddenly the stallion reared up and pawed the air with its front feet. Her heart nearly stopped. With expert ease, Rad controlled the animal, and rode slowly around the enclosure. The twins watched from the fence, their faces aglow with wonder.

For just a moment she felt part of a family. With Rad, the boys, even Hank, Franny and their baby, they were a unit. How she wished this day would never end. That she could stay with

them forever. However, Rad had never given the slightest hint
he wanted her to stay, and she had set her goals from childhood.
Her mother had given up her dream for love. Before her mother
had died, Deidre had promised to pursue the dream.

A dream that didn't include marriage to a gambler who didn't
want a wife any more than she wanted a husband.

Three days later, Rad and Deidre stood side by side in the
parlor as witnesses to Franny and Hank's marriage. Franny
shifted from foot to foot, and glanced at Hank as if she couldn't
believe he'd actually showed up for the ceremony.

Wearing their Sunday best, the twins sat on the davenport
and whispered to the Abrams children, who'd come to watch
their oldest brother take a wife. Their gazes kept shifting to
the cake Deidre had baked for the occasion.

Henry and Rachel Abrams stood beside their son. Although
they weren't thrilled about the nuptials, they'd agreed it was
best for all. Rachel held her granddaughter in her arms, having
declared Christy was the most beautiful baby she'd ever seen.
The young couple had affirmed their love a year ago and their
child was the result of that love. Now they stood before the
minister and announced their commitment to the entire world.

As the minister conducted the ceremony, Deidre glanced at
Rad. He wore his usual black suit and waistcoat. A gold chain
stretched across his narrow waist. He was incredibly handsome.
Her stomach knotted. What would it be like to stand where
Franny and Hank now stood? Would Rad ever declare his love
for a woman and marry? She set her jaw in a determined line.
If he ever did, Deidre wouldn't be that woman. As much as
she loved Rad, she had other fish to fry. By his actions, he'd
made it clear he would take a lover, but he had no place in his
life for a wife.

When the minister pronounced the couple husband and wife,
Franny slid a shy glance at her new husband. Hank kissed her

quickly on the lips and wrapped a possessive arm around her waist. "You're Mrs. Abrams now. And nobody better mess with you."

Franny's face pinked, and Deidre's heartbeat quickened. It was good to see a young couple so much in love. After hugs all around, Rad invited the entire company into the kitchen for refreshments. The children were served cake and punch, and Rad opened a bottle of champagne for the adults.

Deidre had only tasted the bubbly wine once, at the reception in Fort Smith where she'd met Anthony. Shoving that memory from her mind, she waited while Rad toasted the young couple. Even Henry joined in, wishing his son and new daughter all the happiness in the world.

Rad surprised everybody with his next announcement. "Hank, you've done a fine job with Black Star and with the other animals. If you're interested in a permanent job, I'd like you to stay on here. If I decide to build up the ranch, I'll need a foreman who's good with horses. How about it? Interested?"

The young man's grin widened. He stuck out his hand. "Mr. Rad, I'd like nothing better. That stallion is a champion. He'll sire fine stock."

After shaking the man's hand, he turned to Franny. "I'll need a housekeeper, Franny. Miss Dede tells me you're doing a good job. Would you like to stay here, too? You and Hank and Christy can stay in your room, and in time I'll build a cabin for you."

Henry grinned at Rad. "Just a minute. When I loaned my son to you, I didn't mean for you to take him away from me for good."

Taking a cigar from his pocket, Rad handed it to his friend. "Henry, you've three other boys to take Hank's place. It'll be quite a while before mine are ready to work the animals."

The rancher took the cigar. "What say I give them a few acres where my land meets yours? We can put up their house, and they'll be close to both of us."

"Darn, if that ain't a fine idea." Rad slapped Henry on the back. "Let's go outside and smoke these and leave the women to their gossip." He handed a cigar to Hank. "You too, Hank."

"Henry," Rachel stated, her hands on her ample hips, "you know how much I hate those smelly things."

"Yes, dear," Henry said. "But Rad is our host. It would be rude to refuse."

Male laughter followed the men to the rear porch. The twins led the younger children outdoors to play. An awkward silence hovered over the kitchen. Deidre took over as hostess. "I'll make some tea, and we can go into the parlor and talk." She put a kettle on the stove. "Rachel, I'm sure you can give Franny some pointers on being a good wife and mother."

The older woman smiled. "Reckon you could use a little advice about men, too, Miss Parfait. I hear tell that Rad rode that half-wild stallion to rescue you from Magoo."

Her face colored. "He didn't want Magoo to hurt the baby." She turned her gaze to the stove to hide the pain in her eyes. Since Rad had asked Franny to be his housekeeper, he didn't need Deidre any longer. It hurt that he hadn't bothered to mention his plans to her. Well, what did she expect? She'd told him she would only stay until he got a permanent housekeeper. That they'd become lovers didn't change a thing. She should be glad. Instead she felt as if a piece of her heart had chipped off.

"It's a good thing that old buzzard didn't hurt this sweet little thing," the proud grandmother noted. "I'd have strangled him myself."

Deidre laughed to ease her own worry. "You would have had to stand in line."

CHAPTER 11

Rad sank to the davenport and tugged his tie from his neck. After the excitement of a wedding and too much cake, the twins had gone to bed early. Shyly Franny and Hank had said, "Good night," and gone to their room.

He and Deidre hadn't had a moment alone. She'd paled when he'd announced that he wanted Franny as his housekeeper. The announcement had taken them all by surprise—even Rad. He'd been thinking about keeping Hank on, but it was on the spur of the moment that he'd asked Franny to work for him. He'd have thought Deidre would be glad, as she'd made it clear her stay with him was only temporary until they located the mother of the baby. Well, they'd not only found the mother, they'd married her to the father.

A band clenched around his chest. He had nothing to keep Deidre in his home. Not that he wanted to. Things were getting too hot between them for his peace of mind. The night he'd laid beside her after she'd been injured in the mine, he'd been sore-pressed not to make love with her. He'd never felt so needy as he had at that moment. He couldn't come within ten feet of the woman without wanting to sweep her up in his arms and make love with her. That one night they'd spent together would warm his memory for his lifetime to come.

Rad stroked his hand along his throbbing leg—another reminder that he had nothing permanent to offer a woman. And Deidre had made it clear that she would head for San Francisco as soon as her contract expired. Rad made up his mind to help her.

"Rad," she said from the kitchen doorway. "May I speak to you for a moment?"

He sat straighter. "Certainly, come in."

Deidre settled on the rocker in front of the fireplace. She glanced around the room as if sealing it in her memory. "That was a lovely wedding, wasn't it?" Her fingers worked the pleats in her skirt.

"Yes. They looked happy."

"That was very kind of you to offer jobs to both of them. Franny will make a fine housekeeper." She chuckled. "Don't worry, she won't burn your house down."

"I'm not worried."

Silence hovered between them. "I'm sure you're eager to move back into your room. I'll start packing, and ask Mrs. Hansen if I can have my room at the boardinghouse. I'll be out of your way as soon as possible."

"You don't have to go back to the boardinghouse." He wasn't sure how to tell her of his decision.

"Where else could I go?"

"San Francisco."

Her jaw dropped. "I plan to leave as soon as my contract expires."

He stood, too agitated to remain seated. "I'll buy out your contract and pay you for being my housekeeper. That should get you started on your stage career."

She jumped to her feet. "I can't let you do that. I'll honor my commitment."

"I owe you, Deidre." He set his hands on her shoulders. The fresh aroma of her rosewater cologne enveloped him with its sweet fragrance. His fingers stroked the smooth skin at her exposed neck. He knew she tasted as sweet as she smelled.

"You don't owe me anything." She shivered under his touch.

"I do. It was my fault that Winslow left you stranded in Blissful." Guilt washed over him. Her questioning gaze met his. "You were right about his gambling with your money. I caught him cheating, and personally put him on the midnight train."

Her face paled. "You sent him away?"

"I didn't know about you. I'm sorry."

"You should be." She slapped his hands away. "You stole my dream."

"Sooner or later he would have either left you, or stolen your virtue."

"You took care of that, didn't you?"

"I'm sorry about that, too. Now I want to give you back your dream. I'll even buy you a train ticket to San Francisco."

"I suppose that's the least you can do." She spun on her heel. At the hallway, she called over her shoulder, "I'll clear out of your home tomorrow."

Rad's stomach sank to his feet. Part of him was glad to get rid of Deidre; the other part would miss her like he would miss his teeth if they were knocked out. She'd become just as important as each breath he took. But it wouldn't be fair to deny her the chance for her dream. He'd lost his—he would do all he could to make hers come true.

Deidre waited at the station for the train. Tears blinded her to the bright sunshine, and the good-byes of her students and friends. It looked as if half the town had come to see her off. Franny wept openly, pressing her face into Hank's chest.

Mrs. Hansen had been far more gracious than she'd expected. The woman had allowed her to stay at the boardinghouse for the past days, and had assured Deidre that she would personally teach the class until another teacher could be hired. She'd excused the children so they could bid Deidre good-bye. Deidre wondered what it had cost Rad to gain the woman's cooperation.

She scanned the crowd, searching for the tall, dark-haired man she hadn't seen in five days. Five long days of good-byes. Five lonely days, the first of a lifetime stretching ahead of her. The westbound train was due any minute, and still Rad hadn't shown up. Peter and Paul flashed gap-toothed smiles. Each boy had lost a tooth since she'd left the homestead. She kissed them on the forehead, and wished them luck. They told her that Uncle Rad had changed his mind, and that he was looking for a gentle horse for each of them.

Even Sally Jane seemed unhappy to see Deidre leave, or she was upset at having her mother for a teacher. Deidre's gaze shifted to the Silver Spur. The saloon was quiet, as Rad rarely left the homestead until late afternoon. Earlier, Della had sent a note wishing her all the best in her career.

The loud whistle of the train announced its approach. Deidre's heart plummeted. Her stomach was a mass of fluttering butterflies. A new life awaited her in San Francisco. Then why did she feel as if her heart was shattering into a million tiny shards? It took only a few minutes for the arriving passengers to exit, and the conductor called, "All aboard."

Hank lugged her trunk aboard, and, her ticket in her hand, Deidre climbed onto the platform. She pressed her face to the window and watched those she loved slowly drift away. In her last view of Blissful, she knew she would never forget the town that had finally begun to live up to its name.

* * *

Two miserable days later, Rad threw down his cards in disgust. It was close to noon, and he'd been at the table since the night before. At one time he relished this kind of distraction. Now he found it boring. He was at his wits' end. From the shadows he'd watched Deidre board the train and get out of town—and out of his life. How could a man who considered himself intelligent be so stupid? To have let her go—no, he'd insisted she leave—was the dumbest thing he'd ever done.

He sipped the tea and considered going home. But nothing awaited him there. He'd moved back into his room, but signs of the woman were everywhere. Her scent permeated the sheets, and to make it worse, she'd left various items of apparel behind. A chemise remained in the bureau, a stocking had slipped to the floor, and she'd overlooked a haircomb that Rad carried in his pocket.

The man across from him began to deal the next hand. Rad settled back and checked his hole card. As he watched the cards flip around the table, a whisper came from behind him. He didn't have to look around to recognize his nephew's voice.

"Uncle Rad," Paul called. "Teacher wants to see you."

Mrs. Hansen had taken over the class, and now he would have to deal with the woman. When he'd convinced the school board to allow him to buy out Deidre's contract, he'd assured her that his nephews wouldn't cause any disturbances and he would control their behavior. It hadn't taken long for the woman to demand his presence. He gathered up his cards. "I'm out, fellows. I've got a teacher to see."

He picked up his cane and headed to the door. "Take over, Della. I'll be back shortly." When he reached the door, he noticed that Paul had disappeared, apparently not wanting to explain his behavior. Rad shook his head. That boarding school was sounding better all the time.

Fifteen minutes later he approached the schoolhouse. Loud shouts and the laughter of children greeted him as he tugged the team to a halt. Near the woodshed, Peter and Paul were playing marbles on the ground. At least they hadn't been punished. Several girls gathered on a blanket, eating their lunch. He approached the steps and slowly entered the one-room building. He dreaded the confrontation with another teacher. He'd gotten used to sparring with Deidre, and he doubted Mrs. Hansen would be as interesting.

The woman faced the blackboard, her back to him. Either Mrs. Hansen had slimmed down, or she'd succeeded in getting a new teacher. The woman wore a loose shawl over her shoulders and a poke bonnet covered her hair. Something about both was very familiar.

"I'm Rad Christopher. I understand you sent for me." He moved slowly down the aisle. For a second his heart stopped beating. When it started up again, it raced double-time.

She signaled with her arm for him to approach. Rad grinned to himself. "I suppose it's my nephews again. I'd best inform you that you won't have to deal with them much longer."

The woman stilled in writing on the board.

"I'm thinking of taking them and moving away." By that time he'd reached the first row of seats. "I thought San Francisco might be an interesting place to live." He took one step onto the low platform. "Have you ever been to San Francisco, ma'am?"

With a shake of her head, the woman dropped her gaze to a book.

"I hear San Francisco is quite civilized—with libraries, fine schools, theaters, opera houses. Quite a lot of culture for the boys."

He moved closer to the woman. The scent of rose water attacked his senses. "Do you know why I want to go to San Francisco?" Her back stiffened, ramrod-straight. "That's where I sent the woman I love. Fool that I was, I let her go away before I told her that I loved her.'' He slipped an arm around her waist and pulled her hard into his chest. "Do you think she would forgive me if I apologized for stupidity?''

She gasped. "Mr. Christopher, is that any way to treat your nephews' teacher?''

Ignoring her protests, Rad nuzzled the back of her neck with his lips. "Only when the teacher is the woman I want to marry.''

Deidre turned in his arms and splayed her hands across his chest. "Do you propose to all your nephews' teachers?''

"Only the ones that I love.''

"How did you know it was me, and not some stranger? She would have knocked you over the head, or accepted your proposal. Wouldn't that have been something?''

He laughed. The burdens lifted from his heart and Rad felt ten years younger. "I recognized you the instant I walked through the door. I'd know you anywhere. What I don't understand is what you're doing here. I saw you get on that train headed west.''

"So you were watching? Why didn't you come say goodbye?''

"I couldn't bear the thought of losing you. But I felt you needed the chance to make your dream come true.''

She ran rows of kisses over his jaw. "Oh, Rad. I've found my dream right here with you and the boys. I got off the train at the next stop and hired a wagon to bring me back. I didn't know how I was going to convince you to love me the way I love you, but I had to try.''

He met her roving lips with his. The kiss was long and sweet. She tasted of love and forever, of happiness and family, of joy and contentment. Giggles from the doorway tore them apart. He lifted his head and spotted a dozen shiny faces staring at them.

"Looks like we have witnesses. Are you willing to marry a crippled-up gambler?''

"I would be honored to have the handsomest and kindest man in the world for a husband, even if he is a bit of a rogue."

"What about your career?"

"I think I'll become a great singer rocking babies to sleep in their baskets."

Ignoring the children, Rad took her in his arms and whispered, "I can't wait to get started."

She kissed his earlobe, sending rivers of desire through his body. "Neither can I."

EPILOGUE

It looked as if the entire town had gathered for the Harvest Festival. Rad guided his new, larger buggy under the trees where Franny and Hank awaited them. With his growing family, he'd sold his fancy buggy to Della along with the Silver Spur. After a year of marriage, he didn't miss the saloon at all. In fact, he had more than enough to keep him busy on the ranch if he wanted to become a successful horse breeder and trainer.

Deidre hugged his arm. "Do you think it's safe for the boys to race their horses?"

"Sure. They're natural horsemen. Their father was a great rider."

"Like their uncle?"

"Better, I hope. I don't think they'll fall off like I did."

She kissed his cheek, and his heart rate accelerated. The woman excited him more now than she had the day they'd married. Giving birth to twins had enhanced her beauty in his eyes. "You won't, either. I've never seen a man sit a horse better."

Her assurance eased some of his nervousness at his first race in eleven years. He'd trained Black Star and raced Hank on one of the other horses. But he'd hadn't tested the stallion in a pack of equally fast horses.

A whimper came from the baskets in the rear of the buggy. Deidre glanced over her shoulder. "Sounds like one of our children wants attention. I'm betting it's Adam. He's like his father."

Rad laughed. "And Amanda is like her mother. Whenever I come within six feet of her, she reaches out and wants me to hold her."

"She loves her papa nearly as much as her mama."

His heart swelled to overflowing. He stopped the buggy and helped his wife down. Christy spotted them and ran with her hands outstretched. "Uncy Rad," the year-old toddler called.

Rad snatched up the little girl he considered one of his own. Henry appeared immediately, as if jealous that his grandchild had run to another man. His friend's devotion to the little girl surprised everybody, especially Rachel, who adored the child.

"Got those twins back there?" Rachel asked, picking up Adam's basket.

"You don't think Deidre would leave the house without them, do you?" He retrieved Amanda's basket and passed it to Franny. He didn't know how they would have managed without Hank and Franny. The young couple had become not only employees, but close friends. Rad passed the little girl to Deidre.

Henry pulled a cigar from his pocket. "Rad, let's go check out the competition for the races. Some of those fellows have fine animals."

Rad kissed his wife. "I'll see you later."

Deidre watched her husband walk away with Henry and Hank. His limp seemed less pronounced, but he still used the cane. In his usual black suit, he looked every bit the gambler and rogue. Who'd have thought that the scoundrel would turn into a devoted husband and father?

"It was good of Rad to plan this race to raise money for the school," Rachel said. "Men are willing to pay an entrance fee to race their horses when they wouldn't give a dime for charity."

"I think he did it so he could test out Black Star. He wants to enter a race in Kentucky next spring."

"Regardless, the new teacher will appreciate the new desks we ordered."

Deidre had remained as teacher until summer. A young woman from a fine teacher's college had accepted the offer to teach in the small town. Rad had warned the twins to be on their best behavior. He didn't need any more notes from their teacher. That last note had gotten him into a heap of trouble.

The races were scheduled for the afternoon, then there would be a potluck supper on the school grounds, and a dance afterward. Deidre, Rachel, and Franny, with the children, joined the other women in the stands that Mr. Hansen had built in front of the mercantile. Deidre shoved her way to the front row for a close look at the races. The men gathered on the boardwalk in front of the Silver Spur.

"What do you suppose those men are doing over there?" Franny asked.

Deidre had little doubt as to their activity. "Probably placing bets on the races."

"Didn't Mr. Rad give up gambling when he sold the Silver Spur?"

"It would be easier for Rad to quit breathing than to give up gambling," Deidre said with a smile. "He isn't aware that I know his weekly lodge meetings are nothing but glorified poker games."

Rachel laughed. "I'm not supposed to know that Henry attends every meeting."

They settled in their seats and watched the parade of young

riders pass the reviewing stand. The junior races were first, and both Peter and Paul were riding the horses Rad had given them and helped train. The two younger Abrams boys had entered, as had Henrietta Abrams and Sally Jane Hansen.

Deidre blew kisses at her nephews as well as her other former students. When they'd passed by, she leaned over to Rachel. "We can't let those men have all the fun. How about a little wager? I've got a dollar on Peter, and just to hedge my bet, one on Paul."

Behind them, Mrs. Hansen gasped.

Rachel grinned. "It's all in fun. You're on. But let's make it interesting. I bet five on Henrietta."

Not to be outdone, Mrs. Hansen reached over with a dollar. "One dollar on Sally Jane."

Within seconds, other women threw in their money. The men didn't have anything on them.

When a gunshot signaled the start of the race, everybody jumped to their feet. Shouts rang out, encouraging the contestants. At the first loop through town, Peter and Paul were neck and neck in the lead. Another rider began to catch up to them. As they neared the finish line, the pinto nudged out the twins by a nose. Henrietta Abrams had won the race. Deidre hugged Rachel and handed over her ten dollars.

Rachel collected the bets and tucked the money into her pocket. "Next time the men have their lodge meeting, we should get up our own game."

Even Mrs. Hansen laughed at that. "Don't leave me out."

The women settled back as the men paraded before them. When Rad passed close to the stand, Deidre stood and signaled him closer. He'd removed his jacket and rolled up the sleeves of his white shirt. Black Star pranced, eager to get on with what he'd been trained for.

"Give me a kiss for luck," he said.

Deidre leaned over and planted a loud kiss on her husband's

mouth. She slipped the blue ribbon from her wide straw hat and tied it around his arm. "Wear my colors, and win for me."

Rad was certain his heart would burst through his chest. What did he ever do to deserve this beautiful woman and the love she'd brought into his life? He and his nephews had been blessed by her love. The horse shied, and he tugged on the reins to steady the spirited animal. "What do I get when I win?"

She leaned over and whispered for his ears only, "I'll send the children home with Franny and Hank and sing you to sleep."

"I won't sleep a wink tonight." Anticipating a rare night alone with his wife, Rad nudged the stallion toward the starting line.

Win or lose, Rad had already won more than he'd ever dreamed. Thanks to Deidre he'd overcome his fears, and gained a life in exchange. A life full of love and responsibility, and happiness.

ABOUT THE AUTHOR

Jean Wilson lives with her family in Chalmette, Louisiana. She is the author of three Zebra historical romances: *Sweet Dreams, My Mariah,* and *Coulter's Angel* (to be published in May, 1999). Jean is currently working on her next Zebra historical romance, *Christmas Homecoming,* which will be published in December, 1999. Jean loves to hear from readers and you may write to her c/o Zebra Books. Please include a self-addressed stamped envelope if you wish a response.

ROMANCE FROM JANELLE TAYLOR

ANYTHING FOR LOVE   (0-8217-4992-7, $5.99)

DESTINY MINE   (0-8217-5185-9, $5.99)

CHASE THE WIND   (0-8217-4740-1, $5.99)

MIDNIGHT SECRETS   (0-8217-5280-4, $5.99)

MOONBEAMS AND MAGIC   (0-8217-0184-4, $5.99)

SWEET SAVAGE HEART   (0-8217-5276-6, $5.99)

Available wherever paperbacks are sold, or order direct from the Publisher. Send cover price plus 50¢ per copy for mailing and handling to Kensington Publishing Corp., Consumer Orders, or call (toll free) 888-345-BOOK, to place your order using Mastercard or Visa. Residents of New York and Tennessee must include sales tax. DO NOT SEND CASH.

ROMANCE FROM FERN MICHAELS

DEAR EMILY   (0-8217-4952-8, $5.99)

WISH LIST   (0-8217-5228-6, $6.99)

AND IN HARDCOVER:

VEGAS RICH   (1-57566-057-1, $25.00)

Available wherever paperbacks are sold, or order direct from the Publisher. Send cover price plus 50¢ per copy for mailing and handling to Kensington Publishing Corp., Consumer Orders, or call (toll free) 888-345-BOOK, to place your order using Mastercard or Visa. Residents of New York and Tennessee must include sales tax. DO NOT SEND CASH.